Also by Laura DiSilverio

The Reckoning Stones
Close Call

FIRST EDITION
First Printing, 2017

Book format by Bob Gaul
Cover design by Ellen Lawson

Midnight Ink, an imprint of Llewellyn Worldwide Ltd.

Library of Congress Cataloging-in-Publication Data (Pending)
978-0-7387-5253-2

Midnight Ink
Llewellyn Worldwide Ltd.
2143 Wooddale Drive
Woodbury, MN 55125-2989
www.midnightinkbooks.com

Printed in the United States of America

THAT LAST WEEKEND

LAURA DISILVERIO

MIDNIGHT INK
WOODBURY, MINNESOTA

For my Thomas.

I won't say you complete me, because that line's been used, and it's kind of cheesy now, but you definitely make me a better person and give me great joy. Thank you for a quarter century of love, and a life that is more and better because we stride/stumble/crawl/dance through it together.

One

Congratulations hailed down on Laurel Muir, who thanked her supporters and wished herself elsewhere. Anywhere else. The dentist's chair. The top of Pikes Peak. I-25 during rush hour. Anywhere but her parents' Cherry Hills mansion, which seethed with a healthy collection of Denver's movers and shakers, all of whom shook her hand or hugged her before spilling onto the lawn, a swathe of emerald perfection on a late summer day.

"Congratulations, Your Honor." The jowly partner of a competing law firm planted a damp, gin-scented kiss on her cheek. "Remember your friends when you ascend to the bench," he said with a wink.

"Mmm," Laurel murmured noncommittally. "Thanks for coming, Don." He was out of earshot by the time she finished speaking, hightailing it out to the lawn and accosting a waiter to score his third or fourth martini of the day.

She wished she could do likewise, but contented herself with another club soda and lime handed over by an attentive server. She never drank at professional functions. Running the cold glass over her heated forehead, she took a sip and gazed around. The white tent on the lawn, the champagne, the crowd … it all reminded her too much of her and George's wedding reception held here under what might have been the same tent fifteen years ago.

"Darling, I am so proud of you."

George stood there, as if her thinking about the wedding had conjured him, expensive Italian jacket making the most of his broad shoulders, dark brown hair tamed with a dab of gel, skin tanned from a weekend on the links, charm oozing from every exfoliated and moisturized pore.

"You don't get to be proud of me," Laurel said after looking around to make sure no one was within earshot. "And I'm not your darling." She realized he was holding her hand and pulled it away. "The divorce decree specifically spelled out that I was no longer your darling, sweetheart, honey-pie, or snookums—didn't you read it?"

His smile shrank a fraction, but his voice was even. "Laurel, I'm trying to congratulate you on your achievement. Being named a judge is a great honor. You've worked hard for it. Congratulations."

There was a time when his apparent sincerity and the brown eyes smiling into hers, as if she were the center of his universe, would have won her over. That time was long gone. "Thank you. Drinks are on the lawn. You know the way." She turned away to greet the elderly couple making their way across the flagstone patio using matching walkers. "Mr. and Mrs. Ellery, I haven't seen you since Easter. Thank you for coming."

A headache niggled at her temples. How long until she could decently sneak away?

―――――

An hour later, Laurel's headache had blossomed into a troop of baboons banging around inside her skull. Making polite conversation with her well-wishers was taking more effort than usual. Granted two minutes alone by a quirk of party gravity that drew the guests into orbits away from her, she plucked the lime from her tall glass and bit into it, relishing the sting on her tongue. *This party is hard because I'm not sure I want to be a judge.* The thought, as tartly bitter as the lime, jolted her. Club soda sloshed the bodice of her coral sheath. Dabbing at the damp spot, she let herself absorb the truth she'd been trying to squelch ever since her meeting with the governor last week. In the last year, she'd become more and more convinced that she wanted to have a baby, and single motherhood and a judgeship were an uncomfortable match-up. *I might as well be donning a nun's habit,* she thought as she contemplated putting on her judge's robes.

Was it ironic or moronic that now that she had achieved what she'd worked for all her life, she wasn't sure she wanted it anymore? No—that wasn't accurate. She still wanted to be a judge. She just wasn't sure she wanted it more than she wanted a baby. Moronic, definitely. She couldn't change course now just because her biological clock was tick-tocking louder than a bomb in a Jason Bourne movie, and because she was feeling … unfulfilled. No, that was too strong. Restless. She was feeling restless. A gaggle of laughing coworkers came toward her and she smiled a welcome, putting the dilemma aside to think about later.

―――――

It was after eight o'clock and dusk had fallen before she escaped and headed to her LoDo condo. In the elevator ascending from the garage, she removed her pumps and pressed *L*. Scrunching her toes under, she sighed with relief as the elevator rose. The lobby was a distinctive space with marble floors, a rectangular water feature that burbled pleasantly, and floor-to-ceiling glass walls that displayed a mountain view worth pulling out the checkbook for. The mailboxes were tucked into an alcove out of sight of potential buyers. Padding barefoot across the lobby, she stopped to chat with the doorman/security guard, who stood behind his counter.

"How's it going, Miss Muir?"

No matter how she tried, she couldn't get him to call her Laurel. "Fine," she said automatically, and asked how his daughter's soccer tournament had gone. Puffing his cheeks with pride, he gave her a blow-by-blow account of the girl's three goals in one game. When his phone rang, she lifted a hand in farewell and headed toward the mail alcove. *Mail, bath, bed.* She peered into her box. It was crammed full, as she'd suspected it might be since she hadn't had time to empty it all week.

She punched in her combo. The contents sprang at her when she opened the small door. She caught a *Discover* magazine, but circulars and envelopes cascaded to the floor.

"Damn," she muttered, stooping. She collected the bills in one hand and scooped the flyers and other junk into a pile to dump in the trash can in the corner. As she shifted the final piece, a Talbots catalog, it revealed another envelope.

Laurel stilled, staring at the envelope as if it harbored anthrax. It was orange—no, tangerine. Evangeline, possibly the least superstitious person alive, had always said tangerine was her lucky color. It was invitation-sized, with "The Honorable Laurel Muir" and her address inscribed in beautiful calligraphy, thick, dark strokes that stood out against the tangerine color like a tiger's stripes. She hadn't received one of these in ten years, not since the last weekend went so horribly, tragically awry. She considered bundling it with the grocery circulars and dumping it, unopened, in the trash.

Instead, she reached for it, hesitated, and picked it up with her thumb and forefinger. It was heavier than she remembered, the stock a thick vellum from a high-end stationer. She inserted a manicured nail under the flap, but stopped. No, better to open this upstairs, in private. Trashing the junk mail, she crossed the lobby again.

"Not bad news, I hope, Miss Muir?" Dean called.

So much for her poker face. She got on the elevator and turned to face him. "Unexpected," she said, as the doors shut.

———

Dawn Infanti struggled with the dress's zipper and gave up. The human shoulder wasn't made to twist like that. "Ky, can you zip me, please?" She half-squatted beside Kyra's side of the bed and presented her back.

"I'd rather *unzip* you," Kyra said, but she tugged the zipper up.

"Thanks." Dawn turned and gave Kyra a peck on the lips.

"Why so fancy today?" Kyra propped herself on one elbow, the sheet slipping to reveal her small breasts. Short purple hair stuck out at all angles. On some forty-year-old women purple hair would have looked clownish or sad, but not on Kyra. It suited her perfectly.

"Important meeting, new client," Dawn said. She found the gladiator sandals and tied the crisscross laces, and then twisted her unruly hair into a knot and skewered it with an enameled chopstick. She paused in front of the fogged bathroom mirror. There. Professional but artsy.

"Are you going to be late again tonight?"

Dawn pretended to look for her keys so she wouldn't have to meet Kyra's eyes. "Maybe. I don't know yet. Probably." Guilt niggled at her, but she couldn't make herself tell Kyra the truth. Maybe if it turned out the way she hoped. If not, well, she didn't need a replay of the commiserations and sympathy.

"Tell Vera to jump off a bridge if she tries to make you stay late again. It's not like the economy will collapse if your illustration of an amoeba gets finished tomorrow instead of today."

"A virus, actually. A new thogotovirus called the Bourbon virus."

A sardonic grin slanted across Kyra's face. "Of course. Your portrait of the world-famous thuggo virus." She flung the sheet aside and slid out of bed, gloriously naked. "I gotta pee."

Dawn stood, smoothing the tight skirt over her thighs. Had she gained a couple of pounds?

"Oh, I forgot to tell you," Kyra called from the bathroom. "Your mom called yesterday."

"Did she leave a message?" *Of course not.*

"Of course not." The toilet flushing drowned out part of Kyra's next words: " ... won't talk to me."

Dawn supposed she'd have to call her mother back. Her New York friends talked about Jewish mothers ladling out the guilt, but they had nothing on Catholic mothers, especially not Italian Catholic mothers. Teresa Infanti had liked Kyra just fine until the day she stopped believing the fiction she'd created for herself that Dawn and Kyra were only roommates. For the past two years, she'd refused to say a word to her daughter's lover or acknowledge her presence at family gatherings.

Dawn caught sight of the time. "I'm out the door, sweets. See you tonight. I'll try to be earlier. Really."

Her sandals slapped the hardwood floor as she hurried through the narrow hall to the living room. Sunlight blared through the louvers of the shutters she and Kyra had hung two weekends ago, striping the creamy plaster walls. Pausing only to slide her leather portfolio from behind the entertainment center where she'd secreted it, she stepped out of the house into the muggy furnace blast of a mid-summer San Antonio day. Her step was buoyant. Today was the day. She felt it.

———————

Dawn parked her silver Honda Civic at the curb shortly after six o'clock that evening and slumped in the seat. How many times could an artist hear the words, "No, not for us, not the right vibe, doesn't resonate with me, abstracts don't sell, I could take pastels of the Alamo or the Riverwalk on commission if you want to give it a try," before she gave up? Just gave up. Quit painting. Accepted that she didn't have what it took, that her father had had her best interests in mind when he told her to study accounting. That Evangeline had been right. Damn it! She struck the steering wheel with the heel of her palm, bruising it. She sucked on the sore spot.

The building heat forced her out of the car. It might technically be evening, but the sun hadn't heard the news. It was still set to "broil." She eyed the plebeian Civic with disgruntlement. She'd rather drive a Miata like Kyra or, better yet, a Mustang, but scientific illustrators didn't make that kind of money. And artists who couldn't find a gallery to display their work made zippo. She tamped down the spurt of envy. The Civic was more practical for transporting her paintings anyway. She chewed her lip, reluctant to bring her portfolio in and generate questions from Kyra, but it was way too hot to leave her paintings out here. She should just take a flash drive with digital images of her work to the galleries, but there was something enticing about an actual painting, the faint odor of oil paint, the way the light glossed the smooth expanses and danced over the choppier textures she created with a palette knife. She hefted the portfolio and locked the car. With any luck, Kyra would be busy cooking dinner and she could slide it behind the entertainment center again, or under the bed.

No such luck. Kyra was sitting in the living room when Dawn pushed the door open with her foot. Her melon-colored yoga wear contrasted powerfully with her hair. She looked relaxed and carefree after a day at her studio, and for a split second Dawn hated her. Kyra's success as a yoga and meditation center owner—no, her *fulfillment*—burned like lemon juice on a paper cut. It wasn't fair. Then Kyra glanced up from the pile of mail she was sorting, and smiled, and the caustic emotion evaporated as quickly as it had come.

Kyra started to say, "Hey, you're home earlier than I—" but her gaze snagged on the portfolio. "Oh. I'm so sorry, honey. I didn't know you were—"

Her immediate sympathy grated on Dawn. "Why do you assume I didn't get invited to show my paintings? Why the immediate assumption that I got rejected again?"

Kyra straightened, and irritation wiped the concern from her face. "Because when you come home with a face like someone ran over your pet spaniel, then I *assume* no one offered you thousands for the opportunity to display your work."

She rose and came to Dawn, trying to enfold her in a hug, but Dawn shrugged her off and bent to unlace the stupid effing sandals which had rubbed raw spots on her little toes.

"Honey—" Kyra broke off and raked her fingers through her short hair as Dawn kicked the sandals viciously across the room. One slid under the couch and the other bounced off the baseboard. "Honey, you said you were done with this. You said you were satisfied with your job, that you were going to think about teaching classes at that new studio downtown. You said that the two of us being together was enough to make you happy, that you didn't need—"

"I said, I said." Dawn leaned the portfolio against the wall where it would be a reminder of her failure all evening. Like she needed reminding. Some of the frustration leaked out of her, leaving her limp and defeated. She let Kyra hug her, and took a morsel of comfort from the vanilla skin scent of Kyra's neck. "I said a lot of things," she said quietly. Her gaze fell on the pile of mail. The corner of an envelope caught her eye. Her breath hitched. It couldn't be. She pulled away from Kyra. "What's that?"

Kyra turned to see what she was looking at. "That orange envelope?"

"Tangerine."

"Orange, tangerine, or papaya, it's for you. Looks like a wedding invitation—fancy calligraphy."

"It's not a wedding." Ten years evaporated in an instant. Dawn knew exactly what the invitation was for and her blood ran cold. She'd always thought that phrase was the colorful invention of horror writers, but it felt like someone had pumped liquid nitrogen into her veins, raising goose bumps on her arms. Her thumb and forefinger massaged her right earlobe.

Kyra gave her a strange look. "Aren't you going to open it?"

"It might be better if I don't."

———

Ellie Ordahl idled at a four-way stop, hoping one of the other cars would go out of turn so she could lean on her horn and have an outlet for her frustration. If the blue Kia that had pulled up a nanosecond after she did started to accelerate, she could surge into the intersection, blaring her horn to remind the Kia's driver that in a civilized world, we take turns. The Kia's driver politely waved Ellie ahead and she stomped on the gas too hard, making the van lurch into the intersection. She waved and smiled her thanks while hating him for denying her the dual pleasures of being pissed off and feeling self-righteous.

Her son Shane, the older twin by six minutes, leaned forward from the shotgun seat to switch the radio from the country-western station she preferred to the alternative rock noise he liked. "Turn it down," she said at the same time Aidan said "Turn it up" from the back seat.

She used the controls on her steering wheel to turn off the radio. After a "Hey, I like that song," Shane slumped in his seat and concentrated on texting, thumbs tapping quicker than a woodpecker drilling for grubs. Probably texting Hailey, his girlfriend of six months. At least that was one good thing, the only good thing, about him leaving for the University of Alabama—it would put some distance between him and Hailey, a perfectly nice girl, but a needy one. Ellie recognized the type. She'd been Hailey, once upon a time. Needy led to poor life choices and she didn't want Shane's future compromised the way hers had been.

As they pulled into the Target parking lot, a pick-up truck reversed out of a spot, almost dinging them. "Get off your phone and watch what the heck you're doing," Ellie muttered, standing on the brakes and automatically extending an arm in front of Shane as if he were seven instead of seventeen.

"You can say 'hell,' Mom," he said. "We went to high school— we've heard worse."

His comment summoned the memory of Evangeline telling her "use your big girl words" every time she said "frickin'" or "heck" when they were in college. She could never bring herself to do it, although the way people drove these days tempted her.

Aidan griped, "I still don't know why we need to get dorm stuff now. It's two weeks before we have to leave. I told Ryan and Christian I'd hang with them this morning."

"I want black sheets," Shane said, proving he could hear past his earbuds when he wanted to. "With black sheets it won't matter if I don't wash them all semester." He and Aidan bumped fists.

Hoping he was only trying to get a rise from her, Ellie marched toward the store.

Forty-five minutes later, unloading towels, sheets, storage bins, desk organizers, beanbag chairs, socks, and underwear (lots of the latter for fear the boys really weren't going to do laundry all semester) onto the checkout belt, Ellie watched her boys josh around. They were achingly handsome—fit and energetic and sun-bronzed from all the hours in the pool. Shane, the more outgoing, was a shade taller and had hair that was a richer gold. Aidan, more introverted, had the sweetest smile she'd ever seen, a shy flash of teeth that dimpled his left cheek. It was suddenly hard to breathe around the lump in her throat.

The scanner beeped each time the cashier swiped an item and the staggering total mounted up. What was she going to do when her boys left? She only had two more weeks with them, then they were dropping Shane in Tuscaloosa. Two days later, they'd make the trek to Purdue where Aidan had won a full-ride scholarship for swimming. Then ... then it would be home to an empty, quiet house where she'd rattle around purposeless ten hours a day, trying to keep herself from texting the boys—from being *that* mother who couldn't let go, even though she was afraid that's exactly who she was—while Scott worked, doing his mysterious satellite stuff at Schriever Air Force Base.

She smacked a box of pencils onto the conveyor belt. She had her Lia Sophia business, but making a few extra bucks selling jewelry didn't add up to a career. It was nothing more than a part-time job, one step up from the hobby Scott called it. What did she have to show for her thirty-eight years on the planet? Okay, she'd raised two great boys—young men—and that was something, but it didn't feel like

11

enough. Laurel ... now, Laurel had a career. She was a high-powered lawyer, a partner in her father's firm, about to become a judge. Ellie was willing to bet Laurel didn't mope around with a glass of sauvignon blanc in the evenings, waiting for a husband to come home from work and the boys to trickle back from the activities that ate up all their after-school time these days, trying to figure out what she wanted to be when she grew up.

"Ma'am?" The cashier's tone suggested he'd been trying to get her attention. "That's five hundred eighty-seven and fifty-two cents, ma'am. Debit or credit?"

Sheesh. Tuition payments were only the tip of the iceberg.

"Shotgun!" Aidan called, jostling past Shane as they headed toward the exit.

————

Back in their Wolf Ranch neighborhood, Ellie bumped the van up onto the curb by the community mailboxes and nudged Aidan to hop out and check their box. "The price of riding shotgun," she said.

He scooped a handful of mail from the box and began to sort it as she continued to their house. "All junk," he pronounced, letting it slide into the collapsible trash container between the van's front seats.

Ellie pulled into the driveway. The boys jumped out before the van was fully stopped and raced each other into the house, not bothering to take so much as a single bag with them. Ellie hardly noticed. Had she seen a flash of orange? If so, it would turn out to be nothing more than a come-on from a university trying to recruit one of the boys. The car still idling, Ellie pawed through the small trash can. There. An orange envelope. She retrieved it, stained brown on one corner from the contents of this morning's Starbucks cup, and the van jolted forward as her foot slipped.

12

Adrenaline whooshed into her system and she stomped on the brake, stopping the car six inches from the garage door. Scott would have a frickin' cow if she banged up the van only a month after the repairs from Shane's fender bender at the skateboard park. She cut the engine and stared at the envelope in her lap. Not a college come-on. An invitation. An invitation to a girls' weekend. Just like old times.

She wouldn't be able to go, of course. North Carolina was so far. Scott and the boys couldn't fend for themselves—who knew how many appointments and activities they'd miss if she weren't here? Besides, she wasn't willing to give up ten seconds of precious time with the boys, not when they were leaving so soon and she wouldn't see them again until Thanksgiving. There was no point to reading the invitation. She tore open the envelope, her gaze sweeping over the familiar format and details. A month from now, the first weekend in September. The boys would already be gone. Plenty of time to get a good deal on airfare. She didn't even want to go—did she?—not after the last weekend.

Yes, she decided, getting out of the van. She did. Even if it meant revisiting what had happened.

———

Geneva Frost considered the fifteen-year-old girl perched on the edge of the comfy recliner positioned across from her own wing chair. Expensively dressed in the latest logoed teen gear, including a hoodie that she'd pulled forward to hide most of her face, Marta gnawed on her thumbnail and tapped a foot so fast it sounded like a playing card stuck between bicycle spokes. The thought whooshed Geneva back to her childhood momentarily, to her brothers racing their bikes through the neighborhood, playing cards clothes-pinned to the spokes. Jimmie was dead, killed in a drive-by shooting when he was not much older than Marta, and Leland was in prison with another year to serve on his assault and battery conviction. Did kids even ride bikes anymore?

"Do you have a bicycle?" she asked Marta.

The unexpectedness of the question brought Marta's head up. Geneva caught a flash of green eyes behind a scrim of black bangs before Marta looked down again and mumbled. "Yeah. I mean, I haven't ridden it in years. The tires are probably flat." With her chin tucked toward her chest, she glared at Geneva from under her brows. "Aren't we supposed to be talking about my eating, Dr. Frost?"

Geneva ignored the girl's hostile tone. "We can talk about whatever you need to talk about, Marta."

The girl turned her head with deliberation and stared out the office window. Suppressing a sigh, Geneva followed her gaze. Mostly, the view consisted of blue-gray sky impaled by the skyscrapers that surrounded her office building. If she leaned a bit to her right she could glimpse a white-capped Lake Michigan far below. Despite the wind, the sailors were out in force on a bright summer day, their sails neat triangles of color against the gray water. A pigeon flapped heavily against the wind and then gave up, settling on the ledge outside the window and cooing softly. Summons for a mate, or lament for not getting where she'd been trying to go?

"Did you bring your food diary?" she asked Marta.

"Forgot." The girl's tone challenged Geneva to call her on the lie. *Taptaptaptaptaptap* went her foot.

The baby shifted and must have kicked her bladder because suddenly Geneva had to pee. She surreptitiously checked the time. Thirty-six minutes left in her first session of the day. Stifling a groan and the urge to pee, she tried to remember why she'd ever thought counseling girls with body image problems and eating disorders was a good idea. Sure, during her pageant days she'd seen the damage girls could inflict on themselves by buying into society's idea of the perfect body, but right now she wished she'd decided to concentrate on marriage counseling, or any specialty that didn't involve teens.

———————

"What made me think I wanted to work with teenage girls?" she asked Geonwoo when she got home. In her third trimester, she'd shortened her hours, enabling her to beat the rush-hour crowds clogging the train and reach their townhouse by five o'clock, with a quick stop at Jewels on the way. Only months after they married, they'd lucked into the house within walking distance of Northwestern when a Realtor friend gave them a head's up that the owner had died and her heirs wanted a quick sale. He'd said the house was a bit of a fixer-upper—an understatement, if ever there was one—but they'd never have been able to afford the neighborhood otherwise, so they'd gulped and signed on the dotted line.

Geonwoo beat her home every day except Wednesday, when he taught an evening class at the university. She envied him being able to walk to work, and thought for the thousandth time about leaving the group practice she'd joined after getting her PhD five years ago to start a solo practice closer to home. Also for the thousandth time, she thought about how she would miss the interaction with her coworkers, the way they gathered in the break room to discuss their cases and bat around treatment ideas, and talked about kids and spouses and *How to Get Away with Murder* and the shitty state of Chicago politics, and traded recipes for gluten-free dishes or holiday party cocktails. She'd miss that, and she knew the bonds of friendship would fray and get flabby, like old rubber bands, if they weren't seeing each other

15

regularly. The occasional lunch or outing wouldn't cut it. Friends were worth the commute.

"You love those girls and you know they need you. You're just tired," Geonwoo said, taking the grocery bags and putting them on the counter. He opened his arms. She walked into them and looped her arms around his neck, sagging gratefully against his triathlon-hard body.

"A little. The baby was kicking up a storm today. I think she's going to be a soccer player, or an Irish clog dancer."

"She'd stand out in an Irish dance class, I think." He ducked and pressed his lips against her burgeoning belly through the cotton of her maternity blouse. "Lila, you've got to take it easy on your momma. Let her get a good night's sleep tonight, hmm?" He held his ear against her stomach and then looked up. "She says she'll be a little angel tonight."

Geneva made a sound between a giggle and a snort and pulled him upright to kiss him. "You're a goof, but I love you." She'd won the relationship Powerball with this wonderful man, and the gift of a baby girl who would make her appearance in two short months. They were all proof of God's grace, because He certainly knew she didn't deserve them. Quite the contrary. "How was your day?"

"The usual, with the added joy of a departmental meeting. Arguments about candidates for the new endowed professorship, reminders about advising, paperwork for sabbaticals due in triplicate, woo wop da bam." He pulled defrosted chicken breasts and an assortment of fresh vegetables out of the fridge, and slid a knife out of the block.

The clink of the mail slot and slither of envelopes into their front hall interrupted Geneva's commiserations. "Mail's late today," she observed.

With the rhythmic *ka-thunk* of Geonwoo's knife following her, she returned to the foyer. Four envelopes lay on the parquet floor, the one closest to her a bright tangerine color. Her brows rose toward her hairline. She was surprised to see the invitation, but also felt as if it were something she'd been expecting every year for the past decade. A sudden longing for a vodka tonic ambushed her, the strongest craving in years. She fought it back, her hands shaking as she bent to pick up the tangerine envelope. It just might represent the opportunity she'd been waiting for. Ignoring the other envelopes, she bore the tangerine one into the kitchen to show Geonwoo.

Two

In her eighth-floor condo, Laurel put the envelope on the granite counter, poured the bourbon she'd denied herself at the party, and carried it to her bedroom, taking two long swallows on the way. It burned all the way down to her stomach and she relaxed a notch. Shucking off the coral sheath, she dropped it in the dry-cleaning hamper and shrugged into knit loungewear. Her stomach gurgled, reminding her she hadn't paused to eat more than a shrimp or two at the party, and she returned to the kitchen to forage, carefully not looking at the envelope. It wasn't something to face on an empty stomach.

Nuking leftover Thai food, she let her gaze drift over the living room, taking in the cool grays and lavenders that always soothed her after a contentious day of litigation. The space was open, with pale oak floors and a minimum of furniture. No knickknacks or clutter. Some might find it boring, but Laurel found peace in the clean lines and openness. Sectional seating formed a U facing the wall of windows. The colors complemented the stunning mountain view, hidden now by night. *No more litigating*, she thought, parking herself on the chair-and-a-half that was her favorite seat, and tucking her feet underneath her. *The Boys on the Boat*, the memoir she'd started the night before, lay face down on the table beside her, and she tried to read a chapter while forking up her *gaeng daeng* with its powerful aromas of lime and coconut, but she couldn't concentrate.

Her gaze went to the envelope. Annoyed with herself for not being able to resist its pull, she dumped her dishes in the sink and picked it up. She returned to her chair and sat, fingers rubbing the creamy cardstock. *Might as well get it over with.* Sliding a fingernail under the flap, she unsealed it and withdrew the folded invitation. She flipped it up and the fragrance of Opium wafted out, voluptuous notes of mandarin orange, sandalwood, and clove fighting with the leftover smell of coconut from her Thai dinner.

The sense of smell was most closely tied to memories, she'd read. Well, tonight was as good a night as any for memories—the good ones, anyway. She closed her eyes and lifted the card to her nose. She sniffed tentatively and flashed on Evangeline doubled over with laughter in their dorm room, in the dean's office that was the scene of their joint disgrace, and in a jam-packed Raleigh nightclub where they'd been squished so closely together by the crowd that Laurel might as well have sprayed herself with the perfume. She inhaled deeply. She'd thought the scent might carry her back to the first time she met Evangeline Paul, but it landed her in the last weekend instead, the weekend that ended with Evangeline's broken body sprawled on the ground five stories below her bedroom balcony.

Ten years earlier

Laurel let Evangeline pull her into a hug in the foyer of the Chateau du Cygne Noir bed and breakfast, listing to the right with the weight of her suitcase. Crowded with petit-pointed chairs, the gleam of antique wood, dozens of oil paintings by "from the school of" minor artists, and collectibles on every horizontal surface, the inn's entryway oppressed her slightly, as it had the first time they'd come here for spring break. Many people—Evangeline, for instance—were charmed by the Old World figurines and glassware, the Spode plates and decorative mirrors, the vases and lace doilies and candelabras parked atop a Louis Something buffet. For Laurel, the foyer's contents spoke of centuries of heritage and responsibilities and made her feel tired just being in the same room. She turned away from the china shepherdess on the table who looked disgruntled at having been relocated from France to North Carolina along with every stone and timber of the old castle.

"Yay, you're here," Evangeline said, squeezing hard. Her hair tickled Laurel's nose and gave off a hint of Opium. Laurel resisted the urge to sneeze, hugged Evangeline with one arm, and separated. Her friend hadn't changed in the year since she'd seen her. Light brown hair threaded with cinnamon and cognac was piled messily atop her head, and her feet were bare, as they almost invariably were. Her toenails were painted a clear orchid. Her skin was still unlined and lightly freckled, just as it was the first time she'd talked them all into heading for an inland B and B called Castle of the Black Swan for spring break, instead of to the beach where (it seemed) every other student at Grissom University was going for a week of sun and surf.

"Are the others here yet?" Laurel asked.

"Somewhere. You're in the same room as always." Evangeline hefted Laurel's suitcase and yelped. "What have you got in here? Did you rob Fort Knox on the way in?"

"Work."

Evangeline screwed up her face. "No work this weekend," she decreed. "You know the rules."

"Yeah, well, if I'm going to make partner, I'm going to have to work." Just because Evangeline had introduced them to the B and B didn't mean she got to set the rules. Laurel left the thought unsaid and followed her friend. The staircase swept upward from the entryway in a graceful swoosh of mahogany banister and wide treads carpeted down the middle with an Oriental runner. A coil of hair came loose from Evangeline's topknot and bobbed against her shoulder with every step, hypnotizing Laurel. Evangeline turned right when they reached the fourth floor landing and stopped two doors down. "Here we are."

Laurel stepped across the threshold of the room that had been "hers" since the first time they came to Cygne. She crossed the wood floor to the window, pulled the heavy velvet drapes, and opened the door to step onto the Juliet balcony, little more than a foothold with no room for a Romeo. The stone balustrade was cool beneath her hands. The mown lawn and flower beds, and the naturalized area beyond it, a tangle of ferns, hostas, and decorative grasses in early summer, beckoned her. She glimpsed the blue of the small lake past the thicket of live oaks, dogwoods, and magnolias. A gentler landscape than she was used to—no granite peaks or prickly evergreens. Inhaling deeply, she relaxed and turned back to Evangeline, who stood still in that way she had, watching her with a smile in her eyes.

"Do you have a cocktail dress in there?" Evangeline nodded at the suitcase. "For the party?"

"The invitation said to bring one, and you called twice to remind me, so, yes, I have a dress. A new one, actually. I wish you'd tell us what we're celebrating," Laurel said.

Evangeline's face shone with mischief. "All in due time," she said.

Footsteps sounded from the hall, and Geneva and Dawn burst in, full of hugs and greeting and conversation. Laurel smiled and laughed and was glad she'd come.

———————

Ice tinkled as Laurel downed the last swallow of bourbon, breaking her free from the memory. She was glad. She didn't want to think about the rest of that weekend. It had started with such promise and ended in tragedy, suspicion, and a police investigation. Horrible. She crunched on a piece of ice and wondered if the others had received invitations, too. Were they coming? Geneva Frost was the only one she talked to, and not often. She and Ellie exchanged occasional emails and had said they'd do lunch now that she and Scott were stationed an hour down the road in Colorado Springs, but that hadn't happened. She'd last seen Dawn three or four years ago when she and her pre-Kyra girlfriend spent a night in Denver on their way to Yellowstone. It had been fun to catch up, but it hadn't sparked more regular interaction.

Laurel tipped the remainder of her ice-diluted bourbon into the sink. Her gaze fell on the invitation, lying atop *The Boys in the Boat*, and she picked it up. She made as if to tear it in half, but stopped. With a sigh, she returned to the kitchen and stuck it to the refrigerator with an octopus magnet she'd gotten at the Baltimore Aquarium. The orange square stood out among the casual snapshots of friends and family, a graduation announcement, and a baby shower invitation. After a moment, she moved the octopus and invitation to the fridge's side, where she wouldn't have to look at it in the morning.

Three

Ellie got the boys sorted out and walked into the bedroom, where Scott lay on the bed simultaneously responding to emails on his tablet and watching a news program on the television. She gritted her teeth. Couldn't he just once jump in and referee the boys instead of leaving it to her to be the bad guy all the frickin' time? The bedside lamp shone on his bald spot. Other than that sign of aging, he looked much as he had when they met in college. His military-short blond hair showed little gray, and his bare chest and shoulders were tanned and muscular against the pale yellow sheets. She felt a tingle in her groin but ignored it. The sex was still hot, but she wasn't in the mood.

He didn't acknowledge her presence and, after a moment, she crossed to the bathroom and got ready for bed, removing her makeup and applying a retinoid cream and the deluxe moisturizer she'd splurged on two weeks ago, careful not to tug on the skin around her eyes. She was only thirty-eight, but when people heard she had kids in college, they were going to assume she was older, and she needed all the ammunition she had to counteract those assumptions. She'd never been a beauty queen like Geneva, and she didn't have Evangeline's elusive "certain sort of something," but she'd always been pretty in a sporty, girl-next-door way. The blond streaks in her hair might owe more to L'Oreal than the sun these days, but her body was still tight thanks to the swimming. She hadn't given it up, not even when she lost the scholarship or was pregnant with the boys.

Slipping into the extra-large Y T-shirt she used as a nightgown, she came to the bed, turning off the TV on her way past. The pundits spewing doom and gloom gave her nightmares.

"I was watching that," Scott said. A line appeared between his brows, half hidden by the silver rims of his glasses.

"You know I didn't even want a TV in the bedroom." The same old argument. Now he would say, *It's part of my job* ...

"It's part of my job to stay on top of international news," he said, going for the remote. "North Korea launched another missile today."

She snatched the remote away and set it out of his reach on her bedside table. "It's part of *my* job to be alert and well-rested so I can be chauffeur, cook, mediator, maid, and social coordinator."

He sighed heavily, in the way that implied she was being childish or self-aggrandizing, and went back to his emails. Flumping on her side and supporting herself on one elbow, she faced him.

"I got an invitation to the girls' weekend," she said, "and I want to go."

"So go," he said absently, fingers clicking on the keyboard. "I keep telling you, you should have more fun." He scrolled up on his computer. "Is this Susan's idea? Are you going to one of the ski resorts? That'll be fun. Hot tubs."

"North Carolina."

It took him a moment. Then his head jerked up. "What?"

"Cygne Castle." She thrust her chin out a hair.

"Ellie."

"What?" Her look challenged him to spell out his objections.

"It's not a good idea."

"Says who?"

His brows knit together. "Come on. You can't tell me you think it's a good idea. Not after what happened."

"Those women are my friends."

"*Were* your friends."

"Are."

"Besides Laurel, when's the last time you talked to one of them?"

"I keep up with Dawn."

"Facebook doesn't count. Let's analyze your 'relationships' with them. Take Dawn—"

She scooched upwards into a sitting position and crossed her arms over her chest. "Let's not. I am not one of your lieutenants, and I don't need 'mentoring.' If I want to meet up with my friends for a girls' weekend, I will. We'll have a few laughs, catch up, talk about the old days—it'll be fine."

"Fine." He bit the word out. "But don't expect me to pick up the pieces when it all goes to hell."

Ellie flashed on Evangeline's body, splayed and bloody. *Pick up the pieces …* "What a vicious thing to say."

Scott flushed under his runner's tan. "I didn't mean it that way."

Choosing not to believe him and giving him a look that said so, Ellie swiveled toward her nightstand. Tears leaked. She didn't want to be mean to Scott, to push a wedge between them, but sometimes she couldn't help herself. He made it harder when he treated her like one of his subordinates, trying to lead her to decisions he'd decided were the correct ones by guiding her thought processes. She hated that.

She put in the earplugs that would block the sounds the boys made when they came up in a couple of hours, turned off the lamp on her bedside table, and donned the facemask that cut the glare from Scott's frickin' electronic devices. Plumping her pillow, she presented her back to Scott and closed her eyes. After a moment, she pushed the mask up, scrabbled for the remote, and silently passed it to Scott. He took it and turned the TV on, setting the volume at a low level. His hand rested on her hip. She pulled the mask down again, hoping she wasn't about to make the second-biggest mistake of her life.

———————

"I think you should go. I could come with you," Kyra said four days after the invitation came. "I can find someone to run the studio for a couple of days. I'd like to meet your college friends. Geneva's the only one I've met, and I liked her a lot. When she came for the psychology association conference down on the River Walk, remember? We ate dinner at Mi Ti's."

They sat in their sunny kitchen nook, preparing for the day. The sun blasted in, even this early, and a mockingbird sang his plagiarized song from a low tree branch. Kyra had a bowl of muesli in front of her and was slicing strawberries onto it. Dawn poured a diet protein shake into a glass, hoping it would look more appetizing that way. No such luck.

No. Dawn was shocked by her negative reaction to Kyra's suggestion. "No. I mean, you don't know the others, we have so much history, you wouldn't know what we're talking about, the in-jokes, the references to teachers or other friends from college. You'd be bored." That was so weak. Kyra was never bored. She could strike up a conversation with anyone, lose herself in a book, or spend half an hour watching a bumblebee buzz around a lily and be fascinated the whole time.

Kyra popped the last strawberry into her mouth and said thickly, "I thought you said Angela—or was it Deanna?—one of your sisters, anyway, went to one of the weekends."

"That was the year we graduated." The memory of that particular weekend made Dawn shake and the glass rattle against her teeth. She set it down and licked off the creamy moustache. "Up till then, there'd be extras now and then, friends or significant others. Ellie brought Scott one weekend, I remember, and I took Angela. It was awkward." *Understatement of the year.* Awkward didn't begin to describe the humiliation and confusion when Evangeline kissed her in full view of Angela, laid a real lip-lock on her and caressed her breast, making it crystal clear to her younger sister that their relationship had elements their strict Catholic family would not approve of. When Dawn, crying, laid into Evangeline for outing her to her family, Evangeline put an arm around her shoulders and said that her relationship with her family should be based on honesty, and that they would all be closer now. Not so much. Two months later, Evangeline's experiment with lesbianism was over and she left Dawn for the grad student TA of her biology class.

"Honey, they can't stop you from bringing anyone you want," Kyra said into Dawn's silence.

Dawn could tell her feelings were hurt. "It's not that I don't want you to come," she said, rising and wrapping her arms around her lover from behind, hugging her over the chair. "I do," she lied. She didn't want Kyra to come not because she didn't love her, but because she didn't want to associate Kyra in her mind and memories with the girls' weekends, with what had happened at the last one, which was bound to color the upcoming one. Wishing she could say it all in a way Kyra would understand and not be pissed about, she said, "Having other people there changes the dynamic, and—"

"Maybe that would be a good thing."

"It might," Dawn agreed.

Kyra finished her cereal, kissed Dawn's forearm that hung across her collar bone, and stood up. "Why now?" she asked, taking her bowl to the sink and rinsing it.

"I don't know." Dawn had wondered that herself. The invitation hadn't specified. She downed the rest of her diet shake, wishing it were scrambled eggs with a side of blueberry pancakes. "Maybe it's the ten-year thing, like a reunion."

"Hmm." Kyra pursed her lips. "I guess it doesn't really matter." She put her hands on her slim hips and met Dawn's gaze squarely. "The police never figured out what happened, did they?"

"It was an accident," Dawn insisted. "They called it an accident. Evangeline was tipsy, the balcony railings were low ... "

Concern darkened Kyra's blue eyes. "On second thought, I don't think you should go. What if it wasn't an accident? Then one of those women pushed her."

"That's ridiculous. If it wasn't an accident, it was someone else, a staff member, someone trying to rob the place ... " That sounded as ridiculous now as it did ten years ago when she suggested it to the police. She could still feel the sting of the deputy's sarcasm: "What thief would be looking for jewels or electronics on a balcony the size of home plate with no hiding place, not even a potted plant?"

Their tabby cat, Mr. Bojangles, snaked between Dawn's ankles and she bent to pat him. He purred his approval and butted his head into her palm. Even though she didn't want to go back, she also didn't want to be the only one who didn't go, she realized. Besides, she cared about these women. Nothing bad would happen this time. That would be like lightning striking the same place, or the same person winning the lottery twice in a row.

She straightened. "I'm going to go," she said.

Kyra gave her the raised brows that usually meant, *Don't you want to rethink the stupid thing you just said?*

"It'll be good to reconnect." Dawn shivered. Mr. Bojangles' tail had brushed her leg. That's all it was.

Laurel decided that the best thing about being a judge would be not bumping into her ex-husband every day at the office. Both partners at Muir, Delacruz, and Jackson, they had offices on the same floor (although George had a corner office since he'd been a partner far longer), attended many of the same meetings, and had side-by-side parking slots in the garage. When she'd first found out about his secretaries and cocktail waitresses, it had taken every ounce of willpower not to "accidentally" ding the door of his Aston Martin Vanquish every morning when she parked. Carrie Underwood's "Before He Cheats" had been her anthem that summer, but she'd never worked up the guts to buy a Louisville Slugger.

Now, she looked at him over the top of the box stacked high with plaques and mementoes and precariously crowned with two potted violets. It was the last one.

"I'm going to miss you, Laurel," he said, hitching his hip onto her empty desk. His voice was low and intimate, with just the right touch of regret. "It won't be the same around here."

"Same meetings, same coffee, same clients—I don't think it'll be unrecognizable." She hefted the box in her arms, burying her chin in one violet to hold it steady.

"Let me get that for you." He came around the desk and his hand grazed her breast as he tried to take the box. His minty breath told her he'd gargled in his private bathroom, generally a prelude to an amorous encounter, or a post-encounter precaution. He might want to kiss her goodbye. Fat chance. Their goodbye kiss had happened five years after they married, although neither of them had known at the time it was their last kiss. Strange, that, how "lasts" could happen without any fanfare or notice; they could be over and done with before you noticed their significance.

"I've got it, thanks," she said, stepping back.

He cocked his head and didn't fight her for it. Sliding his hands into his pockets, he leaned his shoulders against the now-bare wall. "What are you going to do with yourself before you get sworn in?"

"Relax. Finish *The Boys on the Boat*. Maybe take a trip."

"Really? Where? Alone?"

She knew he took a strange pride in the fact that she hadn't remarried, hadn't even had a serious relationship since they divorced. She suspected he thought she was pining for him, or that she couldn't find a man who measured up. Truth was, she was too damn busy, and it was too exhausting trying to work the hours she worked and date, too. And don't even get her started on how hard it was to find men who didn't live with their mothers, support two ex-wives and assorted offspring, or worship at the Broncos altar to the exclusion of all other activities from August through the Super Bowl.

"With friends," she said, putting the box down. It was getting heavy. "In fact, I'm going to Cygne." She hadn't made up her mind until that moment.

"That castle where you used to go with your college friends? Why?"

Good question. She crossed to the window and looked down on busy Auraria Parkway, twiddling the blinds wand. "We had some special times together at the castle. It's a shame, in a way, that we let the tragedy end our weekends. Those women were—are—important to

30

me. They were part of my life when I went from sheltered high schooler to college woman—"

"You wild thing, you."

"—to lawyer." She turned and gave him a look. He knew how sedate most of her college experience had been; her father had kept him posted. "I wouldn't be the same me now if I hadn't known them. Collectively, they know things about me that no one else does. Like Jackson and I share memories of our growing-up years that won't exist anymore if either of us gets hit by a bus. Does that make any sense?"

Why was she explaining this to him? Because, even though he couldn't keep his dick in his pants, he had a surprising capacity for empathy; it's what had drawn her to him in the first place. And because she was a little bit melancholy about leaving the firm, the place she'd worked for almost fifteen years—twenty, if you counted her time as a summer intern. Lots of memories here, too.

"Of course it does," he said. "Like me and Mark"—his best friend—"or like soldiers and the guys they shared a foxhole with. Even people you might otherwise not like much can be special to you because you experienced something transformational together."

That was it exactly, damn him. "I don't think the military does foxholes anymore, but, yes."

"I'll stipulate that your relationship with those women was important, but maybe you should leave it be. Friendships run their course."

"Like marriages?" She regretted the words immediately and held up an apologetic hand.

He let her comment pass. "I drove out to bring you home after the last get-together," he said, narrowing his eyes and observing her closely. "You were a basket case. I don't think you ate or slept for a week. Remember?"

Was he kidding? "One of my friends pushed another one off a fifth-floor balcony. I was a suspect. Of course I remember." She also remembered a giggly soprano voice in the background when she called to tell him what had happened and begged him to come to North Carolina.

"If you believe that, then why go?"

"*Because* I believe that. Because it's time to figure out who it was so the rest of us can be friends again. Or not, as we choose. It feels like the choice was taken from us, though, and I, for one, want to have the happy memories of our times together back, untainted by suspicion. Did Dawn do it? She was closer to Evangeline than all of us. Did Ellie? Did Geneva lose it because of the coke? They probably all wonder if I did it." She paused. "That was your cue to say, 'No one could possibly think you did it.'"

"I can't see why you would."

Not exactly a ringing endorsement. Laurel exhaled a long breath upward and hoisted the box again. "Rant over."

"Effective closing arguments, Counselor. Give 'em hell."

No one would be calling her "counselor" anymore. After September 15th, it would be "Your Honor." It was almost like getting married and losing her maiden name again. She considered her high heels. She hadn't been able to bring herself to wear jeans to the office on a weekday, not even to clear out her stuff. "Here." She thrust the box at George. "You can help after all."

She would let him carry the box down to her car and then she'd kiss him. That would be their official last kiss, one she could remember, one that would serve as a goodbye to the firm as well, to her life as a lawyer. Then she'd make flight reservations to North Carolina. She rescued the violet as it listed, and strode ahead of him to the elevator.

Four

The ascent angle pressed Geneva back into her seat as the jet climbed out of O'Hare. A pocket of turbulence rocked the plane hard sideways. The man in the middle seat beside her clutched the armrest between them so hard his knuckles blanched white. Afraid of flying, Geneva deduced. He looked so together in a business suit and red silk tie, collar-length hair lightly gelled, the aroma of a lime-based aftershave wafting from him. Irrational fears could fell anyone. Direct comfort or distraction? He was young enough to be embarrassed if she said something like "the worst is over."

"Do you have business in Charlotte?" she asked instead.

His nostrils flared in and out as he breathed hard, and he answered on exhales. "A meeting, yes." Inhale. "I sell shares in a"—inhale—"business jet sharing operation."

She couldn't help but chuckle. It earned her a rueful smile and a quick glance. "I know. Ironic." His fingers relaxed a notch as the plane continued smoothly on with no more bucking. He made a visible effort. "And you? Business or pleasure? Are you from Charlotte?"

"Pleasure, I guess," Geneva said. Unfinished business was more like it, but she didn't need to share the details. "I live here in Chicago. I've been to Charlotte a few times, but never longer than it takes to rent a car. I'm picking one up there, headed to the Asheville area."

———

Geneva had felt so grown-up the first time she rented a car twelve years ago. She stood at the Hertz counter at the Charlotte airport, newly turned twenty-six, handing over her driver's license to an indifferent clerk. She took all the insurance the rental company offered, and sat in the Ford Focus for fifteen minutes, familiarizing herself with the lights and the wipers, and adjusting the mirrors and seat position. She didn't drive much in the city. By the time she hit I-40 west, she was comfortable driving the Focus and singing along with Dolly Parton on the radio. This weekend was all about her and she couldn't wait. Last year they'd celebrated Dawn getting a one-woman showing at a small gallery in Ocean Springs, Mississippi, where she'd been living since the break-up with her latest girlfriend. This year was a celebration of Geneva's new job as an on-air reporter for the CBS affiliate in Chicago. She belted "I-ah-ah will al-way-ays love you-oo-I-ah-ah—"

Two hours after leaving Charlotte, she navigated a hairpin turn on the narrow road north of Asheville, and the Chateau du Cygne Noir bed and breakfast sign appeared suddenly. It featured elegant white script on a lavender background with a black swan. Wide stone pillars on either side of the driveway supported the decorative iron gate that was always open, and she turned in gingerly. The driveway's sharp curves hid the castle until she came around the last bend and it burst into view. Its warm yellow stone seemed to soak up the sunlight and beam it back. Arched windows with their numerous small panes glinted. She'd loved the place the moment she set eyes on it that first spring break, almost as much as Vangie did. It had presence, a personality, the way the House of Usher or Manderley did. She knew Dawn would say "your English major is showing" if she shared her thoughts. The house wasn't brooding, like Usher's house, nor was it grand and forbidding like *Rebecca*'s Manderley, its stony façade repelling the nameless heroine. If Geneva were to assign an emotion to the chateau, she'd have to go with sad. No ... melancholy. The stalwart home that should have been surrounded by fields of lavender and wine grapes, that had presided over the siege of Tournai and absorbed the blood of its scion on the cobbled courtyard and the screams of maidservants treated the way ill-disciplined armies treated women, felt displaced in this verdant corner of the New World.

Geneva parked in the postage stamp lot, laughing a small laugh at the way she read story and feelings into the stone and timbers and mullioned panes. They'd been reinforced and augmented with modern HVAC systems, plumbing, and insulation, she reminded herself, mounting the shallow stone steps, so even if the castle hadn't been assimilated, it had suffered the indignities of modernization. She tried to envision the house plopped down in the Chicago projects where she'd grown up. None of the windows would have an intact pane of glass, graffiti would make the stones wince, upwards of a dozen families would live in it, and a crew of crack-selling gangbangers would stand guard outside, a poor substitute for the liveried footmen the house was used to. Geneva smiled grimly at the sheer impossibility of imagining the house in Englewood.

Dawn could talk about the unsettled "atmosphere," and Ellie could wonder how long it would take to clean the lusters on the chandeliers or dust the intricately carved furnishings, but Geneva loved the castle—its architecture and history, especially. The manager, Mrs. Abbott, a former history professor who managed the B and B, told them it had been brought over stone by stone and timber by timber from France in the early 1800s, after the younger son of a French nobleman killed his opponent in a duel and fled to America. He made his fortune as a privateer during the Civil War and had the family home relocated after inheriting the title and castle when his older brother died of syphilis. Mrs. Abbott had likewise researched the castle's history in France; she told the girls that a previous owner had met his fate on Madame Guillotine days after Marie Antoinette was beheaded, and his successor's young wife had plunged to her death from her fifth-floor balcony only a few years later. The young woman was seven months pregnant at the time, and old documents hinted that her lord suspected the baby wasn't his.

"They say her ghost walks," Mrs. Abbott went on in an unruffled voice, "but I've never run into her." They were touring the castle an hour after arriving that first weekend, standing in the portrait gallery in front of a painting of a snooty-looking aristocrat Mrs. Abbott identified as the beheaded marquis.

Dawn rubbed her arms as if suddenly chilled. Vangie asked, "Which room was hers?"

Mrs. Abbott worked her lips in and out. "The one you're in," she said. In her mid-fifties, the manager carried a few extra pounds, including the belly that Geneva's grandmother called a "menopot." She had jaw-length sandy hair threaded with silver and sported large, plastic-framed glasses she'd probably worn doing grad work in her university library in the early eighties.

"What was her name?" Geneva asked.

"Villette."

"Pretty," Laurel said. "Is there a portrait of her?"

"No. The castle's ledgers have an entry for a fee paid to an artist for 'une peinture a l'huile de Madame la Marquise, Villette nee Desmarais,' but it's either been lost or destroyed." Hammering underscored her words, thudding from a room above them.

"He killed her," Dawn said, her voice higher-pitched than usual. "Her husband. He picked her up and threw her over the balcony. Then he burned the portrait."

"How would you know?" Ellie asked, her voice hovering between curiosity and ridicule.

"I feel her," Dawn said. "She's here. She's still grieving for her lost baby."

Dawn's pale face was so serious, her dark eyes so haunted, and her spirals of long hair so medieval that they were silent for a moment, picturing the scene. Geneva imagined a scared young girl struggling in the arms of an enraged nobleman, screaming as she fell, hugging her belly in a vain attempt to protect her unborn child.

Vangie's silvery laugh dispelled the spooky moment. "You're just being arty again, Dawn. What else is there to see, Mrs. Abbott? I love this place already."

––––––––

Geneva came out of her reverie to find her arms wrapped protectively around her baby bulge and the flight attendant asking if she wanted something to drink. "Cranberry juice," she said, accepting a packet of biscotti. She sipped her juice, appreciating its tartness, and thought how young they'd all been that first weekend, full of excitement at having a week off and feeling sophisticated for having foregone the beach, where the Greek crowd went, in favor of the atmospheric old castle. Vangie had suggested Cygne. She'd grown up in the closest town, New Aberdeen, and knew of the B and B. Now they were about to embark on their eleventh weekend, albeit after a decade's delay. Geneva leaned down to check that the manila envelope with the proof she needed to confront Vangie was still in the front pocket of her weekender bag. It was. She rose awkwardly. The cranberry juice was a mistake—it always went right through her, especially now. Having to pee all the time was the real pisser—pun intended—about being pregnant. The plane lurched and the fasten seat belts sign came on as she staggered toward the lavatory.

————

After seventeen years as a military spouse—she and Scott had married the day he graduated and got commissioned—Ellie prided herself on her ability to pack efficiently. One carry-on bag would suffice for the weekend. She ticked items off her list as she rolled them and stowed them in the bag, including a swimsuit (the castle's website said it had a hot tub now) and a framed photo of the boys. Her eyes misted as she wrapped it in her pajama top. Her boys were gone. In the weeks since she and Scott had dropped them at their universities, she'd heard from Aidan eight times—brief texts and one phone call—and from Shane only twice. One of his two texts had been to complain that his black sheets and towels had dyed his socks and underwear gray when he washed them all together. She was grateful that he'd done a load of laundry, including his sheets and towels. When she texted as much, he confessed that he'd had to since "stuff got spilled" (she suspected "stuff" was code for beer, or worse, vomit) on his bed during a dorm "get together." Read: kegger.

She zipped the case closed. Scott emerged from the bathroom, freshly shaved, hair damp, wearing his lieutenant colonel's uniform. He was dropping her at the airport on his way to work.

He asked, "Ready?"

She nodded. "Just let me grab my sandwich and carrots out of the fridge."

At not quite five o'clock, it was still dark outside when Scott pulled the Subaru into the Departures lane. He switched off the news radio and leaned toward her. "I wish I could go with you," he said, surprising her.

Happiness flared momentarily, but then memories of what had happened the only time he joined them at Cygne extinguished the spark. "Satellites would fall out of the sky if you took a day off," she said with forced lightness.

A car pulled up behind them, disgorging a woman with three small children shrieking about Disney World. They'd be seated behind her on the plane, of course. Its headlights illuminated Scott's face. Ellie wasn't sure what his expression meant. It was a mix of love and something else—sadness? Apprehension? Was he worried that something would happen to her? She leaned in to kiss him. It was a little more than their usual quick peck on parting. The boys' departures had rekindled their sex life, she had to admit, now that they could get naked without worrying about Aidan coming home with the whole swim team in tow, or Shane calling to say he'd locked himself out of the car at the movie theater.

Scott's hand on her arm stopped her from getting out. "Let's get away for a weekend of our own when you get back," he said, surprising her. "Anywhere you want to go. Vancouver, Boston, Charleston. No reason we can't now that the boys are gone."

"That would be fun." How long had it been since they'd traveled together without the boys? Anticipation made her smile. "Charleston. It should be lovely in October and I've never been there."

"I'll look into reservations. Call me when you get there," he said as she got out and retrieved her suitcase from the back seat.

"I will. Do your bit to keep the nation safe for democracy while I'm gone."

"Wilco." He saluted casually and pulled away from the curb.

She wheeled her suitcase briskly through the terminal to the security line. Removing the slip-on loafers she wore when traveling and dumping them with her baggie of liquids into the bin, she felt a little superior to the woman balancing on one leg trying to unlace high-top sneakers, and the man being admonished by the TSA agent for having a full bottle of Gatorade in his carry-on. She shoved her bag forward on the conveyor belt and tried to push away the image of Scott and Evangeline that floated in her head. Scott's words about coming with her had resurrected the scene she'd long tried to keep buried in a deep, inaccessible vault in her mind. For the first time ever, she let herself acknowledge the thought that had been poking at the edges of her consciousness for a decade: Evangeline had deserved it.

The metal detector blared as she passed through it. Her cheeks fiery with embarrassment, she backed out to remove the engraved silver bangle Scott gave her for their fifteenth wedding anniversary.

Five

Having traveled on Friday and spent the night in Charlotte, Laurel was the first one to arrive Saturday morning, and Mrs. Abbott showed her to a room on the first floor. The inn's manager hadn't changed much in ten years, although she must be in her mid-sixties, Laurel figured. There were more strands of gray in her jaw-length bob, her glasses frames were a chic and rectangular lavender, and her knuckles were swollen with arthritis, but she still moved briskly and had the same air of competent alertness.

"I'm sure you were expecting your usual room," Mrs. Abbott said, "but the rooms on the top floors are being renovated. American Castle Vacations, the company that owns the property, has sold it to a consortium that's turning it into a nursing home, and the fifth floor is being gutted so they can kit it out as a medical clinic or surgical suite or some such. In fact, you're our very last private guests. My husband and I turn the keys over to the new owners' agent at the end of the month. Then we're off to Texas to be closer to our grandkids."

"I didn't know," Laurel said. Mrs. Abbott's news was a kick in the gut, but she was also conscious of a feeling of relief. How strange. This really was the last weekend. "Are you sad to be leaving Cygne?"

"It was something of a shock when they sold the chateau out from under us," Mrs. Abbott said, unlocking the door of a room labeled "Dogwood" and pushing it wide. "We've enjoyed being the chateau's caretakers and running the B and B, but it's hard work." She rubbed her swollen knuckles. "Since his hip replacement, Stephen's had trouble keeping up with the unending maintenance and yard work. And I have to admit I'll be glad to give up making beds and doing laundry. I'll miss Cygne, though. It's been our home for over two decades. Sometimes it was easy to forget it wasn't really ours." She ran a proprietary hand across the satin finish of an antique dresser. "The important pieces from upstairs have already gone to auction—they've fetched a pretty penny, from what I hear. More furniture is in the sheds—the contractors moved it out so they could get started on the renovations. The auction house crew will crate the rest of it next week, after you leave, and then it'll all be gone." She gave the dresser a last pat and opened the door to the bathroom. "We can get our own things in a U-Haul, and we'll hit the road to Galveston right after that."

"That's really tough," Laurel said. The room was calming, done in shades of delft blue and white. She hefted her bag onto a fold-out luggage rack. All in all, she decided she was happy with the new room. Fewer memories. "I wouldn't know a Hepplewhite from a Chippendale," she admitted. "Is the furniture worth a lot?"

"Some of the pieces are worth thousands," Mrs. Abbott said. "The dresser, for instance, is Louis XVI—Marie Antoinette had one just like it. There's a Japy Freres wall clock and a sixty-piece set of Puiforcat silver flatware, and other treasures. A lot of it's French—original to the chateau. Other pieces are local, but good quality from the nineteenth

42

century, and some are knockoffs, or too beaten up to be worth much. When we took this job, I made a point of educating myself on the chateau's contents. I took classes, read books, and went to a few auctions with one of the antique dealers from Asheville to learn what I could. Stephen and I put together an inventory. Can you believe there wasn't one before that?" She shook her head in amazement. "Guests could have walked off with a Dresden shepherdess or a creamer from the Revere tea service and no one would have known the difference."

Laurel heard the affection in Mrs. Abbott's voice when she talked about particular pieces of furniture, and she knew leaving the castle was going to be brutally hard for the innkeeper. "Galveston will be a big change."

Mrs. Abbott squared her shoulders. "Well, I might be a bit bored without this place to run, but Alice needs our help with the kids and I'm sure I'll be busy as can be in no time. I've thought about teaching a history class at the community college; I've missed teaching. We'll see. Most of my retired friends say they don't know how they ever had time to work." She laughed, but Laurel detected a hint of uncertainty.

"The change is hardest on Mindy," she went on. "She's been with us almost since we took over, since she graduated high school. She's been my right arm. We're doing what we can to help her find another job. The nursing home people say if she gets her CNA certificate they'll take her on, but it's hard for a single mother. We were okay with having Braden hanging around the place—he's a bright, kind little boy. Now she'll have to make arrangements for him. *Tch.*" Mrs. Abbott shook her head. "Extra blankets and pillows in the armoire, and towels under the vanity. Breakfast from seven to nine. Let me know if you need anything."

The sound of a car crunching over gravel drew their attention. "That'll be one of your friends," Mrs. Abbott said. "You're our only guests this weekend."

She withdrew and Laurel crossed to the window to see who had arrived. She was too late. Whoever it was had already reached the stone portico that shaded the castle's entrance and Laurel couldn't see her. Leaving her unpacking for later, she exited the room, not bothering to lock it, and started down the wide hallway. Excitement and apprehension dueled within her. Voices sounded from outside and she reached the foyer at the same moment one of the large oak doors swung inward, letting in a beam of sunlight and a tall woman.

"Geneva!" Laurel hurried forward, chest expanding with happiness at the sight of her friend. She'd last seen Geneva in March when a case took her to Chicago. She'd dined at Geneva and Geonwoo's house and felt a squirt of envy when they told her they were expecting. They were over the moon, Geneva beaming and Geonwoo treating her like she'd morphed into a Faberge egg the instant his sperm mixed it up with her egg. Laurel celebrated with them, despite the ache of longing lodged like a softball under her breastbone. She wanted a baby, but without a husband—hell, without a date in the last eight months—it didn't look like she'd be needing onesies and a stroller anytime soon.

"Hey, Laurel." Geneva's dark face broke into a wide smile. She dropped her duffel and pulled Laurel into a hug before breaking away. "I've got to pee. Be right back."

She hurried around the corner to the powder room. Laurel shouldered her bag and accepted the key to the "Jonquil" room from Mrs. Abbott. When Geneva returned, protesting that she could carry her own bag, Laurel shook her head. Geneva automatically started up the stairs, but Laurel said, "You're on this level. The place has been sold and the upper floors are closed off."

"Damn," Geneva said. "I was going to count going up and down the stairs as my cardio for the weekend."

Laurel laughed. "Cut yourself some slack. You're due in—what? A month?"

"I am so ready." Geneva patted her belly. "Anyone else here yet?"

"We're the first."

"Great." Geneva squeezed Laurel's hand. "I'm glad to have the chance to catch up with you. Let's dump my bag in the room and go for a walk around the lake."

———

The lake was a glorified pond behind the castle, three-quarters of a mile in circumference. When they'd last been there, Laurel remembered, a foot-wide trail of beaten-down grass close to the water was the only track around the lake. Now there was a breezy path wide enough for three to walk abreast. Cumulus clouds mounded on the horizon, promising rain later, but for now it was a warm and sunny day. The water glittered on their left, still threaded with cattails and marshy grasses. A redwing blackbird trilled, and Laurel tried to spot him.

"Nothing stays the same, does it?" Geneva said as they stepped onto the trail.

"Nope," Laurel agreed. "They're turning the inn into a nursing home."

"No way!"

"This time next year, there'll be a wheelchair traffic jam on this path."

Shade dappled the path and cooled them as they strolled under the trees on the lake's west end. A bird or rodent skittered in the underbrush. Wind ruffled the leaves.

"Why'd you come?" Geneva asked at the same time Laurel said, "What do you think this weekend is about?"

They laughed and both fell quiet. Finally, Laurel said, "I came to find out who did it."

Geneva whistled. "Wow. Uh, wow. You just put it right out there."

"Only to you."

"I'm not a suspect?"

Laurel hesitated a beat too long.

Geneva's face and voice went neutral. "Of course I'm a suspect. No alibi—"

"No one had a decent alibi, including me," Laurel said quickly. Why had she started this conversation? Why hadn't she told Geneva that of course she didn't suspect her? She knew why. Because Geneva had motive, means, and opportunity, and because gut instinct didn't count as evidence. Her stint in criminal defense had taught her that "gut instinct," while perhaps worthy of consideration, was no more reliable than a witness who saw the crime in the dark, from a quarter mile away, without her glasses.

"And I had a better reason than most for wanting to shove Vangie off a balcony. I didn't do it, though." Again, it was a quiet statement, not a plea to be believed.

"Neither did I."

They paused and stared at the lake, not making eye contact. Laurel felt an unsaid *Who do you think did it?* hovering in the air. She didn't verbalize the question; it would be a breach of the friendship they all shared to discuss the others behind their backs. She watched a fish rise and a pair of dragonflies skim the water's surface, darting with jewel-like flashes of color. The not-unpleasant smell of warm mud filled her nostrils and she breathed deeply. It was so peaceful. Her shoulders eased down a notch.

"I always thought I should have been able to figure it out," Geneva said. "If not that weekend, then later, after I finished my degree work. What good is a PhD in psychology if you can't figure out which of your friends threw another one off a balcony?"

"The police couldn't figure it out, either," Laurel reminded her.

"Oh, the police." Geneva dismissed the entire law enforcement community with a wave of her hand. "The police didn't know us. How could they be expected to figure it out? And I'm sure they didn't get the whole truth out of anybody." She slid Laurel a sidelong glance.

Laurel held her hands up in a surrender gesture. "Not from me, at any rate. I told them the truth about where I was when it happened, but I certainly didn't go out of my way to tell them about any issues we might have had."

"Like the way Vangie screwed you over with the cheating thing?"

Laurel nodded once, shying away from the uncomfortable memory. "None of us threw the others under the bus—brought up disagreements or things said in the heat of the moment that the police might have interpreted as motive. I was always proud of us for that."

"You're lucky your motive wasn't a matter of public record—police record," Geneva said with a trace of bitterness.

Laurel squeezed her friend's shoulder. "You got the worst of it."

Geneva managed a small smile. "But in the end, they couldn't pin it on me, even though I was a black woman with a drug arrest. They couldn't pin it on any of us. We all walked away scot-free."

"Except Evangeline. She didn't walk away."

Acknowledging that truth with a small nod, Geneva started forward again. A cloud blocked the sun, and Laurel couldn't help thinking that their discussion had bleached the day of color, turning everything a uniform gray. To fight the effect, she put a purposefully cheery note in her voice and said, "Tell me about the baby. Did Geonwoo get the nursery finished? How long will you take off work after the birth?"

Geneva chattered happily about the baby and her plans until they neared the castle and the throaty roar of a sports car interrupted her. A yellow Mustang blasted into sight a moment later, scattering gravel. It slid to a stop mere inches from Laurel's rental car, and the passenger-side door opened.

———

The rush of driving the powerful sports car kept Dawn in a daze for a split second after she got out. *What a blast.* She'd had no idea. What she wouldn't give to be able to trade in her Civic for something like this. Then, Ellie's voice penetrated the daze.

"You're a maniac," she said, slamming the door. "I'm driving on the way back, Danica Patrick."

Ellie never sugar-coated anything. Dawn couldn't tell if she was really mad or exaggerating for effect. "Fine." She tossed the keys to Ellie over the car's hood. "Every woman should get to drive a car like this at least once."

Geneva, beautiful as ever despite the baby bump, her dark skin glowing, reached them then. Her hair was longer than before, drawn up into a high bun that showed off the sketchable sweep of her cheekbones and prominent line of her nose. She wore a blush-colored knit top and flowy taupe pants. Neutrals with style had always been her vibe. "Give us a hug," she said, opening her arms wide. Her smile lit up the gray day and Dawn was glad she'd come.

Laurel was exchanging greetings with Ellie, and the four of them ended up at the portico together. "Quite the car," Laurel said.

Was she being condescending? She was the only one of them who could afford a car like that. Before Dawn could respond, Ellie said, "The rental company upgraded us because they gave the one we reserved away, and it was the only one left. "It's 'sick,' as my boys would say."

"Lots of fun," Laurel said. Wearing navy linen slacks and a teal blouse, she looked cool and poised. As always. Dawn decided Laurel wasn't being bitchy about the car. She just had that aloof way about her—always had, even in college.

Dawn stepped back from the portico to drink in the castle. The yellow stone was as mellow as she remembered, and the turret still looked like a safe place to hole up if invaders besieged them. Only the chimneys, currently hosting two pigeons, soared higher. She'd tried to paint the castle a few times during college, using photos, but could never capture it satisfactorily. Movement behind the window of Evangeline's old room—Villette's room—made her brows twitch together. *Why would*—"What's with all the scaffolding?" she asked, noticing it for the first time.

"Cygne's been sold," Laurel said.

"It's going to be a nursing home." The voice came from the foyer, making everyone turn. Mindy Tanger, the longtime staff member, stepped out of the portico's shadows and took Ellie's roller bag. She was a weasel-slim woman in her mid-thirties, with large wrists extending past the cuffs of her pink coverall. Soft blond hair hung across her face as she bent for the suitcase, veiling her deep-set blue eyes.

"A nursing home!" Dawn heard the grief in her voice and swallowed. She was astonished by how much the news upset her, but she made herself sound calm. "I mean, why? A nursing home—that doesn't seem right. This is a grand old place—"

"Full of history," Geneva agreed.

"—and it deserves better than to be a way station for old people waiting to die."

There was an uncomfortable silence for a long moment.

Then Laurel, of all people, said, "You're right, Dawn. It's strange to think of this place smelling like antiseptic and boiled peas. I still see aristocratic women in panniered dresses descending the stairs, hair all powdered and pouffed." Her smile was sympathetic. Dawn wouldn't have thought her capable of such whimsy.

"The nursing home people made a good offer, so I heard," Mindy said prosaically. She hefted Dawn's duffel. "I'll show you to your rooms. Everyone's on the first floor because of the construction."

Ellie and Dawn followed her around an ugly plywood shaft, which was obviously going to house an elevator for the incoming geriatrics, and down the hall. Mindy opened the "Cherry Blossom" room and took Ellie's bag inside. Ellie scooted in and closed the door, saying, "Bathroom!"

Mindy led Dawn two doors down and unlocked a door with "Pansy" on it. Nudging it open with her foot, she unslung Dawn's duffel from her shoulder.

"What will you do when the sale goes through?" Dawn asked, curious. As far as she knew, Cygne was the only place Mindy had ever worked.

Mindy straightened and brushed her hair out of eyes, which had muddy lavender circles under them. She looked more careworn than Dawn remembered. Single motherhood and impending unemployment would do that. "I don't know." She sounded defeated. "I just don't know. I could become a certified nursing assistant and maybe get a job on the nursing home staff, but I don't know what I'd do with Braden, especially during the summers. His dad won't help and I can't afford daycare."

Dawn was sorry she'd started the conversation. She was sorry for Mindy—being a single mom was a rough row to hoe—but she wasn't responsible for Mindy or Braden. She wanted Mindy to leave now but couldn't bring herself to say so. And it was her own fault Mindy was latched onto her. When they'd first met she'd gone out of her way to befriend Mindy, who was only three years younger. She'd felt some kind of social justice guilt, embarrassed that she was enjoying a spring break holiday in the castle while Mindy, about to graduate from high school, was stripping the beds and cleaning the toilets. She'd chatted with her while Mindy was making up the room, talked about life at Grissom University, even aired some complaints about her friends. Stupid. Look where misguided kindness landed you. She felt immediately guilty about the thought and wished Kyra had come with her.

"I've got a picture of him," Mindy said, pulling a cell phone out of a pocket and flicking at it. "Here."

She showed Dawn a photo of a gap-toothed boy of nine or so with brown hair falling into his eyes and an engaging smile. He wore a sports uniform and had his arms wrapped around a soccer ball.

"He's a handsome boy," Dawn said. She plopped her duffel on the bed and unzipped it, hoping Mindy would take the hint.

"He loves soccer," Mindy said. "He had his heart set on playing on the same team this year, but we just can't swing it. Not since I had to get new tires on the truck."

Dawn closed her eyes. Would it never end? "I want you to have this for Braden's soccer." She extracted forty dollars from her wallet. "I hope it helps. It's great for kids to be part of a team." Not that she would know. Art club had been her thing; she couldn't throw or catch a ball to save her life, and a PE teacher had once told her she ran like a wounded warthog. That still stung.

Mindy flushed dull red but pocketed the bills with a mumbled "Thanks." She still made no move to leave. "Remember that first time you all came down here? I'd only been working here for a month, and now here we are, twenty years later. That's about half my life." She shook her head wonderingly.

Dawn was groping for a reply that would discourage Mindy's reminiscent mood when Ellie knocked on the door and called out, "Dawn? I'm ready."

Dawn fairly sprang for the door and pulled it open. "I'm coming." Waiting until Mindy sidled past, she shut the door.

Six

Laurel had a moment of surreal detachment, surrounded by the three friends who'd been such a large part of her life from the day she entered college until the last weekend. The four of them were gathered outside the front door of the castle, the sun glittering off dust motes and pollen like sparkles of champagne tossed upward. Geneva's rich chuckle, the corkscrew zaniness of Dawn's curls, the broad expanse of Ellie's forehead—they all seemed too vivid, almost painful to Laurel. Surreal was the only word; she was trapped in a Dali painting. Geneva's baby, Ellie's move to Colorado, Dawn and Kyra's home renovations, an adopted cat, opinions on *The Amazing Race,* a wrecked car a year ago, diets. The topics were varied, not too personal, and they glanced off them, dragonflies skimming a pond's surface, careful not to get too deep. Brief silences caused the conversation to stutter occasionally as they tried to find the old balance and rhythm, but one or another of them would swoop in with a comment or question to keep the awkwardness from taking root. Laurel let the conversation swirl around her, smiling at the right places but not contributing. They'd settled on a plan to explore the grounds and locate the new hot tub (Ellie's idea) when the scrunch of tires on gravel reached them.

The sound cut through the oddness Laurel was experiencing and brought her back to reality, for lack of a better word. She turned. The others fell silent and swiveled to look down the long driveway. The approaching vehicle was still out of sight beyond the curve, but Laurel's muscles tightened. She took a rib cage-expanding breath, lowered her shoulders, and wiggled her fingers. She couldn't decide if the fluttering in her stomach was anticipation or dread. Both, perhaps. Ellie whispered something to Dawn, but Laurel didn't catch it.

A van, newish and white with North Carolina plates, trundled around the corner. Drawing up in front of them, it came to a stop. The driver cut the ignition and got out in one motion. He loped around the van's rear, tall and dark, good-looking in a flashy way with a deep tan, black hair curling below his ears, and rock-hard tattooed biceps displayed by a short-sleeved T-shirt advertising a gym. Late thirties or a little older. Almost before Laurel could wonder who the hell he was, he was coming toward her, hand out.

She automatically extended her hand and he shook it, his palm callused and hard against hers. Definitely not a lawyer's hand. This man didn't work in an office. "Laurel, right?" he said with a big smile. Light crow's feet fanned the corners of his brown eyes.

The look he gave her was disturbingly intimate, as if they'd known each other for years, and she couldn't even figure out how he knew her name. Before she could answer or ask who he was, he was turning to Dawn, saying, "And I'll bet you're Dawn. Your art—wow, it's amazing."

"Thank you—" Dawn started, looking as confused as Laurel felt.

He moved on to Geneva and Ellie, identifying each of them and sharing hearty handshakes with them.

"I'm sorry," Laurel said, "but who are you?"

He looked disconcerted, but then laughed. "I'm Ray. Didn't she tell you my name?"

Laurel glanced at Geneva, who shrugged in an "I've got no clue" way.

Before the man could say more, a click heralded the slow opening of the van's rear passenger door. A lift folded out. Laurel glimpsed the wheel of a wheelchair before Ray blocked her view by bounding forward to maneuver the chair and its occupant onto the lift. A mechanical whir accompanied the lift's descent.

An upwelling of tension gripped Laurel. Blood thrummed loudly in her ears. Anticipation twined with something very like dread. No, that was silly. There was nothing to dread. She tried to find another name for the emotion as the wheelchair and its occupant sank to the ground and Ray maneuvered it off the lift.

"I can't believe you didn't even tell them my name," he said in a mock-disappointed voice.

A silvery laugh answered him and brought an involuntary smile to Laurel's face. The laugh was the same as before, the happy trill that had brought heads around at orientation that first day at Grissom. "Loverboy, I didn't even tell them you existed. I wanted you to be a surprise, a wonderful surprise."

Evangeline propelled the wheelchair toward them, rocking forward when it stuttered over the gravel. Ray moved to help her, but she waved him away. Her face was thinner than Laurel remembered, but the hazel eyes still sparkled. Lines on her forehead suggested it was frequently furrowed with pain or worry, but they were the only sign of aging or her trauma—other than the wheelchair, of course. Her light brown hair, untouched by gray, was piled messily atop her head and the sun warmed the cognac-colored highlights. Her shoulders and arms, bared by a sleeveless blouse, were tan and muscled, and a light blanket covered her lap and legs. Gladness lanced through Laurel at the sight of her college roommate, quickly followed by anger, guilt, and disquiet. She'd been both looking forward to and semi-apprehensive about this encounter, unsure of how she'd react, and she couldn't sort out her feelings. Part of her felt the way she used to at the start of each new school year, excited to see Evangeline again and catch up after the summer. Part of her felt there was too much water under the bridge, too much suspicion and history and pain lurking under that bridge, like the trolls from a children's book.

Evangeline clapped her hands together near her chin. "Oh, it's so good to see all of you again. I'm so very, very grateful we could all be together to celebrate my engagement."

Ray put a hand on her shoulder and she nursed it to her cheek. "You've already met, but this is my dearest Ray." She tilted her head up toward him, and he bent to kiss her lips lightly.

For a moment, the rest of them were still, held in check by surprise, the constraint of ten years apart, or … something else. Laurel's skin prickled. She got an impression of resentment or dismay and looked around to spot the source, but she couldn't sort it out before everyone surged forward, surrounding Evangeline, congratulating her, saying how good it was to see everyone after such a long time. No mention of Evangeline's non-functioning legs or how she came to be paralyzed. Laurel's gaze lifted briefly to that fifth-floor balcony, and then she leaned forward to hug her friend, getting a whiff of Opium from Evangeline's hair.

"I'm not the only one with something to celebrate," Evangeline said. "You're going to be a judge. Judge Muir. It has a good ring. Congratulations."

"Thanks."

Gravel crunched under the wheelchair as Evangeline powered it forward. Ray leaped to help, but she suggested he get their suitcases and move the van out of the way. When he pulled the bags out of the van and drove off, Evangeline looked around with a melancholy smile. "It's going to be a nursing home, you know. I went to the town hall meetings to lobby against the zoning change, but the fix was in. Remember when I thought I was going to buy it and run the B and B? I had such plans!"

Was she kidding? Of course they all remembered. Laurel scanned the others' faces as they fell silent. Geneva's face was blank, and Dawn's half-hidden by a curtain of hair as she looked down and dug a hole in the gravel with the toe of her shoe. Only Ellie looked saddened by the memory, murmuring, "Of course we do."

How could they not remember when Evangeline had made such a big deal of it that last weekend, announcing that she'd come into some money and was buying Cygne. She'd orchestrated the whole evening, insisting they dress up, arranging for a fancy dinner and special cocktails—"sidecars," made with a special French brandy to celebrate the house's French origins, she said. She'd looked spectacular in a blue chiffon dress with a beaded bodice and a vaguely 1920s vibe to it. Her eyes had sparkled brighter than the chandelier's crystals. She'd been delighted by their surprise and clapped her hands. "It's been my dream forever," she'd reminded them, flitting about the room, hugging Ellie, squeezing Geneva's hand, inviting them all to be delighted with her. "Forever."

Congratulating Evangeline with a hug, Laurel had caught sight of Mr. Abbott over Evangeline's shoulder. Dressed in the dark pants and white shirt he used for serving at table, the man had been standing in the dining room doorway, expressionless. The sidecar glass he was holding tilted, and the liquid leaked down his hand and soaked into his white sleeve. Hours later, Evangeline lay on the ground beneath her balcony, paralyzed from the waist down.

Of course, they hadn't known that then, Laurel remembered as they traipsed around the house to eat lunch on the patio in the back at Mrs. Abbott's invitation. At first she'd feared Evangeline was dead— all that blood, and she'd lain so still—but there'd been a pulse and the ambulance had arrived quickly. They had all scattered back across the country once the police said they could leave, but they'd kept in touch for a while, trading news of Evangeline's operations, her therapy sessions, the diagnosis that meant she'd be in a wheelchair forever. Once it became clear her paralysis was permanent, Evangeline had refused to talk to any of them for two years, so they'd relied on stilted conversations with her mother for updates. Her impending purchase of Cygne had faded away without fanfare, since the old mansion with its multiple staircases wasn't wheelchair-friendly and all her money was going toward hospital bills.

Ironic, Laurel thought, that the place was going to be overrun with wheelchairs and walkers now. She cast a look at Evangeline's profile, wondering how she felt about it, if returning to Cygne reminded her of what might have been, of how differently her life might have turned out. Then she snorted gently. Of course it did. Why had Evangeline gathered them here again? Why now? She watched Ray, who had reappeared after parking the van, plant a kiss atop his fiancée's head as he maneuvered the wheelchair over the rough ground.

Geneva inched close and whispered in her ear. "You'd think this would be the last place she'd want to have an engagement party, wouldn't you?"

Laurel shrugged. "Maybe she's exorcising old ghosts."

Geneva's "hmph" said she was unconvinced. "That sounds more like Dawn. And who is this Ray, anyway? I'd swear Vangie never mentioned him."

"Do you talk often?" Guilt tugged at Laurel that she'd totally let go of her relationship with Evangeline. It had been at least three years since they'd talked, maybe longer. Semi-annual emails and Christmas cards didn't count.

"Every few months. She never mentioned Ray or this party, for that matter. My invitation for the weekend came out of the blue." She winced.

"You okay?"

"Just the baby kicking." Geneva patted her belly. "She's a lively one."

"I've been thinking about having a baby." The words spilled out before Laurel could dam them back. She immediately wanted to recall them. She hadn't told anyone. Not her mom, not her coworkers, not her friends in Denver. She'd been quietly researching her options, not sure she was brave enough to go through with it, not sure that a pregnant single woman wielding a gavel would go over well with the Denver judicial establishment.

"I didn't know you were involved with someone!" Geneva exclaimed, bringing Dawn's head around.

Laurel shushed her with a look and said quietly, "I'm not."

Geneva caught on immediately. "Well, I think you should go for it, if that's what you want. No reason you shouldn't. Being a single mom is hard—just ask my grandmother—but if anyone can do it, you can." She gave a self-conscious laugh. "Look at me—giving advice before I've even spent two seconds with my own baby. Talk to me in a couple months and I may be singing a completely different tune. I may be telling you to save your sanity and your money. You don't want to know how much Geonwoo and I have spent baby-proofing the house. Historic fixer-upper homes were not made for babies. It's a wonder any of our ancestors survived to adulthood. Are you thinking about *in vitro*?"

Something relaxed inside Laurel at her friend's casual acceptance of her plans. She wasn't crazy or irresponsible for wanting to have a baby alone. "I've looked into it."

"I want to hear all about it," Geneva said as she joined the others at the pre-set table. "Don't you dare leave this weekend without filling me in on every detail. Promise?"

"Promise." Laurel smiled and pulled out a chair between Ellie and Ray. Maybe this weekend was a good idea after all.

Seven

After lunch, Ray announced he was going to explore the castle and Evangeline waved him away good-naturedly. She leaned back in her wheelchair, lifting her face to the sun, and shut her eyes. Geneva said she needed a nap and Laurel disappeared for a run. No wonder Laurel was still so slender and fit-looking, Ellie thought. Her great figure would be wasted under a judge's robe.

"Do you still dance, Dawn?" she asked, and then wondered if she was being insensitive to Evangeline. Her friend didn't open her eyes, and Ellie relaxed. "I remember you used to take dance classes."

"Not for years, unless you count the occasional zumba class. I do a little yoga, a little walking. 'Little' being the operative word." Dawn's finger drew swirls in the condensation on her tea glass. "I keep saying I'll do more, that I'll lose five pounds, but when push comes to shove ... " She shrugged. "Blame my Italian genes."

"For what?" Evangeline had opened her eyes and was leaning forward. "For that gorgeous hair? I always wanted hair like yours—thick and curly. Mine is too wispy." She spun the chair around. "Why don't we go into the sunroom and catch up?" She was already wheeling herself in that direction by the time Dawn and Ellie pushed their chairs back and rose.

Ellie blinked in the dimness of the sunroom and took off her shoes, appreciating the tile's coolness under her feet. She settled onto a rattan armchair and tucked her feet up so she was sitting "criss-cross applesauce," as the boys' kindergarten teacher called it. Back in the day they'd said "Indian style," but that wasn't PC anymore.

"I'll go get another pitcher of tea," Dawn said, exiting toward the kitchen.

"Do you need anything? Can I get you anything?" Ellie asked Evangeline, uncomfortable with her disability and not knowing if she was being helpful or insensitive.

"I'm fine, Ellie. Relax. I'm handicapped, not helpless. Tell me about how the boys are doing at college. Scott says Aidan's at Purdue and Shane's at Alabama, or do I have that backwards?"

Time slowed. Ellie felt as if everything in the room was mired in transparent molasses, moving in slow motion. Evangeline's eyelids descended, oh so slowly, in a blink, and then rose again as she brushed a fly away from her face with an endlessly graceful flick of her wrist. Evangeline's lips were moving, but no sound registered over the thrumming in Ellie's ears.

Her lips were numb and her tongue as thick as after a tooth filling. "You talk to Scott?" She finally got the words out. Scott had never said a word about being in touch with Evangeline since their college days. Had they been communicating all these years, or was it a more recent connection? Was it coincidence that Evangeline had lured her into *this* of all possible rooms to drop her bombshell?

"Now and then." Evangeline smiled innocently. "Oh, thanks, Dawn."

Ellie swiveled to see Dawn approaching with a tray holding three glasses and a pitcher. It rocked as she lowered it to the coffee table, and Ellie grabbed for a glass that was tipping. She missed, and it toppled to the floor and smashed on the tile. Glass shards exploded outward. "Damn," she said, too loudly.

Evangeline wheeled her chair back from the spreading lake of tea. "It's no big deal."

"I'll get—" Dawn started, but Ellie cut her off. "No, it's my mess. I'll get some paper towels. Sorry." She stood, forgetting she was barefoot, and pain bit into her heel. "Ungh." She raised her right foot to see a one-inch triangle of glass lodged in her heel. Wincing, she jerked it out and blood dripped to the floor.

"Oh my God, Ellie. You're bleeding." Dawn started toward her, but Ellie held her off with an outthrust hand.

"Yes, I noticed," she snapped. "Sorry. I'm fine. I'll get a Band-Aid." Wanting only to get away from the whiff of deceit Evangeline had introduced, and the room where she'd walked in on Evangeline and Scott going at it like horny rabbits, she picked up her sandals and hobbled out, leaving blood splotches at eighteen-inch intervals.

She didn't really feel the pain until she reached the powder room off the foyer; then, her heel began to sting and throb. Finding paper towels under the vanity cabinet, she folded one into a pad, lifted her foot onto the marble counter, and applied pressure to stop the bleeding. She caught a glimpse of herself in the gilded mirror and was surprised to see she looked just like always. Her face was a little pinker, maybe, but that could as easily be from the sun during their patio lunch as her conversation with Evangeline. If she'd had her cell phone on her, she would have called Scott on the spot, but it was in her room. *Just as well.* She needed to think about what she would say, and how she would ask him if it was true that he was carrying on a relationship of any sort with Evangeline Paul, no matter how platonic or incidental. She took another moment to compose herself and hobble-hopped to the kitchen to hit Mrs. Abbott up for a Band-Aid.

By the time she returned to the sunroom with her heel bandaged and paper towels in hand, Dawn had picked up all the glass bits and stacked them atop a magazine. The two women sat facing each other, Dawn on the rattan loveseat with her arms crossed over her chest, and Evangeline leaning forward in her wheelchair as if trying to convince Dawn of something. Ellie wondered if she was imagining the tension in the air. They looked toward her when her sandal slapped against the tile.

"I'm fine," she said, forestalling their enquiries. She lifted her sandaled foot so they could see her foot was properly bandaged. "It's what I deserve for being such a klutz." She stooped to sop up the tea, dropping drenched paper towels into the bowl she'd filched from the kitchen.

"Dawn was telling me about her art," Evangeline said brightly. "She's going to start teaching."

Ellie cocked her head to look up at Dawn. "That's great, Dawn. Kids or adults?"

"Adults." Dawn tugged on her earlobe. "It's not for sure yet. I've been working on new pieces and I haven't had time to finalize things with the art center."

"It sounds like fun." Ellie straightened, plopped the last paper towel in the bowl, ripped off another one to dry her hands, and sat. "I need to find something like that to fill my time now that the boys are gone. A new hobby."

"My art is not a hobby."

Dawn is too freakin' sensitive. "I didn't mean it like that. I know it's not. I meant that I need to find something worthwhile to do with my time now, something as meaningful to me as your art is to you."

"Nice recover," Evangeline said.

Ellie glared at her. "It's not a—"

"Whatever happened to my paintings?" Dawn interrupted. "The ones you bought for Cygne. When the sale fell through, what did you do with the paintings?"

Ellie's brows rose slightly at the tremor in Dawn's voice. She sounded more like she was asking about the fate of a kidnapped child than about some paintings. Evangeline, strangely, seemed pleased with the question.

"My favorite, the one with the teal and turquoise streaks on the—"

"I know the one."

"Of course you do. Anyway, it's hanging in my living room. It really makes the room. Everyone who visits comments on it."

Dawn did not look appeased. "What about the others?"

After the briefest of hesitations, Evangeline said hastily, "Well, they're in a storage unit for now. I don't have room ... Anyway, when Ray and I get married, I'm sure we'll find a place for them. I still think they're brilliant, just brilliant."

Dawn's mouth drooped.

"Could I buy one of them from you, Evangeline?" Ellie heard herself say. Scott hated abstracts and their budget was stretched with both boys in college, but Dawn looked so dejected, and the words popped out before she thought about it. "Or"—she looked at Dawn— "do you have any new work that's for sale?"

Dawn jumped up in a flurry of flying hair and snapping eyes. "I don't need any pity purchases," she ground out between clenched teeth.

"I didn't mean—" Ellie started, but Dawn was out of the room almost before she'd started talking. Ellie exchanged glances with Evangeline. "I didn't mean—"

"Of course not. She's oversensitive, always has been," Evangeline said soothingly.

That was so close to what Ellie had been thinking moments before, she should have felt vindicated; however, the image of Dawn's furious and hurt face haunted her. "I need to catch her." She hurried after Dawn, foot throbbing, leaving Evangeline alone in the sun-splashed room.

———

There was a dinner planned for that evening. They weren't getting too dressed up, and Laurel was certain there wouldn't be sidecar cocktails, but even so, it felt too much like the last time. *Don't be silly*, she told herself, kicking off her shoes in her room. *We have to eat, after all.* Pounding hammers and a saw's shriek from the upper floors made it sound as if a giant were ripping the roof off the old castle. She changed into workout gear, eager to escape for a quiet, solitary run.

She saw no one as she exited through the front door and jogged slowly down the long driveway. Rhododendrons, bare of flowers at this time of year, turned the driveway into a tunnel. Funny she hadn't noticed it so much driving in, but her slower pace, or maybe passing clouds, made it feel dark and confined. Relieved when she reached the road, she turned right and set an easy pace, tension draining from her shoulders, chest, and thighs with each yard she put between her and Cygne. The trees had started to change, and flashes of scarlet, gold, and orange lifted her spirits. The humidity brought on a quick sweat, but running was easier here, at less than half of Denver's altitude, and she picked up the pace. Timing herself, she reckoned she'd run almost three miles and was ready to turn around when the sound of a car approaching from behind made her step off the paved road into a slight ditch filled with soggy leaves left over from last year. No poison ivy, she hoped.

It was the white van. It blasted toward her at speeds more suited for a Ferrari, and Laurel glimpsed Ray's profile as the van barreled past, peppering her with heat and road debris. He seemed to be alone; at any rate, no one sat in the front passenger seat. His attention was fixed on the road ahead, and she was sure he hadn't spotted her. Where was he going in such a hurry? She eased back onto the pavement and headed toward the inn. She pushed herself hard for two miles and was breathing heavily by the time she slowed for a cooldown. Ray seemed nice enough, she mused, although she'd learned surprisingly little about him over lunch. She'd assumed a guy as gregarious as he appeared to be would be forthcoming, but he'd turned her questions—about where he'd gone to school, what he did for a living, and how he'd met Evangeline—aside in a way she might not have noticed if she hadn't dealt with lawyers and clients who employed similar tactics.

"Have you known each other a long time?" she'd asked.

He smiled, teeth very white against his tan skin. Wiry black hairs poked from the neckline of his T-shirt, and Laurel glimpsed the top of a tattoo that crossed his collar bone. "It feels like all my life. You know, I'm trying to teach that woman to love basketball. I mean, we live in the heart of NCAA country with Duke and NC State right down the road. I'm a Blue Devils fan myself—have been since high school when I played a little ball myself as a Blue Demon. Almost the same, right?" Not waiting for a reply, he drank some tea and continued, "I wasn't good enough to play in college, though."

"Oh? Where did you go to—" Laurel started.

"Anyway, I've got a friend who gets me Blue Devils tickets a few times a year. Do you know how hard those are to get? You got a better chance of being hit by lightning than of scoring Devils tickets without connections. I got Evangeline to go to three or four games with me, but she said watching ten sweaty men fight over an orange ball didn't do it for her." He laughed, apparently not overly dismayed by Evangeline's lack of interest, and gestured with the hand holding half a club sandwich. "I'm getting her a Duke T-shirt for Christmas, though. You know, kind of a gag gift. Don't tell her. It's a secret."

He raised his voice on "It's a secret," so Evangeline broke off her conversation with Dawn and asked with a smile, "What's a secret, love? Husbands and wives aren't supposed to have secrets from each other." She spoke gaily, kidding him.

"We're not married yet," Ray had replied, raising his iced tea glass to her in a toast. "But I'm counting the days." He half-rose from his seat and leaned across Dawn to kiss his bride-to-be.

Such mushy, in-your-face romance seemed like something from a Hallmark movie, but it was sweet. Laurel knew she and George had never made goo-goo eyes at each other. She laughed inwardly at the idea of sophisticated George making goo-goo eyes at anyone. Not his style. Geneva seemed pleased by their display, if her sappy smile was any indication. Ellie, though, eyed the couple skeptically, and Dawn looked vaguely nauseated as she scooted her chair back.

Most likely, Laurel now figured, Ray was off to pick up something for the dinner tonight. A rustling in the underbrush presaged a squirrel's dash across the road and she took a startled step back as it passed mere inches in front of her toes. She laughed and the squirrel froze at the sound before skittering up a tree. Buoyed by the encounter, Laurel picked up her pace. She spotted Cygne's gates when she rounded a curve and was conscious of a slight feeling of oppression. She shook it off. She had time for a soak in the bathtub, an indulgence she didn't usually make time for, before dressing for dinner. If Geneva was ready a little early, maybe they could have that chat. She found herself suddenly eager to discuss the possibility of having a baby.

———————

In the event, Laurel couldn't get any hot water in the bathroom and settled for a frigid, one-minute shower. She slid into the navy sheath that was her go-to for occasions ranging from networking functions to church, clipped on the enameled dragon earrings George had given her, applied eyeliner and a flick of mascara, and slipped into her medium-heeled nude pumps. Footsteps sounded in the hall and seemed to pause outside her door. She was about to ask who it was when they moved on and faded away.

She eyed her reflection in the mirror with dissatisfaction. With the exception of the earrings, swirls of green flecked with gold scales, her outfit was boring. *It's appropriate*, her lawyer side said. *You look stodgy*, an almost-forgotten part of her replied. On impulse, she loosed her hair from its customary low ponytail and ruffled it with her fingers. It fell heavily around her face, a blunt-cut swathe of chestnut hanging between chin and shoulders. Now she looked more like she had in college. The thought brought her up short. She wasn't one of those sad women trying to relive their college days, was she? Pining for the dewy complexion of a twenty-year-old and breasts that sat an inch north of where they were now? She would have corralled her hair again, but the clock on the dresser said she was already five minutes late, so she left it and hurried from the room.

Mindy emerged from Geneva's room and dumped a small trash can into her rolling housekeeping cart, sorting recyclables first, it looked like. A young boy with curly brown hair dug his hand into a compartment on Mindy's cart, coming up with foil-wrapped squares, and asked, "Can I put the mints on the pillow, Mom?" Without waiting for a reply, he dashed through the room's open door.

"Looks like you've got a great helper," Laurel said with a smile.

Mindy's head jerked up, as if she hadn't noticed Laurel before. "Oh, uh, yeah." She smiled in return. "Yeah, Braden's great." The boy reappeared and she rumpled his hair. "He's my helper, all right."

He ducked away from her hand, saying, "Mo-om."

Laughing, Laurel said good night and headed down the hall.

From the foyer, she followed the light and conversation to the sunroom, a space with floor-to-ceiling windows on three sides that was much more modern than the castle's original structure. She was relieved that they weren't gathering for pre-dinner drinks in the parlor, as Mrs. Abbott called it, where they'd started their ill-fated evening ten years ago. The sunroom was Laurel's favorite, a bright, happy place during the day, looking out on the rear gardens and the lake. At night, like now, blinds were lowered to shut out the dark and the room was lit by mismatched table lamps and a ceiling fan fixture with brass trim from the 1990s. The sofa, chairs, and tables, too, were more modern, also mismatched but comfy and cheerful. A portable trolley in one corner sported liquor bottles and an ice bucket. Mr. Abbott, a tall man of near-cadaverous thinness, stood behind it, gray-white hair slicked into obedience with a gel that showed the comb's furrows, and a bow tie askew at the neck of his white shirt. A plinking sound puzzled her, but then she recognized it as rain.

Laurel surveyed the room before entering. Evangeline held center stage in her wheelchair. She was laughing at something, head thrown back so the tanned column of her neck arched, most of her hair piled atop her head with romantic tendrils draping across her brow and around her cheeks. An off-the-shoulder gold lamé top gave her skin a sallow cast, or maybe her tan was fading. Geneva, leaning over her and laughing hard enough to make her eyes squint into crescents, seemed to glow. Baby hormones. Ellie, holding what looked like a gin and tonic, seemed more relaxed than Laurel had yet seen her in skinny jeans and a silky halter top that made the most of her swim-toned arms and shoulders. Of all of them, her fashion style had stayed the most consistent over the years, Laurel thought, remembering Geneva's experiments with big hair and heavy eye makeup and Dawn changing her look from sweats to goth to punk to "artist." She was in full artist mode tonight, colorful broomstick skirt swirling around her ankles, blue-painted toenails on display in strappy sandals, and no makeup other than a swoosh of blue eyeliner.

It took Laurel a minute to figure out what was missing from the happy gathering: Ray. There was no sign of Evangeline's fiancé. She moved into the room, greeting her friends, and asked about Ray.

Evangeline pouted. "I'm so disappointed. He got called away on business. I really wanted you all to get to know him, and him to know you, but what can you do?" She shrugged one shoulder. "That's what happens when you're the boss, and we've all got to pay the bills, after all. He's hoping to make it back by tomorrow afternoon. If not, well, he'll send someone back with the van to get me. That's one of the worst things about this." She banged her palms on the wheelchair's arms. "Transporting it is such a pain. But that might not be a problem for too much longer." She put on a mysterious look.

"Why not?" Ellie asked bluntly. She pulled an ottoman forward and sat on it, favoring her injured foot.

Evangeline hesitated. "Well, I wasn't going to tell you until later—I wanted it to be a surprise—but I've been in Mexico for the last few months. You know that their health system is a little less … regulated than the U.S. system. Our government stifles innovation—do you know how long it takes to bring a drug to market here?" She wrinkled her nose. "The doctors down there are trying new things, experimenting with treatments that U.S. doctors can't use because of all the FDA rules and the like. Anyway"—she took a deep breath—"I had an operation. Three, in fact. Very cutting edge."

She paused so they could groan at the pun. When the laughter died down, she continued. "There was also some drug therapy. Also experimental. And expensive. There were some unpleasant side effects"—she put a hand on her abdomen—"but it was all worth it." She took a slow, deep breath and looked into each of their eyes in turn. "It worked. I'm going to walk again. I *have* walked, in my PT sessions. Just a few steps, but I walked! Before this weekend is over, I'll show you what I can do with only my cane, if someone will lend me an arm." She beamed.

The four of them erupted in a babble of exclamations and questions. She turned aside questions about the procedures, saying the technicalities were beyond her, that she'd need a medical degree to understand it all, much less explain it. During the treatments, she'd lived in a small bungalow on the hospital grounds, in a suburb of Mexico City. "Did you know Mexico City was my first international flight, back when I was with the airline? I remember I could hardly wait to shoo the passengers off the plane so I could explore. The altitude zapped me, but I still saw the Frida Kahlo Museum, the National Museum of Anthropology, Chapultepec Castle, and I managed to get a nasty case of Montezuma's revenge, all in a twenty-four-hour layover." She laughed. She said she wasn't yet sure how mobile she'd be, or whether she'd always need a cane or walker, but anything would be better than being chained to the chair. "In a couple of months, when I can get rid of this thing"—Evangeline smacked the wheelchair again—"you can all come back for the ceremonial wheelchair burning. Or maybe I'll push it over a cliff. I haven't decided."

Laurel listened to the questions and answers, happy for Evangeline. Another emotion gave her a sense of lightness and she tried to isolate it. Relief. She felt relieved, as if Evangeline's recovery had freed her from a guilt she didn't know she'd been carrying around. It all went back to that last weekend, she realized. She'd felt a sort of communal responsibility for what had happened to Evangeline. And she'd felt guilty about not staying in touch with her former roommate, with letting their connection dry out and get brittle and finally crumble like a dried prom corsage stuck in the back of the fridge. She excused herself to get some chardonnay from Mr. Abbott at the portable bar. The glass looked fragile in his large, work-roughened hand.

"I hear you're moving to Texas," she said, making polite conversation. "It'll be nice to be closer to your grandchildren."

He didn't return the smile. In fact, his mouth turned down, carving deep lines in his sunken cheeks. "You think so?" His deep-set eyes challenged her. "When you get kicked out of a job you've poured your sweat equity into for two decades, then you tell me how nice it is." His heavy jaw shifted from side to side. "We'd be prepping for the move this week if Nerys hadn't insisted on accepting your reservation. For old time's sake, she said. Pah."

"It's got to be hard. I'm sorry." Taken aback by his hostility, Laurel didn't know what else to say. She tried to excuse his behavior by reminding herself that the move had to be a scary and depressing change to make at the Abbotts' time of life.

73

Luckily, Dawn appeared beside her and asked Mr. Abbott for a glass of merlot. When he handed her the glass, she told him, "The hot water in my bathroom isn't working."

"Mine either," Laurel said.

"I'll have a look at the hot water heater when I get a chance," he said, bottles clinking as he stowed them back in the cooler. His expression and tone implied they'd asked him to clamber up Mount Everest. "It acts up sometimes, like old things do."

Laurel and Dawn edged away from the bar. "Doesn't sound like he's going to hop right on it, does it?" Laurel asked sotto voce.

Dawn shook her head, making her curls dance. "He's always been a surly bastard. He scared me to death that first weekend, all stern-faced and grim. He reminds me of Christopher Lee in one of those old horror movies."

Laurel stifled a giggle at the idea. "I can see that."

They stood a ways apart from the others, both of them watching Evangeline. She was in her element as the center of attention, laughing and gesturing widely with her champagne glass. Ellie began to wheel her toward the dining room, with Geneva leaning down to say something to her.

"Quite the miracle, isn't it?" Dawn said, her gaze tracking Evangeline.

Laurel couldn't read her tone "Sounds like it."

Dawn tugged at her earlobe, jingling a delicate silver chandelier earring. "Evangeline was always the luckiest of us," she said. Before Laurel could ask what she meant, Dawn followed the others into the dining room.

Eight

Ten years earlier

For once, Dawn wasn't even the slightest bit reluctant to attend one of their girls' weekends. In fact, she'd set out to make the drive from New Orleans a full half-day before she needed to, with the result that she had to kill three hours in a café in Asheville so she wouldn't be the first to arrive. Her red Ford Fiesta was a wreck on its last legs, but now that the exhibit and sales had gone so well, she could afford to replace it, or at least get the brakes fixed and buy new tires. The memory of Wednesday's phone call from the gallery, saying she'd sold all of the pieces in the exhibit, made her float. People *did* appreciate her art. She *could* make a living as an artist. Maybe she'd xerox the check when it came and send the copy to her dad, to show him how wrong he'd been. Rattling up the driveway, noting the way sunlight blaring through the rhododendrons streaked the leaves with viridian, she wondered if it was too soon to resign from her teaching job.

She greeted Mrs. Abbott and then Mindy with cheery hellos, climbed the stairs to her usual room, and hurriedly unpacked, slotting the yellow organza monstrosity into the wardrobe after fluffing it out. She was trying to move to an artier style and the dress didn't fit her image, but beggars couldn't be choosers. She'd worn it in her sister's wedding two months ago and had packed it because Evangeline had insisted on everyone bringing "festive" attire for a celebration she was being very secretive about. Evangeline got off on being mysterious. Dawn couldn't imagine what she wanted to celebrate. Surely she hadn't gotten engaged. A new job? Whatever, Dawn was happy to whoop it up. Once she deposited the gallery's check she could buy a new dress if she wanted, something that didn't shout "prom" or "bridesmaid." She was twenty-eight, for heaven's sake. Twenty-eight and finally on her way to success. She pirouetted three times, arms out, hair flying, making herself dizzy. Laughing at her silliness, she took the stairs down two at a time. Where were the others? She wanted to tell them.

Muted clanging of pots and pans sounded from the kitchen, indicating dinner preparations were underway, and Dawn glimpsed Mindy running the vacuum in the dining room. She didn't want to tell her—rejoicing in her good fortune when Mindy barely got by seemed callous—so she was glad the vacuum's roar drowned out her footsteps. She wound her way through the rarely used parlor and music room and headed for the sunroom. Through its open door and long windows, she spotted Geneva and Evangeline making their way toward the lake. She started through the sunroom, eager to catch up with them, but a muffled sob halted her.

Blinded by the room's brightness, she didn't see anyone. As her eyes adjusted, she made out tanned legs drawn up on the papasan chair and encircled by strong arms. Long blond hair spilled over them, hiding the woman's face against her knees. "Ellie?"

A gasp, little more than a quickly indrawn breath. Ellie lifted a tear-stained and puffy face to stare at Dawn. "Oh! I didn't hear you come in. I was just ... I was just ... " She stopped, mouth slightly open, apparently unable to come up with a reason for her presence or her tears.

Dawn closed the distance between them and put a hand on Ellie's shoulder, worried. Ellie was an athlete, stoic. She'd never seen her cry. "You're crying. What's wrong?"

Ellie snuffled loudly. "I hate this room."

She said it with such intensity that Dawn looked around, almost expecting the room to have darkened, a hairy spider to have appeared, or Villette's ghost to be lurking in the corner. She'd never sensed Villette in here, though, probably because the room hadn't been part of the original castle. The space was still light-filled and cozy, brimming with thriving potted plants in shades of green ranging from chartreuse to forest to emerald.

She pulled a wicker chair up beside Ellie's. "Why?"

Ellie bit down on her lip, drawing a bead of blood. Then the words burst out of her as if no force could contain them. "This is where I saw them."

Dawn blinked in confusion. "Who?"

"Evangeline and Scott. There." She pointed to the overstuffed sofa with its pilled upholstery and plethora of bright throw pillows.

"Is Scott here?" Dawn hadn't known Ellie's husband was coming. "Isn't he home with the boys?"

"No!" Frustration strangled Ellie's voice. "Not now. When we were juniors. The third time we came here. Remember, Scott came with me." Waiting only long enough for Dawn to nod, she barreled on. "I saw them. Saturday afternoon when everyone else was playing horseshoes. I came back because I cut my hand and needed a Band-Aid, and I saw them. They were having sex."

"Evangeline and your Scott?" *Holy shit.*

Ellie hugged a pillow to her chest. "He was sitting on the sofa with his shorts around his ankles. She was in his lap, riding him, her hair falling around her face, making little noises like my cat used to when you scratched under her chin." Ellie dug her knuckles into her ears as if trying to scrub them clean.

Ellie's story shocked Dawn, but didn't really surprise her. She could remember the electricity that had hummed between Evangeline and Ellie's boyfriend that weekend, the way his eyes lingered on her ass under the cut-off jean shorts, and the way her pointy tongue licked her lips when she was talking to him.

"Well, that was a long time ago ... " Dawn didn't know what to say and shifted in the chair, uncomfortable with Ellie's confidences, shying away from the images her words evoked. Why now? "It was before you got married ... "

"It's why we got married!" Ellie sat straight up and planted her bare feet on the floor. Her eyes were wide, her jaw set. She looked like a vengeful Amazon.

Ellie's declaration made no sense. Dawn half-formed a couple of questions and settled for a simple, "I don't understand."

"When I saw him with her, I knew that I was losing him." Grief colored Ellie's voice as if the wound was still raw and weeping. "I knew that if I didn't do something drastic, that he'd—that we—I loved him. I love him. I was a virgin, saving myself for marriage." She choked on a laugh. "That sounds so pretentious, so, I don't know, holier-than-thou. But it was important to me, and Scott and I had talked about it, and I thought he understood, but then ... But then I saw him with Evangeline and I decided that I had to, well, that is, I knew he was the one, so I ... "

"You slept with him." Dawn said it so Ellie wouldn't have to.

"Yes," Ellie whispered. "Two weeks later. After the world championships. I won gold in the 200-meter breaststroke. Scott got a silver with the men's four by two hundred freestyle relay team. It was a celebration and it just seemed right. We did it wearing nothing but our medals, in the pool after everyone had left."

She fell quiet, and Dawn got the impression she'd drifted into her memories. Who'd have known Ellie had it in her to break so many rules and behave so wildly? She was so disciplined about her swimming and her eating and her classes. Dawn was getting a new perspective on a friend she thought she'd known pretty well. Obviously not. "I still don't see."

"I got pregnant." Ellie dabbed at her eyes and nose with her shirt hem. "That first time. You'd have thought all the chlorine would have done something to the sperm, but no. It turned my hair green but couldn't kill off a few microscopic cells. There I was: twenty years old, pregnant with twins, no job and no husband. I lost my scholarship, of course, when I couldn't compete, and I had to drop out of college."

"Why didn't you tell me any of this?" Dawn burst out. "I would have helped. I thought you quit school because you and Scott were so in love you couldn't wait to get married. That's what you said." Hurt that Ellie hadn't trusted her enough to tell her warred with sadness for Ellie. It must have been hell.

Ellie scraped her blond hair back with one hand and the sun struck her strong facial planes. Her high forehead gleamed and tear residue was sticky on her cheeks and chin. She sniffed. "He asked me to marry him when I told him. To give him his due, he never even hinted at an abortion." She paused. "Evangeline suggested it, though. She offered to go with me and to pay."

"You told Evangeline?" Dawn asked slowly. Just because she and Ellie had been roommates didn't give her the rights to Ellie's confidences. Still, it rankled a bit.

"She guessed."

Guilt mixed it up with the jealousy. *She* should have guessed. She had lived with Ellie, for heaven's sake, shared a dorm room no larger than a walk-in closet, and she hadn't been tuned in enough to notice her roomie was knocked up.

Ellie seemed to sense something of what she was feeling because she leaned forward and said, "I was really careful around you, Dawn. I didn't want you to know, to think less of me. Evangeline, well, something she said made me wonder if she'd been pregnant before, if she'd maybe had an abortion. I think that's why she noticed. I had a miscarriage ten days ago."

It took Dawn a long second to process Ellie's words, delivered like a non sequitur in the same tone she'd used to speculate about Evangeline's possible abortion. When their import hit her, she reared back and her chair scraped across the tile floor. "What? My God! I'm so sorry. What are you doing here?" Maybe this was why Ellie was sobbing her heart out in the sunroom and spilling her guts. It wasn't really about Scott and Evangeline hooking up years ago; it was about her lost baby, and maybe hormones. Leaning forward, she grasped Ellie's hand and squeezed hard. "Oh, El, I'm so sorry."

Ellie gripped her hand painfully and tears leaked again. "I'm sorry. I thought I was done crying about it. I was fourteen weeks along. A little girl. Scott—we—thought that I should come here as planned, that it might help take my mind off it."

Dawn knew how much Ellie longed for a baby girl and wished she could say something that would lessen her friend's pain. She wasn't good at this crisis stuff. She tried to channel her mother, who had seen eight kids through emotional breakdowns of various sorts ranging from not being invited to a six-year-old friend's birthday party to a cancer diagnosis. "Look, let's get you some tea or a shot of whisky—"

"Tea."

"And a box of tissues."

"Two."

Dawn laughed gently. "Okay, two boxes. And I'll find a cold wash-cloth so you can wipe your face. Then maybe you'd like to lie down for a while before dinner?" She helped Ellie out of the awkward papasan chair and led her, as if she were a little child, out of the sun-room and upstairs, making soothing noises the whole time. Her excitement at selling her art and her drive to share her news had faded into the background; the important thing was to take care of Ellie.

———————

After settling Ellie for a nap, Dawn worried that her friend wouldn't be up to joining them for dinner, but Ellie was in the parlor talking to Geneva when Dawn came down. Wearing an above-the-knee dress with heavy beading at the neckline and a not-too-clingy fit, Ellie was pale but otherwise showed no sign of her earlier distress. A brave slash of red lipstick brightened her face and she smiled uncertainly when she saw Dawn. Dawn read her expression as a combination of "thank you" and "please don't tell the others." She gave a slight nod of acknowledgment and accepted a sidecar cocktail from Mr. Abbott, who was playing bartender, his black suit and white shirt making him look like an undertaker. Did the man even know how to smile?

Dawn didn't want to like the sidecar—it was just like Evangeline to pre-determine what they were all going to drink and make it something pretentious—but she did. The richness of the Cointreau and the sprightly taste of citrus blended well and went straight to her head. Holding the glass up, she enjoyed the swirl of amber and gold, the almost oily vein that ran through the liquor when the light hit it. Maybe she could paint an abstract series based on cocktails. New Orleans was a city that liked its hurricanes and absinthe, God knew; she could do limited editions that would sell like hotcakes.

Laurel Muir came in then, dressed in an understated black dress with openwork detailing at the hem and a neck that put it just barely in the "cocktail" category rather than the "funeral" category. How a woman who made the kind of money Laurel did could dress so drably was beyond Dawn. She glanced down at the pouf of yellow she was wearing. People in glass houses shouldn't be catty about other women's clothes. Laurel came toward her, smiling, and they exchanged real hugs and complimented each other's dresses.

Dawn wrinkled her nose. "It's a bridesmaid dress."

Laurel nodded sympathetically and smoothed a hand down her thigh. "I never know what to buy and always end up in black because you can't go wrong with black, right? Hey, I heard you sold some pieces. Sold out your whole exhibit, as a matter of fact. Congratulations!"

Dawn beamed. "Thank you. It's validation—finally. You can't imagine the high, knowing that total strangers were moved enough by what I created to spend their money on it. I think I'm finally on the brink of being able to do art full-time."

"Fingers crossed," Laurel said, holding up twined fingers. "Tell me about the exhibit. I saw the catalog, but I want to know what it was like."

Dawn launched into a detailed account of the exhibit opening and reception, a description of the pieces, and a list of the things she hoped to do with the money. Only after Mrs. Abbott sounded the dinner gong and they were seated around the table did she wonder where Laurel had gotten the news.

The meal was delicious, and the conversation flowed easily with lots of laughter. Even Ellie seemed to be genuinely enjoying herself. They caught up on Geneva's progress on her doctorate, heard about a big case Laurel was handling, and discussed Ellie's recent move to Virginia and how her boys were doing, Evangeline leading a tour group in Italy, and Dawn's art show. They amused themselves through dessert—a tart rhubarb-strawberry cobbler—with ever more outrageous suggestions for how Dawn should spend the money she'd made: a cruise, dreadlocks, a donation to good ol' Grissom U so the art building could be named after her. Dawn swallowed the last of her third sidecar and said that her eight thousand dollars was unlikely to impress the university's trustees that much.

Finally, Evangeline, who had shimmered with suppressed excitement the whole evening in a royal blue dress that brought out her eyes, tinged her fork against her glass. "Everybody. Everybody!" she said, speaking louder and faster than usual as a result of the sidecars or her excitement. "I have an announcement."

"You're getting married," Geneva suggested.

"You're moving to Australia," Ellie guessed.

"You won the lottery," Dawn said, "and if that's right, I hope you're about to tell us you're splitting it evenly with your best friends."

They dissolved into raucous laughter at that, all of them (except Geneva, who didn't drink anymore) at least tipsy. Evangeline quieted them by tapping her fork on the glass again. "No. Better than any of that." She paused to build the suspense. "I'm buying Cygne. I've come into some money, and I made an offer to the company that owns the castle, and they accepted it. It's what I've always wanted, a dream come true. Come June, it's a done deal. That's when we close. And you guys get to stay here free whenever you want, forever."

The sound of shattering china broke the momentary silence that followed her announcement. They swiveled in their seats to see a white-faced Mrs. Abbott standing over the remains of a tureen, twisting her apron in white-knuckled hands. After a moment she hurried out, muttering about fetching a dust pan. Then they exploded in congratulations and questions, surrounding Evangeline, who responded to all the questions in fits and starts, laughing the while and smiling triumphantly.

Dawn participated through a sidecar-fueled glow, pleased for Evangeline, pleased for herself, happy that they were all together, that they loved each other enough to get together every year, that they could count on each other, that her dress was yellow, wondering how soon her check would arrive and thinking about giving each of them matching pins or necklaces. Nothing too "sorority," but something special that would remind them of their ten years as friends. Something related to Grissom or here? A G? Too blah. A tiny castle charm? A swan!

Her head whirling, Dawn smiled at having hit on the perfect thing and tuned back in to Evangeline, who was motioning for them all to follow her. They trooped after her like obedient little ducklings, if ducklings wore organza and silk instead of feathers. Dawn heard herself giggle and realized she was drunk. Who cared? She tripped over the threshold of the music room and Geneva caught her arm with a sympathetic smile. A grand piano dominated the room, filling an embrasure by the window, and Dawn remembered someone saying that one of the earlier owners had been a concert-caliber pianist. She hummed "Für Elise." A sheet was draped over rectangles leaning against the wall. They must be planning to repaint. There were gold velvet drapes and a cream wool carpet patterned with gold, yellow, and pale green leaves. Laurel, Ellie, and Geneva sank onto a brocaded couch while Evangeline stood near the piano like a conductor about to strike the downbeat. Dawn drifted to the harp in one corner and plucked a string, eliciting a soft *bong*. Evangeline was saying something about redecorating and Dawn made an effort to listen.

"Obviously I won't be throwing out any of the antiques that give the castle its character, but I want a more eclectic style. Lighter. So I'll be mixing in chairs and tables and art bit by bit to modernize—no, that's not the right word. To vary the décor a bit. And I've found just the pieces to start with." With a sideways glance at Dawn, she whipped the sheet away.

At first, Dawn couldn't process what she was seeing. She must be drunker than she realized because it looked like all the paintings from her exhibit were here at Cygne, lined up against the wall, one after another. She frowned and squinted. With gathering dismay and confusion, she realized they *were* her paintings. How had they gotten here? Evangeline's voice broke through the cocktail fog.

"…couldn't think of anything more perfect than some of Dawn's art. I'm going to hang them the day after the castle becomes mine." She beamed, inviting them all to smile or clap or crown her queen of the fucking world.

"You bought my paintings?" Dawn heard her own voice as if from underwater, thick and ugly.

An uncertain look clouded Evangeline's face. "Yes. I love them. I—"

"All of them?" She hated that her voice cracked. She refused to look at her friends' faces, keeping her gaze glued to Evangeline.

"Well, one had already been sold when I—"

Dawn had heard enough. More than enough. She whirled, wanting nothing except to escape before she started to cry or scream. The quick movement made her head spin. She grabbed for support, but her grasping hand encountered only the harp's strings. They tore into her palm, making a whizzing sound as she slid to the ground. She barely registered the pain as she vomited all over the rug, spewing a slick of rhubarb red tinged with bile that clashed dreadfully with the delicate yellow and green.

Nine

They dined in the formal dining room, redeemed from the darkness of rich wood paneling and mulberry velvet drapes by a multi-tiered crystal chandelier and numerous candles, at a table covered with a snowy tablecloth and set with china patterned with scenes of French village life. The china looked old. Geneva surreptitiously tilted her salad plate to examine the mark. Limoges. The flatware was equally elegant—heavy sterling silver engraved with the Vendome et Falaise family crest. The Abbotts must be getting some mileage out of the good stuff before packing it away. What would happen to all the dishes, linens, and collectibles? The nursing home certainly wouldn't need them. There'd be an auction or estate sale. The thought of antiques dealers and bargain hunters traipsing through the house, fingering the snuff box collection and crystal, scuffing at the Oriental and Aubusson rugs, and joking about the portraits of the family members made her melancholy. She almost felt like slipping a monogrammed fork or embroidered napkin into her purse to remember the place by. A better idea came to her. She could buy the nineteenth-century cradle that was part of the décor in the room she stayed in every other time she'd come to the castle. It would be perfect for baby Lila.

Geneva looked around the table at her friends. She was glad, in a way, that Ray had been called away. It was nice to be just the five of them again. The flattering glow of the candlelight eased away wrinkles and made them all seem younger and more relaxed. Despite that, a thin membrane of tension stretched between them or around them. Oh, they were reminiscing and laughing, complimenting the food and toasting Vangie's engagement, but beneath the banter was a strain revealed by Dawn drinking too much, just like she had last time; Ellie's white-knuckled grip on her knife as she cut into the too-rare beef that left bloody puddles on all their plates; Vangie's too-frequent and too-loud laughter; and Laurel's watchfulness. Geneva caught Laurel's eye for a moment and they exchanged smiles and a recognition that something felt off about this party. Lila rolled over and Geneva stroked her belly. One more month.

She refilled her glass with water from the pitcher and turned to Vangie on her left. "Tell us about the wedding."

A chorus of "Oh, yes, when is it? Where are you having it?" rose up. "Just don't make your bridesmaids wear yellow organza," Dawn put in drily.

Geneva thought she was being self-deprecating, making a joke at her own expense, but the reference to their last disastrous dinner was unfortunate. For a beat, there was silence, and then Vangie laughed and made a calming motion with her hands. "We're too old for all the frou-frou stuff," she said. "We're going to keep it simple—no gown with ten-foot train, no darling little flower girls strewing rose petals, no ten-thousand-dollar bar bill. I think we'll just decide to do it one day when it feels right. We'll elope, maybe go to a justice of the peace, or Ray has a friend who's licensed to marry people. Then we'll go away for a week, have a honeymoon. A week's about all Ray can spare from his job. We'll keep it simple and easy and inexpensive, like Ellie did." Vangie smiled at Ellie.

"We kept it simple because I was pregnant, so we had to pull the whole thing together in a month," Ellie said bluntly. "I would have loved all that frou-frou stuff, as you call it. I went through bride magazines from the time I was ten, cutting out pictures of the dresses I liked and trying to decide if my bridesmaids would wear salmon or sapphire or celadon. Whenever I made a new friend, I sealed our friendship by telling her she could be one of my bridesmaids. It's just as well we had a small wedding," she added, cracking a smile, "because I must have promised at least twenty-five girls over the years that they could be in my wedding."

Everyone laughed.

Geneva was unexpectedly touched by an image of tomboy Ellie sitting cross-legged in her room, carefully scissoring around photos of models in strapless gowns with fluffy tulle skirts and pasting them onto construction paper. She'd bet Ellie still had the binder or envelope she'd used to store her photos. Despite her efficiency and practicality, she had a sentimental streak. "Do you still have the photos?" Geneva asked.

A wistful smile played around Ellie's lips, but she said, "I haven't seen my 'Ellie's Wonderful Wedding' folder in years. Probably lost in one of our moves. If I'd had a daughter, I'd have shared it with her." She stopped and swallowed hard. Dawn reached across Laurel to squeeze Ellie's hand where it lay on the table. She gave Dawn a small smile before withdrawing her hand.

What was that about? The baby kicked again and Geneva's abdomen contracted with a force that startled her. "Ooh," she breathed, hunching forward.

"Are you okay?" Laurel put a hand on her shoulder.

"Braxton-Hicks," Geneva said, straightening as the pain faded. "Nothing to worry about. Totally normal."

"Do you have a name picked out?" Vangie asked.

"Geonwoo does," Geneva said. "Lila Grace."

"I like it," Vangie said. "It's distinctive, but not weird." She pushed her plate aside.

She hadn't eaten much, Geneva noticed, just cut up the steak and rearranged the pieces. No wonder she was so thin. "I want to name her after my grandmother, but she strictly forbade me from saddling any child with Hortense."

Dawn made a face. "Hortense is old-fashioned, certainly," she said diplomatically.

"What does it mean?" Laurel asked, pulling out her cell phone to answer her own question. "Gardener," she said after a moment. "Did she garden? What was her favorite plant?"

"Marigolds," Geneva said, the memory bringing a smile. "We had marigolds every year, yellow and orange, in window boxes and in the little patch of dirt out front. The years we couldn't afford to buy any, she'd take the three-quarters dead ones the big box stores tossed out and nurse them back to health. I used to hate their scent—kind of bitter—but now I can't smell it without tearing up."

"What about Marigold as a middle name?" Dawn said. "After your grandma. Hortense means gardener, and she planted marigolds, so ..."

"I like it," Geneva said slowly. "Lila Marigold. That would honor my grandmother without having to christen the baby with a name Mama

Gran hated all her life." Her eyes misted. "I'm not going to cry." She dabbed at her eyes with the cloth napkin. "Stupid hormones."

"Of course you're not," Vangie said. "It's a happy thing. The circle of life and all that." She circled an expansive arm.

"Have you and Ray talked about having children?" Dawn asked. She leaned forward, elbows on the table, peering across Geneva at Vangie. One dark curl came dangerously close to dunking itself in Geneva's water glass and she slid it away.

Vangie's blue eyes went flat. It was an eerie trick of the light, Geneva decided, the way the pupil appeared to expand into and consume the iris, just as the candle guttered and the change in the light made the cornea seem two-dimensional. "I can't. Not since—well, you know." Her voice matched her eyes.

Shock or discomfort rippled around the room and Dawn stuttered an apology.

Vangie pressed her palms together in front of her chest and smiled a forgiving smile. "I'm about ready to turn in. It's been a long day, and I want to be up early tomorrow so we have as much time together as possible before you all have to leave. Laurel, maybe you could help me get ready for bed. I can do for myself if I have to, but there's a couple of things that are easier with a helping hand. Ray knows what I need, but now—" She rolled her eyes in the age-old way of women deprecating their men's absences.

Geneva opened her mouth to offer to help just as Laurel said, "Of course." Geneva stayed silent. She could wait. There'd be another opportunity to confront Vangie privately.

Leaning forward, Vangie blew out the candle nearest her. Smoke wisped up, dark gray at first, then dispersing to ghostly nothingness.

An hour later, near eleven, Laurel tapped on Evangeline's door. She found herself oddly nervous at the prospect of helping her, unsure what would be required and too aware of the fact that she'd never been called on to nurse or care for anyone. Her parents were still vigorous, knock on wood, and her grandparents had all had the good grace to die in circumstances that had precluded her being involved in caring for them: on the other side of the country when she was young (her mother's parents), of a sudden catastrophic heart attack (Grandpa Muir), and peacefully in her sleep at a nursing home (Gran). *Don't be silly*, she told herself as Evangeline called "Come in." *You're helping her unzip her top, not inserting a catheter.*

She pushed the door open and stepped into the room. Evangeline sat in front of a delicate vanity, head bowed, hands behind her neck, wrestling with the clasp of her necklace. A gilt-framed mirror reflected the top of her head. The bed was already turned down, and a foil-wrapped chocolate barely dented the middle of the pillow. Laurel thought of Braden enthusiastically distributing the candies and smiled. A water glass, half full, sat atop a cloth napkin as a makeshift coaster on the bedside table, beside a book laid face down. She couldn't read the title. A space heater hummed in one corner, making the room several degrees warmer than the hall, and Laurel was suddenly grateful for her sleeveless dress.

"I'm always cold," Evangeline explained, her eyes tracking Laurel's movements in the mirror. "Mrs. Abbott dug up that heater for me. She's so considerate."

"Let me help." Laurel stepped forward and bent close to Evangeline's neck to examine the sticky clasp. It had a hook and a small safety chain, and it took her a moment to undo them both. Evangeline's skin was warm and slightly damp under her fingers, and the scent of

Opium seeped from her pores. Laurel stepped back in relief when the necklace came free.

"Thanks." Evangeline grasped the hem of her gold lamé shirt and pulled it over her head, messing her hair and freeing small breasts.

Laurel had seen plenty of strangers' breasts in locker rooms over the years, and she'd seen Evangeline nude before when they roomed together, but something about the situation—the heat or their non-relationship for the past few years?—made her itch with discomfort. Her gaze slewed away from the sloping breasts with their unusually large areolas, and she asked in a would-be nonchalant voice, "Do you have pajamas somewhere?"

"In the drawer of the bedside table."

Laurel retrieved the nightgown, a soft blue cotton printed with clouds, and noted that Evangeline's book was a biography of Ernest Hemingway. "Is it good?" she asked, handing over the nightgown.

"He was an interesting man," Evangeline said, slipping her arms into the nightgown and wriggling it down to puddle at her waist. She shrugged off her pants and pulled the nightgown into place.

"Toss me some socks from my bag, will you?" Evangeline said. She gestured to the suitcase laid open on a luggage rack.

While Laurel hung the slacks in the wardrobe and rummaged through the weekender bag for socks, Evangeline said, "So, you're going to be a judge, huh? Dispense justice, sentence criminals to life in prison, condemn evildoers to death?"

Her tone was light, but the question grated on Laurel. "I'm going to be on the appeals court. I won't be hearing capital cases at the trial level."

"The death penalty seems to be going the way of the dodo with more and more states foreswearing society's ultimate revenge. Pity. Some crimes are so heinous they deserve death, don't you think?"

Laurel refused to be baited into a death penalty argument at this hour. She found a pair of rolled-up socks and tossed them to Evangeline, who fielded them neatly. "Need help?"

"I've got it," Evangeline said. She bent to pull up the socks, hair flopping over her face. Voice slightly muffled, she said, "I've thought a lot about justice the last ten years, as you might imagine. I've come to believe there's no such thing, not really."

Her voice remained detached, but Laurel tensed. They hadn't talked about it in ten years, not since those first awful weeks when Evangeline had alternately flung accusations at each of them and begged them to tell her the truth. When she left rehab and gave up hope that her memory of the fall would return, she never brought it up again. It was that uncertainty, Laurel suspected, that had disrupted their friendship, poisoned all their friendships, really. She hadn't been able to see Evangeline afterwards without wondering if she suspected her, and she was sure Evangeline relived the smack of hands on her back, jolting her over the balcony's low rail, every time they talked. Despite that, Laurel felt guilty about abandoning their friendship.

Evangeline straightened and rolled her chair toward the vanity, where she picked up a brush and began drawing it rhythmically through her hair. "Seriously, though, does it make you uncomfortable—the idea of judging people? You've been judged before, after all, and it wasn't pretty." Her mirrored eyes locked onto Laurel's.

Laurel knew what Evangeline was referring to. The shame, humiliation, and dread of those awful couple of weeks during the spring semester of their junior year came back. The sidelong glances, the silences. Her hands trembled and she fisted them at her sides. The summons to the Dean's office. Her surprise at finding Evangeline there as well. The accusations and tears. Her shock when Evangeline confessed to copying large chunks of her poli sci paper, saying that since they had different professors she'd been sure the similarities in their papers would never be noticed. Her father's disappointment that Laurel wouldn't be following in his steps and her grandfather's steps by going to Yale Law School. God, that still stung. Her mother's gentle consolation. Her brother's hoots of laughter that the perfect sibling was on the verge of expulsion.

"Why bring that up now, for God's sake?" Laurel put her hands on her hips and stared down at Evangeline, a line between her brows.

"I don't know … you becoming a judge. It makes me think about miscarriages of justice, I guess. Let's face it—that was a doozy."

"You confessed."

"I did." Evangeline rolled the chair back and forth, a foot in each direction. "What if I were to retract my confession? I imagine the powers that be who appoint judges in Colorado might be interested in the tale." She shrugged. "Or maybe not. They'd realize that either I lied back then, or I'm lying now—my credibility is suspect regardless, right? Still, it might be interesting." Her tone was lightly speculative, as if it didn't matter to her one way or the other, as if she were postulating trivial questions like whether or not Pluto would be reinstated as a planet or M&Ms would put out a purple candy.

Laurel stilled. "Are you threatening me?" The words came out louder than she intended. She couldn't believe the turn the conversation had taken.

Evangeline gave a puckish smile. "Do I detect a hint of paranoia?" Her trill of laughter grated on Laurel.

"This is total bullshit, and you know it. Say what you want. Tell whoever. I earned my judicial appointment," Laurel bit out, keeping her voice low. "I worked hard for it. I gave up a lot. Getting married again, having a baby—"

Evangeline rolled her chair over the bathroom threshold and reached up to turn on the lights. They shone on her head, creating a halo effect from staticky hair filaments energized by the brushing. "Probably just as well. You were always a bit too invested in your career to be a good mother, weren't you?"

The casual cruelty of it and the accuracy stung beyond bearing. Laurel tried to tell herself that Evangeline didn't know, that she *couldn't* know … but it was too much. Evangeline had jammed a cattle prod into an open wound and exposed Laurel's hidden doubt about her own suitability as a mother. Twenty years of friendship be damned. A lifetime of measured responses, of keeping her cool in all situations, be damned. "I hope you don't need help wiping your ass," Laurel said through clenched teeth, "because I'm out of here."

Stalking to the door, she wrenched it open, letting in a breath of cool air. She stepped into the hallway with relief and a sense of having dragged herself out of quicksand. Her leg muscles trembled, like they had the time she climbed the Incline in Colorado Springs, and the weakness made her mad. She pulled the door closed with a *whack*, cutting off Evangeline's laugh.

Ten

Ellie and Geneva lingered in the dining room after the others left, talking about having babies and taking care of them. When Mindy and Mrs. Abbott came in to clean up, they moved to the sunroom, Ellie limping because her heel hurt. It was a little weird, Ellie realized, that she was the only one of their quintet with children. The urge to text the boys came over her, but she'd left her phone in the room again and she'd already texted them once today; that was the limit she'd set for herself. One "what's going on with you I love you" text per day. Geneva had lots of questions, and Ellie happily shared her advice about birth and the first year with an infant. They had only turned on one table lamp, and beyond their puddle of light, shadows cloaked the sunroom. The furniture was all new: rattan chairs, tables, and a love-seat with pastel plaid upholstery. The plants were as abundant as ever.

"Is Geonwoo excited about the baby?" Ellie played with a corn plant's long leaf, pulling it through her hand like she would a dog's floppy ear.

"Oh, heavens yes." Geneva chuckled. "He's so ready to be a dad. He's read twice, three times, as many books about parenting as I have, convinced that there's a formula for raising babies, just like there is in chemistry. He's sure that if he can figure out the formula and apply it, everything will go smoothly."

"He's in for a rude awakening." Ellie kicked off her sparkly sandals and pulled her legs up so she was sitting cross-legged on the loveseat. "But it's sweet that he's so invested." Scott had been invested, too, as much as his Air Force job allowed. He'd never shied away from changing diapers, and before they weaned the twins, he'd always gotten up at night with her and burped or changed one twin while she nursed the other. A hollow spot opened up in her chest. *Why, I miss him.* The realization first took her aback, and then made her smile. Maybe absence really did make the heart grow fonder.

"You must miss the boys," Geneva said, sipping at the herbal tea Mindy had brought her before they left the dining room. Gingery steam rose from the mug.

"Like I'd miss my arms," Ellie confessed, trying to sound wry instead of desperately, pitifully sad. "Or at least my big toes. I don't really know who I am without them around. Pathetic, huh?" She forced a smile.

"Not at all." Geneva clicked the mug down on the glass-topped table. "Totally normal. There's a woman in my practice going through the same thing. Her youngest started at Arizona State last month and she's convinced he went there because it's so far away from her and his dad. She talks about how empty the house is, how quiet, and says she's ready to move into a tiny bungalow, only then she won't have room for her grandbabies when they come along."

"But if she works with you, she's got a job—a real career, a source of identity other than her kids." Ellie saw that she'd shredded the leaf and dropped it guiltily. "It's not the same."

"Probably not." Geneva's voice was calm. "It's more same than not, though." She pushed herself out of her chair with a groan, one arm wrapped under her belly. "Bedtime for me and Lila Marigold."

"I'm kinda wired," Ellie said. "I'm going to poke my head outside and call Scott. It's only nine thirty in Colorado."

They hugged good night and walked together as far as the foyer. When Geneva turned past the plywood elevator shaft toward the bedrooms, Ellie opened the front door and stepped out into the silky night air. The rain had stopped for the moment. She stood still, letting her eyes adjust to the darkness. Gradually, she made out the dark forms of trees, shrubs, and the contours of the castle. She tilted her head back, searching for the moon, but found nothing but a lighter spot in the sky where clouds were shrouding it. Thunder grumbled. She settled on the top step and dialed Scott's number. Should she ask him about keeping in touch with Evangeline?

He picked up almost instantly and she could hear the snark of Fox News commentators in the background. He must have muted it because the voices cut off when he said, "Hi, El. How's it going?"

His voice, steady and familiar, brought a lump to her throat. What the heck? She swallowed and said, "Hi, honey. It's going great. Evangeline's engaged."

Did she imagine his hesitation? "Really? That's great. Who's the lucky guy?"

He sounded totally unconcerned, and she let out a breath she hadn't been aware she was holding. "No one you know, or me either. His name's Ray. I'm not sure what he does." Crinkling her brow, she realized she'd picked up remarkably little about Ray. She didn't even know his last name. "Seems nice enough. They act like teenagers in love for the first time, hands all over each other. I can't decide if it's nauseating or sweet."

His laugh warmed her. "I'd be happy to get my hands all over you."

She could just see him waggling his brows suggestively and a wave of longing surprised her. "Me too. When I get home." She bit her lip. She had to ask. "Evangeline mentioned that you and she had talked," she said in a would-be casual voice. "I didn't know you were in touch?"

"She said we talked?" The confusion in his voice seemed genuine, and her throat relaxed a notch.

"Um-hmm. She knew what schools the boys were going to."

"Not exactly a state secret," Scott said drily. "That's on my Facebook page."

"You're Facebook friends?" Not that she was happy they were in touch at all, but Facebook was pretty innocuous. She stopped herself from asking who'd sent the friend request.

"Yeah, I think so. For a few months now. Aren't you?"

Come to think of it, she wasn't. The last time she'd looked for Evangeline on Facebook, she hadn't found her. *Huh.* She let the subject drop. They talked for five minutes about his work, the chores he had planned for Sunday, and the surprising news that his group commander, a woman in her early forties, was pregnant. Midway through that discussion, he broke off to say, "Oh, Aidan called today. He's met a girl. He's in love." He turned "love" into "luuuuv."

Aidan had called Scott, not her? Ellie quickly checked her texts. Nothing. "Hmm," was all she could manage. Being jealous that your son talked to his dad was beyond petty. She knew that, and yet she couldn't help feeling hurt. "Does she have a name?" she made herself ask.

"Cyndabelle, with a Y," he said.

Despite herself, she laughed. They discussed Aidan's love life for a few minutes and her worry that Shane was doing more partying than studying. Then the first heavy raindrops chased Ellie inside with a hurried exchange of I love yous and good nights. She entered the B and B feeling more secure about Scott and looking forward to their Charleston weekend. Maybe being an empty nester wouldn't be *all* bad.

———————

Balked of a shower by the still-icy water, Dawn slipped on the white satin pajamas Kyra had given her for Christmas two years back and called her lover, in the mood for a spot of phone sex. The phone was picked up with a breathless "Hi!" on the fourth ring.

"Kyra?" Dawn asked, knowing it wasn't.

"No, this is Flannery," the young voice said. "Kyra's not here. Can I take a message?"

May, Dawn mentally corrected, and who the hell was Flannery? "This is Dawn. Who—"

"Oh, hi, Dawn," Flannery said, greeting her as if they were best buddies. "Kyra's told us so much about you that I feel like I know you. I'm in her hatha yoga class. Mondays, Wednesdays, Fridays at eight. I've been taking class with her for two years now and it has totally changed my life. Totally!"

"Um, why are you—?"

"In your house? Kyra asked me to pet sit your cat, your precious Mr. Bojangles. Who's the best kitty? Mr. Bojangles is, yes he is."

Her voice got muffled. She must have bent over to pet the cat. "Where's Kyra?" Dawn asked, beginning to lose patience.

"Oh, I don't know," Flannery said sunnily. "She didn't say, and it really wasn't my business to ask. I've got her cell phone number, if you want it."

"I have it," Dawn said. *Idiot.* "Do you know when she's coming back?"

"Before Wednesday, for sure," Flannery said. "I'm teaching classes on Monday and Tuesday for her, but she didn't ask me to do Wednesday, so I'm thinking she'll be back by then."

Dawn hung up with a curt goodbye, hoping Mr. Bojangles survived Flannery's airheadedness. She dialed Kyra's cell number, but it went straight to voicemail. Where the hell was she? Unsettled now, Dawn paced the room, the wide pajama legs flaring. Kyra had been miffed when Dawn made it clear she wanted to come to North Carolina by herself. Was she acting out? She couldn't have gone to see Lexie, could she? A spark of jealousy flared as Dawn thought about Kyra's former girlfriend, a svelte history professor at Rice University in Houston. Easy weekend distance.

That was ridiculous. She and Kyra were solid. She would call soon. Her mother! Maybe her mother had fallen again. Dawn almost dialed Kyra's folks' number, but it was coming up on midnight in Pennsylvania. She would wake them and scare the crap out of them if there was nothing wrong. She opened the door and stepped into the quiet hall, which was dimly lit by a sconce midway down its length. A strip of light showed under Evangeline's door, but that was all. She considered knocking and actually stood outside the door for a moment, listening. No voices. A *snick*, like a drawer opening, or maybe just an old board creaking. As soundlessly as possible, she moved away, padding down the hall barefoot. Talking to Evangeline would only wind her up again. And she couldn't guarantee she wouldn't feel the old attraction, the magnetic pull that was part chemistry and part witchcraft and had to do with the mischievous sparkle in Evangeline's eyes, her long, sensitive fingers, the fragrance of Opium and warm skin, her laugh. She'd been conscious of the old feelings, dormant and muted but not gone, ever since Evangeline arrived.

Dawn passed the ugly plywood box around what would be the elevator shaft and began to ascend the stairs. Now, with the workmen gone, might be the only time she could peek upstairs. The floorboards were chilly against her soles.

She automatically turned right at the top, getting a whiff of sawdust and raw lumber. She tried the light switch but nothing happened; the construction crew must have the electricity turned off to this part of the castle. She started down the hall, moving slowly in the dark. It was echo-y without the drawings and prints that had always hung on the walls, the baronial chair that used to sit just off the landing, the piecrust table in the window embrasure that had held three or four potted violets. She couldn't see that they were gone, but she knew it. Cleared out to make room for the renovations.

Halfway down the hall, she barked her shin and stubbed her toe on something stacked against the right-hand wall but extending into the middle of the hall. The pain brought tears; she was sure her big toenail had ripped up from the bed. "*Aagh.*" Hopping on one foot, she steadied herself with a hand on the wall. She leaned over to inspect her toe and her hand slipped. One moment, the wall was supporting her, the next her hand sank into emptiness and she was tipping. The elevator shaft! Fear lit up every neuron, and Dawn hurled herself sideways, away from the emptiness. She landed with a thud on the floor and lay for a moment, panting.

Sawdust grains impressed themselves on her cheek. She raised her head slightly to brush them off and a glimmer, fainter than a firefly's glow, grayed the dark near Evangeline's old room—Villette's old room. Blinking, she tried to focus on it, but her eyes swam. Had she hit her head when she fell? She rubbed her eyes and her hand came away damp. Tears. She pushed to a sitting position and dried her eyes with her sleeve. Her gaze sought the faint light. It resolved into a womanly shape, misty and undefined. Villette! Her heartbeat quickened with the thrill of it. She wasn't afraid—Villette's was a sad spirit, not an angry or vengeful one. Using the stack of drywall or lumber that had tripped her up, Dawn levered to her feet. Before she could take a step toward the ghost, it melted into the room.

Favoring her injured foot, Dawn hobbled after it. As she neared the room, a breath of cooler air washed around her. Her silk pajamas absorbed the chill, and she wrapped her arms around herself. It didn't deter her, though, and she crossed the threshold without hesitating. Her head swiveled as she searched the room for the wraith. A sense of movement took her toward the French doors that opened onto the balcony. She hesitated. The door was slightly ajar, and the wind was teasing a single forgotten sheer panel. It fluttered, wisping toward Dawn, and she jolted back.

Embarrassed by her reaction, she reached to pull the French door wider, eased it fully open with a *cree-eek*. The wind tangled her hair. She could smell the approaching rain. She didn't approach the balustrade, now topped with a foot-high iron railing, but hovered in the doorway. This was as close as she wanted to get to a memory she'd avoided touching for ten years. Closing her eyes, she strained to sense Villette and felt a force willing her onto the balcony, drawing her to the rail. Panic welled, making her blood pulse loudly in her ears. "No," she whispered, and then more loudly, "No!"

A crack of thunder and zigzag of lightning chased her back into the room. She shoved the French door shut, tugging on it to be sure it had latched. Rain pelted the glass. She quickly retraced her steps and descended the stairs, balancing on her heel to spare her mangled toe, and resolved not to mention her midnight wanderings to the others. She could just hear them explaining away her experience as a slight concussion from the fall, Villette's manifestation as a trick of moonlight, the open window as evidence of the workmen's careless practices. She was tempted to tell them, tempted to cling to the rationale she knew they would offer, but you couldn't reason away the truth, not even when you wanted to.

———————

Clutching the manila envelope in both hands, Geneva listened at her bedroom door. When she'd passed Evangeline's room earlier, Laurel had still been there, and they'd been arguing. She'd listened only long enough to figure out that they might be a while yet before continuing to her own room. She'd been on the verge of setting out fifteen minutes ago but had heard a door open and close, and then soft footsteps. She couldn't imagine where Ellie or Dawn or Laurel would be going at this hour. It was coming up on midnight. Being back at Cygne might be affecting all of them, making it hard to sleep. Maybe someone was off to the kitchen for a snack or a calming cup of chamomile. She yawned. If she didn't do it now, she'd fall asleep. The baby tired her out.

The urge for a drink, dormant for years, burbled up again as she eased her door open and slipped into the hall. Should she find an AA meeting in Asheville? No need. She could hold out for another day until she was back in Chicago. She was still dressed in the clothes she'd had on earlier. Pajamas and a robe would not give her the confidence she needed for this encounter. The hall was dimly lit by a sconce. Light made a faint line under Ellie's, Evangeline's, and Laurel's closed doors. Steeling herself, she passed two empty rooms and neared Laurel's. She paused, listening, and thought she heard the toilet flush. She crossed the hall to Evangeline's room and laid her ear against the door's smooth wood. The action released memories of listening at Mama Gran's door before sneaking out to meet her friend Shalimar and their boyfriends in high school. She'd heard recently that Shalimar was in rehab and her four kids in foster care.

There was a sharp click and the hall got inky dark. Geneva startled, and then realized the bulb in the sconce must have blown. The envelope crinkled loudly as her hands tightened involuntarily. She relaxed her grip, telling herself the sound hadn't traveled. Anger, no longer white-hot after almost a decade but nonetheless powerful, drew her shoulders back. It was time, way past time, to have it out with Evangeline. Her therapist had been suggesting for years that she write a letter to Evangeline and put it behind her, but Geneva insisted she had to do it in person. She raised her hand to knock.

A stair tread groaned, whipping her head around. Was that—? Yes, a footstep. Another. Someone was coming down the stairs. She didn't want to have to explain why she was hovering outside Evangeline's room at midnight. Moving silently, she hurried to her room and slipped inside, leaning her back against the door when she closed it. Her pulse beat too fast, and Lila's head wedged under her rib cage made it hard to breathe. She'd waited this long. She could wait until tomorrow. Placing the envelope on her bedside table, she got into bed and lay on her side, the only halfway comfortable position this late in her pregnancy. She was drifting off to sleep before she wondered who she'd heard on the stairs, and what they'd been doing wandering around the deserted upper floors in the middle of the night.

Eleven

When Laurel entered the breakfast parlor, Geneva, Dawn, and Ellie were already seated. Sun streaming through the windows seemed extra bright, as if the night's rain had washed the air clear of pollens and dust that had previously muted it. Only one table was set, with a red-and-white-checked tablecloth and white stoneware, a far cry from dinner's formality. Happy daisies bloomed in a centerpiece, and a large coffee urn sat on a buffet. The Abbotts brought in platters laden with fluffy pancakes and scrambled eggs, and the aroma of coffee and crisp bacon pervaded the room. "I'll bet you won't miss cooking breakfast for a dozen or so people every morning," Laurel said, filching a piece of bacon from the serving tray.

"You've got that right." Mrs. Abbott shoved her glasses up her nose with the back of her wrist. "I've told Stephen that we're eating at the IHOP or Denny's every morning. I don't plan to even own a waffle iron or griddle." She set the platter down and bustled out as they laughed.

"Did you sleep okay?" Laurel asked Dawn, who was seated beside her. The other woman seemed quieter than usual, and she'd limped when she rose to get coffee from the urn. Even her curly hair seemed subdued, lying flatter against her skull and draping over her shoulders without its usual verve.

"So-so," Dawn said. "The storm."

"The rain woke me, too," Geneva said. "I left my window open and it came blasting in at about—what? One or so?" She dunked an herbal tea bag in the white ceramic pot Mrs. Abbott had left her. "I can't wait to go back to caffeine. At the beginning of this pregnancy, I told Geonwoo I might kick my caffeine habit forever, but that was just stupid talk. Now I'm counting the days until I can have a cup of extra dark coffee. No sugar, no flavorings, just pure unadulterated coffee. Mmm."

Her expression, reminiscent of a puppy hankering after a juicy bone its owner was dangling, made all of them laugh.

"A cup of coffee at this point isn't going to fry Lila's brains," Ellie said. She added, "I'd forgotten how noisy old houses are. Thumps and creaks and what sounded like mice gnawing inside the walls kept me awake half the night." She helped herself to a heaping spoonful of scrambled eggs.

"Where's Evangeline?" Laurel asked.

The others shook their heads, and Geneva said, "Haven't seen her this morning. She might need help getting ready. I'll go check on her." She started to rise.

Feeling guilty about the way she'd walked out on Evangeline the night before, Laurel waved her back. "You sit. I'll go." She took a big swallow of coffee to fortify herself and headed toward Evangeline's room. Pausing outside the closed door, she listened for a moment. No rustlings, running water, or *shush*ing of wheels over carpet. It didn't sound like Evangeline was up. She tapped lightly. When that got no response, she knocked a bit harder and called, "Evangeline?"

Silence. A silence so deep it was beginning to creep her out. Hesitantly, Laurel turned the knob. It moved smoothly under her hand and the door sighed open. A blast of heat smacked her, raising instant sweat on her forehead—the space heater working overtime in the closed room. *Whew.* The room held the quality of dusk, the sun trying to burn through the cotton drapes providing barely enough light for Laurel to make her way in. One step inside the door, the smell grabbed her. The toilet had overflowed, or a sewer line had ruptured, she thought. How could Evangeline stand to be in here? Another step showed Evangeline's bed. The linens were smooth, the bed clearly not slept in. Unease tickled at Laurel. Something was off. Something more than the plumbing problems.

"Evangeline," she called sharply. She flicked on the overhead light.

A scene of chaos met her widening eyes. A floor lamp had tipped over, knocking the shade askew and shattering the bulb. The thin glass bits winked in a beam of sunlight that infiltrated through a narrow gap in the drapes. Evangeline's suitcase was upended on the floor, her undies and shirts and socks bleeding out of it. The collapsed luggage rack lay beneath it. The wheelchair was on its side in the middle of the room, and Evangeline sprawled half in and half out of it, torso twisted and arched in a horrible spasm. One hand reached toward Laurel, the fingers curled into a claw. Two of the painted nails were broken off, lying like tiny tangerine smiles on the dark rug. The other arm was trapped under her body. The worst part was her eyes, wide open and filmed, and her mouth, stretched open in a silent scream. A glass had rolled not far from her outstretched hand; Laurel had almost kicked it.

"Oh my God. Evangeline!" Even as she breathed her friend's name, Laurel knew it was futile. Nevertheless, she crouched and placed her fingers on Evangeline's wrist. The flesh was tepid and still beneath her fingers, with much the texture and density of a block of mozzarella. She jerked her hand back hastily. A sudden urge to vomit came over her, her body's sympathetic response to the acrid stench of bile from the fluid splashing Evangeline's chest, arm, and chin. Laurel rose and backed into the hall, careful not to touch anything even in her flustered state. She leaned back against the wall, getting control of her breathing and her stomach. When she was reasonably sure she wouldn't throw up, she pulled her cell phone from her pocket and dialed 911, telling the dispatcher there'd been a death.

She answered the woman's questions as best she could, noting with surprise that her voice was level and calm. She didn't sound like she'd sustained the biggest shock of her life. When she hung up, she stayed in the hall for a moment pinching the bridge of her nose. It was all too much to take in. She breathed deeply and returned to the breakfast parlor. She must not have looked as calm as she sounded talking to the dispatcher, because Ellie immediately said, "Good heavens, Laurel. You look like you've seen a ghost. What's wrong?"

She started to answer but her voice didn't work. She cleared her throat and tried again. "Evangeline. Evangeline's dead."

"What? She can't be." Disbelief sounded in Ellie's voice.

They all stood, chairs scraping against the wood, and Dawn put a hand on the table to steady herself, as if she were dizzy. Geneva's cocoa-colored skin had taken on an ashy tinge, and she wrapped both arms around her belly.

"I'll go check," Ellie said, with the same tone, Laurel suspected, that she'd use to tell her husband she'd find the mustard in the fridge when he said it wasn't there.

When she moved to block Ellie from compromising the scene, Dawn streaked past them, hair flying out behind her, calling, "Evangeline! Evangeline!"

Glancing at one another, the three others quickly followed. When they reached the hall, Dawn's tear-thickened voice howling "No, no, no!" stopped them. She'd fallen to her knees in Evangeline's doorway, arms stretched up to clutch the door jamb on either side. Her whole body shook.

Ellie reacted first, hurrying toward her. She put her hands on Dawn's shoulders and stood behind her, crouching slightly and murmuring to her. Laurel caught the exact moment that Ellie understood the scene in the bedroom: she swayed, and Dawn yelped as if Ellie's grip had tightened.

"I don't want to see this, do I?" Geneva asked. Her nostrils flared. "The smell—"

"No, you don't. Think about Lila. Stay here." Laurel closed the gap between herself and the women in Evangeline's doorway. "We shouldn't be here."

Ellie turned a shocked face toward her. "It's awful. Poor Evangeline. She's all twisted and—you didn't say—what the hell happened to her? Why's it so hot?" Anger seeped into her voice and snapped her brows together.

Laurel had seen it before. Some people found it easier to cope with tragedy if they got angry. It kept the anguish at bay ... for a while. "Help me get her up," Laurel said, hoping to distract Ellie. They each put a hand under Dawn's arms and hauled their unresisting and now quietly sobbing friend to her feet. "Come on. I called the police. They'll be here any minute."

They steered Dawn toward where Geneva waited, and the four of them returned to the breakfast parlor together. Geneva guided Dawn to a chair and brought her some juice. "Drink it." She held the glass to Dawn's lips. "The sugar will help." Dawn drank, the glass chattering against her teeth.

Ellie came to where Laurel stood near the door listening for the police to arrive. "It looked like there was a fight in there," she said. "The wheelchair knocked over, the lamp."

"It doesn't look like a natural death," Laurel admitted. The weight of what she'd seen pressed down on her. Unshed tears made her sinuses ache, but she couldn't cry. Not now. "We all need to stay here until the police have done what they need to do."

Ellie bridled. "You're saying…you're saying…What are you saying?"

Leaving Dawn to finish the orange juice, Geneva made her way over to them, shaking her head back and forth very slowly. "Poor Vangie. She seemed to be doing so much better. Her life was on track…she was going to walk again. She had Ray. Oh my."

Ellie shot her a sharp look. "You think she killed herself?"

Geneva looked puzzled. "Laurel said it didn't look natural."

"What did it look like to you, Laurel?" Ellie asked.

She could tell from Ellie's voice and her expression that they shared a fear about Evangeline's death. "I'm not going to speculate," Laurel said, annoyed with Ellie for putting her on the spot. The Abbotts came in—why hadn't they come running when Dawn screamed?—and she broke the news of Evangeline's death matter-of-factly, eliciting a gasp from Mrs. Abbott and a frown from her husband.

The doorbell bonged and everyone stilled. Exchanging a look, both Abbotts hurried toward the front hall. Breakfast was forgotten, eggs hardening on the plates and syrup pools congealing. The fatty bacon smell hanging in the air that had been so appetizing earlier made Laurel's stomach turn. The bright sunshine now seemed an affront; even as Laurel had the thought, Geneva stepped to the windows and lowered the blinds. The sound of muffled voices carried from the foyer.

The Abbotts returned, looking shell-shocked. "The officer took one look and called for the sheriff," Mrs. Abbott said. She removed her glasses and polished the lenses with her apron hem. Her hand shook. "This is only the second death we've had at the castle in all these years. Diabetic coma, the other one was, maybe six years back."

"Ray," Geneva said suddenly. "Someone needs to tell Ray."

"The police will do that." Ellie pulled a chair forward. "You should sit."

"I'm not an invalid."

Ellie stepped away as if she'd been stung. "I didn't say you were," she said.

"Oh, Ellie, I'm sorry. I didn't mean to snap at you," Geneva said. Contrition scrunched her face. "I'm not used to this."

"None of us are," Dawn observed, surprising them. She set down the juice glass and stood, one hand braced on a chair back, hair straggling over her forehead. Her eyes were bloodshot and red-rimmed. She gave a brittle laugh that had no humor in it. "Or, maybe we all are. Used to it. This is all too much like that last weekend, isn't it? Maybe Evangeline will turn out to be alive this time, too. Another miraculous resurrection from a near-death experience." She flung up a hand like a magician flourishing a wand.

The hint of hysteria made Laurel eye her with concern. She was about to reiterate that Evangeline was truly dead when a heavy footstep made her pause. They swung around as one to observe the newcomer on the threshold.

Laurel's heart sank at the sight of the wide-shouldered figure backlit in the doorway. It was like an effect from a cheesy western. Of all the bad luck…

"The usual suspects, I see," said Sheriff Judah Boone.

Twelve

His voice, rumbly and rich as cocoa, had the soft edges and slow cadence of North Carolina. It released a flood of memories in Laurel. The four of them waiting in the cold glare of fluorescent lights at the hospital to find out if Evangeline would live. Coffee from the ICU waiting area vending machine that tasted like burned mud. Mrs. Paul's piercing shrieks when the doctors told her Evangeline was paralyzed. Then-Deputy Boone's penetrating brown eyes, and the questions he whipped at them like a pitcher tossing curve balls. His conviction that Evangeline's fall hadn't been an accident, and the thwarted look on his face the day he told them they were free to return to their own homes. "Don't ever play the lottery," he'd said on parting, "because you've used up all the luck you get in this lifetime."

Now he stepped into the breakfast parlor and Laurel had to make herself not retreat. He was a shade under six feet tall but he had a presence that made him seem larger. He hadn't changed much in ten years, although he must be pushing fifty. More gray grizzled his wiry black hair, and the corrugations on his rich brown forehead were deeper, but the wide-set eyes that gave him a deceptively open look were the same, as was the rumpled uniform shirt pooching over the hint of a belly. He was still fighting the good fight against middle-age spread, Laurel thought, imagining him on a softball field with his deputies, or playing basketball in an over-forty league. He had hands that could palm a basketball, strong and long-fingered. His voice was his only exceptional characteristic; that, and an intellect as sharp as any Laurel had ever come up against in court. He'd lulled her initially with his lawman-from-the-sticks routine, with his disheveled persona and laconic questioning, but it hadn't taken her long to recognize the penetrating mind behind the slow speech.

There was a satisfied glint in his eyes when he said, "Stay put. I'll be back to talk to you once I've seen the deceased. No half-measures this time, I hear." Without waiting for a response, he left, directing a veteran patrol officer to stay with them.

The spark in Boone's eyes made Laurel think of a boxer getting another chance at the heavyweight title after having been beaten. She knew it had grated on him when he'd had to let them go ten years ago. Milling about in nervous silence after he left, she and the other finally settled into chairs, not making eye contact. Laurel sat beside Geneva, who shifted uncomfortably for five minutes before pushing herself up and telling the officer, "I've got to pee."

The policeman, standing with his arms crossed and his back against the wall leading to the hall, grunted his permission.

As if Geneva's initiative had freed them, Mrs. Abbott began to stack dishes. Her husband joined her. The clatter of stoneware and the clinking of utensils chased away the silence.

Dawn pulled out her cell phone, dialing a number and frowning with frustration when it apparently went to voicemail. "Call me as soon as you get this," she said. "Please."

"He didn't say we couldn't talk," Ellie said in a low voice, coming to sit in the chair Geneva had vacated. She turned it so her back was to the officer. "Tell me what you think. Could she have killed herself?" Ellie's clear blue eyes looked into Laurel's.

"Of course she could have," Laurel said, "but I don't see why she would have."

Her words lay between them for a moment before Ellie said regretfully, "No, I suppose not. If she was going to do that, it would have been years ago, right after she was paralyzed and had to go back to living with her mom. I'm going to call Scott. I don't know what he'll say. He didn't want me to come." Tapping her smartphone, she moved away.

Laurel wished she had someone to call. Last time, she'd called George. This time, there was no one. She gave a second's thought to how the Denver papers would play the story: "New Judge Interrogated as Murder Suspect." Murder. The word lingered in her brain, flashing and crackling like a neon sign on the fritz. Such soft syllables, almost like "murmur," for such an ugly act.

The sound of the front door opening and closing and of more footsteps tromping through the hall made Laurel look up, even though she couldn't see into the foyer from where she sat. She mentally ticked off the probable arrivals—medical examiner, crime scene techs and photographer, more cops—all of them with shoes and boots muddied by last night's storm.

She was rising to help the Abbotts clear the last of the dishes when Sheriff Boone reappeared.

"Who found the body?" His gaze swept the room.

Laurel stepped forward, unconsciously squaring her shoulders. "I did."

His eyes met hers and his lips thinned and lengthened in a way that creased his cheeks but wasn't really a smile. "Ms. Muir, right?"

"Good memory."

"The lawyer."

"Judge, now."

One brow quirked up. "Congratulations, Your Honor. Come with me and let's chat about what you were up to when your friend was murdered."

Laurel followed him from the room, suddenly not nervous. She had done nothing wrong. In fact, she and Boone were on the same side because they both wanted to get at the truth. She caught up with him before he entered the dining room where they'd eaten last night and seated herself at the table while he adjusted the rheostat so the chandelier overhead glared its brightest.

"Make yourself comfortable," he said drily, sitting across from her. A jug-eared deputy appeared and settled himself in an inconspicuous corner, laptop at the ready. Despite the notetaker's presence, Boone put a notepad on the table. Then he pulled five or six butterscotch candies from a pocket and set them beside it. She'd forgotten his butterscotch habit. He clicked his pen and poised it over the paper. "Name and address."

Laurel supplied them, and asked, "Do you know the cause of death?"

"Not until after the autopsy."

"What's your best guess?"

"I don't 'guess,' Your Honor," he said, giving the words a twist Laurel found highly annoying.

She refused to rise to his bait. "Well, you wouldn't be talking about murder if the ME suspected food poisoning, so I'm going to guess poison."

Leaning back in the chair, he rolled his hand in a "continue" gesture. His expression was that of a man prepared to indulge her whims. It made her want to slap him, or impress him. Angry with herself for the latter thought, she decided not to play his game; she'd keep her speculations to herself for now.

"Tell me about finding Ms. Paul's body. Why were you in her room? What did you touch?"

Laurel told him about everyone gathering for breakfast and missing Evangeline. "We thought she might need help, so I went to see."

"Why you?"

"I helped her get ready for bed last night, so it made sense for me to go."

He unwrapped a butterscotch and popped it in his mouth. She caught a whiff of the buttery aroma and said, "I knocked. When she didn't answer, I opened the door." Cold crept over her as she recounted finding Evangeline. "I'm pretty sure I only touched the light switch and her wrist." She cast her mind back, and then nodded decisively. "Yes, that's all."

"Then you returned to the breakfast room and told your friends. How did they react?" Boone leaned back in his chair, fingers interlaced on his broad chest, eyes fixed on her face.

Laurel hadn't prepared herself for that question. She drew her brows together. "Just how you'd expect—they ran to check on her, but no one went in the room. They were shocked and upset."

"I don't have any expectations about people's behavior," Boone said, "so spell it out for me: who was shocked, who was upset, and what did they say, specifically?"

Laurel told him, as best she could remember, ending with, "Ellie asked me what I thought after Geneva reacted like it was suicide."

"And you said?"

"That I wasn't going to speculate." She lifted her chin a notch, wishing she had on one of her power suits rather than the comfy chinos and lemon-colored polo shirt she was wearing.

"Let's go back to last night, Your Honor—"

"Stop calling me that!"

His wide mouth dented in at one corner and she could have slapped herself for giving him the satisfaction. "You say you helped her get ready for bed…so you were the last person to see her alive?"

The idea made Laurel's fingertips tingle, as if the blood flow were constricted. She rubbed them together. "I might have been. I don't know. I suppose it's possible someone else came by, or that she called her fiancé."

"Fiancé?" Interest flashed across Boone's face. "What fiancé?"

"Ray. This whole weekend was about celebrating their engagement. We made a small party of it last night."

"Ray what?"

Laurel crinkled her brow. "You know, I don't think I caught his last name. We hadn't met him before. Evangeline sprang him on us as a surprise."

"What did he do? Where was he from?"

Laurel was forced to shake her head again. "I don't know."

"You spent an evening with the man and you learned nothing about him?" Boone gave her a skeptical look.

"He wasn't here for the party. He got called away—work, Evangeline said—in mid-afternoon. He was a Blue Devils fan," she offered.

"Wonderful. That narrows it down to half the male population of North Carolina," Boone said. "Anything else you want to tell me?"

Slowly, Laurel said, "You know, I think he was deliberately vague about himself. I asked about what he did for a living and where he went to school, how long he and Evangeline had known each other—stuff like that—and he didn't give me a single straight answer. I didn't notice it so much at the time, but looking back, it feels like it was deliberate."

"Maybe he's just one of those guys who don't like to talk about themselves," Boone said dismissively.

"No such thing," she shot back.

That earned a real smile. Small, but real. He quickly suppressed it. "Thank you, Your Honor. I suppose I don't need to tell you not to run off. I'll have more questions for you." As she started to rise, eager to get outside and process things on her own for a bit, he said, "One more thing. Ten years ago. Who pushed her off the balcony?"

Her mind scurried around possible answers. She didn't want to point a finger at one of her friends; even if she'd been willing to, she didn't know who. She'd thought about it off and on for ten years, had visualized each of her friends on that balcony, shoving Evangeline off in a fit of anger, but she couldn't fix any of the images in her mind for long. No witnesses, no physical evidence, no alibis. The kicker was that all of them had motives. She considered ducking the question by reminding the sheriff that it had been ruled an accident, but she no longer believed that, if she ever had. After a good thirty seconds of silence, she finally said, "How do you know it wasn't me?"

She locked gazes with him for a long moment, not sure what to make of his expression, and then turned and walked out. She kept going, down the hall, through the foyer and out the door. The humidity bathed her face. Pulling out her cell phone, she called her father. She'd ignored two calls from him already this weekend, but now she returned his call to tell him she wouldn't be back in Denver as scheduled. She explained why and fended off his offers to help. "Tell Mom not to worry and I'll keep you updated about my return plans," she said, preparing to disconnect.

"You're not in any danger, are you?" he asked, and the real concern in his voice cut through her irritation. Every time she got fed up with him, he did or said something that reminded her he loved her, and not just because she was a credit and an asset to him.

The thought had never crossed her mind. "I don't think so. It doesn't feel like a random thing. Evangeline was clearly the target."

"Hmph. I never liked that gal. Not since she tarred you with that plagiarism charge."

Laurel cringed at the reminder. She could hear pigeons cooing in the background, and traffic sounds, and suspected he was walking to the courthouse, a short but commanding figure that people instinctively made way for.

"She was a cool customer, that one. Smart as a whip, but always working the angles. That Thanksgiving she came home with you, I watched her put the moves on Jackson and I warned him to watch himself."

"She did? You did?" Laurel had totally missed all that. She had an overwhelming urge to call her brother and see if he'd hooked up with Evangeline. *Better not to know.*

Her father sucked air through his teeth the way he did when he was considering something, making a *feezing* sound. "I'll have Berenson do a backgrounder on everyone involved, including your friends, the staff, the executives at the corporation that owns the B and B, and the sheriff. I'll pass along anything interesting."

Ari Berenson was the firm's lead investigator, a former FBI agent who'd signed on with them after a bust gone bad had put him in the hospital for eight months and ended his government career. "Dad, don't—"

"I have a right to keep my daughter safe," he said, in the voice that told her further argument would be useless.

She sighed. "Fine. I'll let you know when I'm going to get back. Kiss Mom for me."

She disconnected before he could huff and puff any more. Wandering into the shade of the massive live oak on the front lawn, she gazed at the house's impassive façade and forced herself to confront the truth: someone in the castle, most likely one of her friends, had killed Evangeline. Unease pricked at her with the realization that she was probably sharing living quarters and meals with a murderer. She resolved to lock her bedroom door and make sure she wasn't alone with anyone. Having to take such precautions and be on guard against her friends made her sick to her stomach, and her footsteps dragged as she returned to the house.

Thirteen

On her way to the dining room cum interrogation chamber, Dawn thought she was prepared for anything Sheriff Boone might throw at her. She could account for her movements last night and this morning; she had nothing to hide, not a thing. While waiting her turn for questioning, she'd visited the loo, brushed her hair, and splashed cold water on her pale face, pinching her cheeks to bring up some color. She looked into the brown eyes reflected in the mirror. What would the sheriff read in them? Sadness, confusion, shock? She wasn't sure which feeling was uppermost.

When she entered the dining room, Sheriff Boone rose politely and gestured her to the chair across from him. His skin was the rich brown of autumn leaves and she cocked her head, wondering whether a hint of terra rosa or maybe Venetian red would capture its warm undertone on canvas. While she was considering, he threw her off her game with his very first question.

"Why are you limping?"

Dawn startled. "Oh, ah, I stubbed my toe last night. I almost ripped the whole toenail off."

"Where?"

She forced a tiny laugh. "There's a reason that construction sites are off-limits. I'm afraid I was poking around upstairs and smashed into a pile of lumber. I bled like a stuck pig."

"What were you doing upstairs?"

She shifted on her chair, not wanting to go into the mix of feelings—melancholy, guilt, curiosity—that had pulled her upstairs, and certainly not wanting to mention Villette to this coldly logical man. "They're turning this place into a nursing home. Did you know that?" Not waiting for his answer, she continued. "I guess I wanted to say goodbye, you know? I don't suppose I'll ever be back here again. We spent a lot of weekends here and this place is special to me."

"Hmm." He jotted something on his notepad and she itched to see what it was. "What time did this nocturnal farewell session take place?"

She felt herself blush at his description of her actions. *Bastard.* "I don't know exactly. Eleven? Ish. I came upstairs after dinner about ten and called my girlfriend. Then I lay down for a while but couldn't sleep, so I got up and went exploring."

"Did you see Ms. Paul, or talk to her?"

Her hair caressed her neck as she shook her head. "Not after she left the dining room. I thought about it—I even stopped outside her door—but I didn't hear anything, so I decided it was too late to knock." She realized she was massaging her earlobe and released it, sitting on her hands so they wouldn't betray her nervousness.

Boone scratched near his armpit. "Ten years ago, you said you thought the castle ghost had caused Ms. Paul's fall. Do you think she—what was her name?"

"Villette," Dawn whispered.

"Do you think she was involved in whatever happened last night?"

"No. No, I don't, because—" She stopped, dismayed by what she'd almost said.

"Because … ?"

Dawn hesitated, and then said quickly, "Because she was with me. Last night. In her old room. She tried to get me to go out on the balcony, but I wouldn't."

Boone ran his tongue along the inside of his mouth below his full lower lip. "Uh-huh. The ghost. And you don't think she could be two places at once?"

"Don't mock me, Sheriff," Dawn said with quiet dignity. "There are things in this world that we don't any of us understand."

"Oh, I'll give you that all right," he said. "Like the popularity of that Kardashians show, like the fact that North Carolina doesn't have a major league baseball team"—he got louder and spoke slower with each item—"like the fact that a woman can get tossed off a balcony and her four 'friends' deny any knowledge of what happened. They protect a would-be murderer. Well, now that murderer is more than 'would be' and I'm going to find her." He slammed his forearm and palm onto the table with a loud *smack* that made Dawn jump.

She leaned in, lips parted, before he could throw her with another question. "You're acting like there's some connection between what happened ten years ago and what happened last night. There doesn't have to be. Even if last time wasn't an accident, there doesn't have to be."

"You think there are two people in your friend group with homicidal instincts? Two people who hated Ms. Paul enough to kill her?" The sheriff's brows soared. "If that's the case, I have to ask: Why were you all friends with Ms. Paul?"

Dawn ducked the question, although she'd asked herself that more than once. It wasn't something she could explain to someone who didn't know Evangeline. "It doesn't have to be one of us. There's the Abbotts, Mindy, Ray ... " She scrabbled desperately to think of other people who could conceivably have hurt Evangeline. "I'm sure there must be others."

"And why would any of those people want to kill her?"

Forgetting her resolve to sit on her hands, Dawn flung them up in frustration. A tension headache was building behind her forehead. "Lots of reasons! I don't know. Isn't it your job to find out? Ray was her fiancé—don't the police look at spouses and boyfriends first? The Abbotts were really upset when Evangeline almost bought the castle out from under them. Mindy, well, Mindy snoops. She's in and out of everyone's bedrooms and I'm sure she's found things, seen things—"

"What kind of things?" Boone tilted his head ever so slightly, reminding her of a large, shiny raven about to grab a hapless grasshopper. The urge to paint him had disappeared.

"How would I know? Personal things." She knew she needed to shut up, to answer his questions as succinctly as possible, but the words kept spilling out. "Evidence of, of illicit sex or, or sex toys. Credit card receipts. Drug paraphernalia."

"You know this from personal experience?"

"No! Of course not." Dawn glared at him. "Aren't we supposed to be talking about Evangeline's death?" She began to tear up and bit the inside of her cheek, hard, to distract herself. She was not going to cry in front of this soulless man.

"You're the one who wanted to talk about sex toys," he murmured. "I think I have all I need from you now," he continued, ignoring her gasp of outrage. "I'd appreciate it if you'd stick around for a couple of days." He stood and she felt his gaze on her as she hurried out of the dining room, trying not to limp.

———

Ellie walked briskly three times around the lake despite the sting in her heel, working up a healthy sweat and wishing there was a pool. She wanted to swim a half-mile to work out the tension building in her neck and shoulders. She needed the cool water flowing over her, drawing out the stiffness and worry, emptying her mind of everything except "stroke, stroke, stroke, breathe" and leaving only trembling muscles and the odor of chlorine. She stopped on the far side of the lake, as far from the castle and Sheriff Boone as she could get, and lobbed a pebble into the still water. She was good at skipping stones, the family expert, but today she wanted to hurl them higgledy-piggledy, flinging them overhand as far as she could and watching them plop into the water.

Scott was coming. The first flight he could get was on Tuesday, so he'd suggested he should hop in the car and drive straight through, but she told him Tuesday was fine. She'd teared up when he told her; she hadn't expected such immediate and concrete support. It made her feel guilty for the times she'd resented his long hours at work, or snapped at him for emptying his pockets onto the kitchen counter, or felt jealous of his bond with the twins. He was there for her. He always had been. When she got pregnant. When her father died. When she'd gotten meningitis in Germany. When she went back to college in Alabama and finally got her degree. There was only one time he hadn't been at her side during a crisis. Was she there for him the same way, or did she still keep a little distance, hold something of herself back, because she'd seen him with Evangeline? The thought appalled and saddened her. She'd think about it later, when she had time and mental space that wasn't concerned with what she knew would turn into a murder investigation.

The knowledge of Scott's coming was the nugget of comfort she had clung to during her interview with the sheriff. She stooped for another handful of stones and hurled one, feeling the tug in her lats and shoulder. *Splish*. Not that it had been much of an interview. She'd sat in the chair he indicated, crossed her legs at the ankle, and rested her hands in her lap. Calm, she was very calm. She supplied her name and address and then said she wouldn't answer any questions without a lawyer present. She could see that her pronouncement took the sheriff aback.

He exhaled heavily, washing the aroma of butterscotch over her. "You're not a suspect, Mrs. Ordahl." He twiddled his pen between his fingers but kept his eyes on her.

Sure she wasn't. "Good to know."

"So you don't need a lawyer."

"My husband suggested I not talk to the police without a lawyer, and I'm following his advice." She stood.

He remained seated, studying her face with his lower jaw shifted to one side. "Does your husband think you have something to hide?"

His words had rooted her to the spot for a moment, lightning striking through the top of her head, traveling down her body, and exiting through her foot, leaving a tingle and a scorched odor. When she could move, she had turned and left, but his words taunted her now: *Does your husband think you have something to hide?* Why had Scott told her not to say anything? She hurled a larger rock. It didn't go as far, but it fell with a satisfying *plonk* and fountained up a geyser of water.

Ten years ago, when Evangeline fell and then-Deputy Boone made all their lives a living hell for a week, Scott had been deployed to Afghanistan

128

and the Air Force wouldn't give him leave to come home. Not since they'd let him have two days for her miscarriage less than two weeks earlier. His parents were with the boys. She'd downplayed the situation in their phone calls, not wanting to worry and distract him while he was facing IEDs and snipers and combat. That might have been the wrong decision, she thought now, because it left him feeling she was hiding something from him. She'd sensed his unease during their first Skype session after Boone let them leave North Carolina.

Scott had been wearing desert camo BDUs, even the helmet with his captain's insignia on it strapped tightly under his chin. His face was dust-streaked and grim, and a map of the region served as a backdrop for their conversation. She'd gotten home—Virginia, at the time— only two hours earlier and spent most of that time reconnecting with the boys who were hyped on the donuts, Pop-Tarts, and other sugar their grandparents allowed them. She sat in the alcove off the kitchen where they kept the computer and paid the bills. From there, she could watch the boys playing on the jungle gym in the backyard.

"So, Evangeline's going to be all right?" Scott had asked.

"She's going to live, if that's what you mean," Ellie said, piqued to hear him seemingly concerned about Evangeline. "I don't know if you can call paralyzed from the waist down 'all right.'"

He was silent for a moment, and a pair of soldiers with rifles slung over their shoulders passed behind him. "God, what a mess," he said finally. "But the police said it was an accident? They're sure?" He took off his helmet and scrubbed his hand over his buzz-cut hair. A red trench showed where the helmet had rested on his forehead.

Ellie flashed on an image of Deputy Boone and his scowl when he told them they were free to go, that Evangeline's fall had been ruled an accident. "Yes," she said. "They're sure."

"Why do I get the feeling you're not telling me everything, El?" Scott kept his voice low and looked over his shoulder as if to make sure no one was eavesdropping.

"There's nothing more to tell." Not unless she wanted to mention the tension vibrating between the four of them once it became clear that the police suspected one of them might have pushed Evangeline, the veiled attempts to ferret out each other's alibis, Deputy Boone's rough interrogations, the worry about Evangeline, and then the sadness over her prognosis. Her fear that the deputy would learn that she had a potential motive for wanting revenge on Evangeline, who, by sleeping with Scott, had put in motion a chain of events that had led to the loss of her scholarship and her hasty marriage. None of which Scott needed to hear about while he was in a combat zone. As if she needed a reminder, a thin whistling sound was followed by a *whumpf*, and the laptop screen went blank. A moment later, it shivered back to life. Scott had his shoulders hunched forward and people were running and yelling behind him.

"Mortar round," he said. "Lucky for us those bastards can't aim. I wish I could have been in North Carolina with you, El. I'd have told that detective that you're not capable of the kind of viciousness it takes to push someone off a fifth-floor balcony, that you don't have it in you."

She'd thanked him and kissed two fingers and touched them to the screen before changing the subject, thinking, *If only he knew.*

She put thoughts of the past behind her. She would get the car keys from Dawn and drive to the nearest grocery store and pick up some fruit and pre-packaged meals. All the vomit in Evangeline's room … Until the sheriff said she *hadn't* been poisoned, she was taking no chances. Hurling the remaining pebbles at once so they *plip-plipp*ed into the lake, she started back toward the castle, pulling out her cell phone to text Shane and Aidan. Surely being a murder suspect was a good enough reason to break her one text a day rule?

Fourteen

Geneva sought out Laurel after her session with Sheriff Boone. It hadn't been as bad as last time—she was less fragile in her sobriety, stronger than she had been—but it had still been ugly. Partly because it dredged up the slimy memories, and partly because he'd made her choose between betraying the truth or her friends. She'd made the painful choice and now she needed to tell Laurel. To warn her.

She searched the ground floor for her with no luck, and paused in the foyer, deciding Laurel must be out for a run, when a noise made her look up the staircase. Laurel was descending it. "What were you doing up there?" Geneva asked.

Brushing dust off her crisp slacks, Laurel said, "Looking around."

Geneva didn't bother asking why. They were all aware this would be their last time at the castle. "Anything left up there?"

"No, not really. Everything's off the walls and the furniture's gone, off to auction like Mrs. Abbott said. It should fetch a fortune, wouldn't you think? The rooms look a lot bigger without the Louis the Whatever beds and the Queen Whoever dressers. They're widening the doorways—to accommodate wheelchairs?—so all the rooms on the third floor have no doors right now. It's weird. Are you going to check it out?"

Geneva made a snap decision. "Nope. I want to remember it the way it was."

Laurel smiled. "Does that make you a romantic?"

Geneva shook her head. "A coward."

Laurel looked like she might want to pursue that, but Geneva forestalled her. "I've got to tell you something."

A crime scene technician emerged from the hallway leading to the bedrooms, and the women fell silent until he was out the door. "Not here," Geneva said. "Let's find someplace more private."

Laurel flinched the tiniest bit and Geneva caught on immediately. The thought that her friend was afraid of her was heartbreaking.

"I'm not trying to lure you to a dark corner so I can do you in." She met Laurel's gaze levelly.

"Oh, Geneva, I know that. I'm sorry. It's just that—"

"I get it." Geneva flashed a forgiving smile. "It's a strange situation. It's bound to disrupt our dynamic. Intellectually, I can see that it would be smart not to be alone with any of you—wait, that's an oxymoron, isn't it?" She chuckled.

"I know what you mean. Why don't we drive into town?" Laurel suggested. "I don't know about you, but I could do with a break from this place, from … " She gestured upwards. "Unless you think I'll run us both off the road in a spectacular murder-suicide."

A sense of peace poured into Geneva at the thought of leaving the castle. "I'll take my chances. Let's get out of here."

On the two-lane road leading away from the inn, Laurel rolled down the windows and let the wind buffet them. Geneva closed her eyes and let her head fall back against the headrest, forgetting for a moment why she'd even wanted to talk to Laurel. The wind grazing her face and hair blew away the ugliness.

"What did you want to tell me?" Laurel asked, bringing Geneva's eyes open.

She turned her head to look at her friend's profile, its straight nose and strong chin revealed by the wind blasting her hair back. "I had to tell the sheriff that I heard you and Evangeline arguing last night. I feel so bad about it, Laurel. He asked me point-blank if I knew of any quarrels or bad feelings, if I'd witnessed any tensions between anyone and Evangeline."

Blanched knuckles revealed that Laurel's grip had tightened on the wheel. "Don't worry about it, Gen," she said, keeping her eyes on the road. "You did the right thing." She dropped a hand from the wheel to squeeze Geneva's hand. "It was no big thing. While I was helping Evangeline get ready for bed—I'm not sure why she asked for help, actually, since she seemed perfectly capable of doing everything for herself—she brought up the plagiarism incident. I got a little heated."

"Of course you did," Geneva agreed. Something in the way Laurel focused on the road ahead gave her the feeling that there might have been more to it. At least Laurel wasn't asking awkward questions about why she'd been eavesdropping outside Evangeline's door. She felt like a hypocrite—she hadn't told Boone about her own grudge against Evangeline, after all. She hovered on the edge of confessing, but instead asked, "Why in the world would she want to stir *that* up after all this time?"

Slowing the car as they reached the outskirts of New Aberdeen, Laurel said, "You got me. It was weird, actually."

They were passing a high school and had to wait at a crosswalk for a gaggle of teens to cross. A large blue-and-white sign announced

133

"New Aberdeen High School Blue Demons—Girls 3A Champions" over a poorly executed painting of a basketballer. A drugstore across the street advertised a back-to-school special on Pepsi products and binders, and a fast food joint next door to it did a steady stream of business, mostly hungry teenagers, it looked like.

"I'm hungry," Laurel said. "Want to get something to eat?"

Realizing she was starving, Geneva said, "Yes, indeed. I only ate a couple of bites of breakfast before … Well, I could eat the proverbial horse."

Laurel cruised slowly down the town's main drag, a two-lane street shaded by overarching oaks that must have been planted about the time Sherman was burning Atlanta, Geneva thought. Businesses, some looking decidedly seedy and a few thriving, lined both sides of the road: a printing shop, a bank, a dollar store with a rack of clothes pulled out onto the sidewalk, a storefront church, a tattoo parlor with soaped windows, an ice cream parlor, and a small café with two round tables outside. What would it be like to raise a child here, in small town America, rather than in Chicago? Easier? Or just as hard but in a different way?

Laurel pulled into a slanted parking slot in front of the café and when they'd ordered their food at the counter, they sat at a table on the sidewalk. Laurel adjusted the red umbrella so it shaded them and sipped her iced tea while Geneva sucked hard at the straw plunged into her vanilla milkshake. The creamy sweetness was heaven on her tongue. "I haven't had a milkshake in … oh, I don't even know how long. I'm having one every day between now and when Lila comes. Pregnant women are supposed to gain weight, right?"

Laurel laughed. "Absolutely."

"That's the sign of a true friend," Geneva said, licking her tongue around her mouth. "Not even trying to tell me how hard it will be to lose extra baby weight."

A young waitress brought their sandwiches and napkin-wrapped utensils. A skateboarder whizzed by, and a car horn blared down the street. It would have been an idyllic fall day, Geneva thought, without the specter of possible murder and another police investigation hanging over them. "Sheriff Boone asked me something weird this morning," she said. "He wanted to know if I'd ever had trouble with 'things going missing' from my room here. If I'd ever suspected Mindy of stealing."

"And?" Laurel bit into her sandwich.

Focusing on squirting mustard onto her pastrami and rye, Geneva said, "I don't think she stole, but she did mention once that she'd taken a vodka bottle from my trash and recycled it. I got the feeling she was after something more than reminding me to recycle."

"Like what?"

"Like"—Geneva hesitated, remembering the awkward encounter—"like if I'd acted embarrassed at all, she might have ... I don't know. In the same conversation, she mentioned that she'd had to replace two tires on her car and how expensive it was. It sounds silly, but I got the feeling she was hinting that I should give her some money."

"Blackmail?"

"Maybe? I didn't take the bait and she never brought it up again." Geneva grabbed for her napkin as the wind tried to whisk it away. "Hey, do you think you could find Vangie's house?"

"I only went there a couple of times, and she was driving, but I might be able to. Why?"

Geneva shrugged, not sure why she wanted to see the house. "I don't want to go back yet, and, I don't know ... it seems like paying our respects, somehow."

"Sure," Laurel said, rising. "We can give it a whirl. Do you remember the street name?"

"Willow-something? Willowbrook? Willowdale?"

Twelve minutes of driving in circles and wandering down streets that boasted a house or a tree that looked familiar but turned out not to be what they were looking for, finally led them to Willowglen Lane. It was a short street featuring 1980s vintage two-story houses. "That one," Geneva said, pointing to the third house from the end on the right.

Laurel pulled the car to the curb and idled, both of them staring at the house. It showed signs of neglect: faded paint; a scruffy yard that hadn't been weeded, seeded, or mowed in far too long; a wheelchair ramp leading to a concrete stoop that listed to the left; and windows so grimy they looked opaque, like eyes filmed with cataracts. The eerie thought made Geneva shiver. Like a goose had walked over her grave, as Mama Gran would say. A "For Sale" sign was the cleanest, brightest thing about the property.

"Evangeline was selling up?" Laurel asked. She cut the engine.

"I guess so." Geneva got out of the car, stumbling a little on the curb. "She must have moved into Ray's place, don't you think? It doesn't look like she's done anything to this place since her mom died. That was six months ago, right? Did you come for the funeral?"

Laurel joined her on the sidewalk and said, "No."

"Me neither." She'd had a raft of reasons why she couldn't leave Chicago—clients, home renovations, the pregnancy—but they seemed petty now. "We—I—should have come. She was our friend."

Laurel kicked at a trio of acorns and they skittered off the curb. The front door opened, surprising them. A young couple appeared, accompanied by a sixtyish woman in a green linen suit. The trio stopped when they saw Laurel and Geneva hovering on the sidewalk. Geneva was stuttering for something to say when Laurel broke in with, "We saw the house was for sale and wanted to take a look. Are you the listing agent?"

"No," the woman said, "but I can give you his number. He represents the bank handling the foreclosure." She scribbled on the back of a business card and handed it to Laurel.

The trio drove off in the Realtor's Lexus, and Laurel and Geneva returned to their rental. Geneva braced herself with her hand on the warm hood, and Laurel stood with her back to the car, staring at Vangie's house as if she were trying to puzzle something out.

"You know," Laurel said, "the Realtor said the house was foreclosed on. I wonder if Evangeline was having money troubles. I'm sure her medical expenses over the years have been astronomical, and traveling to and from Mexico for whatever procedures she was having there must have been expensive, too. Did she have that kind of money coming in?"

"Ray might have been funding her. He looked well off. Did you notice that gold bracelet? And his athletic shoes cost upwards of two hundred dollars. I know because one of my clients—fourteen years old, mind you—came in with the same shoes a couple weeks back and bragged about them."

"Huh." Laurel stood silently for a moment, making no move to get in the car. The breeze stirred her hair. "I wish I'd learned more about him. Did you talk to him, get his last name, learn what he does or where he's from? I don't even know if he and Evangeline were living in the state. I assumed she was living here"—she gestured to the house—"but it's clear she wasn't."

Geneva cast her mind back, disconcerted to realize that despite half an hour's conversation, she didn't know much about Vangie's fiancé, either. "He was raised by his grandmother, like I was," she said. "I don't know how we got onto that—I think I said something about Mama Gran—and he told me he and his brothers were brought up by his grandmother, too. I learned a lot about his grandma, but not much about him." Geneva was irked by the realization. "Why are you so curious about Ray?"

Laurel opened the driver's-side door. "He's an unknown quantity. Women are more likely to be killed by spouses or boyfriends than by anyone else. Given the situation we're all in—again—I think it might be wise to have a little ammunition to counter Sheriff Boone if worse comes to worst."

Sobered by the thought, and impressed with Laurel's farsightedness, Geneva got in the car and pulled the door closed.

Fifteen

Sheriff Boone snagged Laurel when she came through Cygne's front door at two o'clock. He looked as worn down as she felt, with his eyes slightly bloodshot and cushioned by the hint of pouches beneath them. "Your Honor," he said, breaking off a conversation with a deputy as she came in. "I've been looking for you."

His tone invited her to explain her absence but she merely said, "You found me."

"Come with me." Without waiting to see if she was following, he disappeared down the hall leading to the bedrooms.

Laurel followed reluctantly. Boone stopped, as she knew he would, in front of the open door to Evangeline's room. A breeze wafted from the window, opened to disperse the heat and odors, Laurel figured. Gooseflesh chilled her arms as Boone made room for her beside him in the doorway. His bulk was warm and almost comforting in the circumstances. Her first glance told her Evangeline's body was gone, and she slumped slightly with relief.

"Tell me what's different from last night when you helped her get ready for bed," he ordered.

She gave him a disbelieving look. "Everything. It's a mess. None of that"—she waved a hand at the disorder in the room—"was like that."

"Try. Is there anything in the room that wasn't there when you left last night? You can go in—we're done processing it."

The last thing Laurel wanted to do was enter the room where her friend had died, but she took a small step forward and then another until she was almost centered in the room. *Focus.* The wheelchair was immediately to her right, tipped on its side. She touched a finger to the upright wheel and it spun with a faint whisking sound. The impotence of it struck her—a wheel spinning in mid-air, nothing to bite into, nowhere to go. She stepped back. Clothes were still strewn around, the lamp on the floor, although someone had swept up the shattered bulb. Someone had also taken a stab at cleaning up the vomit and other bodily fluids. An overpowering odor of harsh cleansers lingered, searing her nostrils. She breathed shallowly through her mouth and looked around, wanting now to find something out of place, a clue that spoke to another person's presence in the room after she'd left, but there was nothing new. She shook her head. "I'm sorry."

"Did this all happen when you fought with the victim?" Sheriff Boone asked.

Her gaze flew to his face. His hooded eyes were fixed on her, evaluating her reaction. "What? No! We argued, we didn't *fight.*"

"About?"

"Ancient history." She should share the details of their conversation, she knew, but it didn't have any bearing on Evangeline's death, so why go into it? She sought for something to distract him. She swiveled her head, only now remarking the absence of men's clothing and effects. "There's nothing of Ray's in here."

Boone didn't act surprised; he'd undoubtedly already noticed.

"Don't you think that's strange?" she persisted when he didn't respond. "Evangeline said he was coming back."

"It's noteworthy." He wasn't going to speculate with her, she knew. From the corner of her eye, she spotted the Hemingway book half-under the bed, pages crumpled, and it struck her that Evangeline would never finish it, never read another book, and the sadness of that, the emptiness, roiled her stomach. "I have to—" She shouldered past Boone and burst into the hall, where she bent over, hands on her thighs and hair flopped over her face, panting. She concentrated on not throwing up. After a moment, the wave of nausea receded and she slowly straightened.

He stepped through the door and closed it, not commenting on her hasty departure. "Thanks for your help, Your Honor. We'll chat again tomorrow." He gave her a considering look but didn't say anything more as he led the way back to the foyer.

———

Dinner that night was awkward and late. Sheriff Boone and his team hadn't left until almost seven, and he'd dropped a bombshell on them as he departed. Evangeline Paul, he said, had died of strychnine poisoning. The medical examiner had completed his autopsy, working overtime on a Sunday, and had no doubts about the cause of death. Toxicology results would verify it in a couple of weeks. With a long look at each of them, Boone said he'd be back in the morning to interview each of them again. He recommended Ellie have her lawyer on hand because he was going to insist she answer his questions. There was dead silence when he left, and then Geneva asked Ellie if she had a lawyer. She sheepishly confessed that she didn't, and went to her room to call Scott for his advice. The others went to their rooms, too; at least, that's where Laurel had gone, and she assumed the others had done the same.

When the dinner gong sounded, the four of them gathered in the breakfast parlor rather than the dining room. A pall of unease and even suspicion hung in the air. Laurel hated thinking that one of her friends could have murdered Evangeline, but she couldn't help analyzing their expressions and postures, what they said and what they didn't say. What did Ellie's sidelong glance at Dawn mean? Where was Geneva when Evangeline died? Come to think of it, Geneva's room was at the far end of the hall from Evangeline's—how had she overheard their argument? Why was Dawn so fidgety, twiddling her spoon, tinging her finger against her water glass, jiggling her foot?

Mrs. Abbott brought in a hearty lentil stew, and Ellie excused herself. When she returned three minutes later, she carried a microwaved pot pie.

"What?" Her gaze challenged each of them as they stared at her. "Someone poisoned Evangeline. I'm not taking any chances." She thrust a defiant fork into the pie which showered pastry flakes on the table.

"You think one of us killed Evangeline?" Dawn asked. A line appeared between her brows.

"Well, duh." Ellie wasn't giving an inch. "One of you or one of the Abbotts or Mindy, maybe Ray. Either way"—she gestured toward the pie—"I'm playing it safe." She took two bites while the others fiddled with their stew without eating it.

Laurel finally swallowed a spoonful of the savory stew, trying not to think about how the cumin and oregano could conceal the flavor of poison. She was not going to be paranoid. "It's good." She took another bite, and first Geneva and then Dawn began to eat. Geneva asked Dawn about her recent vacation and conversation stumbled forward.

Ellie, midway through the meal, burst out, "Let's just talk about it," interrupting Dawn, who was describing a temple she and Kyra had toured in Bangkok. "One of us probably murdered Evangeline, and now we're trapped here together until Sheriff B. figures out who it was. That's creepy. I'd like to ask the guilty party to turn herself in so we can all go back to our lives."

Laurel was simultaneously discomfited by and appreciative of her bluntness. Maybe it was time for them all to be a bit more blunt.

Dawn slewed around to face Ellie. "Why do you assume it was one of us? Even if it wasn't suicide, it—"

"I can't imagine it was a suicide," Laurel broke in. "Not using strychnine. It's a horrific way to die. Barbiturates and alcohol, or carbon monoxide poisoning would have been painless."

Dawn dipped her chin. "Fine. Even if someone killed her, it doesn't have to be one of us. I know you're going to say that there has to be a link between what happened to her ten years ago and this, but there doesn't." Her hands gripped the table's edge, shifting the tablecloth enough to put their glasses in jeopardy. "It could have been one of the Abbotts, like Ellie said. Mindy. Ray. Someone in her life we don't even know about. If it was poison, there's nothing to say the person who gave it to her even had to be here, right?"

"That's true," Geneva murmured, looking struck. "But you said it looked like there'd been a struggle …?" She queried Laurel with a raised eyebrow.

"I googled strychnine poisoning after Boone told us," Laurel said. She kept her voice steady, although the photos of poisoned rats accompanying the article had appalled her. "I think that what looked like a struggle was actually caused by Evangeline. Strychnine causes horrible, violent spasms—victims sometimes even break their spines with the force of the convulsions. The lamp and everything—it probably happened while Evangeline was—" She trailed off and no one made her finish the thought.

"So, Ray could have put it in her—I don't know—mouthwash," Dawn said, sounding triumphant. "Then he made up a bogus crisis at work so he wouldn't be here when her body was discovered."

Some of the tension had dissipated, and Laurel suspected it was because they were all focusing on Ray as Evangeline's murderer, rather than on each other. She hoped Sheriff Boone had similar ideas. She topped off her wine glass with Chianti and passed the bottle. Everyone except Geneva, who was drinking water, refilled their glasses. Laurel's forefinger tapped nervously on the wine stem. She didn't know quite how to say what she needed to say, so she decided to spit it out. "I think we should make a pact."

"What kind of pact?" Ellie frowned.

"To stick it out this time. To stay here until we know what really happened to Evangeline." She ached with the need to convince them. If they left Cygne without knowing, they would drift apart forever, and she knew with sudden clarity that she didn't want that.

There was silence around the table. Dawn met her eyes briefly, and then dropped her gaze to her wine glass. Geneva stared off into space. Ellie dipped her napkin in her water glass and dabbed at a spot on her blouse.

"The sheriff can't make us stay, but I think we should. We owe it to Evangeline, and to each other." Laurel kept her voice quiet and level. If the others didn't want to stay, shouting and pleading weren't going to change their minds. She held her breath. She owed Evangeline, and she'd let her down last time by being too chicken to search out the truth. She was going to see it through this time, whatever the others decided.

"I'm in," Dawn said. She tucked her hair behind both ears so the perfect oval of her face was easy to read. Resolve shone in her eyes.

"Me too." Ellie nodded.

"I can stay for maybe a week," Geneva said, "but then I've got to go home to have this baby." She patted her belly.

"Great," Laurel said, relieved. "We'll give it a week. If we don't know by then, we probably never will. We don't need to twiddle our thumbs and let Sheriff Boone do all the work this time. As long as we're here, we might as well chip in, whether he likes it or not. So," she started carefully, "it might be helpful if we tell each other what we were doing last night, to clear the air."

"Establish alibis?" Ellie said. She took a long swallow of wine, put the glass down, and challenged them with her stare. "Someone's been lying for ten years—it's not like they're going to start telling the truth now."

"We all lie every day," Geneva said quietly, "in big ways and little, by omission and on purpose, by telling ourselves that white lies are kind, or by convincing ourselves that no one will be hurt."

"That's a cheery outlook," Ellie observed.

Geneva shrugged. "Experiencing it during my therapy sessions has made me more sensitive to it in myself and my relationships."

"What do you lie about?" Laurel asked, intrigued despite the way the conversation had wandered from her original purpose.

Geneva knit her brow. "There's a friend I get together with every six weeks or so even though she brings me down with her constant complaining. We're not really friends anymore, but I don't have enough backbone to tell her that, so I agree to lunch with her when she calls. Our whole relationship is a lie, in a way. Then there's the little things, of course, like telling a coworker her lemon cake is delish when it tastes like mulch, and faking the occasional orgasm because I'm too tired to try for the real thing and I don't want Geonwoo to feel bad."

145

Dawn smiled in a way that implied she'd done the same, and Ellie spit out a few drops of wine on a startled laugh.

"I lie to myself." The stark words came from Dawn. Her smile had disappeared. "I tell myself that I'm okay with being a scientific illustrator, that I'm still an artist, but I don't believe it. Not deep down. And then I tell myself that it doesn't matter whether or not I'm an artist of any kind, that it'd be perfectly okay if I, if I sold shoes or was an airline pilot, but that's an even bigger lie. What I'm coming to realize is that if I lie to myself all the time, I'm by default lying to everyone else, especially Kyra. I told her I'd given up trying to place my art with a gallery, but that was a lie. Short of the way I feel about Kyra, there's not much in my life that isn't a lie." Her lips curved in a bleak approximation of a smile. "No wonder she hasn't returned my phone calls since I came here."

Her honesty and vulnerability pierced Laurel. There was no adequate response.

"That sucks, Dawn," Ellie said. "Really. I'll bet a therapist could help you work through the artist thing, the job thing. Have you tried one? It sounds like we could all use one—I certainly could. Do therapists offer group discounts?" she asked Geneva.

Fractured laughter greeted her attempt to lighten the atmosphere.

Geneva shook her head and directed a look at Laurel. "You?"

She rolled her wineglass between her palms. She'd felt this moment creeping up on her since arriving at Cygne. Now it was here, nudging her off the thirty-meter platform diving board. Her stomach seemed to swoop and collapse as she took the plunge. "I've lied to all of you for years." A chair shifted back, and Dawn's knife clattered to the floor. Did they think she was going to confess to pushing Evangeline off the balcony? She hurried on before she could back away—again—from telling them. "I cheated." She swept them all with her gaze. "In college, the poli sci paper. I copied Evangeline's paper. She took the blame. When I got called into the dean's office, and saw Evangeline there, I knew it was over. I was going to be expelled. There would be no law school, no joining my dad's firm. I was shaking like an aspen leaf. And then, before I could say anything, Evangeline piped up and said she'd copied my paper. I could have spoken up. I opened my mouth, but nothing came out. The moment went past, and then a whole minute where I didn't hear a thing the dean was saying, and then, well, it seemed like it was too late."

She swallowed hard. "I've never known why she did it, and I never had the guts to set the record straight. Well, she's dead and it's too late, but you should know she didn't cheat. I did." Her teeth chattered from nerves and she ground them together for a moment. "We never talked about it, strange to say. I was too ashamed to bring it up, and she—well, I don't know why she never mentioned it until this weekend. The strangest part is that even though I knew I should be grateful to her, I resented her taking the blame. Ridiculous, I know. She saved my ass, and it made me wary of her." Geneva opened her mouth as if she was going to say something therapisty, but then shut it, shaking her head. "That's part of the reason I came back," Laurel finished. "I've always felt I owed her. I'm sorry."

There was silence as the others absorbed her confession. Laurel sat as if turned to spun glass: immobile and fragile. Would they forgive her? God knows she hadn't yet managed to forgive herself. Would they shun her? The thought made her tremble, and she laid both palms flat on the table to steady herself.

Dawn crossed her arms over her chest. "I feel bad that it was easy to believe Evangeline had cheated," she said. "I never suspected it was actually you. Never. We don't know each other as well as we think we do, do we? I always thought you were a straight arrow, but now it turns out you're a cheater. Maybe you're a murderer, too."

Her voice was reflective, not accusatory, but still the words burned like acid. "I'm not. I'm sorry," Laurel said again. "There's no excuse. I was under a lot of pressure, worried about getting into Yale ... there's no excuse. It's the worst thing I ever did."

"My worst thing was way worse than that," Ellie said with a minatory look at Dawn. "But it wasn't murder."

"It was a despicable thing to do," Geneva said, "cheating and letting Vangie take the blame, but it doesn't make us—me—hate you. You screwed up—you're human." Her brown eyes reflected her disappointment.

"It was a long time ago," Ellie offered.

Almost two decades. Laurel knew that the ameliorating effect of time had taken some of the sting out of her confession for her friends. Would they have been angrier if she'd told them the truth right away? A couple years later? She inhaled through her nose, inflating her lungs, feeling like it was the first breath she'd taken in long minutes—maybe years.

"I notice no one's copped to lying about pushing Evangeline or poisoning her," Ellie said after a moment, "so I guess we're back to alibis."

"Knowing where we all were after dinner doesn't really tell us much, though, does it?" Dawn put in. "Not if the poison could have been added to something she already had with her. Does it have to be ingested or would skin contact do it?" She focused on Laurel for an answer.

"The website I looked at said it can be fatal if inhaled, swallowed, or absorbed through eyes or mouth," Laurel said. "It supposedly has a bitter taste."

"Eye drops!" Ellie said. "Ray could have put some strychnine in her eye drops. Did she use eye drops?" She looked around, brows raised, but got only shrugs in reply.

"I'm going to find out more about the mysterious Ray," Laurel declared. If Dawn was right, if the murder wasn't connected to Evangeline's fall, then Ray was as good a suspect as any. Better, in fact, than the four of them, none of whom had seen Evangeline in years. She shared her thoughts with them.

"How will you find him?" Ellie asked, at the same time that Geneva said, "Don't you think the police have a better chance of locating him?"

"They don't know what he looks like," Laurel said. "About the only thing he told me about himself is that he played basketball as a 'Blue Demon.' When Geneva and I drove to town today, we passed a high school whose teams are called the Blue Demons. What if he's from right here in New Aberdeen, like Evangeline? I'm going to visit the school tomorrow and see if their library has yearbooks. Maybe I can find his picture."

"That's a great idea," Ellie said.

"We need to go at this like we're creating reasonable doubt," Laurel said. "We know Sheriff Boone thinks one of us did it, so we need to make him focus on an equally viable suspect or suspects." Taking charge energized her. The shock of finding Evangeline's body and the news that she'd been murdered had immobilized her. Well, that was over. She wasn't going to sit around with her head in the sand while Boone built a case against one of them. "To do that, we need to find out more about Evangeline's recent life," she went on, thinking aloud. "There could be all sorts of things going on in her life that we know nothing about. Do you all want to help?"

"I do," Dawn said immediately.

"Sure," said Ellie, and "Tell me what to do," said Geneva.

Dinner forgotten, they pushed plates out of the way. Ellie pulled a receipt and pen out of her purse and prepared to take notes. Geneva propped her elbows on the table and rested her chin on her fisted hands. Dawn pulled her hair back with both hands, twisted it into a knot, and secured it with a pair of hair elastics she'd been wearing around her wrist.

"Okay." Laurel smiled grimly. "Let's figure this out. One of us needs to get a copy of Evangeline's mother's will—it should be a matter of public record—and suss out her financial situation."

"I'll try to do that," Geneva said.

"Ideally, we'd get her bank and credit card records, too, but there's no way," Laurel said regretfully. "The police will pull those. Was she working?"

Dawn half raised her hand. "She was last time I saw a Facebook update, but that was before she started all those treatments in Mexico. If she was out of the country a lot, she might have quit. She was doing medical billing and insurance work for an orthopedic clinic here in town. She hated it."

They fell silent, remembering Evangeline's joy when she landed her first job as a flight attendant—she had always wanted to travel "to every place worth seeing in the world"—and her bitterness when she realized her paralysis would make it impossible to continue as the international tour guide she'd become after five years with the airline.

"Would you be comfortable talking to her coworkers?" Laurel asked.

"Not really. It feels like we're invading her privacy, but I'll do it."

"I'll go with you," Ellie volunteered.

Dawn gave her a grateful look. "What do we ask?"

"Okay, good," Laurel said. "Try to find out what they knew about her personal life. When did she start dating Ray? Where did they meet? Were they having any issues? Was she involved with any groups outside work—church, a book club, a support group? Get details, names if you can. Was she worried about money ... or anything else?

Where did she go in Mexico for her treatments? Were there any conflicts at work? Really, just get someone talking and listen hard."

A brief silence fell as they thought about the tasks they were taking on. Geneva broke it. "I was thinking … as long as we're going to stay, I think it would be nice to have a memorial for Evangeline. Nothing fancy, just us sharing some memories. By the lake might be nice."

The others nodded. "That's a lovely idea," Dawn said. "We can say our own private goodbyes." She choked up on the last word. Ellie silently passed her a tissue and she dabbed at her eyes.

After a moment, Geneva stretched and yawned and said she was turning in early. She and Dawn left together. Ellie announced she was taking a short walk before going up, and might talk to Scott. Soon, Laurel was alone. She let her gaze wander idly over the glasses, crumpled napkins, and crumbs. Finding Ray and poking about in Evangeline's life were all good and well, but she wasn't going to blind herself to the fact that everyone in the castle had a damn good reason for wanting to kill Evangeline.

Sixteen

Motive wasn't enough, Laurel reminded herself, gathering up the remaining glasses and napkins and heading toward the kitchen, a table knife in her right hand just in case. And, as far as she knew, all of their motives were dusty with age, practically ancient history. Of course, that didn't mean the wounds were completely healed, or that old slights had no power. Look at how she'd fired up when Evangeline threatened to make an issue of the plagiarism. Still, they'd all had opportunity, staying at the castle where no one locked their doors. As for means, well, if strychnine was used as rat poison, how hard would it be for any of them to buy some?

Using her hip to bump open the kitchen's swinging door, she overheard Mr. Abbott saying, "... know what the police will ... poking around."

The couple were seated at the kitchen table, its round maple top pitted and scratched from years of hard use. Mrs. Abbott was slumped over a steaming mug, and Mr. Abbott was leaning over her, one hand on her shoulder. Laurel wasn't sure if he was reassuring her or shaking her. They both turned when the door swooshed shut, and Mrs. Abbott sloshed what looked like coffee, and smelled like it had a tot of bourbon in it, onto her hand.

"Ooh!" She shook droplets off her hand and her husband handed her a handkerchief.

"Did you need something?" Stephen Abbott directed a look at Laurel that made her remember he'd been something high-powered on Wall Street before they took over managing the B and B.

"Just bringing you the rest of the dishes," she said, hefting the glasses in her hands and then placing them and the knife on the counter. The bulk of their dinner dishes were piled nearby, and a pot full of soapy water soaked in the deep stainless steel sink. A lemony scent rose from it. "I know it's Mindy's day off, so I thought I'd bring these through." She rinsed her hands under the faucet. Her gaze trailed around the room and her eyes widened at the sight of a mousetrap tucked into the slot between the commercial-sized refrigerator and the lower cupboards.

"That was thoughtful of you," Mrs. Abbott said with an effort.

"It's sad that your last week here has been spoiled," Laurel said.

Mrs. Abbott turned a grave face her way. "It's sad that Evangeline got killed," she said. "Tragic. We had our differences, but I wouldn't wish a death like that on anyone."

Gesturing toward the mouse trap, Laurel asked, "Are rats a problem in this area?" If she looked under the sink, or in the pantry, would she find rat poison?

Mr. Abbott took a step toward her, large hands balled into fists at his sides, chin jutting. "Here, you've got no right to imply that," he said. He turned back to his wife. "I told you we should have turned down this booking. I told you." Without another word, he flung out of the screen door, letting it bang shut behind him.

"I'm sorry," Mrs. Abbott said. "He's under a lot of pressure. The move and everything. We've lived here so long. It's hard on him, hard on both of us. At our time of life, to be laid off without so much as a 'thank you,' to have to pick up and ... well." She rose and put on a determinedly resolute face, retying her apron strings as if latching up her armor. "Would you like a cup of coffee to take to your room?" she asked, in what was clearly a dismissal. "Or perhaps some cocoa?"

Laurel declined the beverages, thanked her, and left. She walked down the hall toward the public rooms. She'd known the Abbotts off and on for those first ten years and hadn't given them a thought in the past ten. What did she really know about them, other than that they ran the B and B efficiently and had been devastated when it looked like Evangeline was going to buy it out from under them? Now that American Castle Vacations had actually sold the castle, what did that mean to them? If tonight's scene was any indication, leaving Cygne was harder for them than they were letting on. Still, that didn't give them a reason to kill Evangeline. Laurel flashed on an image of Jack Nicholson as the crazed hotelier in *The Shining*, and she shook her head to clear it. *Redrum.* Stephen Abbott might be pissed off and worried about the move or something else, but he wasn't an ax-wielding maniac.

As Laurel reached the foyer, the front door creaked and started to open. Heart beating a shade quicker, Laurel stopped well back from it as the door gapped wider.

Dawn came in. She was sliding her phone into her pocket and her eyes glistened. She let out a sharp "Oh" when she spotted Laurel.

They were all edgy, Laurel realized. "What's happened?" Laurel asked, Dawn's obvious distress dissolving her instinctive caution.

Dawn shook her head, a curl or two pulling loose from her top-knot. She shut the door. "I can't get hold of Kyra. She should be home, but she's not. She got someone to stay at the house, and she's just … disappeared. I'm afraid …" She sniffed.

"I'm sure she fine," Laurel said. "She might have had a … a meeting or yogi convention she forgot to tell you about."

Dawn lifted her tear-streaked face. "She didn't want me to come. What if she's—" She stopped again, and Laurel wondered what she was truly worried about. "She was right. I shouldn't have come this weekend. I thought—well, it doesn't matter now, does it?"

"What did you think, Dawn? Why did you come?"

Laurel's genuine interest seemed to cut through Dawn's distress. She stilled, hands hanging limply at her side. "I thought that this weekend could be about closure, or moving on, I guess," she said. "The last weekend was so horrific, the worst thing that ever happened to me, and it seemed to cancel out all the good times we'd shared, you know?"

Laurel nodded.

"So, I thought that if we got together again, shared a few laughs, and caught up on each other's lives, that it might—I don't know—cover up what happened last time." Her laugh was tinged with hysteria. "But it didn't work that way. It didn't work any better than spraying one of those scented products in the bathroom to cover up the odor. Shit smells like shit. Instead of re-connecting, we're farther apart than ever, asking each other for alibis, wondering which of us slipped Evangeline a dose of rat poison. I hate it. I just hate it. And now Kyra might be hooking up with her old girlfriend!" Dawn broke down in noisy tears.

Laurel slipped an arm around her shaking shoulders and nudged her toward the bedrooms. "Why don't you go to bed? Things will look more manageable in the morning, once you're rested." Good Lord, she sounded like her mother. Well, her mother was good at managing the fallout from emotional crises. "I'll get you a cup of chamomile tea from Mrs. Abbott."

Entering the hallway, they stumbled to a halt at the sight of the crime scene tape and closed door barring access to Evangeline's room. After a brief moment, Laurel swallowed hard and urged Dawn forward. Neither of them commented. Dawn's bedroom door was slightly ajar and Laurel pushed it wider.

Dawn balked on the threshold. "I locked my door," she said, pulling the key from her pocket. "I know I did. Since Evangeline..."

"Mindy probably left it open after turning down your bed," Laurel said, nudging her into the room and flipping on the light. "Or Braden did. He was putting mints on the pillows last night. Why don't you get into bed and I'll get you a cold washcloth?" She crossed to the small bathroom and unfolded a washcloth from the stack atop the toilet. As she was dampening it, a brief, sharp scream came from the bedroom.

Laurel bumped her hip on the sink as she rushed to return to the bedroom. Dawn stood in the middle of the room, panting, finger extended toward the bed. "A—a—" she gasped. "Snake." She finally got the word out.

Laurel's eyes widened. She approached the bed cautiously. She wasn't afraid of snakes in the abstract, and merely trekked around them when she came upon one on a hike, but caution seemed like a good idea until she knew what they were dealing with. Dawn had pulled the covers partially down, and it wasn't until she was two feet away that she glimpsed the slithery coil of scales curled up against the pillow. She took an involuntary step back. "That's a snake, all right," she said, trying to steady her breathing. The snake didn't move, not so much as a tongue flicker. She stepped closer to the bed.

"Be careful," Dawn breathed from behind her. "We should get—"

Still clutching the damp washcloth, Laurel lofted it so it landed almost on top of the snake, tensed to jump back if it struck. The reptile didn't move. She let out a breath she didn't know she'd been holding "It's not alive. Plastic, maybe?" She leaned in to study the snake. "No. It's a real snake, but it's flat in the middle. Road kill, I'd guess."

"How did it get in my bed?" Anger and astonishment seemed to be edging out Dawn's fear.

"Someone's idea of a joke?" Laurel wasn't sure she believed that herself, not after what had happened to Evangeline. "Braden?"

"If so, he should be spanked until he can't sit down for a week." Dawn's hands clenched on the fabric of her skirt.

Laurel went to the closet, got a hanger, and used it to snag the poor snake and drag it off the bed. It dangled from the hanger's hook, about three feet long and black. "I don't know what it is," she said, "but it's not poisonous."

Dawn eyed it with repulsion. "No way am I sleeping in that bed," she said. "I can camp out on the sofa in the sunroom." She swept to the closet and pulled down the extra blanket and comforter stored on the shelf.

"You get settled in there," Laurel said, "while I get rid of him"— she raised the hanger six inches—"and make you some tea."

"Thanks," Dawn said, suddenly sounding weepy again. "Really— thanks, Laurel. I don't know what I'd have done if you weren't here. What a shitty day this has been." Her thin shoulders drooped.

They parted in the foyer with Dawn traipsing off to the sunroom, and Laurel returning to the kitchen, holding the hanger and snake at arm's length. She was disconcerted to find it deserted, with one dim light glowing over the sink. What the heck was she going to do with the snake now? She'd been planning to turn it over to Mr. Abbott and ask him and his wife about where it could have come from. They might know if Braden had played similar pranks before. If not … she bit her lip. If not, the snake felt like a threat or a warning of some kind, but she couldn't imagine from whom, or why it had been left in Dawn's bed. The idea of an unknown someone sneaking into their rooms at will made her shiver.

The quiet was a shade unsettling. While she waited for the tea kettle to boil, Laurel found a two gallon zip lock food storage bag in the pantry and sealed the snake into it. She'd keep it under her bed overnight and give it to the Abbotts to dispose of in the morning. She drifted to the outside door, now closed and locked, and peered through the window. Thunder rumbled in the distance.

She had a view of the wall shielding the row of trash cans, and a corner of the parking lot. The flames from the gas burner reflected weirdly on the glass, and she couldn't make out more than shadowy shapes. What sounded like a truck engine growled, but a clap of thunder drowned it out. She listened as the thunder faded but heard nothing more. *Huh*. Who would be arriving at Cygne at this hour? With her peripheral vision, she sensed movement in the dark, in the direction of the Abbotts' cottage, but when she tried to focus on it, she saw nothing. A chill tickled her arms, and she tested the deadbolt—locked—before common sense reasserted itself. *Don't be ridiculous. It's a friend of Stephen Abbott's, stopping by for a nightcap or to watch a ballgame.* It wasn't all that late—not quite nine. Hard to believe it was only twelve hours ago they'd found Evangeline's body. The tea kettle shrilled and she hurried to take it off the burner. Warm mug in one hand and plastic bag in the other, she glanced through the window again on her way out, but all was still.

She delivered the tea to the sunroom where Dawn had turned on a lamp, made a nest of blankets on the comfiest sofa, and was studying

158

her cell phone screen. She dropped her phone when Laurel came in and it clattered on the tile.

"Sorry," she apologized. "I'm a little jumpy." She accepted the tea, thanked Laurel, and said good night. Laurel headed toward her room, the sunroom's light soon swallowed by the hall's darkness. She glanced over her shoulder several times as she hurried to her bedroom, unable to shake the feeling that she was being watched. Dawn would say it was Villette wandering Cygne, mourning her dead baby. Laurel would take a grief-stricken ghost over a murderer any day, if she believed in ghosts. A creak came from overhead and she quickly unlocked her door, slipped inside, and relocked it. Feeling paranoid, she shoved a tufted bench against it for good measure.

Seventeen

Laurel was downstairs at seven o'clock Monday morning to hand the snake over to the Abbotts in the kitchen. Mrs. Abbott gaped at her when she told them where she and Dawn had found it, and swore that Braden would never, ever do such a thing. Mr. Abbott accepted the bag silently and stomped outside with it. The clang of the Dumpster's lid spoke to the snake's resting place. Unsatisfied, but not knowing what else to do, Laurel entered the breakfast parlor to find Sheriff Boone draining coffee from the urn into an insulated cup. His solid presence immediately made her relax. She hadn't realized how tense she was about being cooped up at Cygne with multiple murder suspects until the tension drained from her muscles at the sight of him. He screwed the lid on his cup and she saw it was decorated with images from Disney's *Frozen*.

"You have kids?" Laurel couldn't help the exclamation. She'd never thought about Boone's personal life and was having trouble fitting a Disney princess-loving daughter into her mental image of him.

He sipped from the cup seemingly without embarrassment and without answering her question. "Been for a run yet this morning? I seem to remember you were a runner."

"Not today." Laurel got a plate and helped herself to a muffin and a carton of yogurt. She hoped Boone would leave, but he settled at the table with his coffee, legs stretched out in front of him, looking as relaxed as if he were in his own home. Pouring herself a cup of coffee and adding a dollop of milk, she chose a chair two away from him and sat.

"Dawn Infanti found a snake in her bed last night," she said conversationally.

His thick eyebrows corrugated his forehead. "Come again?"

She told him the story and repeated Mrs. Abbott's assertion that Braden wasn't responsible.

He ran his tongue along the inside of his cheek. "I'll take your word for it that it didn't get there on its own."

"Not unless it dragged itself there from the road after getting run over," she said drily.

"Why would someone do that?" he asked. His gaze didn't leave her face, and she got the feeling he thought she knew more than she was saying.

"It makes no sense." She suddenly remembered something. "Dawn said her door was locked."

He looked unimpressed. "She says. Even if it was, these locks wouldn't keep out anyone with a credit card or paper clip and the manual dexterity of a four-year-old."

She conceded the point with a nod.

"So, Your Honor," he said, cocking his head in a way that signaled a change of topic. "I'm curious. Why did you come back? You got away with attempted murder ten years ago—and when I say 'you,' I mean the collective all of you," he clarified as she opened her mouth to object. "So why come back?"

Laurel leveled a look at him over the lip of her coffee cup. "Don't you need a sidekick taking notes?"

"This isn't an interrogation," he said. "It's friendly breakfast table conversation." He smiled, mostly with his eyes, and even though she knew she couldn't trust him as far as she could throw the table, she had to stop herself from returning the smile.

"Truthfully?"

"That would be a nice change." His tone was dry but not hostile.

"I wanted to figure out what happened last time." She tore the lid off her yogurt and licked it. "Like you, I never thought it was an accident. Oh, I wanted to, but Evangeline was no more than tipsy that night, not nearly drunk enough to fall by accident. You know—the BAC tests showed that."

"So you came back to see justice done?" Skepticism flickered in his eyes. "How noble."

She wasn't going to let him irritate her. "Not noble. Just … " She searched for a word. "Necessary. To me."

"You thought—what? That you'd all sit around, catching up, and one of your pals would confess? 'Oh, by the way, the last time? I shoved Evangeline off the balcony?' You're not that dim, Laurel."

His use of her first name took her aback. His southern accent lengthened it and gave it more resonance than she was used to. Her eyes locked with his. "No," she said after a moment, dropping her gaze to the yogurt cup. "No, I guess I'm not. I don't know why I came." She certainly wasn't going to tell him about her personal turmoil about the judgeship and her ticking biological clock, tell him that she'd needed some distance from her Colorado life. She thought about what Dawn had said last night, and knew she'd wanted to do something similar—not erase the last weekend so much, but purge it of its ugliness by talking about it, like lancing a boil. Pleasant image. She wrinkled her nose. But once lanced, the infection could heal. She realized with a pang that she wanted these women in her life and that wasn't going to happen until they knew the truth. She shared none of that with Sheriff Boone, who was eyeing her silently while she thought.

"You know what I think?" he asked.

"Do tell."

Her gentle derision didn't seem to faze him. "I think that whoever pushed Evangeline off that balcony was jealous. Soul crushingly envious. Evangeline had something—I don't know what—that the murderer didn't or couldn't have. And even though Evangeline didn't die, she was paralyzed, imprisoned in a wheelchair. And that was enough. Until … " He held up a finger and shook it gently. "Until you all showed up here and Evangeline was happy—engaged to be married, and on the brink of walking. The green-eyed monster rose up again."

He didn't sound self-satisfied with his theory; in fact, he sounded matter-of-fact, perhaps even a little sad. He'd learned a lot during his interviews yesterday, too. His insight astounded her. His theory about jealousy … could he be right? She tucked his ideas away to think about later. "You're different this time," she said slowly. "Not so cocky."

"And you're not so arrogant."

Her jaw dropped a fraction. Before she could think of a comeback, he said, "Life has a way of doing that, doesn't it, taking us down a peg? Especially the kind of lives you and I lead, where we spend more time than the average person looking at the ugly things people do to one another." He fished a butterscotch from his pocket but didn't unwrap it. "Tell me about the vic. Who was she? What made you all friends?" He sipped from his insulated mug but kept his gaze on her face.

Facing Elsa's long blond braid and limpid blue eyes, Laurel voiced a sudden thought. "I'll bet you don't even have kids. I think you use that silly Thermos mug to distract people, or take them off guard."

For answer, he flicked his smartphone screen and held it out to show her a photo of a sprite in a purple bathing suit. "Ciara. She's ten. Her mom has custody."

Flushing and feeling stupid for her semi-accusation, Laurel thought about his question. "I can't explain Evangeline—you had to know her," she said when he shifted in the chair. "She could be prickly and controlling, but she had so much energy, so much zest for life—she was fun to be around. You never knew what was going to happen. And she could be very kind, generous to a fault, even. She lived on Ramen noodles and peanut butter fall semester our sophomore year after giving her spending money to a friend who needed to fix his car so he could get to and from work and classes. And she ran a fund-raising campaign—put dozens of hours into it—for an international student, a girl from India, so she could be independent of her parents and not have to take part in an arranged marriage." She found herself wanting to tell him more but bit back the impulse.

She fell silent, thinking of all the laughter and good times, about the effervescent sparkle that hung around Evangeline, and for the first time since learning she was dead for real, she felt tears welling up. She dabbed at them with a napkin but they kept coming. "I'm sorry," she said, groping for another napkin. "I didn't mean to—"

"It's okay." He passed her a packet of Kleenex from his pocket.

Blowing her nose, she managed a watery smile. "I don't usually do this."

He leaned back and rubbed his broad nose. "What? You don't do human? Crying is the natural human response to grief and loss. It's part of how we cope. The people who *don't* cry—now, they're the ones who worry me. Do they keep all that emotion bottled up? Not good. They're likely to explode. Or, worse, do they not feel sorrow when someone they're close to is injured or dies? I'll tell you," he said as she blew her nose again, "the worst part about being a man is the way our culture views a man who cries—he's a wimpy loser. Women get a pass, but a man who cries, especially on the job or in public—look out, he's a total write-off. Nothing is more toxic to a fella's manly image than a few tears."

"Nothing?" she asked, trying to lighten the mood. She appreciated what he was trying to do, and it was working; she felt better and the tears had dried up.

"Well, man purses and talking about 'window treatments,' maybe."

She gave a gurgle of laughter and his mouth crooked up on one side.

"Thank you," she said.

"You're welcome."

He was attractive, Laurel realized with some surprise. Not her usual type, but funny and warmly human—when he wasn't treating her like a murder suspect. Or, maybe this was how he treated all murder suspects, with a degree of humanity that put them off-guard. She scrambled to fill a suddenly awkward silence. "Are we done—" she started, just as he chipped in with, "We're done for now. I'll have more questions after talking to the others."

His voice was brisker, almost brusque. Did he regret letting down his guard? Scooping up the pile of damp tissues, Laurel left the room without looking back. She bumped into Mrs. Abbott coming out of her bedroom with an armful of towels. "Where's Mindy?" Laurel asked. The younger woman usually took care of their rooms.

"Now that's the sixty-four-thousand-dollar question, isn't it?" Mrs. Abbott asked sourly, nudging her glasses up her nose with the back of her wrist. A washcloth dropped and she squatted to retrieve it. "She hasn't come in today, no, nor called either."

"I hope Braden isn't sick," Laurel said.

"More like she's decided that since this job is gone anyway, showing up late won't make any difference. Come to think of it, she's probably correct. It's not like she can be fired when she's already been 'laid off.'" She gave the final words an emphasis that said the distinction between "fired" and "laid off" didn't mean much to working people with bills to pay.

"Have the police talked to you?" Laurel asked on impulse.

"Of course." Mrs. Abbott's eyes narrowed behind her glasses. "That man is not walking away without a suspect in handcuffs this time. You know," she said, her pale blue eyes meeting Laurel's gaze squarely, "he asked us who we thought did it, not just this time, but last time, too."

Laurel didn't want to gratify her by asking, but her curiosity got the better of her. "What did you say?"

"The first time, I said I thought it was Ellie Ordahl," Mrs. Abbott said matter-of-factly, "because there was something about the way she used to look at Miss Paul. It wasn't hate in her eyes, exactly, but something wounded. I can't describe it. Stephen, though, he put his money on Dawn Infanti. He's of the opinion that anyone who sees ghosts is a loony. It's his finance background," she said excusingly.

Laurel made to move past her, sorry she'd asked the question, but Mrs. Abbott shifted to block her. "When that sheriff asked us the same question yesterday, I told him I thought it was you." Light streaked her lenses, making it hard for Laurel to see her eyes. "For this one, anyway, because it took brains. I say more power to you. I'm sure the sheriff won't be able to pin it on you," she added. "You're smart enough to dance circles around him. I told him so."

Laurel stood stunned as the older woman moved off. She wasn't sure what bothered her most—that Mrs. Abbott, a woman she'd known off and on through her twenties, thought she was capable of murder, or that she'd applauded her for supposedly killing Evangeline.

———

It was after eight by now and Laurel figured classes would be in session at the local high school. Suddenly desperate to escape from Cygne and the miasma of doubt and suspicion that pervaded the place, she brushed her teeth, grabbed her purse, and half-jogged down the hall to the main door. As she passed the roughed-in elevator housing, she wrinkled her nose at the thought that the workmen would be back today, too, with their pounding and shouting. In the parking lot, she noted Mindy's dew-covered car parked beside her equally wet rental and hoped that she didn't get docked for coming in late. Mindy undoubtedly needed to hoard every penny she could earn until she found a new job.

At New Aberdeen High School, a friendly secretary in the main office gave her a bright smile, directions to the library, and a yellow pin-on button that said "Visitor!" The halls were hushed, with only the hum of voices behind closed doors and an occasional laugh punctuating the silence. A bright, airy space, the library looked to have more computers than books. The flooring consisted of red and orange carpet tiles laid in a checkerboard pattern and Laurel blinked. She crossed the objectionable carpet to the counter, resisting the urge to only step on the orange squares. A slight man looked up when Laurel stopped at the counter where he was using a scanning device to record books from the "Returns" bin. Fiftyish, he wore his graying brown hair in a short ponytail that brushed the collar of his button-down shirt.

"Hi." She gave him a winning smile and explained that she was interested in perusing old copies of the yearbook, without telling him why.

He listened with a gravely courteous air and then shepherded her to a section of metal bookshelves that held yearbooks. "All the way back to the first graduating class in 1961," he said. "You're welcome to look at them here, but I can't let you take them if you're not a student or faculty member. I'm Kyle, if you need anything else."

She thanked him and, as he returned to his tasks, dropped to her knees to pull five books off the lowest shelf. Lugging them to the nearest table, she settled down to the tedious task of scanning all the faces in each graduating class. What she wouldn't give to be able to turn this task over to the firm's team of investigators. Her gaze snagged on at least one young man every other page, and she despaired of ever being able to identify Ray from a twenty-year-old photo. Even if he was here, which he probably wasn't, she thought glumly, turning a page in the 1996 yearbook. A bell rang, and the clatter of students changing classes momentarily interrupted her. Lockers clanged, hundreds of feet shuffled past, and teens called to each other, adding to the hubbub. Only two kids came into the library, though, and she returned to studying the seniors' photos when another bell rang and quiet fell once again.

She found him in the 1997 book. She had already turned the page when some instinct made her flip back. She studied the photo of one Raimondo Hernan. The teen in the photo was slimmer than Ray, and his hair was longer and fuller, so she couldn't see his ears or face shape too well, but something about the way he held his head, the way he looked into the camera … she was ninety-five percent certain he was

Evangeline's fiancé. She flipped ahead a few pages and found a young Evangeline Paul smiling from the middle of a row of photos, easily recognizable. She and Ray had been classmates. Why hadn't either of them mentioned that? Laurel distinctly remembered Ray giving her a vague answer when she'd asked how they'd met.

Tucking the yearbook under her arm, she carried it to Kyle and asked if she could make a copy of the page. He laid the book on the copier, handing her the warm page when the machine spit it out. She had piqued his curiosity, she could tell, and she gave him a considering look. He was old enough to have been here in 1997. When she asked, he confirmed that he had started at the high school in 1995 after getting his Masters in Library Science. "There've been a lot of changes in the library world in the last twenty years," he said in a voice that led her to infer he didn't think all the changes were for the better. He continued to work while they talked, stacking the returned books onto a cart. "I need to shelve these."

She followed him as he pushed the cart across the dreadful carpet to the racks. "You don't seem to get too much student interaction," she said, gesturing to the near-empty library.

"No, that's one thing that's dwindled, and I hate it." He slotted a book into its space with more force than necessary. A blue stone glowed from a silver ring on his right pinky. "Now when the kids come in, they're glued to a computer screen, not asking me about books or for help finding another series they might like if they enjoyed Harry Potter." Moving an out-of-place book, he returned two more to a shelf and trundled the cart to another row.

"Did you by any chance know Raimondo Hernan?" Laurel asked.

"I wondered who you were interested in." He gave her a sidelong glance. "What's Ray to you?"

She bit her lip and decided on a partial truth. "A friend's fiancé. She doesn't have the best history with men, and well, I thought I'd do a little background check. I don't want her to get hurt again. I'm a lawyer."

He nodded and looked almost approving of her snooping on a friend's behalf. "She can do better."

"Oh?"

Kyle swiveled his head, as if making sure no one was in earshot, and said, "That young man was trouble. He didn't graduate. He was expelled three weeks before graduation. The rumor was a random drug search with dogs turned up drugs in his locker. More than for personal use—at least, that's what I heard."

"And you believed it?"

"Oh, yeah. I caught him once myself, handing a packet to another kid right over there." He raised his chin to indicate the far corner of the library, a reading area with tall potted plants. "Back then, it was the biography section. By the time security got here, he'd managed to get rid of the evidence. That kid had a smirk on him when he walked out of here that made me want five minutes alone with him in a dojo." Remembered anger added grit to his voice. "I'm a third degree black belt," he explained. "I got into it when I was a Marine."

"You were a Marine?" Laurel couldn't help the exclamation. He looked so mild and average.

He smiled, apparently not offended, and deep creases appeared in his cheeks. "Semper Fi. I enlisted out of high school. Did my four years and let them pay for my college. I talk to the kids here all the time about the benefits of enlisting in the military for a tour, especially if they don't have a focus yet."

"Have you seen him since he left school? Ray?"

"Not to talk to, but he's still in the area. I bumped into him in the Harris Teeter, oh, two or three years back. I remember all he had in his cart was a case of Red Bull and three watermelons. He got that same smirk on his face when he saw me and said, 'Hey, Kyle, how's it going?' like we'd been buddies rather than staff and student." His nostrils flared.

A girl came toward them and hovered nearby, clearly wanting to ask Kyle a question, so Laurel thanked him and left, mulling over what she'd learned. Hope and relief fizzed within her. Ray was looking more and more like a viable suspect. She would give the copied yearbook page to Sheriff Boone and enjoy the look on his face. He could take it from there; no way could he afford to ignore Ray Hernan as a suspect now that he'd been identified and a long-term connection between him and Evangeline established. She was feeling damn proud of her detective work when her phone rang. Geneva. She'd call her back from outside the school. She silenced the phone, returned her visitor button to the secretary, and left.

Eighteen

Hands shaking, Geneva left a message for Laurel to please meet her at the sheriff's station and tucked the phone into her purse. She lifted a strained face to Sheriff Boone, who was ready to escort her to his car. "I don't understand why we have to go to the station," she said, finding it hard to talk around the lump in her throat.

"As I explained," he said, "new evidence has come to light and it would be better to discuss it at the station. Please." He gestured with a large hand for her to precede him out the door. His demeanor was polite but reserved, and it unsettled her.

At least there weren't handcuffs this time, Geneva thought, giving in to the inevitable. The sun was bright as they descended the steps, and the lawn a glorious green. A pick-up truck pulled up as she and Boone came down the steps and stopped with a puff of dust. Three construction workers scrambled out of it and began to unload tools from the lockbox in the back. "Can I drive myself?" she asked.

"If you like," he said.

She breathed more easily. She wasn't under arrest. When they rounded the corner of the castle, she crossed to her rental, trying to keep her pace measured so it wouldn't look like she was running away.

"You can follow me," Sheriff Boone said, getting into his sedan with the discreet lights in the grille, "in case you don't remember the way."

Geneva got into the car, fighting the feeling of hopelessness that sluiced over her like a cold wave. How could she ever forget?

———————

She'd been twenty-six that weekend, giddy with the excitement of landing a job as an on-air reporter at Chicago's CBS affiliate. She'd parlayed her communications and English majors and her beauty queen title into her dream job. Mama Gran had beamed with pride when Geneva shared the good news, saying, "Oh, lordy. Watch out, City Hall, my baby girl's comin' for you."

She arrived in North Carolina for their annual weekend three days later, gleeful at the thought of springing her news on the others. She waited till cocktail hour, when they were all gathered together, and then had the Abbotts bring in the pink champagne she'd brought for the celebration because it seemed fun and classy. Her friends overwhelmed her with congratulations and hugs and an impromptu dance-off to Aretha Franklin's "Respect," which Geneva belted at the top of her lungs. They killed all four bottles of champagne and never got around to eating dinner.

The others set up outrageous news scenarios and made Geneva deliver fake reports on the "events of the day," ranging from a politician caught in *flagrante delicto* with a trio of Swedish gymnasts—Ellie did a hysterical Swedish accent as one of the "interviewees"—to an alien invasion and a tidal wave rolling in off Lake Michigan and washing away half the city. Geneva wanted to celebrate all night long, and when they ran out of champagne and Vangie said she knew where they could score some coke, she hesitated only briefly.

"You'll love it," Vangie promised. "It's a great high—like someone set off a sparkler inside you and filled you with energy. Only this once because we need to keep celebrating. What can it hurt?" She dangled her keys and said she'd drive.

Laurel demurred, saying she was exhausted and needed to go to bed. Geneva and Evangeline exchanged a look that said Laurel was a prude. Dawn backed out, too, saying she'd tried coke once and it made her manic. "It interrupts my creative process," she said in what Geneva couldn't help but think was a pretentious way. Really, no one could say the words "my creative process" without sounding pretentious. Ellie muttered, "I'm a mother—I can't," making Geneva wonder who switched your fun button to "off" when you had a baby.

"Just you and me, then," Vangie said gaily, sweeping Geneva out of the house and into her car before she could change her mind. Dance music at high volume kept the doubts at bay as they sang their way to the rendezvous Vangie had arranged via a quick phone call. They pulled into an alley behind a small convenience store and that's when it began to feel furtive and real. The odor of rotting food from the nearby Dumpster drifted in the open windows and roiled Geneva's stomach. Despite the champagne haze, she knew this was a very, very bad idea. Vangie flashed the headlights three times in quick succession. A car parked at the alley's far end flashed its lights twice briefly in response. It was too late to back out, and Geneva hunched in the passenger seat, hands gripped tightly, staring into her lap, trying hard to avoid looking at the man who sauntered toward their car. He was only a dark shadow, glimpsed for a moment when he leaned in to hand Vangie a packet and take rolled-up bills from her. They exchanged a few words, Vangie laughed, and he returned to his car.

"Here." Vangie tossed the packet at her and Geneva caught it automatically.

It was when Vangie put the car in gear and started to back out that the blue and red lights striated the night behind them, and a siren whooped once. The other car tore out of the alley's far end, but Vangie, after one convulsive movement, cut the engine and put her hands on the steering wheel to await the officers' arrival.

"I'll tell them it was all my idea, that you were just along for the ride," Vangie said in a fierce, tight voice. A dim security light from the rear of the convenience store limned her profile, making her straight nose and sharp chin look as flat and chiseled as an image cut into a coin. "It was my money. I made the buy. You tell them that, too. It'll be okay."

It wasn't, of course. Nothing was okay for a very long time after that. They were both arrested and processed and spent what was left of the night in a jail cell together. Reporters from the local rag got wind of the story somehow and took photos of them leaving the jail the next morning. Geneva looked like an addict in the photo that got published, dark circles under her eyes, hair sticking out, eyes blank with misery that the newsprint's pixels made look like the emptiness of a habitual offender. As first-time offenders, she and Vangie received a conditional discharge with community service and probation, but the network fired her before she ever started her reporting job and her grandmother was ashamed of her. Hortense Frost didn't tear into Geneva or read her the riot act. No, it was worse than that. She leveled a sad look at her over the wire rims of her glasses and said softly, "We reap what we sow, baby girl. We reap what we sow." Geneva had turned away, unable to bear the tears trickling down the seamed cheeks.

Geneva reached the outskirts of New Aberdeen on autopilot and slowed, still caught up in the past. She had fallen apart, unable to envision a future that didn't hold a reporting job. She started to drink when she got home after a round of fruitless job hunting each day, worn down by the doors shutting in her face, the judgmental looks, the "Sorry, I don't think you're a good fit here" refrains. Vodka, just like her mother. Funny thing was, she didn't even like it. The drinking was as much about punishing herself as it was about oblivion. She fell into a relationship—if you could call getting drunk together and sometimes ending up in bed a relationship—with a man she'd known in high school, an "underachiever," Mama Gran called him with a sniff, and it wasn't until he hauled off and belted her one evening that she woke up to what she was doing to her life.

Making the turn into the station lot, Geneva blinked and came back to the present. Rotating her shoulders to loosen them, she maneuvered herself out of the car and stood for a moment, repeating the mantra she'd adopted during therapy: *Be strong. Be kind. Breathe.* A squat, tan brick edifice that had surely gone up in the 1960s, the sheriff's station, located two miles west of New Aberdeen, looked innocuous plopped down on two acres with cows grazing in a nearby field. Two large urns on either side of the door held white chrysanthemums. They seemed an incongruously soft and decorative touch. A pair of uniformed officers came out the door, laughing. The sun was warmer today, and sweat sheened Geneva's cheeks and brow as she squared her shoulders and entered. A blast of air-conditioning cooled her, and Sheriff Boone stepped forward, having parked behind the station and entered through another door.

"In here." His impassive face gave nothing away.

She hardly had time to note that the reception area had been completely re-done since she was here twelve years ago, and catch a whiff of popcorn, before he had her settled in an interview room with pale peach walls she knew were designed to be calming. Fat chance. Her gaze flew to the one-way mirror on the opposite wall and she hoped no one was back there watching. She practiced her Lamaze breathing to calm herself while Sheriff Boone got a video recorder going and stated his name and hers. When he sat across from her and began to read the Miranda warning, the laminated card lost in his big hand, she stiffened. Pain shot through her abdomen and she wasn't sure if Lila had kicked her or if it was shock from the knowledge that she was a real suspect.

"Wait—I'm a suspect?" she interrupted him.

He finished Mirandizing her and then said, "Just routine."

"Bullshit, Sheriff." The part of her that had grown up in Englewood surfaced. The survivor part of her that had lain dormant for a few years. The part that had seen cops railroad her brother's friends, their neighbors, and others, that had seen what happened when you were poor, black, and from a gang-infested neighborhood and got caught in the system. The legal system might have been designed to be fair and color-blind, but its practitioners in Geneva's world wouldn't recognize fair if it bit them in the ass. Good to know that Englewood Geneva was still there when she needed her. "As you may recall, I've been down this road. I'm not saying anything without a lawyer present." Crossing her arms, she leaned back in her chair.

"That's your prerogative, of course," Boone said, apparently unperturbed. He rested one ankle on his knee, giving her a glimpse of colorful socks that surely weren't part of the official uniform. There was gray at his temples that hadn't been there ten years earlier and a new two-inch scar, still slightly pink against his dark skin, arcing from near his ear to mid-cheekbone. He seemed less tightly wound than before, too, she thought, the therapist in her considering what might be responsible for the change. "You can call one in a minute. Before you do, though, I want to show you something."

Geneva feared it would be photos of a dead Vangie, but he pulled an ordinary glass out of a box she hadn't noticed beneath his chair. It was encased in a plastic bag, and he centered it on the table between them. "I can't ask you any questions without a lawyer since you've requested one, so I'll assume for the moment that you recognize this as being from the B and B where you're currently a guest."

Geneva licked her dry lips. "Could be," she said.

"It has your fingerprints on it." When she said nothing, he used his forefinger to push it toward her. "And traces of strychnine inside it. We found it in the victim's room." He delivered the words with all the emotion of someone saying he'd located the dog's lost chew toy under the sofa, or a misplaced glove in a jacket pocket.

The words hit her like a shotgun blast, but she bit back the instinctive denial. Through suddenly numb lips, she said, "Lawyer."

His face went grave and he shook his head sadly as he packed the glass back into the box. "You know that insisting on a lawyer makes you look guilty, like you've got something to hide when I'm sure there's a logical explanation. I want to have a simple conversation, clear this up right now so you can leave. Waiting for a lawyer is going to drag this out. You could be here all day."

A tap at the door made him look up with a twitch of annoyance. A uniformed officer poked his head in. "Sorry, Sheriff, there's a woman here says she's Ms. Frost's lawyer." Before Boone could respond, Laurel Muir sailed past the officer. Geneva had never been so glad to see someone in her life. Relief gushed through her. She stood and Laurel hugged her. She hung onto her friend convulsively. "Thank you," she whispered.

"I got your voicemail and came as fast as I could." Laurel pushed Geneva gently back into the chair. "You didn't say anything, did you?" When Geneva shook her head, Laurel turned to face Boone. "What's going on? Why did you bring my client down here, Sheriff?" She put her hands on her hips and managed to come across as if she was wearing an Armani suit rather than casual khakis with a Grissom University T-shirt. Geneva suppressed a smile of admiration, feeling more hopeful about her situation already.

"Your client? Don't you think there might be a little conflict of interest in that relationship, Your Honor?" Boone had risen when Laurel came in, a polite gesture Mama Gran would have given him full marks for, but his tone was acerbic. He faced Laurel across the table, a tic of frustration jumping at the corner of his mouth.

"I haven't been sworn in yet," she said. "I need to consult with my client, so if you'll give us the room …? And don't forget your recorder."

Laurel remained standing until Boone had turned off the recorder, picked up his evidence box, and exited, closing the door with more firmness than necessary. Then she sank into the chair beside Geneva. "Tell me what happened. Why did he drag you down here?"

Geneva met her friend's eyes and said baldly, "He has the glass used to poison Vangie. It has my fingerprints on it and he found it in her room." From the way Laurel's mouth tightened, Geneva knew her situation was serious.

"Have you any idea how it could have gotten there? Think hard—this is important."

Geneva was shaking her head before Laurel finished speaking. "I know that, damn it, but I can't think of anything. I've been wracking my brain since he told me, but nothing comes to mind. I swear to God, Laurel, I never set foot in Vangie's room this weekend." She heard the nerves making her voice quaver and hated it.

"That's actually bad," Laurel said. "If you'd been in her room earlier that day, we could have made a case that you touched the glass then." She furrowed her brow, looking troubled. "Look, fingerprints on a glass are hardly conclusive. They could be mere smudges, or a partial. Maybe the Abbotts' dishwashing practices aren't as sanitary as they ought to be. Yuck."

Geneva refused to smile, even though Laurel's last comment invited her to. "I didn't do this, Laurel. I did not kill Vangie."

"Of course you didn't." Laurel clasped her hand and squeezed.

"I thought about it, you know," Geneva said in a low voice. "After the arrest. When I was a drunk, I'd sit at the bar some nights, the vodka heating up my blood, and I'd think of ways to do it. I blamed her for talking me into going with her that night to buy cocaine, for the arrest, for my getting fired. I blamed Vangie, and the icky, slimy part of me I'm not proud of wanted revenge. When I got sober, though, and got myself into therapy, I let myself accept that I had gotten into that car of my own free will; Vangie didn't tie me up and force me to go. I wanted to go." The words still tasted bitter, but she said them again. "I wanted to go. It seemed exciting, daring, something a glamorous, jet-set TV reporter would do."

"You don't have to tell—" Laurel started.

"I know. But I want us to be real friends again, so I want you to know who I really am."

"I know who you are."

"Bullshit." She didn't think she'd used the word in over two years, and now it was the word du jour. "We haven't talked enough in these past years for either of us to really know who the other is. We can fix that." Should she tell Laurel why she'd come back this weekend? What she'd said was true—Vangie hadn't forced her to buy coke—but it wasn't the whole truth. Problem was, the whole truth and what was in that envelope gave her a pretty damn good motive for hurting Vangie, and even though she trusted Laurel almost a hundred percent, she had Lila to think about now. She couldn't risk it. She dragged a hand down her cheek. She'd missed Laurel these past years, and felt like someone had taken a knife and sliced away her college years and her early twenties so there was nothing but a gaping hole where that part of her life had been. She wanted to fill it in.

Laurel's expression softened. "I'd like that. I really would. Let's get through this first. It's probably best to let Sheriff Boone back in and answer his questions. Keep your responses short and don't expand on anything. I'll interrupt if there's a question I don't think you should answer." She paused, biting her lower lip. "Or I can make a few calls and get you a local lawyer. Boone's got a point about the potential conflict of interest. If I killed Evangeline, I'd have a vested interest in making you look guilty. Mrs. Abbott thinks I did it." She slanted a wry smile.

"No way!" Geneva's eyes widened at the surprise of it, and then she chuckled. It released some of the pent-up tension and she was able to take a deep breath for the first time that morning. "I want you," she said firmly. "Let's get this over with."

Nineteen

Ellie and Dawn connected in the breakfast parlor where dirty dishes testified that Geneva and Laurel had already eaten. Dawn wore an airy blue tunic, and her hair was loose, corkscrewing over her shoulders in glossy abundance. Ellie experienced her usual mild jealousy over the romantic spirals that were so different than her own straight blond locks. She reminded herself that Dawn's hair would be a bitch to shove under a swim cap, and even more of a pain to shampoo and dry after her morning swim. Mrs. Abbott came in bearing two steaming plates of French toast, a harried expression on her usually calm face. Over the *shree* of a power saw slightly muted by being two or three floors above, Ellie asked her if she knew where Geneva and Laurel were.

"I don't know when they left," she said, setting French toast in front of Dawn. "But I noticed their cars were gone when I let the appliance repairman in. Washing machine's on the fritz." She slid the other plate onto Ellie's place mat. The line between her brows deepened.

"Mindy's car is in the lot, though, which surprised me. I haven't laid eyes on her this morning—can't imagine where she's got to. If you run into her, please tell her that I need to speak with her."

"Will do," Ellie replied, opening a yogurt she'd bought the day before and stirring in granola she had also purchased. "Diet," she said when Mrs. Abbott gave her an astonished look.

Collecting the dirty dishes and the plate in front of her, Mrs. Abbott sniffed and bustled out.

"I found a snake in my bed last night," Dawn said.

"A reptile or a low-life man?" Ellie asked on a laugh, thinking she was joking.

"Reptile," Dawn bit out. "Dead, thank God."

"You're serious."

"As a heart attack. Which the damn thing nearly gave me."

Ellie listened, forgetting to eat, as Dawn told her about finding the snake.

"I meant to spend the night on the sunroom sofa, but I felt too exposed and ended up with my comforter and pillow in the Mustang. Surprisingly comfortable with the seat reclined, and more secure than any room in this house," Dawn finished. "Mrs. Abbott gave me a new room this morning. If we hadn't promised Laurel that we'd stay until we know what happened to Evangeline, I'd have been out of here at first light."

Tempted to tease her friend about sleeping in the car, Ellie remembered her own private grocery stash and shut her mouth. "Don't forget we came in the same car," she said tartly. "Don't run out on me."

"I won't. Want to interview Evangeline's coworkers this morning?" Dawn asked, running a piece of French toast through the syrup pooled on her plate. "I went through old Facebook posts last night and found the name of her office. Then I mapquested it and got directions." She held up her phone.

"Good thinking," Ellie said. "Might as well get it over with." When Laurel suggested they try investigating, she'd been fired up, but a night's reflection had made her wonder what they were doing. Who did they think they were—Rizzoli and Isles? Scott had echoed her thoughts in their phone conversation. "You should let the police handle it, El," he'd said in his measured way. "There are procedures."

As the commander of a satellite operations squadron, Scott was all about procedures. It drove Ellie crazy when he wanted to "procedurize" their household routines, but this time she mostly agreed with him. However, it wouldn't hurt to drive into town and ask a few questions at Evangeline's office, and it would help kill time. Consequently, she knotted a light cardigan around her shoulders while Dawn fetched her purse, and they set out.

Ellie let Dawn drive. It was clear Dawn got a kick out of *vroom*ing the Mustang down the road, and letting her drive the powerful car made Ellie feel mildly sacrificial and therefore virtuous. A win-win. Dawn's speeding didn't scare her, not after she'd taught Shane and Aidan how to drive and ridden in the death seat while they got their mandatory hours to earn their licenses. Last night's storm had left puddles on the road and Dawn steered the car through them deliberately, splashing up rooster tails of muddy water.

"We should have a story," Dawn said, breaking the silence as she parked the car in front of the two-story medical building where Evangeline had worked. She turned in her seat to face Ellie. "We can't just walk in and say, 'Hey, anyone got anything they'd like to tell us about Evangeline Paul?'"

Ellie tapped a forefinger on her lower lip. "Good point. We could say we're helping to organize the funeral and wanted to know if there was anyone she was particularly close to who might want to speak?" She said it doubtfully, but Dawn looked at her like she was a genius.

"That's brilliant," Dawn said.

They walked side by side into the building and located Orthopedics Specialists of New Aberdeen on the second floor. Taking a deep breath, Ellie pushed the door open. A quick scan of the waiting room revealed padded plastic chairs with metal frames; a coffee bar emitting an aroma that made Ellie wonder if it would be tacky to help herself to a cup; a handful of patients, some with crutches, casts, or complicated braces, looking resigned to a long wait; a television broadcasting a home-repair program; and a receptionist's counter with a sliding frosted pane.

They approached the latter and the receptionist gave them a professional smile, showing teeth grayed near the gums like Ellie's mom's. "Checking in?"

"Uh, no," Ellie said. "We're friends of Evangeline Paul's and we—"

A shuttered look came over the receptionist's face. "She doesn't work here anymore. If you're bill collectors, I have to remind you that—"

"We're not," Dawn cut in. "We—she's dead."

It wasn't the way Ellie would have chosen to break the news, but it silenced the receptionist. Her mouth fell open, making her look like a goldfish gasping for air. "Dead? Evangeline? How? What happened?" Before they could answer, she craned her neck and said to someone they couldn't see, "Jasmine, did you know that Evangeline had died?"

"No!"

Another woman appeared in the aperture. In her early forties, Ellie guessed. Her golden skin, dark hair, and large dark eyes pointed to Indian or Pakistani heritage. "Is it true?" she asked. "Evangeline's dead?" She didn't have the singsong accent Ellie half expected; she sounded like she came from the Midwest, maybe even Nebraska, where Ellie had grown up.

Ellie and Dawn nodded. "We're friends of hers," Ellie said again. "We're helping to plan the funeral."

"Perhaps you'd better come back. There's a door just there, to the left."

By the time Ellie and Dawn reached the door, the woman had it open and gestured them into a hallway floored with beige linoleum and walls painted a soft blue. Closed doors on either side probably led to exam rooms.

"I'm Jasmine Dent," she said, offering a slim hand for them to shake. She wore a short-sleeved gold polyester blouse that brightened her skin and a brown pencil skirt that emphasized full hips and thighs. "I'm the office manager. I probably knew Evangeline as well as anyone here did."

Ellie and Dawn introduced themselves and followed Jasmine past the closed doors to a break room with a table and six chairs, refrigerator, microwave, sink, and coffee maker. A wall clock's hands pointed to 9:07 and the second hand jumped as it moved. A bulletin board plastered with photos and notes from grateful patients hung on one wall. "Coffee?" Jasmine offered.

"Oh, thank God," Ellie said, making Jasmine smile.

"I know what you mean," she said. "I'm lucky if I can dress myself before I get caffeine in the morning. Please sit." She gestured them to a round white table where half a loaf of a homemade zucchini bread sat in a nest of Saran wrap and crumbs. Jasmine busied herself pulling mismatched mugs from a cabinet and filling them from the full carafe. She brought them to the table, along with a ceramic container of sweetener packets and a pint of milk from the fridge. Ellie ran a napkin around the rim of her mug and peered into it, wondering who it belonged to and how often it got washed. They all took first sips in silence, and then Jasmine leaned toward them. Her gold bangles clinked against the table's edge. "Tell me, please, what happened to Evangeline."

Her shoulders hunched forward slightly, and Ellie thought she glimpsed fear in the woman's eyes. She decided to be blunt. Maybe she could shock a reaction out of her. "Evangeline was murdered. At the Chateau du Cygne Noir."

"Murdered." Jasmine barely breathed the word. A multi-ringed hand went to her mouth, and Ellie got the distinct impression that she was both surprised and relieved.

"That's awful," Jasmine said, recovering a bit. "How…?"

"The police aren't sure yet," Dawn put in before Ellie could mention the poisoning. It was smart to keep it vague, Ellie decided, giving Dawn an almost imperceptible nod of approval. Dawn continued. "We're sorry to spring it on you like this. Did you work with Evangeline a long time? We're, uh, helping to arrange her funeral and we wondered if you or any of her coworkers here would want to, uh, say anything."

"Oh, I wouldn't think so … " Jasmine started before apparently realizing how abrupt her words sounded. "That is … " She gave up trying to explain and made a moue. "Evangeline left here six months ago." When they didn't react, she added, "Under somewhat strained circumstances."

"That's about when her mother died," Dawn said hesitantly. "Did she leave because of her mother's death, or perhaps she inherited enough so that she didn't have to work any longer?"

"I didn't get that impression," Jasmine said. She dropped her gaze and concentrated on stirring a packet of sweetener into her coffee.

Just spit it out, Ellie wanted to shout. Instead, she put on an enquiring look.

"Did you know Evangeline well?" Jasmine's gaze went from Dawn's face to Ellie's and settled there.

"Since college," Ellie said.

"Oh, so you knew her before she was paralyzed."

Ellie nodded, and Dawn said, "Yes, we've been friends for twenty years."

Off and on. Ellie didn't say it aloud.

"Well, I don't know what she was like before her accident, obviously," Jasmine said, pleating an empty sweetener packet, "but in the two years I knew her, she became increasingly bitter about her paralysis. It began to affect her work, her interactions with the patients and staff. I sometimes thought that this was the worst possible place for her to work." She must have seen Ellie's confusion, because she said, "It had to be hard on her, watching patients come in here with broken bones, some of them with spine issues not unlike hers, and seeing them get surgery and PT, walk, become, well, *whole* again. They returned to their 'normal' lives, driving and skiing and dancing, some of them with limitations, sure, but not wheelchair-bound like she was. I sometimes wondered why she didn't quit and get a different kind of job. I guess she needed the money." She wrapped both her delicate-fingered hands around the mug and drank deeply.

The refrigerator made a sudden grinding noise, like a cat working to spit up a hairball, and ice cubes clinked into the freezer bin. Footsteps passed the break room, and a man and a woman carried on a low-voiced conversation outside the door.

Ellie cleared her throat, thinking about what Jasmine had said. "So, when she left, was it to go to Mexico?"

"She didn't leave—she was let go," Jasmine said drily, "and I can't imagine she had the money for an international vacation."

"Not a vacation," Dawn said. She pushed her curls behind her ears. "Medical procedures. She went to Mexico for surgery, and it worked. She told us she was walking again. Just a few steps, but still."

Jasmine's face went blank with astonishment. "There's no—I can't comment on a patient's situation." She folded her lips in.

"Was Evangeline a patient?" Ellie asked.

Crinkling her brow, Jasmine said, "Well, no, not officially. This practice wasn't open when she suffered her trauma. She did bring her MRI report and images in once, early on, and—it's a gray area, but I really don't think I should comment. Patient privacy is paramount." She pushed her chair back from the table, distancing herself from them, or preparing to end the conversation.

"Okay, then," Ellie jumped in, searching for a way around Jasmine's restrictions. "Would it be fair to say you would have been surprised to hear that a patient with similar injuries was walking again?"

Jasmine pursed her lips and said, as if coming to a decision, "Let's just say that any doctor—Mexican or otherwise—who promised Evangeline she would walk again was on a par with those Nigerian princes sending emails that say they'll give you a million dollars if you only send them your bank account info." She raised her brows in a "does that answer your question?" way. She stood and it was clear the interview was over.

Ellie downed the rest of her coffee in a gulp, and she and Dawn rose. Escorting them to the waiting room door, Jasmine asked, "When is the funeral?"

"Um, a date hasn't been set yet," Ellie said, her conscience twitching. "The police ... "

Jasmine nodded. "Well, the office would like to send flowers, so if you could let me know when a date's been arranged, I'd appreciate it." She handed Ellie a business card and gave them a polite smile of farewell.

Before she could close the door, Dawn asked in a rush, "When we told you she was murdered, you looked more than surprised. Almost relieved. Do you mind telling me why?" Dawn asked it like it was important to her personally, her eyes fixed on Jasmine's, and Ellie wondered at both her sensitivity to Jasmine's initial reaction and her nerve.

"I suppose I thought you might say she'd committed suicide, and anything, even murder, seems preferable to that, doesn't it?"

She closed the door firmly on the questions her statement made Ellie want to ask. She and Dawn exchanged a look and left the medical center, with Ellie pondering Jasmine's words and wondering if she believed that being murdered was a better way to go than suicide. On the whole, she decided not, especially if being murdered entailed a lot of pain and fear, as Evangeline's death must have.

She mentioned that to Dawn once they were back on the road, and Dawn thought about it a long moment, her eyes fixed on the highway. "I suppose most suicides are suffering a different kind of pain and fear before they decide to end it, wouldn't you think? Psychic pain, emotional pain."

"I can't see too many of those people electing to suffer unnecessary physical pain if they decide to off themselves. If we'd told Jasmine how Evangeline died, she wouldn't have thought 'suicide.'"

"Probably not." Tears welled in Dawn's eyes and when she took a hand off the wheel to dash them away, the car swerved into the oncoming lane. Ellie instinctively gripped the dashboard. Dawn overcorrected and the tires spun on the muddy verge for a moment before gripping the pavement again.

Ellie bit back the words that sprang to her tongue, knowing how defensive they would have made her boys, and released the dash, mildly surprised it didn't retain an impression from her fingers.

Trees flashed past. It seemed like more leaves had turned yellow overnight. Within days, they would all fall, leaving the branches bare until spring. She'd be gone before the last leaf fell, and this might well be her last memory of North Carolina.

Twenty

Laurel rose from the table shortly after ten, largely pleased with how the interview had gone. Geneva had stuck to the script, giving Sheriff Boone one-word answers to his questions. No, she didn't know how her prints got on the glass. No, she didn't know why that glass was in Evangeline's room. No, she hadn't been in that room at all this weekend, and no—slight hesitation—she had no idea who would want to harm Evangeline. Laurel didn't fault her for the hesitation; she figured none of the four of them could have said "no" to that without a pause for reflection. No, she'd never bought strychnine, as far as she knew, and no, she hadn't spoken to Evangeline recently and was surprised when the invitation arrived. No, no, no. It had gone on like that for half an hour before Sheriff Boone gave up.

"Thanks for your help," he said with a hint of sarcasm, switching off the recorder. His gaze landed on Laurel and she knew who he blamed for the interview's sterility. Too bad.

"I've got something that might help," she said when Geneva hurried out of the interview room to visit the restroom. Pulling the copy of the yearbook page out of her purse, she passed it to Sheriff Boone.

"What's this?" He smoothed it out on the table.

"Evangeline's fiancé," Laurel said, unable to keep the triumph out of her voice. "Ray. Raimondo Hernan."

"Where did you get this?"

"The high school." She explained her thought process and detailed her visit to New Aberdeen High. "The librarian there remembered Ray, said he'd been a troublemaker and that he was possibly expelled for selling drugs."

Boone looked at her with what she read as reluctant respect, but quickly put on a scowl. "Maybe you're being so helpful about pointing the finger at another suspect to divert attentions from your client—or yourself."

She ignored his half-hearted accusation. "You're welcome. So now you can harass Ray instead of my client."

He looked at her from under his brows. "We didn't find Ray's fingerprints on the glass used to poison the victim."

Laurel couldn't explain away Geneva's fingerprints, but she said, "She didn't do it. I know it."

"Like you knew none of your friends pushed her off the balcony ten years ago."

Choosing not to respond to that, Laurel asked instead, "Does anyone benefit from Evangeline's death? Did she have a will?"

"We're checking," Boone said repressively.

One place the police would be checking was Evangeline's house, or wherever she might have moved to. She thought about the empty house from yesterday. "Do you know where Evangeline was living?

We drove by her old place, her mom's home, but it's for sale and it doesn't look like anyone has lived there for a while."

"I don't need you poking around in my investigation, Your Honor."

"I helped," she said indignantly, gesturing to the yearbook page.

Scratching the scar that curved up from near his ear, Boone relented. "Fine. Yes, we know where she lived. She rented one-half of a duplex off of County Line Road. We searched it yesterday."

"Did you find anything?"

He started for the door. "I am not revealing any of the details of an ongoing investigation."

"If you'd let me go through the house, maybe I'd spot something you missed."

He turned, his brows twitching together so the line between them deepened. "We do know the basics of homicide investigation out here in the sticks."

Laurel flushed. "I didn't mean to imply you didn't. I just thought, since I knew Evangeline, that I might have some insight that would be useful." If she could see Evangeline's house, she might have something to offer; she'd lived with the woman for four years, after all, and knew a lot about her habits.

"Amaze me," he invited, digging a hand into his pocket and tossing something to her.

She snatched it out of the air automatically. Keys. She looked from them to him. "Really?"

"Why not? We've finished with the place. I think I can trust you not to run off with the family silver—not that there was any. Lock up when you're done." He reeled off an address.

Geneva returned before Laurel could respond. She didn't know what she'd have said anyway.

"You okay?" Laurel asked Geneva as they walked to the parking lot.

"Tired," Geneva said, massaging her belly. "And worried. This isn't how this weekend was supposed to be."

"No. I don't suppose it's what's Evangeline had in mind, either," Laurel said. She glanced at her watch. "Look, it's not even lunch time. Boone gave me the keys to Evangeline's house"—she dangled them—"and permission to visit it. Let's go look. Maybe we'll run into Ray."

Geneva stopped in the middle of the sidewalk and a woman behind them, texting as she walked, bumped into her. They exchanged "sorry's" and Geneva grabbed Laurel's arm. "Don't you think it's weird he hasn't come back? I mean, he was only supposed to be gone for what—a day? He might not even know she's dead."

"Or he might be the reason she's dead, and that's why he hasn't come back." Laurel played with that idea in her mind. If Ray had poisoned Evangeline, wouldn't he have come back to Cygne, to make it look like he'd had nothing to do with it? His absence was suspicious—surely he couldn't be stupid enough or arrogant enough to think the police wouldn't identify him?

They arrived at Laurel's car, parked at the curb. Geneva shivered. "There's something really cold-blooded about that idea. I'm tired. Baby Lila Marigold is wearing me out. I'd rather just go back to Cygne, if you don't mind. I might lie down for a bit."

"Want me to drive you?" Laurel asked. "We could pick up your car later."

"No, I'm good." Geneva hugged her hard and waddled off in the direction of her rental.

Laurel got into her car and checked her email. There was one from Ari Berenson, the firm's top investigator. It had several attachments. Her father must have called him ten seconds after she talked to him yesterday, and paid his exorbitant overtime rates. She knew he did it because he was worried about her, and she felt a rush of affection for him. Opening the email, she scanned Ari's note—preliminary results, more in depth later, hoped she was well, yada yada. The attachments were labeled Boone, Abbott, Ordahl, Frost, American Castle Vacations, Infanti, and Tanger. The thought of prying into what were likely to be private financial and professional details on her friends made her vaguely queasy. It would be a horrendous invasion of their privacy. She decided she was not going to even open her friends' files unless something happened that made it imperative. She knew it was a sentimental decision, and that it might handicap her in her attempt to solve Evangeline's murder, but she couldn't make herself do it yet.

Giving in to temptation, she opened the Boone document. She felt a tad guilty doing so, but told herself that he had undoubtedly compiled an even more complete dossier on her. *Yeah, but he's not a person of interest in a murder case*, her conscience reminded her. Ignoring it, she began to read the report couched in Ari Berenson's usual concise prose. Several items of interest jumped out. One of five boys, Boone attended Duke University on an academic scholarship and majored in philosophy, of all things. *Huh.* Apparently recognizing that a working knowledge of Kant and Nietzsche was unlikely to pay the bills, he got a Masters in Public Administration before attending the police academy and becoming a beat cop in Raleigh. Two commendations for bravery and a citizen's complaint of excessive force, unsubstantiated by the review committee, leaped out of his record. He got married, moved to New Aberdeen and joined the Sheriff's Department, got divorced after four years of marriage, and three years later ran for sheriff and won. He'd been sheriff ever since and enjoyed an 89 percent approval rating, which "reflects his competence and honesty but also the fact that his predecessor was caught having sex with three prostitutes in the sheriff station's holding cell. I was unable to ascertain whether this was a single incident involving four persons having sex, or whether the former sheriff had relations with prostitutes in his holding cell on three separate occasions," Ari wrote with the dry wit that made his reports more entertaining than most.

Closing that file with a chuckle, Laurel opened the one labeled "Abbott." The first page was narrative and the second financials, which showed a bottom line that wasn't going to make for a comfortable retirement. She skimmed the first paragraph with dry facts about birthdates, parents' occupations, and the like. She started reading more carefully when she got to their college years. Nerys Abbott (nee Silverstrim) had majored in history at a small college in Pennsylvania before going on for her doctorate at NYU. She'd met Stephen Abbott in New York after she started teaching at SUNY. He was a graduate of the University of Maryland and worked for Goldman Sachs. Laurel was a bit surprised to see that he'd only been on Wall Street for six years. He had left Goldman Sachs and embarked on a series of entrepreneurial enterprises. "He didn't lose his shirt on any of them," Ari Berenson wrote, "but none of the businesses made the return on investment that Abbott (and his investors) expected."

The next paragraph documented Nerys Abbott's arrest, and made Laurel sit up straighter. *Hello!* She slumped when she read the arrest was for participating in a campus protest that got rowdy. The couple left New York for North Carolina in 1993 when they landed a job as co-managers of Chateau du Cygne Noir. They applied for and were granted a loan to buy the B and B, but the sale never went through.

The Abbotts had two children, Alice Ruth Abbott Drummond and a son, Ronald Justin Abbott, who'd died of pneumonia when he was five. *How awful.* Laurel felt a pang of compassion for the Abbotts. He'd died four months before the family's departure for North Carolina. They must have wanted a new start, someplace free of memories. She couldn't blame them. Their son's death must have colored everything in their world—their jobs, their neighborhood, their relationships. The tragedy might help explain Stephen Abbott's habitually dour aspect—maybe he was still mourning his lost son. How do you get over a child's death?

How do you get over wanting a child? Beyond mentioning it to Geneva, Laurel hadn't been dwelling this weekend on the decision she was contemplating, and the melancholy thought ambushed her. *By having a baby.* The answer leaped into her head. But it wasn't that simple ... or was it? Could it be that the barriers she perceived—her professional obligations, her reputation, her parents' likely disapproval, wondering whether it was fair to the baby to bring him or her into the world without a father, the logistical and financial difficulties—were not that high? She keyed the ignition to get some air conditioning into the overheated car, and her energy revved along with the engine. *You get over wanting a baby by having one.* Over and over, the thought scrolled through her head, repeating like the severe weather warning crawl at the bottom of the television screen.

Unable now to concentrate on the Abbotts' file, she closed out of it and tucked her phone into her purse. She fingered the keys Boone had given her. One was for a deadbolt and the other for a doorknob lock. *You get over wanting a baby by having one.* She banished the thought. Now was not the time, not with Evangeline's death hanging over them. Laurel dropped the keys onto the passenger seat and put the car in gear. No time like the present.

———

Leaving the courthouse, Geneva briefly considered trying to locate a copy of Evangeline's mother's will, but she flat-out didn't have the energy. Tomorrow would be soon enough for that task. On her way out of New Aberdeen, she cruised through a drive-through fast food joint and ordered a large milkshake. What she really craved after the police grilling was a vodka tonic; she could almost taste the tart sting of it on her tongue and feel the warmth washing through her, but those days were behind her forever. *For. Ev. Er.* This weekend had brought back some of the urges, true, but nothing would make her go back to who she'd been when she was drinking—not Evangeline's murder, not even being arrested for it, if it came to that, which she sure as hell hoped it didn't. She rubbed her belly, sucked hard on the straw, and pointed the car toward Cygne, one hand on the wheel and the other holding the sweating milkshake cup.

Driving one-handed, it seemed to take more effort than usual to make the turn out of the McDonald's lot, but once on the main drag, the car picked up speed without a problem and Geneva relaxed. Buzzing the window down, she enjoyed the damp earth smells that floated in and the way the wind brushed her hair back. Just what she needed after the tight interview room that had smelled vaguely like a locker room. She'd take a shower when she got back, the longest, hottest shower of her life, to scrub away any microscopic bits from criminals and perverts that might have adhered to her in the police station. Good grief—she was beginning to think like Ellie. Maybe a phobia about germs was a side effect of motherhood. She tried to remember if Ellie had been germophobic before she had the twins.

Somehow, her thoughts drifted from germs to poison. Who had killed Evangeline? She tried to dispassionately consider each of her friends in turn, evaluating them with her psychologist's eye rather than a friend's eye. Laurel had the brains and the expertise to plan and get away with murder, she was sure, and she'd confessed that Vangie had threatened to disclose the truth about the plagiarism incident. Would that have affected her judge appointment? *No idea.* Regardless,

Laurel had a lot of intellectual pride and the disclosure would have humiliated her. Dawn was the most mentally fragile, the most prone to taking offense where none was intended. She'd also been in love with Vangie at one time. Even back then, Geneva had known it was going to end badly, because Vangie was clearly having a fling while Dawn was hopelessly besotted.

The road swung to the left, and Geneva had to put muscle into steering the car through the turn. She frowned. She'd call the rental company when she got to Cygne to let them know the car was acting up. The inn was only a mile or so ahead. She returned to her mental inventory of her friends. Ellie was the strongest of them all physically. If there'd been a fight, Ellie would have prevailed. Ellie held on to her grudges, too. She couldn't see a motive for Ellie, though. Of all of them, Ellie had had the.most standoffish relationship with Vangie. Geneva passed the small farm that was the last building before the Cygne turn, and a Border collie charged toward the road, barking like he intended to fend off the Huns. She tried to give the wheel a twist to dodge the dog, but the car didn't respond. Fear shot down her spine.

The tight turn that hid Cygne from sight loomed in front of her, and Geneva stomped on the brake as the car sailed straight ahead. Dropping the milkshake, she grabbed the wheel with both hands. Putting the force of her shoulders into turning the car, she felt a zip of pain up her side. The car responded sluggishly, turning enough that she didn't barrel off the road and into the wide-trunked sycamore at the curve's apex. The passenger-side tires slipped off the pavement and the car lurched hard enough to yank the steering wheel out of her hands. Geneva instinctively wrapped her arms around her belly as the car stopped hard, slinging her against the steering wheel.

Hands trembling, she unfastened her seat belt but found she was shaking too much to open the door. She bent forward and rested her head against the steering wheel while the collie carried on outside. Thank goodness the dog had charged the car so she realized before she came to the sharp turn that the steering wasn't working. If she'd gone into it at full speed ... she didn't want to think about it.

Twenty-One

The map app on Laurel's phone guided her to a semi-rural area two miles past the town limits. She knew when she left the city because the road devolved from smooth asphalt to a grooved surface that buzzed as the car's wheels traveled over it. She almost missed the turn-off to a small collection of rickety duplexes and bungalows huddled under a faded sign announcing "Welcome home to Green Meadows." If a healthy collection of weeds gone to seed counted as "green," then the sign wasn't lying. A field stretched beyond the rear of the housing area, harvested down to unidentifiable stalks, maybe tobacco. Acrid smoke irritated Laurel's nose as she parked the car in front of Evangeline's duplex and got out; someone was burning refuse.

Young kids argued in a backyard a couple of houses away, but she couldn't see them. Other than that, there was little sign of occupation. Most of the area's residents, she presumed, were at work on a Monday. The duplex wasn't old, she decided on closer inspection, just thrown up quickly with shoddy construction techniques. The concrete pad that fronted the building had cracks in it, although a container of healthy red begonias and a yellow-and-teal welcome mat by the "A" unit made it cheerier. The duplex was set up so the entry doors were side-by-side, a mere two feet between them. Laurel inserted the keys into the door marked "B." They turned easily. The door was level with the concrete outside, obviating the need for a ramp, and the door swung inward.

Laurel hesitated. She'd wanted the opportunity to poke around in Evangeline's house, but now that she was here, it felt invasive. Chiding herself for being ridiculous, she stiff-armed the door wider and stepped in. The interior was muggy, with no air conditioner running, and tasted like water from a canteen, slightly stale and metallic. A drip sounded from somewhere.

Her gaze swept the room, and she realized after a disconcerting second that she almost expected it to look like the apartment they'd shared their senior year, which was stupid. That was the environment she most closely associated with Evangeline, though, so she'd automatically looked for the denim bean-bag chair that had squatted near their television; the two-foot-tall fake Christmas tree they'd kept on a plant stand year-round, decked with blinking lights shaped like chili peppers; and the trunk claimed from beside a trash can that they had spray-painted cream with gilt trimming and used as a coffee table. None of those items were here, however. Instead, a living room suite upholstered in oatmeal tweed that could have been stamped "so boring it will fit with any décor" was arranged around a glass-topped table stacked with medical journals and brochures. No end tables or rugs. Perhaps the minimalist approach made it easier to maneuver the wheelchair? Not a *Cosmo* or a wedding mag in sight. No photos, no art on the walls. Evangeline had lied to Dawn about hanging her painting. How sad.

She drifted into the galley kitchen. Clean. Opening a few drawers and cabinets, she found nothing unexpected or out of place. The fridge likewise revealed nothing. A six-pack of beer, one missing, some condiments and salad dressings, a hunk of Parmesan, a half-full container of wheat germ, and some apples made up its contents. Feeling like a Peeping Tom, Laurel walked into the bedroom. It, too, was furnished with rental pieces—dresser, queen-sized bed, single bedside table—that made the space feel like an anonymous hotel room. Only the pale green duvet splashed with flowers and the apricot blanket folded at the foot of the bed brought Evangeline's personality into the room. Like the living room and kitchen, the bedroom was neat—almost too neat, like Evangeline had been expecting company. She hadn't been a slob when they'd lived together, but clutter didn't bother her the way it did Laurel. There was no book open on the made bed, or litter of lacy bras, jeans, and shoes on the floor. The wheelchair had probably changed Evangeline's habits; she wouldn't have been able to wheel it over clothes on the floor.

Wishing she'd made more of an effort to stay in touch, that she knew more about what Evangeline's life had been like, Laurel reached for the stuffed unicorn propped against the pillows. Rainbow. Her fingers caressed the thin plush. The unicorn had been a grubby gray, rather than snowy white, by the time she'd come to Grissom with Evangeline. Rainbow had watched them study and make out with boys and grouse about unfair tests. If Laurel remembered right, Rainbow was a gift from an aunt, and Evangeline hadn't been one whit embarrassed about giving her childhood stuffie pride of place on her dorm room bed. Laurel had hidden the remnants of her own blankie in a drawstring bag under her pillow.

Hugging the soft toy to her chest, she sank onto the bed. Her chest felt tight, and she coughed roughly. Part of her wanted to cry, but the tears refused to come. Her throat and sinuses seemed clogged by burrs rather than by tears, and she coughed again, a jagged sound in the silence. She should finish up and get out of here. She squeezed Rainbow and positioned her carefully on the pillows.

Her gaze strayed to the bedside table. It held a lamp and alarm clock and nothing else. Tugging on the iron pull, Laurel slid the drawer open. A couple of pens, a bookmark, and a phone charging cord. If there'd been a phone or an address book, the police must have taken them. The closet was equally unrevealing, holding a meager collection of women's clothes and shoes. No men's stuff, so Ray must not have stayed over often. Maybe Evangeline stayed at his place, which would account for how few clothes were in the closet.

Laurel closed the closet door and approached the bathroom. It was large enough to accommodate the wheelchair, but windowless, with fluffy apricot towels and washcloths, and tile floor that extended without break into the handicap-access shower area, which had plenty of grab bars and a shower head with a flexible hose set within easy reach of someone in a wheelchair. This room felt more like Evangeline, with cosmetics chosen for their pretty compacts or sleek tubes corralled in an acrylic organizer on the counter, and a collection of fancy perfume atomizers and bottles lined up atop the toilet tank. She recognized some of them with a pang. Evangeline had kept the collection on a windowsill in their dorm room. Fingering a pink glass bottle, Laurel remembered how pretty it looked with the sun shining through it.

A scraping sound from the front of the house brought her head around. Before she could begin to wonder what the source was, a voice called, "Hey, you, thief! I've called the police. Don't even bother trying to get away because I also wrote down your license plate number. You are one dumbass burglar." The voice was female and fearless and held more Texas twang than North Carolina drawl.

"I'm not a thief," Laurel called out, unsure whether to be nervous or laugh. Hands held unthreateningly at shoulder height, she walked to the bedroom door. From the end of the short hall, a woman peered at her, frying pan held in a batter's position over her shoulder. She was shorter than Laurel, with a wiry build, and cinnamon-colored hair that kinked around her head in a vast cloud. With skin a shade lighter than her hair and blotched with large freckles on her bare arms and face, she could have been any age between forty and sixty. She wore blue hospital scrubs.

"I was a friend of Evangeline's," Laurel said, stepping cautiously into the hall. "The police gave me a key. Look." She reached slowly into her pocket and brought out the key, dangling it so the woman could see. The frying pan lowered a fraction of an inch. "Are you a neighbor?"

"Next door," the woman said, nodding toward the wall connecting the duplexes. She let the frying pan drop to her side. "I was just about to fry up an egg when I heard someone moving around in here. These walls are paper—you can hear the proverbial pin drop. I knew Evie was away—I've been picking up her mail—so I knew it wasn't her. You say you know Evie?"

The unfamiliar shortening of Evangeline's name threw Laurel for a moment, but she caught up and said, "Yes. We were roommates in college, friends."

"Haven't seen you around before," the woman observed, eyes narrowing.

"I live in Colorado."

Apparently accepting that, the woman said, "Do you know what's up with Evie? I got off shift from the hospital this morning and found a note from the police tucked under my door saying they wanted to talk to me about her. She's dead, isn't she? You keep using the past tense."

She didn't sound grieved by the idea, so Laurel said bluntly, "Yes, she died Saturday night. You say you haven't talked to the police yet?"

"I'm gonna give 'em a call after I've had my breakfast." The woman moved closer, hand outstretched, and a wave of stale cigarette smoke wafted off of her. "Tisha Jackson. Can I offer you an egg?"

Tisha's handshake was strong and straightforward. "Laurel Muir. I'd love an egg."

Settled at Tisha's dinette table fifteen minutes later with a hard fried egg, a slice of toast, and a glass of orange juice in front of her, and Tisha seated across from her tucking into a similar breakfast, Laurel asked, "Did you know Evangeline well?"

Tisha shook her head, frizzy hair shimmying. "She only moved in six months ago. I knew her to say 'hey' to and we kept an eye on each other's places. There's a coupla teens down the other end of the housing area who aren't above chucking rocks into windows or breaking mirrors off cars for the hell of it. She watered my plants when I traveled, and I was picking up her mail this weekend, like I said." She tipped her head backward to indicate the profusion of potted African violets, ferns, ivies, and other plants growing from every horizontal surface in the cheery kitchen. "Other than that … she stayed in a lot." She finished her egg and lit up a cigarette. Exhaling a stream of smoke, she said, "You'd think a nurse would know better, wouldn't you?"

"Did you look after her place while she was in Mexico?" Laurel chewed a bite of the rubbery egg.

"Mexico?" Tisha laughed. "Unless she went there and back in a day, she hasn't been to Mexico since she lived here. I don't even think she worked. Spent all day on that computer of hers."

Laurel hadn't seen a computer and supposed the police must have taken it. She frowned slightly. Why had Evangeline lied about going to Mexico? Was it possible she meant she'd been there before her mother died? She tried to remember if Evangeline had said anything specific about the dates of her surgery, or if she'd only assumed it was very recent.

"Rarely went out, even though she had that van with hand controls so she could drive it. The miracles of modern science—and good insurance." Tilting her head up, Tisha blew out a long stream of smoke.

"Did she have visitors?"

Tisha cocked her head. "What's it to you?" Some of her earlier suspicion returned. Her gaze slid to the stove, as if she was assessing how long it would take to grab the frying pan again. She didn't move, however.

Laurel decided to go with the truth. "She was murdered. I'm trying to figure out who did it."

Tisha didn't gasp or exclaim with horror. Instead, she looked thoughtful. She tapped her cigarette ash into an ashtray shaped like an armchair. "Why? Why not let the police figure it out?"

"My friends and I are suspects." Laurel met the other woman's gaze without blinking. "I didn't do it, and I don't think any of them did. The police do, so they're not casting a very wide net."

"So I invited a murder suspect into my kitchen?" A slow smile spread over Tisha's face, creasing her freckled cheeks. "I suppose I've had worse."

Laurel smiled ruefully. "I like to think 'murder suspect' is only a small part of my identity."

Tisha chuckled. "Good one. Anyway, the only visitor I ever saw was a man, a burly guy with black hair. Her age, give or take."

"Sounds like her fiancé, Ray."

"Her fiancé, huh? Last time he was here, they argued like they'd been married twenty years. They had the music turned up so I couldn't hear what about, but I could hear the yelling, even over the radio."

"When was that?"

"Middle of last week. Wednesday? Thursday?" She dragged on the cigarette and the nicotine hit seemed to spur her memory. "Wednesday. I was getting ready for the last of three night shifts in a row, and praying one of my patients, a woman I'd grown to like, had made it through the day. She didn't. I work on the oncology ward." She said it matter-of-factly as she stubbed out the cigarette.

No wonder the talk of death didn't faze her, Laurel thought. "Did they argue a lot?"

"I only ever saw him two or three times, counting Wednesday." Tisha yawned. "Look, I'm coming off a twelve-hour shift and I've got to get some sleep, and I've still gotta call the cops, so ... "

Laurel was standing by the time she finished. "Thanks for your help. I appreciate your time."

"Good luck finding your murderer. Or maybe it would be bad luck for you to find him. Or her—I don't want to be sexist." She gave a tired laugh and showed Laurel to the door.

Twenty-Two

The first person Laurel ran into when she returned to the castle near noon was Mrs. Abbott. Her normally pristine apron was smudged and flour streaked her nose, as if she'd pushed her glasses up while baking. She was hanging up the squat, old-fashioned phone that sat on a table in the foyer when Laurel entered.

"Is anything wrong?" Laurel asked, and then berated herself mentally. Of course something was wrong—a guest had been murdered in her B and B, it was being turned into a nursing home, and she was moving to Texas.

"That was the mother of Braden's friend, the one he stays with sometimes. She says Mindy was supposed to pick Braden up first thing this morning—her family needed to leave early to drive to Atlanta for her mother-in-law's funeral—and she hasn't heard from Mindy. Her cell phone goes straight to voicemail, the woman says. She's hopping mad—says she's on her way here now to drop off

Braden." Anxiety creased Mrs. Abbott's face. "I can't take care of the boy, not on top of everything else."

Laurel bit her lip, concerned about Mindy's continued absence and her failure to pick up her son. She'd parked beside Mindy's car, which hadn't moved. "Shouldn't Braden be in school?"

"Oh. Oh, yes," Mrs. Abbott said, her face clearing. "Stephen can run him over to the school—he was going into town to visit the farmers' market anyway. I'll just catch him before he leaves. Excuse me."

Laurel hesitated only a second after Mrs. Abbott disappeared before dialing Sheriff Boone's number. In normal circumstances, the police wouldn't get too excited about a grown woman missing for a day, but these were not normal circumstances, and someone would have to figure out who should have charge of Braden if Mindy didn't turn up by the time school let out. She was relieved when Boone took her concerns seriously.

"She's been missing how long?"

"I'm not sure, exactly. I don't know when she dropped Braden off with his friend. Her car's here, and I think it might have been here all night, maybe longer. It had dew on it this morning." While Laurel talked, her gaze rested on a Tiffany-style lamp with stained glass peacocks.

"Shit," Boone muttered under his breath. "Okay, look. I was headed out there anyway. I'll send an officer around to her house, and have a conversation with this woman who's been taking care of the kid. We'll go from there." He hung up without saying goodbye.

Dawn came into the foyer while Laurel was talking to Boone, purple maxi skirt wisping around her ankles. "What's up?"

Laurel filled her in.

"Mindy's missing?" Threading her fingers through her curls, she said, "Surely she's just late. Maybe she stayed over with a boyfriend."

Laurel didn't know Mindy well enough to guess if that was plausible, or if she would have neglected to pick up Braden, if so. "Her car's been here all night."

"The boyfriend could have picked her up."

"Possible," Laurel conceded, "but there's still Braden." They started toward the kitchen so Laurel could tell Mrs. Abbott that the police wanted to speak with the woman dropping Braden off and not to let her leave.

"Speaking of cars," Dawn said, "did you hear what happened to Geneva?"

Laurel halted. "Geneva? No. The baby—?"

Dawn made calming motions. "No, no. They're both fine. It's just that on her way back here from the police station, her steering went kaput. She couldn't make it around that curve just before you get to Cygne if you're coming from town, and she went off the road. She didn't roll or anything, didn't even scratch the rental. She's napping now."

Relieved that Geneva hadn't been hurt, Laurel let out a long breath. "How did—"

"Ellie and I came up on her about ten minutes after it happened. She was pretty shaken up, as much by Sheriff Boone interrogating her as the accident, I think, but not hurt at all." Dawn put her hands on her hips. "I can't believe he dragged a pregnant woman down to the station. I don't care where he found her fingerprints. Can you see Geneva sneaking into Evangeline's room and dumping strychnine in her water glass?" Her nostrils flared. "It's ridiculous. Absurd. Anyway, the Triple A guy came out pretty quick and had a look. He says there was a hole in the power steering line and all the fluid had drained out."

"Did he say if it looked deliberate?"

Dawn's winged brows came together. "Why would you think that?"

211

Laurel resumed walking. "Evangeline's murder, the snake in your room, Mindy missing ... all sorts of strange things are happening around here. You think it's coincidence?"

Dawn pondered Laurel's question for a full thirty seconds before saying, "Well, if it was sabotage, I wonder if it was meant for her or you? You're driving an identical car, after all."

Laurel thought she preferred the idea that someone was after her and hadn't intended to hurt Geneva. Of course, draining the power steering fluid wasn't a sure-fire recipe for grievous bodily harm, as Geneva's non-accident had proven. If someone really wanted to hurt one of them, wouldn't he or she have cut the brake line? But if the saboteur hadn't intended serious harm or death, why bother at all? Maybe it was a simple accident ...

They emerged into the kitchen, where Laurel told Mrs. Abbott what Boone had said. She overrode the innkeeper's exasperated "And how'm I supposed to do that?" by asking if Mindy had a boyfriend.

Mrs. Abbott knit her brow. "She had kind of an on-and-off thing going with a man from Weaverville, the next town over. It's possible she had a date with him. Jimmy Willett, that's his name."

"Should we look for her? Put together a search party?" Dawn asked.

"It couldn't hurt," Laurel said. Normally she'd have counseled waiting a bit, but unease pricked at her. There had been too many unexplained happenings since Evangeline died.

She and Dawn passed through the foyer, planning to ask Geneva and Ellie to help hunt for Mindy.

"You don't suppose ... " Dawn started, and then shook her head. "No."

"What?"

Dawn slowed. "Could Mindy's leaving have anything to do with Evangeline's death? I mean, do you think she could have … been involved?"

Laurel frowned. "You mean you think Mindy killed Evangeline and now she's taken off? Gone on the run? What motive could she have for killing Evangeline?"

Shrugging, Dawn said, "I don't know. But they both lived here in the same town. There could be something between them that we don't know about. An old grudge, a boyfriend thing. It makes as much sense—more—as thinking you or I or Geneva or Ellie did it." She knocked on Ellie's door.

What Dawn said *did* make sense. Laurel had no idea what Mindy's relationship with Evangeline might have been, if any, outside of Cygne. Was Mindy devious enough to plot Evangeline's death by strychnine, to acquire the poison and then wait until the inn was full of possible suspects before administering it? There was a certain slyness to Mindy, a hint of opportunism, and Laurel suspected the younger woman had gone through her things once or twice while cleaning her room, but she had trouble seeing her as a premeditated murderer.

The most likely explanation for Mindy's absence was that she had hooked up with a friend or lover and blown off work because she was losing her job anyway. She'd probably forgotten that Braden's buddy wouldn't be going to school today because of his grandmother's funeral and that the mother wanted an early pickup. Garden-variety lack of consideration—nothing sinister.

Ellie unwittingly confirmed her analysis after Dawn told her about the search party. "That's way overreacting," she said, flapping a dismissive hand. "The woman's in her thirties—she's not sixteen. She won't thank us for making a big fuss if she's sneaked off for a booty call. You can't much blame her for not showing up for work, not when they've yanked her job out from under her."

"Hey, what's up?" Geneva appeared in her doorway, face pillow-creased, blinking.

"Sorry to wake you, Gen," Laurel said. "Are you okay? I heard about your accident."

"Oh, it wasn't even an accident. Power steering failed—no big deal. What's this about Mindy?"

Dawn answered. "She hasn't shown up for work, and she forgot to pick up Braden from a friend's house. Sheriff Boone's coming to talk to the friend's mother, and we were discussing whether we should look for her."

"Of course we should," Geneva said immediately. "It won't hurt anything, and it might help. Let me put my sneakers on."

"You should stay here and rest," Ellie said. "You look worn out."

"I'll quit if I get tired—promise."

They paired up, with Dawn and Laurel searching the top three floors and Geneva and Ellie searching the bottom two and the outbuildings. If one team found something, they would call the other pair. They agreed to meet in the sunroom in an hour if no one had an update before then. Any hesitation Laurel felt about their going off in twos was mitigated by the workmen's presence. They were all safe, she told herself.

"Start at the top and work our way down?" Laurel suggested to Dawn when the other pair left.

"As good a plan as any," Dawn said.

They climbed the stairs side by side and the sound of hammering got louder.

"Have you heard from Kyra?" Laurel asked.

"Not a word," Dawn said, her clipped tone making it plain she didn't want to discuss it. Laurel suspected she was seesawing between anger and worry and let the subject drop.

On the fifth-floor landing, they ran into two men in work clothes, hard hats, and goggles reframing a doorway. Dust motes floated through the air, sparking to gold as they drifted through a sunbeam. The excised drywall lay against the wall in a pile of jagged chunks.

One of the men moved to block them. Shoving his goggles onto his forehead, he said, "Hey, you can't be up here. It's a construction area. It's not safe."

Laurel explained that they were looking for Mindy.

"Attractive gal, mid-thirties, brown hair, got a kid?" he asked. When they nodded, he said, "I've seen her around, but not today. I can tell you she's not up here."

"We'd like to look to make sure," Laurel said politely but firmly. "We won't be long."

"My insurance won't cover it if you get hurt," he complained, but he handed them each a yellow hard hat. "Here. Watch your step."

"We'll be quick and careful," Laurel promised, plunking the hat on her head.

Dawn did the same and they entered the first bedroom on the left. It was immediately clear Mindy wasn't there—denuded of furniture, the room also lacked a closet door. Spackle speckled the walls. The next two rooms were the same, and both smelled of sawn lumber. They ran into an electrical contractor in one, colorful loops of wire over his forearm, shouting through a gap in the ceiling at a helper.

"This is depressing," Dawn whispered as they neared Evangeline's old room. "It's like they've given Cygne a lobotomy, cut out all its personality."

"That's exactly what it's like," Laurel agreed, struck by the analogy. She dodged a pair of sawhorses set up in the middle of the hall and pushed open the door to Evangeline's old room. "Looks like they haven't gotten this far yet."

Dawn hovered in the doorway as Laurel peeked into the closet. No Mindy. Instinct urged her toward the balcony and, after a brief hesitation, she pulled open the stiff French doors and stepped out. Sunlight made her blink. Drawn by a macabre impulse, she put her hands on the cool iron railing that topped the balustrade and looked over, half expecting to see—what? Mindy's body? Don't be ridiculous, she told herself. History didn't repeat itself—not like that. She spotted Sheriff Boone talking to a woman driving an old station wagon but couldn't hear what they were saying. Stepping back into the room, she said, "Not here."

"No one's here," Dawn said.

It took Laurel a moment to figure out that she might be referring to Villette. Laurel had never seen or felt the ghost of the castle's former mistress, but she didn't completely discount the idea that some sort of energy lingered. They retraced their steps, giving the yawning elevator opening a wide berth, and descended to the fourth floor.

Laurel sneezed. The construction dust was giving her a headache. "Hey, I forgot to mention—I found Ray."

"You did?" Dawn's eyes widened.

"Well, I found out who he is." Laurel explained how she'd located him and filled Dawn in on her conversations with Sheriff Boone and Geneva.

"It is strange that he hasn't come back," Dawn agreed. "Really strange."

"Did you and Ellie get anything from Evangeline's coworkers?"

Dawn swept aside a musty-smelling shower curtain to look into a tub and said, "She didn't seem to like the job much, and they didn't seem to like her much. It was sad. I know what it's like to work at a job that drains you, that's no more than a paycheck. One interesting thing: the woman we talked to—the office administrator—was pretty convinced that no surgery on earth could have made it possible for Evangeline to walk again."

Laurel frowned. "How weird. Evangeline said..." She trailed off, thinking. "You know," she said slowly, "there was no cane in her house, or in her room here."

"What?"

"No cane. Evangeline didn't have a cane with her. I know because I was in her closet and her duffel when I was helping her the night she died. Remember she said she was going to show us how she could take a few steps with only a cane for support? If she didn't have a cane with her, how was she going to do that?"

"It's been an hour. We should meet the others. Maybe it was in the van and Ray ran off with it by accident."

"That's possible," Laurel conceded, not sure why the missing cane seemed important. She turned it around in her brain but didn't come up with anything by the time they entered the sunroom, shortly after one o'clock. Ellie and Geneva were there before them, Ellie hugging a pillow on one chair and Geneva half-reclining on the loveseat, her bare feet on the glass-topped table. They were puffy and swollen, as were the ankles peeking out from under her slacks. Laurel felt a twinge of guilt for not stopping her from joining in the search.

"Anything?" Geneva asked when they came in.

Laurel shook her head. "You?"

"Not a sign of her," Ellie said. "Our only excitement was Stephen Abbott going all rabid on us when he found us poking around in one of the storage sheds. It was packed to the gills with furniture. No way was Mindy in there." A wisp of cobweb clung to her bangs and she fluffed at her hair to get rid of it.

Sheriff Boone strode into the room, bringing an unsettled energy with him. Their heads swiveled toward him. His brow was damp with humidity and his hands were shoved into his pockets.

"Anything?" Laurel asked him before he could speak.

"We don't have any news about Mindy Tanger, no. Ivy Burrelsman, the friend who had Braden, says Mindy dropped him off Saturday afternoon so he could spend the weekend. She was supposed to pick him up on her way to work this morning and take him to school. She has no idea where Mindy is, but gave me the name of a boyfriend I could check with."

"Jimmy Willett," Laurel said.

He cocked a brow. "Yes."

"And?"

"Nothing yet. We haven't gotten hold of him by phone. An officer is stopping by his house."

Sheriff Boone settled himself in a scruffy chair, laying his arms on the armrests and sinking back as if he were planning to spend the day. "We got a copy of Ms. Paul's will," he said conversationally.

A provocative note in his voice boded ill for one of them. Laurel tensed and felt a piquing of interest from the others.

Boone spoke into the silence. "Mrs. Ordahl, can you tell me why Ms. Paul left you twenty thousand dollars?"

Ellie goggled and dropped the pillow she was holding. "Me? She left me money?"

Boone nodded, never taking his eyes off her face. "Yes."

Wanting to draw his attention away from Ellie, Laurel asked. "Who else benefited in her will?"

Boone switched his gaze to her. "No one. Eleanor Jane Ordahl is the sole beneficiary of a checking account with twenty thousand dollars in it. Ms. Paul's duplex is a rental, as is most of the furniture it in. The odds and ends that aren't rental are to be sold and the profits divided between a charity that helps disabled people and one that does spine research. Ditto for the proceeds from the sale of her mother's house, although a Realtor friend of mine says she was underwater on the mortgage."

"Why didn't she give the money to charity, too?" Ellie asked.

"Good question. Perhaps you'd like to take a stab at answering it?" Boone leaned forward now, his clasped hands hanging between his thighs. Laurel could tell he was sucking on a butterscotch.

"I can't! I have no idea—I hadn't talked to Evangeline in a year and a half," Ellie said.

"We'll be checking your phone records."

"Go ahead." Anger and fear thinned Ellie's voice. "I have no earthly idea why she would have left me money, any money, never mind all her money." She raked her left hand through her hair several times.

"Twenty thou will make a nice dent in college tuition bills," Boone suggested. "Quite an unexpected windfall for you, if it's indeed unexpected." His tone said he suspected otherwise. "That kind of money, a nice round figure like that—well, it looks to me like a payoff of some kind."

"A payoff?" Ellie gaped.

"What are you suggesting, Sheriff?" Geneva asked.

"He's suggesting Ellie was blackmailing Evangeline over something," Dawn said in a tight voice.

His interested gaze swiveled to her. "Actually, I was thinking more along the lines of Ms. Paul paying Ms. Ordahl for undertaking a task of some kind, potentially something illegal, or repaying a debt. But if you have a reason for thinking Ms. Ordahl was blackmailing the vic ...?" His voice invited her to continue.

"No, of course not." Dawn leaned over to grasp Ellie's hand. "I wasn't saying that at all. You know I wasn't."

"I know." Ellie held on to Dawn's hand, but her gaze tracked Boone.

Laurel judged it time to intervene. "Ellie and Dawn visited Evangeline's former workplace this morning. Tell them what you learned."

Ellie and Dawn exchanged looks, and then Ellie spoke. "We talked to the office manager, who was Evangeline's boss. She made it clear that Evangeline's work wasn't up to par and that she was let go right about the time her mother died."

"Also," Dawn cut in, "she more or less said it was impossible for Evangeline to walk again, ever."

"So?" Boone seemed unimpressed.

"So," Laurel said impatiently, "she lied to us. She said she was going to show us how she could walk with a cane. Did you find a cane in her room here?"

Boone shook his head. "No, but I don't see that it matters."

"It matters because if she lied about being able to walk, maybe it was all a lie." Laurel felt the others' eyes on her but focused on Boone. He was the one she needed to convince of the outlandish theory that had come to her, born from the cane's absence, her visit to Evangeline's excessively neat apartment, and the news of her bequest to Ellie. "Her neighbor told me Evangeline didn't go to Mexico. Maybe Ray is a lie, too."

"We met him," Ellie objected.

"I know. I mean, what if the engagement was a sham? There wasn't a single photo of him at her place, no men's clothes, nothing to hint he spent any time there. If the engagement was real, where's Ray? Why hasn't he come back or gotten in touch with the police? By now he either knows she's dead, in which case he should be here grieving and organizing a funeral, or he should be so worried that she hasn't been in touch with him that he calls the police for a welfare check. He's done neither. That's not just weird, it's suspicious."

"Okay … so?" Boone looked more alert now, and Laurel got the feeling he knew where she was headed.

"So, the engagement was bogus. The paralysis cure was bogus. Thus, Evangeline's happiness, her 'my life is coming up roses' routine, was an act. Without the engagement or being able to walk again, she had no reason to be so happy. Her mother—who was her caretaker, by the way—had died, she'd had to leave their house and get a rental place, she was unemployed, almost broke, and had no prospects for anything better. Additionally, her house was so clean she might have been expecting guests, and there was nothing to speak of in her fridge, as if she had deliberately emptied it."

Geneva sucked her breath in sharply. "You're saying—"

Laurel steeled herself. "I'm saying I think Evangeline killed herself."

Twenty-Three

No *damn way*. That was the first thought that lit up Geneva's brain. Evangeline wouldn't do that to herself. She wouldn't kill herself, and in such a way.

Ellie echoed her thoughts. "I don't know," she said doubtfully. "I'm not saying you're wrong about Ray or about her walking again, but she died of strychnine poisoning. Even if she was suicidal, she wouldn't choose a death like that. No sane person would."

"Do you have an answer for that, Your Honor?"

"Actually, I do," Laurel said coolly. "I think she purposefully picked a method that would all but rule out suicide. I think she wanted her death labeled a homicide."

A rapid *thunk-thunk-thunk* from a nail gun overhead punctuated her words.

"What would be the point?" Boone asked impatiently. "A little notoriety? An article about her death in the newspaper? That dog won't hunt."

Understanding came to Geneva in a swoop of clarity and sadness. *Oh, Evangeline.* Regret drained through her like water through sand, rearranging her beliefs about truth and friendship and making her doubt her qualifications as a psychologist. She should have spotted the depths of Evangeline's distress and anger; her own agenda for the weekend had kept her from reading Evangeline with more sensitivity. She licked her dry lips. "She wanted it to look like murder because she wanted to get back at us."

Laurel nodded once, emphatically. "Exactly."

Boone started to say something, stopped, and finally announced, "That makes no sense. If I hear you right, you're saying she summoned you all here—this get-together was at her invitation, right?"

They nodded.

"She gets you all together so she can kill herself in the most painful way possible, so—what?"

"So we can be murder suspects." Laurel's voice was calm, but her wounded eyes expressed her disillusion.

Dawn clearly felt it, too. "This is her revenge for last time," she said. "She never knew who pushed her, but she knew—thought she knew—that it was one of us. Maybe she thought we were all in on it, or that we all covered up for whoever pushed her." She rubbed her hands together. "That's why there's evidence pointing at each of us."

"You mean … " Geneva still struggled with the idea that Evangeline could have been so calculating. "You mean she deliberately used a glass with my fingerprints on it for the poison?"

Laurel nodded. "I'd guess she got it from the dining room, and she avoided touching it so her prints wouldn't be on it—"

"The napkin," Boone said unwillingly. "There was a cloth napkin in her room."

223

"And the will?" Ellie asked. "She put me in her will so it'd look like I had a reason to kill her? Fuck her. Fuck her, fuck her, fuck her." Rage made each syllable as brittle as ice on a puddle.

Ellie never used the f-bomb, but it seemed appropriate for the occasion. Geneva felt like dropping "fuck" and "bitch" into the conversation herself. Murder and betrayal could upend anyone's habits and values.

"And she picked the fight with me," Laurel said. "That last night. She threatened me. It felt weird at the time—now I know why."

"What about me?" Dawn asked. "There's no evidence pointing to me."

"Maybe it just hasn't turned up yet," Laurel said. "Job's comfort, I know. If the police search your phone, maybe they'll find that you googled 'strychnine poisoning.'"

Dawn put her hand over the lump her phone made in her pocket, and Geneva guessed she was trying not to pull it out and check her search history.

Boone had been sitting quietly, but now he shook his head again. "I don't buy it. Even if I could believe that the vic was Machiavellian enough to put all this together, I can't see anyone sacrificing themselves just to screw over someone they were pissed at."

Geneva laboriously lifted her legs off the table and planted her feet on the floor. She leaned in, her top gaping to reveal cleavage deepened by pregnancy. "I suspect that whatever Evangeline felt went well beyond 'pissed off,' Sheriff," she said. "As she saw it, her life was ruined when she was paralyzed. She's had ten years to steep in that knowledge. We don't know how long it took for her to accept that she was never going to walk again. Maybe that realization came only recently. I'll bet she really went to Mexico at some point, hoping for a cure. When she learned there was no chance, when she lost all hope … well, I guess that's when her sense of loss turned to bitterness and hate. And we were the targets for her disappointment. That's too mild a word, of course." Geneva dragged a hand down her cheek, stretching the skin. "As for Evangeline sacrificing herself to control someone's life … she's got quite a history of that."

"She almost got herself expelled from Grissom for me," Laurel said. "It put me in her debt, even though neither of us ever acknowledged it in so many words."

"She spent money she couldn't afford buying up all the pieces I had at an exhibition," Dawn said in a tight voice.

"How is that a bad thing?" Sheriff Boone asked.

"You wouldn't understand." Dawn barely got the words out. Ellie squeezed her shoulder hard enough to make her wince.

"She slept with my boyfriend where the chances were good I'd see them," Ellie said.

"She slept with Scott?" Laurel exclaimed.

Ellie gave a small nod of confirmation. "Before we were married."

"And she got herself arrested on drug charges along with me so I'd lose my job," Geneva said. "In fact—" She hesitated. No, it was time for the whole truth. She hugged her arms around her belly. "In fact, she set up the whole thing—the arrest, the newspaper coverage."

"What?" Laurel slewed to face her.

Geneva folded her lips in and nodded. "At the time, I thought we were the victims of the world's worst luck. I mean, how does a woman—me—making her very first drug buy get busted? What are the odds? And then for it all to end up in the newspaper so I lost my job … I felt like it was karma, that I deserved it for being such a fool." Lila kicked and she winced. "Settle down in there. As you all know"—she looked at each of them—"I dove into a vodka bottle for a while. It wasn't until I was sober that I began to think about that night with any clarity."

Ellie leaned forward. "What did you do?"

"I was an investigative reporter once," Geneva said wryly, "before I threw it away. I investigated. I got hold of the reporter for the New Aberdeen paper who was at the courthouse that morning. She was younger than I was—a kid. Nothing wily about her. She admitted right off that she'd gotten an anonymous call from a woman saying she could get a good story if she showed up at the courthouse. I've got an affidavit from her in my room." She tilted her head toward the bedrooms. "Finding out why the cops were there was harder, but the reporter helped me. She got one of the arresting officers to admit that they'd received an anonymous tip, too. Easiest bust he ever made, he told her. Ruined my life, but what the hell."

Bitterness had bled into Geneva's voice. Eyes narrowed, she locked gazes with each of them, stopping with Boone. "If you can think of anyone else besides Vangie who could have tipped off the cops and the reporter, I'm all ears."

"When did you find all this out?" Boone asked.

She nodded at him. It was the right question. "A few weeks before that last weekend. I came down here intending to … I don't know what I intended. To have it out with Vangie, to end our friendship, or just let her know that I knew? I never got the chance."

"Or maybe you did." Grim lines bracketed Boone's mouth.

Ellie interrupted their tense staring contest. "What about this time? Why did you bring the affidavit?"

Geneva inhaled slowly until her ribs complained. "Somewhere between then and now, I accepted that I had to own what happened that night. Still, I needed to let her know that I knew what she'd done. I needed to tell her that friends don't fuck friends over like that. Then I was going to rip the papers into confetti and drop them at her feet before walking away. Dramatic, right?" She winced, and this time it wasn't Lila. "When she turned up dead, I felt so small and ugly and

226

guilty. God, I want a drink. Anyone have some vodka?" She was only half-joking.

Dawn put an arm around her shoulders and squeezed. "How about apple juice instead? Lila wouldn't like vodka."

Ellie leaned away and crossed her arms over her chest. "Did you push her?"

No one called her out on it, and Geneva sadly acknowledged they were all thinking it. "I don't know why you'd believe me, but no." She bit her lip hard enough to taste blood. "When we found her, though, my first thought was 'she deserved it.'" Her voice was barely more than a whisper, and she hoped none of them had heard her clearly.

Laurel cleared her throat. "Geneva's investigation is further evidence of how far Evangeline was willing to go to manipulate people's lives."

"All right, all right." Boone stood and faced them, palms facing out in a "slow down" gesture. "You've cobbled this theory together out of speculation, reinterpreted history, and wishful thinking." Stopping Laurel's protest, he said, "You don't have a shred of proof. I'll grant that the no-show fiancé is suspicious, but to my mind, that points to guilt on his part, not suicide on the vic's. All this medical mumbo-jumbo … the vic has been in a wheelchair for a decade. It's hard to believe she suddenly decided she couldn't stand it anymore. I can see where she'd blame one of you for putting her there. Hell, I blame one of you—I just don't know which one." His stern gaze swept them all. "But I don't see how that translates into framing you all for murder. No, I don't buy it."

"You had to know Evangeline," Dawn said simply.

A ruckus in the hall, a shout and thudding footsteps followed by a clatter and raised voices, broke the tension in the sunroom. A workman appeared at the door, his face pale with dust or shock. His yellow helmet was askew. Every muscle in Geneva's body tensed. She wished she could put her fingers in her ears to block what he was going to say.

"A body. There's a body. A woman. Dead. At the bottom of the elevator shaft." Having spit out the words, he turned away and vomited into the hall.

Twenty-Four

S*o much for that theory.* The thought slipped through Ellie's mind before she could stop it. Laurel had almost convinced them that Evangeline had committed suicide, but Mindy's body in the elevator shaft deep-sixed that. Two bodies in the space of two days was no coincidence; Boone wasn't going to buy Laurel's theory now. Too bad. They had all frozen for a split second, but then Geneva said, "Do you think it's Mindy?" and they rose as one to investigate. Ellie wanted to say, *Of course it's Mindy—who else could it be?* but she kept silent. Geneva's question was reflex, or denial.

Despite Sheriff Boone's order to "stay here," they followed him into the hall. The stench of vomit stung Ellie's nostrils and she breathed shallowly through her mouth. What looked like every construction worker in the state of North Carolina was clustered around the plywood box housing the elevator shaft. It was probably only eight or ten men, but Ellie could see nothing over the sea of yellow hard hats.

"Police. Let me through." Boone plowed a path with an efficiency Ellie admired.

She trailed him, eeling through the spaces he opened before they could close up again. The odors of sweat and dirt and something with a sickly sweet edge made her stomach lurch. Someone had slid away the heavy sheet of plywood that had blocked the shaft opening, and a hard-hatted man knelt inside the roughly four-foot-by-six-foot space inside. At first, Ellie thought he was trying to aid Mindy—could she still be alive? She caught her breath. But then she realized he was praying, his lips moving silently. He stood in response to Boone's hand on his shoulder and backed away, revealing a sight that would haunt Ellie forever.

Mindy lay sprawled on her back on a two-foot-high stack of lumber. Her torso hung over the boards, head tilted awkwardly on the floor with her hips and legs twisted above her, resting on the rough planks. Her arms were flung out over her head like she was making a referee's "goal" symbol and her hair splayed out, matted with blood. A gleam of white bone stuck out of her thigh, and a depression in her temple made one staring eye bulge. Ellie couldn't tear her gaze away from Mindy's open eyes, filmed and flat, clearly lifeless and yet accusing. Blood was splattered everywhere. Suddenly, it was too much. She backed away hurriedly and bumped into Laurel.

Laurel was paler than usual, but she steadied Ellie and helped push through the workmen to open space. Ellie bent and put her hands on her knees, letting her hair flop over to hide her face. She fought down the urge to throw up. "Sorry," she managed.

Laurel rubbed her back. "Let's get some fresh air."

Ellie straightened, and they headed for the front door and sunshine. Outside, she blinked back tears. The brightness, she told herself. She'd hardly known Mindy, after all. "Sorry for falling apart on you," she said to Laurel, slightly embarrassed. She was the mom who stanched bloody noses and calmly took her sons to the ER when they broke arms falling out of trees or got concussed on the lacrosse field. She hadn't turned a hair when Shane came home with a bleeding gash in his shin from skateboarding that needed thirty-eight stitches; she wrapped it tightly in a clean dish towel and got him to the ER in record time. Why was she all shaky?

"It got to me too," Laurel said. "We should have been smart, like Geneva, and not looked. There are things you can never unsee."

Ellie hadn't realized that Geneva had hung back. A thought struck her as they moved into the shade of the huge live oak thirty feet from the door. "Braden. Oh, that poor boy. His mother's dead. Who will tell him? What will happen to him?" Braden's tragedy suddenly loomed larger than Mindy's. Mindy was dead, and no matter how that had happened, she was beyond pain. Braden was about to be blindsided with the worst news of his life, much worse than his father leaving. Tears stung behind her eyes again and she pinched the bridge of her nose to dam them up. Her biggest fear from the time the boys were born was of dying before they didn't need her anymore. She wondered if Mindy's last moments had been tortured by thoughts of her bereft son. She hoped, for Mindy's sake, that she'd died instantly, without time to worry about Braden.

"It's just like Evangeline," Laurel said in a low voice, almost as if she were talking to herself. "She was so ... broken. She had to have fallen from the fifth floor, don't you think?" Her gaze, sharp again, queried Ellie.

"Do I look like an expert on how screwed up you get by falling five stories versus four?" Ellie asked, not wanting to think about it.

"Of course not. Sorry."

An ambulance's whoop broke in on them, and the vehicle swayed around the last bend in the driveway, lights flashing. It skidded to a halt, spraying gravel, and the EMTs sprang out.

"I guess no one told them there was no hurry," Ellie murmured, watching them disappear inside.

Two police cars and an unmarked sedan pulled up beside the ambulance and she felt the first prickings of fear. First Evangeline, now Mindy. Where would it end?

Leaving Ellie under the tree, Laurel walked toward the lake, suddenly needing time alone, distance from humanity, from the kind of person who would shove a young mother into an elevator shaft and let her fall five stories to her death. She didn't for one second think Mindy had fallen accidentally. She hadn't known Mindy well enough to mourn for her personally, but there was something to that "no man is an island" idea, and the young woman's death saddened her. And, if she was honest, frightened her a little. Two deaths already ... would there be more? The sun's heat coaxed rich smells from the mud at the lake's edge and a heron hunted in the shallows, sharp blue death for any frog or minnow fooled by his stillness.

Who was fooling them? The thought teased at Laurel as she left the path and wandered to where the land sipped at the water. Water striders skidded busily across the surface, and dragonflies flitted. She'd been convinced Evangeline was fooling them, that she'd spun an intricate web of lies and calculation designed to ensnare one or more of them with a murder charge. But now ... Mindy's death changed things. She couldn't make it fit. Who among the people at the castle hated both Evangeline and Mindy enough to kill them? Or, could

Mindy have killed Evangeline for some reason, and then, out of guilt or remorse, committed suicide?

That would be a neat answer, a solution that didn't implicate one of her friends, but Laurel couldn't make herself believe it. If it weren't for Braden, maybe. But she couldn't see Mindy jumping down the elevator shaft and leaving her son to fend for himself. Another possibility presented itself: Mindy had seen Evangeline's killer. For some reason, she hadn't spoken up immediately, and the killer had silenced her to protect himself or herself. Laurel swatted at a gnat buzzing around her ear. This idea felt more likely than the murder-suicide scenario, only why hadn't Mindy told the police if she'd seen Evangeline's killer?

The heron stabbed the water suddenly and then tossed his head back triumphantly, letting a snip of silver slither down his throat. Feeling the damp seeping through her sneakers, Laurel moved on. The heron gave her an affronted look and flapped his heavy wings, rising up only far enough to glide to a spot a hundred yards away. A bleat from a siren, quickly cut off, brought her head around in time to watch the ambulance leaving. It was probably empty; Mindy's body would stay where it was until a medical examiner had looked at it and Sheriff Boone's team had finished with photos and evidence collection.

She debated returning to the house to face the music. Boone must be ready to start his interrogations by now. A strangely rebellious feeling rose up. She didn't feel like being the responsible citizen right now, the duty-bound judge. She noticed a paneled delivery van pulling up to one of the outbuildings, down a slope behind the castle. It backed up to the shed door and the driver got out to let down a ramp. Mr. Abbott appeared, walking slowly from Cygne's back door, and unlocked a padlock securing chains that linked the building's sliding doors. He and the driver each pushed one door aside. Laurel headed toward them, wondering if the Abbotts had even heard the news.

They'd known Mindy for many years; her death would undoubtedly devastate them.

By the time she reached the men ten minutes later, sweat trickled between her breasts and at the small of her back. The men were hefting a carved armchair with a brocade seat into the van, Mr. Abbott saying, "Careful, Nat. Don't scratch the finish."

He was inching up the ramp with his back to her, and he lurched and almost dropped the chair when she said, "Mr. Abbott." He regained his grip on the chair and his head swiveled. A flush stained his cheeks when he spotted her.

"What the—? Put it down, Nat."

The other man set the chair down inside the truck and mopped his brow with a handkerchief. "Hot," he observed. He was a pleasant-looking man in his mid-thirties, with a round, open face and receding blond hair only partially concealed by a Texas Longhorns ball cap.

With his brows beetled together, Mr. Abbott stepped toward Laurel. "What are you doing down here? You don't belong—"

"I didn't know if you'd heard," she said, forcing herself not to back away from the fury in his face. What the hell was he so revved up about? She'd cut him enough slack; getting laid off didn't excuse his continued rudeness to a paying guest. "About Mindy."

He half-turned away from her and flapped a dismissive hand, as if her news didn't interest him. "Has she turned up? Better have, or her paycheck won't be as fat as she's expecting come week's end."

"She's turned up," Laurel said. "Dead." So much for breaking the news gently. The man rubbed her the wrong way with his touchiness and ill temper. Had he always been like this? "Didn't you notice the police cars?"

"I thought they were here about the other one, that Evangeline," he said, scraping a heavy knuckle against his temple. His eyes shifted uneasily. "I'd better get back to the house. Nerys will be having a fit. Mindy had her ways, but she was a good worker and Nerys was fond of her. Nat, we'll have to finish up later. Serve the company right if this stuff is late to the auction house."

"But—" Nat began.

"Later." Stripping off his heavy work gloves, Abbott marched away, the set of his shoulders telling Laurel he didn't want her company.

Nat lingered only long enough to loop the chain around the shed doors before starting up his dirty truck. Laurel backed away hurriedly as it lurched forward, stirring up a dust cloud. She coughed. She watched it trundle down the hill and sighed. Might as well go back and face the music.

———

Ellie was just leaving the dining room when Laurel came down the hall. "His royal sheriffness is asking for you," she said, "and he's in a pissy mood. Can't blame him, I guess. Scott's coming tomorrow. He's convinced I'm next on the killer's agenda and he's taking me out of harm's way." She looked gratified. "My knight in shining armor." Her voice held a little wonder, as if she wasn't used to thinking of her husband that way.

"He's a good man," Laurel said. She'd always liked Scott. In college he'd had a serious streak, a hint of gravitas, that set him apart, something that went beyond the ROTC uniform he'd had to wear once a week.

"Yes, yes he is." Ellie smiled, but it faded quickly. "Sheriff B's on the warpath. I think he's looking to crucify one of us." She whisked around the corner toward the bedrooms, and Laurel entered the dining room.

Boone sat at the head of the table, writing in a notebook. With his head down, he didn't immediately notice her. One hand massaged his scalp. The sun beaming through the window behind him glinted off the silver flecks in his hair; Laurel hadn't realized he had so much gray. As if sensing her presence, he looked up. With the light behind him, his eyes were hooded, unreadable, but Laurel got an impression of mingled anger and weariness.

"Sit." He beckoned to her. "I guess that puts paid to your suicide theory," he said when she joined him at the table. There was no satisfaction in his tone. "Unless you want to argue that Evangeline's ghost, or that other one Ms. Infanti talks about, pushed Mindy Tanger down the elevator shaft?"

Laurel met his gaze levelly and didn't answer.

He sighed. "When did you last see Mindy Tanger?" The laconic, half-mocking tone was gone, as if he were too tired to bother with the persona.

She fought the urge to touch his hand where it lay on the table. Really, what was she thinking? She cast her mind back. "Saturday lunch maybe? I don't think I ran into her after that."

He crunched down on a butterscotch. "It has been suggested," he said carefully, "that Mindy might have helped herself to odds and ends from customers' rooms." He leaned back and waited to see what she would say.

"Are you saying she was a thief?" Laurel shook her head. "I can't imagine—I mean, I know money must have been tight for her as a single mother, but a thief? The staff here was small—I don't know how she could have gotten away with stealing for twenty years." She hesitated, trying to decide if telling him about her conversation with Geneva would be betraying a confidence. Not in the current situation. "Geneva mentioned that Mindy might have tried to blackmail her once with ... with something she found in her room."

"'Might have tried'?"

The way he said it made her think the idea of Mindy as black-mailer was not new to him. "Geneva didn't go for it."

He made a note and looked at her from under his brows. "Can you account for your whereabouts last night? If so, you'll be the only one. Everyone else was in bed asleep, alone." He repeatedly thumbed the pages of his notebook so they *zzp*ed.

"Add me to that group," Laurel said. "We all had dinner together, and then I talked to the Abbotts in the kitchen for a few minutes at roughly eight thirty. Mr. Abbott stomped out in a huff. Then Dawn and I chatted for a while and found the snake, and I went back to the kitchen to get some tea. The Abbotts were both gone by then, but I thought I heard a car or truck go past, headed toward their house."

"At nine o'clock at night?" Boone's brows went up. "Did you see who it was?"

"No," she said apologetically. "I took Dawn her tea and went to bed. That's it." She bit her lower lip, debating, and then said, "I presume you've considered the possibility that Mindy saw something related to Evangeline's murder?"

He gave her a tight smile. "You're free to presume whatever you want, Your Honor."

"Stop it." The exasperated words were out before she had time to think about them.

"I beg your pardon?" Boone said with an exaggerated look of affront.

"You know what I'm saying. Yesterday, you let me look through Evangeline's apartment. Today—"

"Today I have another murder on my hands," he said.

"You don't think I'm a killer." She stated it as a fact.

He twisted his mouth to one side and finally said, " My contacts on the Denver force say you're okay, for a lawyer."

"You asked about me?" Of course he had. She was a murder suspect. She wondered what rumors were floating around the cop shop now. None that would make it easier for her on the bench, she was sure.

As if reading her mind, he said, "Don't worry about your rep. I didn't mention that you were a suspect. I let them think I had a personal interest in you." His tone was matter-of-fact and she could read nothing into it.

"Oh, that's much better." She found herself wondering if he might find her attractive, and was mad at herself for the thought. He was a small-town lawman who couldn't be bothered to iron his uniform, who was hooked on butterscotch candies, for God's sake, and enjoyed needling her with his "Your Honor"ing. Not her type at all, so why did she care what he thought of her?

"As for Mindy Tanger, smart money says the deaths are connected. However," he continued, raising a hand when she started to break in, "I already fucked up this case once, maybe twice, and we've got another body as a result. I'm playing it by the book from here on out."

In answer, Laurel pulled the key to Evangeline's apartment from her pocket and slid it across the table to him. He pocketed it without comment.

"It wasn't your fault." She wanted to erase the self-blame tightening his mouth and knifing a line between his eyes.

His expression bleak, he said, "You have no evidence to support that theory, Your Honor. If I'd put one of you in prison ten years ago, none of you would be back here now, in all probability. Ergo, this chain of events wouldn't have been set in motion, and a young boy would still have his mother." Boone shoved back from the table and checked a text. When he finished reading, he closed his eyes for a moment and then snapped them open. "We've located Mike Tanger. I'm off to tell a man his ex-wife is dead and that his son is motherless. I'll be back."

Twenty-Five

Her head whirling through the possible scenarios, Laurel went for a long run and returned an hour later, at three o'clock, dripping with sweat and eager for a shower. Passing no one as she entered Cygne, she headed for her room. About to step into the tub, she spotted the empty shampoo and conditioner bottles; the room hadn't been serviced. No wonder, with Mindy dead and the Abbotts coping with the police presence and probably notifying the corporate owners that another murder had occurred on the property. After a brief hesitation, she slipped into the robe with the cursive *C* embroidered on the chest and walked barefoot down the hall to the housekeeping closet where Mindy's cart resided when she wasn't using it.

The closet wasn't locked. The cart was shoved just inside the door, blocking access to the shelves lined with towels, cleaning supplies, and box upon box of tiny shampoos and conditioners. A bucket, mop, broom, and vacuum occupied a narrow vertical niche. A metal flap labeled "Laundry" covered the entrance to a chute that undoubtedly took dirty linens down to the castle's laundry room. Reaching across the towels stacked on top of the cart, Laurel grabbed one of the small shampoo bottles from the recessed bin. Her elbow unbalanced the towels, and the top few began to topple. She grabbed for them and managed to catch two, but another two slid to the floor. As she was retrieving them, wondering if she should refold them and put them back on the cart or toss them down the laundry chute, a rustling sound caught her attention.

She shook the towel she was holding, and a brown paper bag dropped out. Curious. She stooped to retrieve it and was about to plunk it into the cart's garbage can when she felt the outline of a box through the bag. Reaching in, she pulled out a rectangular cardboard box with a cartoon depiction of a dead rat lying on his back, legs in the air, long whiskers crinkled and broken. Rat poison.

The implications swept over her and she fumbled the box, almost dropping it. Cursing herself for having added her fingerprints to whoever's were on the box, she slid it back into the paper bag. Something blocked it and she used her thumb and forefinger to pull out a slip of paper. A receipt. Warier now, she pinched the corner between the fingernails of her thumb and forefinger and lifted it so she could read it. It was dated three weeks ago and came from a ranch supply store in San Marcos, Texas.

She went cold. San Marcos was just up the road from San Antonio, where Dawn lived.

"Hey. Can you grab me a towel while you're in there?"

Laurel whirled at the sound of Dawn's voice, banging her elbow on the cart so it sang with pain and her forearm and hand went numb. The bag dropped. She casually slid her hand with the receipt into the robe's pocket.

Dawn bent and retrieved the bag, handing it to Laurel without peeking inside. "You all right?" she asked. Concern shone from her brown eyes. "You look peaky."

"Ran too long in the heat," Laurel managed. She couldn't believe it. Not Dawn. Dawn had been half in love with Evangeline for years. Surely she wouldn't ... Experience in the legal system fought with her memories. Nine times out of ten, a murderer turned out to be someone who "loved" the victim—a spouse or boyfriend, a mother or father, occasionally a son or daughter. Realizing Dawn was still studying her, she said, "I just need a shower, need to cool down. I'm fine, really." She edged past, burning to get away and think this through.

"Okay." Dawn grabbed a towel and washcloth from the cart. "Geneva said something about all of us getting together for dinner in town to give the Abbotts a break from cooking. Are you up for that?"

"Sure. Good idea." It took a slight effort to turn her back on Dawn, and Laurel hated that she was afraid of her longtime friend. She resisted the urge to look over her shoulder, but she felt like she had a target on her back as she walked to her room. Not until the door closed behind her did she relax a little. Setting the paper bag with its incriminating contents on the dresser, she shucked off the robe, stacked clean clothes atop the closed toilet lid, and plunged into the shower, shivering under the cold needle-spray until the castle's hot water heater kicked in. The warming water seemed to release the stranglehold that surprise and fear had on her brain. The analytical facilities she'd long relied on snapped into action.

The rat poison box did not mean Dawn had poisoned Evangeline or killed Mindy, any more than her own fight with Evangeline was proof she'd killed her, or Geneva's fingerprints on the glass, or Ellie inheriting twenty thousand dollars. The thoughts washed through her mind as clear as the water cascading off her shoulders. The more she thought about it, the more she was inclined to stick with her original theory: Evangeline killed herself and tried to frame one of them. A bright eucalyptus-mint scent filled the stall as she shampooed her hair and seemed to bring further clarity to her thinking.

Her scrubbing fingers stilled as another possibility occurred to her. What if someone else was doing what she thought Evangeline had done? What if someone else killed Evangeline and was distributing clues that would make each of them look guilty? Could Geneva or Dawn or Ellie be that calculating, that diabolical? The Abbotts? It was almost impossible to believe any of them guilty of killing Evangeline in such a way, and harder to suspect them of being evil enough to frame someone else for the murder. Merely considering the possibility felt like a betrayal. But wait … whoever it was might not be trying to convict someone else for the crime, but only looking for a way to establish reasonable doubt if she ever came to trial. That was actually brilliant, Laurel conceded, if true. The conflicting thoughts bashed against each other and brought frustration. Without more evidence—proof—she couldn't think her way through this puzzle. Ducking her head, she let the water sluice the shampoo from her head. Swirls of soap circled the drain.

She turned off the faucets and wrung her hair between her hands. Pushing aside the shower curtain, she found herself face to face with Dawn.

Twenty-Six

Dawn clutched the paper bag from the housekeeping cart between her hands. Steam from the shower spun her glossy hair into tight curls around her face and her white teeth indented her bottom lip. She looked fierce and determined.

Laurel recoiled, and one foot slipped. She reached out instinctively and grabbed a handful of shower curtain. It slowed her fall, but then the rod gave way and crashed onto her head. She went down in the bottom of the tub in a welter of fabric and metal rod. Her head banged against the tub's side, and her knee whacked into the faucet. She lay stunned for a moment in a dark cocoon of shower curtain, knee aching viciously, before the fabric covering her head was ripped away.

Dawn stood over her, distress imprinted on her face. "Oh my God. I'm sorry, so sorry. I didn't mean to scare you like that. I wanted— here, let me help you out of there." She finished scooping the shower curtain out of the tub and bent toward Laurel.

A knock sounded on the door. "You okay in there?" Geneva's voice called. "I heard a great thump."

Dawn grabbed Laurel under the armpits and helped her stand. Laurel shrank away from the contact and steadied herself with a hand on the tiled wall. "I fell in the tub," she called to Geneva. "Come on in." She didn't want to acknowledge to herself that she was uncomfortable alone with Dawn, but she was glad to hear Geneva's voice.

Dawn hurried out to open the door. Laurel carefully stepped out of the tub and wrapped a towel around herself. The rat poison box was half out of the paper bag, soaking up water from the bathmat. She lifted the bag between a thumb and forefinger, even though her precautions were ludicrous now that both she and Dawn had handled the bag and its contents. She placed the packet on the counter. Feeling shaky, she dried herself, wincing as pulled muscles and bruises made themselves felt, pulled on jeans and a T-shirt, and ponytailed her dripping hair. She returned to the bedroom with the bag to find that Dawn had let Geneva in and was feeding her a story about also having heard Laurel fall.

Laurel summoned a smile. "I'm a klutz," she said by way of greeting.

Geneva studied her. "Are you okay?"

"I'll live." Her knee was already swelling, and her right shoulder and ribs felt bruised.

"Okay, then. I'm on my way down to see if Mr. Abbott can tell me how to go about purchasing the antique cradle that used to be in my room. Geonwoo and I haven't bought a crib yet, and now I know why. This cradle was meant for Lila Marigold. I've always loved it. Hopefully he knows when and where they're going to auction it. Can you believe I've never been to an auction in my life? I'll ask Mrs. Abbott to bring you some ice. That knee looks nasty." On that note, she left.

"I didn't do it," Dawn said in an impassioned voice, as if Geneva hadn't interrupted them. Her arms were straight at her sides, fists

244

clenched. "I didn't. You have to believe me. I didn't kill Evangeline or Mindy. The way you acted in the hall, I knew something had happened, and I remembered what you said about us not finding the clue that would implicate me yet. You were behaving so oddly, and you practically snatched that bag away from me ... I had to know what you'd found. I had to." She gestured toward the box. "I've never seen it before, never. I certainly didn't buy it. I don't know how to convince you, but I didn't do it." Her eyes were moist with unshed tears, but her voice was strong.

"I'm going to sit," Laurel said, annoyed by how shaky her voice sounded. The fall had really rattled her. She hobbled to the bed and sat.

"I'm truly sorry," Dawn said. "I didn't think. Are you sure you're okay?"

"I'll be stiff tomorrow, I'm sure." She eyed her friend. After a moment, she lifted the bag, pretty sure that what she needed to say was not going to be well-received. "Look, I have to give this to Sheriff Boone—"

Dawn took a hasty step forward. "You can't! He'll think—"

"—and tell him how I found it. It was rolled up in a towel in Mindy's cart. I have no idea how it got there, if Mindy hid it or someone else, but I need to turn it over to the police."

"Do you think I killed her? Killed Evangeline?"

It was the first time, as far as Laurel knew, that one of them had asked the question outright. *Did* she think Dawn had killed Evangeline—had snitched a glass with Geneva's fingerprints from the dining room, slipped a dose of strychnine into an after-dinner drink, and offered it to Evangeline? She couldn't picture it. "No, I don't."

"Then don't do this!" Dawn burst out. "What good will it do? You know I didn't kill her, so why put a target on my back by giving it to the police?"

"I have to."

"They'll arrest me."

"I don't think so. They'll question you, sure, but they've got physical evidence against Geneva and they didn't arrest her. Her fingerprints on the glass, remember? With any luck, you were somewhere else at the time this was purchased—at work, or with Kyra. You can prove you couldn't have bought it."

"Right," Dawn said. "Like anyone can remember where they were at 5:08 on a Friday three weeks back."

"The store might have cameras. If you—" Laurel stopped herself and rephrased. "You weren't there, and you'll be able to prove that somehow. It might be best if you come with me to turn this over to Boone."

"I thought you were my friend," Dawn said in a quiet, bitter voice that stunned Laurel.

She swallowed the saliva that suddenly collected in her mouth. "I am. But I'm also an officer of the court. It's my duty to—"

"You've always valued duty, your 'responsibilities,' over everything else, even friendship," Dawn said, anger or desperation flushing her cheeks. "Always. Two weeks into our first semester you had to turn in those guys four doors down for smoking marijuana in the dorm, a little harmless weed. And—"

"They were selling marijuana and oxy," Laurel said. "Don't you remember all the skeevy people that—"

"—and of course you became an RA sophomore year so you'd have a reason to run around enforcing the rules, doing your duty. Did you know you were the most hated RA in the dorm? The other RAs turned a blind eye to toaster ovens or a little underage drinking, but not you. Oh, no. You had to do your 'duty.'"

Her scornful tone was like fingernails dragging across Laurel's skin. "I did my job, what I thought was right," she snapped. "I tried to keep people safe." She hated how defensive she sounded. "Okay, I might have been a little overzealous, but I was nineteen years old. This isn't the same thing at all, and you know it. You can come with me or not, but I'm taking this to Sheriff Boone." She rose stiffly on the words and headed to the door. With her hand on the knob, she turned back. Dawn hadn't moved. Her head was bent, hair falling forward to curtain her face. "Don't you want to know who killed Evangeline?"

Dawn slowly raised her head, a blind look in her eyes. It took a moment for her to focus on Laurel. "No. No, I don't," she said. "It doesn't matter to me. The three of you and Kyra are my best friends in the world, the whole world, and if one of you killed her, I don't want to know. I don't want to compound the tragedy by seeing one of us end up in jail. I guess that's where you and I are different, huh?"

"If by that you mean I want justice for Evangeline and Mindy, and you don't, I guess you're right."

Laurel held Dawn's gaze for a long minute, knowing the anger and hurt she saw in Dawn's eyes were reflected in her own. Was this the end of twenty years of friendship? Dawn started to say something but shut her mouth, shook her head as if words were pointless, and brushed past Laurel into the hall. Laurel followed her, wanting to bridge the gully opening between them. She reached out a hand. "Dawn, wait."

Dawn didn't turn. She picked up her pace and pounded toward the foyer. A moment later she rounded the corner and disappeared from view. The front door wheezed open and then closed with a bang.

———

Laurel saw Boone's car pull up as she was passing through the foyer, and she went to meet him. His expression was somber, heavy with the burden of having to tell a man the ex-wife he'd loved once upon a time was dead, and it lightened only slightly when he spied Laurel. His gaze went immediately to the paper bag she held. "What's that?"

She handed it to him, explaining what it was, how she'd found it, and apologizing for both her and Dawn's fingerprints on the box. "My fingerprints will be on the receipt, too." She didn't mention her bathroom encounter with Dawn, even when he eyed her elbow and said, "Where'd you get that bruise?"

"Slipped in the tub."

"I'll pass this along to the lab," Boone said, putting the bag and its contents into a plastic evidence bag. "We'll see what they make of it. They'll be able to tell if the rat poison was the source of the strychnine ingested by the victim. You predicted this would turn up, didn't you? Evidence pointing toward Ms. Infanti."

She didn't like the way he eyed her. "It fits the pattern," she said coolly. A dust devil snatched up a handful of leaves, whirled them around, and dropped them. One came to rest on Boone's foot, a bright red maple leaf. He dislodged it with a small kick.

"Keep in mind that patterns can be deceptive, especially when you don't have all the pieces," he said. "What you think is a horse may turn out to be a unicorn when you turn over the last puzzle piece."

"How whimsical, Sheriff," she said.

"Don't knock unicorns," he said, unfazed by her light sarcasm. "Ciara tells me they fart rainbows. I'm thinking about hiring one or two to lighten up the air in the squad room after a night of beer and brats." He pounded his fist on his sternum and belched lightly to illustrate.

"Lovely."

He grinned, creasing his cheeks and lighting up his whole face. "You'd better stay on your side of the law enforcement fence, Your Honor, where the shit doesn't stink like it does in the trenches."

"We're on the same side, Sheriff." Laurel cocked her head, suddenly impatient with him. "Don't bother with that good ol' boy routine around me. A black man from the city with a philosophy degree fits no one's definition of a country hick. You're more Mr. Tibbs than good ol' boy."

If anything, his grin widened at her annoyance. "It helps come election time. Besides, I'm not so far off good ol' boy as you might think. I work hard, I like to fish and have a couple beers after a softball game, and I make the best barbecue sauce in the county. I've got a blue ribbon that says so."

Before Laurel could respond, a paneled truck lumbered up the driveway, dripping water. Now that it was mud-free, Laurel could make out red lettering spelling out "Drummond and Sons," with a logo of two cartoon men carrying a stack of armchairs, tables, beds, and lamps capped by a piano. Nat tooted the horn and waved as he drove past, angling onto the dirt road that cut toward the sheds.

"Who's that?" Boone asked.

"One of the guys taking the furniture to the auction house," Laurel said.

Boone lost interest. He started toward the front door, and Laurel fell into step beside him.

The beginnings of a headache made her massage her scalp. "I hate this," she burst out. "The deaths, the suspicion. I came here this weekend hoping I could figure out what happened ten years ago, but this is all more than I expected and so much worse. Evangeline dead, Mindy dead, Cygne being gutted ... I feel like *I'm* being gutted, like someone's taking my memories of our times together and ripping them up, rearranging them so that none of them are what I thought they were. I don't know what was true from those years. I feel like part of my history, part of me, has evaporated. Poof." She opened her fingers in a starburst, as if releasing something into the air. She sucked in a harsh breath that hurt her throat. Why was she telling Boone this?

Before she could apologize and excuse herself, he gripped her shoulder. His hand was heavy and warm through the thin cotton of her blouse. She could smell the butterscotch on his breath, and it was oddly comforting. "Murder is like that always. Always," he said. "We focus on the havoc it wreaks physically on the victim, but that's the tip of the iceberg. It damages the survivors, too, mentally and emotionally. If the murderer was someone trusted, the victim's spouse or friend, or, God forbid, someone related to us, we question our judgment in liking that person, in not suspecting that they could take a gun or a knife or their bare hands and steal the victim's life. If the killer was a stranger, a psychopath, we question our understanding of the world as a place of order. We go through life believing that if we take reasonable precautions, interact with each other on a basis of goodwill, that we'll be safe. Oh, we don't think it explicitly," he said, "but we believe it nonetheless. Then, murder happens and rearranges our perception of the world, like twisting a kaleidoscope so all the patterns shift."

"That's it exactly," Laurel said, both taken aback and intrigued by his understanding. "You've thought about this a lot."

"Of course I have," he said, his hand dropping from her shoulder. A slight breeze stirred her hair. "I've investigated twenty-two murders. Of course I've thought about it."

He sounded almost angry, and she couldn't tell if the anger was directed at her or something else. Dawn would say that his philosophy major was showing. "How do people get past it?" she asked.

"By catching the murderer and seeing that justice is done," he said promptly. "That's the first step. After that, well, different people go about it different ways. Therapy, prayer, quests for revenge, alcohol. Some turn their experience into a cause, like Amber Alerts or Mothers

Against Drunk Drivers. Most just muddle through. I don't have you pegged as a muddler," he said with a ghost of a smile.

"Not usually," she admitted.

Ellie came into the foyer and stopped when she spotted them outside the open door. "I'm looking for Geneva. Have you seen her?"

Laurel shook her head. "Last I saw her, she was going to ask Mr. Abbott about that cradle she's always been mad about."

Boone's cell phone buzzed with a text notification. He glanced at it and cursed under his breath. As if feeling the women's eyes on him, he looked up and said, "My daughter just threw up and her basketball coach needs me to pick her up."

"Poor thing," Ellie murmured, as Laurel asked, "Her mother…?"

"Out of town on business. I've got Ciara for three days. Unless she's in really bad shape, I'll get a sitter and be back here as soon as possible. Don't go anywhere." His gaze fixed on Ellie. Without giving her a chance to reply, he moved away, already speaking on the phone to someone at the station to let them know his whereabouts.

———

Boone hadn't been gone five minutes when Laurel's phone rang. Recognizing Ari Berenson's number, she answered it.

"Your father will kill me for this," he said without preamble. She could picture him in his office surrounded by stacks of folders and documents, feet in their high-top basketball sneakers propped on his desk while his chair teetered on two legs. He was probably running a hand over his bald head. "I'm only passing this along because I'm going to miss seeing you around here when you put on your judge's robes. Consider it a goodbye present."

"What have you got?"

"An address."

A clunk told her he'd dropped his chair onto all four legs. "For Ray Hernan?"

"One and the same. Thing is, the info is perishable. You don't need all the deets, but poking around in Hernan's files led me to a DEA buddy who admitted Hernan's been his CI for the past two years."

"Ray's a confidential informant for the DEA?" Laurel couldn't keep the surprise out of her voice.

"Yeah. Took me by surprise, too. He's been dealing drugs for years, apparently, since high school, and got caught in a DEA sting two years ago. He agreed to become a CI and help make the case against his supplier, a Mexican cartel the DEA's been after for years. He's already helped them put one of the big bosses in prison. My buddy's high on Ray, and he only gave me the address because he owes me big time. You've got to get onto him immediately, though, because he's due to travel to Oaxaca tonight. Whatever you do, don't scare him off because my buddy will have my balls if Hernan does a runner."

"What if he killed Evangeline?"

"Let him go to Mexico and get it sorted later," Ari said in all seriousness. "The cartels are good at sniffing out traitors. Chances are he'll end up dead anyway, in a particularly ugly fashion, and you can tell yourself justice was done. Maybe I shouldn't give you—"

"I need to talk to him. Just give me the address, Ari." Laurel copied it down as he read it out, surprised to see it was in New Aberdeen. "My dad need never know," she said.

"Unless you get caught in the crossfire and he's called to ID your body," Ari said morosely.

"Won't happen," Laurel promised. "Thanks, Ari. I owe you one."

When he hung up, she put her phone away slowly, thinking through her options. With Ari's warnings about not scaring Ray in mind, she knew she couldn't tell Boone and let him interview Ray. He would be furious if he ever found out she had Ray's address and didn't share it with him, but that couldn't be helped. She couldn't afford to hesitate if Ray was on his way to Mexico in a few hours. She thought about asking Dawn or Ellie or both of them to go with her, but decided she couldn't put them at risk. Ari knew where she was going; if she didn't return, he'd call the cavalry. She texted him to say that she was off to meet Hernan and that if he didn't hear from her in an hour to call the police.

Feeling she'd done what she could to protect herself, and wishing she had the gun she kept in her bedside table at home with her, Laurel found directions and set out.

Twenty-Seven

Pregnancy multiplied the effects of heat and humidity by about a thousand, Geneva thought. Sweat trickled down her face as she plodded across the grass to the shed where she and Ellie had seen the antiques. Mrs. Abbott, tracked down in the industrial-sized laundry room, had suggested distractedly that her husband might be there. Geneva felt a twinge in her abdomen but rubbed it away with the heel of her hand. Less than four weeks. Was she ever ready. Despite the heat and the baby's weight making her lower back ache, she walked briskly, dried grass crunching underfoot. The thought of being able to buy the cradle made her smile. She could see the cradle's mellow wood in the corner of her bedroom and imagine herself reaching from her bed to rock it gently if Lila got fussy during the night. When Lila outgrew it, she could use it for a doll, and maybe someday for a baby of her own. Geneva's smile grew.

The shed was quiet when she drew near, its sliding doors pulled most of the way closed. Geneva grimaced. If Mr. Abbott wasn't here, she'd have busted her butt getting down here for nothing. She slid one door a bit wider and stepped into the cool dimness. She sniffed. The space held hints of lemon furniture polish, cigarette smoke, and motor oil. It took her eyes a moment to adjust, but then she saw that the shed was empty, all the furniture gone. Of all the lousy luck. She'd been hoping to see the cradle, to stroke its satiny curves. No matter. So the cradle was stacked in an auction house somewhere, awaiting cataloguing, rather than sitting here at Cygne. Mr. Abbott would know what company had it and she could call them to get the auction dates.

She felt rather than saw movement to her left, and was starting to turn when a hard hand clamped onto her wrist.

"What are you doing here?" Mr. Abbott growled. His eyebrows beetled over his deep-set eyes and his overalls were dusty and stained. The hand that wasn't gripping her wrist held a broom.

Geneva jerked her arm free. "I came to ask about the furniture." She kept her voice even. "I'm interested in a cradle, the one from the 'Periwinkle' room. Maybe you remember it—maple, with wide rockers and scrollwork on the headboard and footboard?"

"It's gone." Mr. Abbott moved away from her and plied the broom vigorously so a cloud of wood shavings and dust enveloped her. "It's all gone."

"I see that." She coughed. "I want to know where."

He stopped sweeping and faced her, blinking rapidly. "You're working for them, aren't you?"

"What? For who? I'm not—"

"For American Castle Vacations. That Mindy must have called them like she threatened to. God damn it, I thought she was giving me time to get the money together, but she'd already called before … it was none of her business! Nerys and I poured ourselves into this place, and what did we get in return? A pink slip, a thank-you-very-much-we-don't-need-you-anymore note, and not a goddamn thing else. We deserved more, but they had all the lawyers. If they weren't going to do the right thing, then I was going to get what they owed me another way." His voice dripped bitterness. "They sent you, didn't they? Is that why you've all been poking around here? That other one was down here earlier, that lawyer. She works for them, doesn't she? I told Nerys we shouldn't have let you all come, but she wouldn't listen." He shook his head in disgust. "She thought we could pocket a little extra, off the books, and booked your rooms behind my back. We had words about that, I can tell you. I tried to get you to leave—the cold water, the snake, the car—but you've got some brass ones between you. Or you aren't smart enough to know what's good for you."

He sprang toward her and grabbed her wrist again, dragging her close, twisting her so her back slammed against his chest. Before Geneva could even struggle, he dropped the broom with a clatter and wrapped his other arm across her breasts.

"I'm not—you've got it all wrong." She tried to sound calm but heard the fear in her voice. His mention of Mindy had scared her, and his barely coherent babbling made her wonder if he was totally sane. Despite his age, he was wiry strong, and she struggled against him in vain. "Help!"

She screamed the single word before his hand clamped over her mouth, fingers digging into her cheeks.

"Oh, no you don't," he muttered against her cheek, his peanut-butter-scented breath making her gag.

A vicious cramp knotted her abdomen and she tried to double over, but his hold kept her straight. "Ungh," she groaned against his hand. Her next action came from instinct. She bit down on his hand, grinding her teeth into two of his fingers. The coppery thickness of blood made her stomach heave.

He jerked his hand away and she got out another half scream before he spun her and belted her across the mouth. Her lip split. The blow knocked her off her feet, and pain tore through her side. "My baby—" she moaned.

"What to do with you?" he asked, pulling a dirty handkerchief out of his pocket and stuffing it in her mouth.

The ball of cloth filling her mouth made her panicky and she concentrated on breathing through her nose. The cotton absorbed all her saliva, leaving her mouth dry. Yanking her to her feet, he dragged her toward the rear of the shed and held her with one hand while he searched a rickety metal cabinet.

"Know it's here somewhere. That damn Nat better not have—ah, here." He pulled a roll of duct tape from a bin full of odds and ends, and bit off a length with his teeth.

Desperate, Geneva swung a knee up toward his groin, but her belly slowed her and altered her balance and she caught him on the thigh. Snarling, he punched her in the temple. Her vision blurred and she went limp, on the verge on unconsciousness. She felt herself melt toward the ground. Abbott took advantage of her wooziness to wrap the duct tape around her wrists several times behind her back. By the time her vision cleared and she was thinking straight again, he'd also taped her ankles together. She lay on her side, her face pressed into the gritty boards. Her head throbbed and her shoulders ached from the strain of the unusual position.

"There," he said with satisfaction. "That should hold you for a while. When it's dark and the police have gone, I'll figure out what to do with you. You shouldn't have come here." His tone placed the blame for her current situation squarely on her shoulders.

His words echoed Geneva's thoughts. She shouldn't have come for the weekend, and she for damn sure shouldn't have come to the shed. She'd put Lila at risk, and for what? A cradle she coveted. Tears choked her but she fought them back, knowing that if she gave into them and her nose got clogged she wouldn't be able to breathe. The thought shoved her to the brink of panic. Lifting her head, she tracked Abbott as he shambled away from her, opened the door and let in a slice of sunlight, and then slammed it closed. The chain jangled and the snap of the padlock carried to her. Her head slumped to the floor, but then another contraction ripped through her and she moaned.

When it passed, she forced herself to assess the situation. She focused on breathing slowly through her nose—in, two, three, out, two three. She was uncomfortable but not in immediate peril. Laurel and Dawn knew where she was—they'd come looking for her eventually. That thought brought a measure of calm. She wasn't going to lie here, trussed like a sacrificial virgin, waiting to see if they found her before Abbott came back. *No virgin ever had this belly.* Well, only one. The thought almost made her smile. Almost. Abbott wasn't going to let her live, not when he'd more or less confessed to killing Mindy. She coached herself as if she were one of her own clients: *It'll be okay in the end; if it's not okay, it's not the end. Let's think this through. Prioritize.* First, get off the floor. Second, get rid of the gag. She needed to be able to breathe freely. Third, check out the cabinet where he'd gotten the duct tape. With any luck—and she was due for some luck—there'd be something she could use to saw through the duct tape. Then ... her mind blanked. No matter. When she'd accomplished the first three items she'd reassess the situation.

First things first. Normally lithe and limber, she felt like a shackled whale with her arms behind her back, her ankles taped together, and her distended belly. Rolling onto her front, she mentally apologized to

Lila for compressing her space, planted her forehead on the ground to steady herself, and hitched her knees in with small, jerky motions until her thighs were tucked under her hips. *Should've kept going to Pilates.* Her stomach was scrunched between her thighs and the floor and Lila complained with a vicious kick to Geneva's kidney. *Sorry, sweetie. I'm trying to get us out of this.* Grit embedded itself in her forehead from the pressure, and the shed's rough wood flooring scraped her knees raw. She did her best to ignore the pain, telling herself fiercely that it was for Lila. She stopped for a long minute to catch her breath, and then curled her toes under, glad she was wearing thin Keds gym shoes. Rocking back and forth, she tried to get enough momentum to shift her weight backwards and drag her torso up.

Her first five efforts failed. Each time she thought she had enough momentum, her heavy belly pulled her down. Running out of energy, she put everything she had into a final attempt, flinging her head and shoulders back and straining with her thigh muscles. *For Lila, for Lila.* She swayed, clenched every muscle, and managed to hold her torso upright. Sweat trickled down her face, and she rested for a moment in the glow of victory, small though it was. Her kneeling posture brought a vision of Mama Gran to mind: back straight, head bowed, praying at the AME church they'd attended throughout Geneva's childhood, her light weight barely denting the kneeler's brown velvet. Geneva bowed her head and offered a short, fierce prayer for strength and deliverance.

As she breathed "Amen," she rolled from her toes to her heels and pushed up and back with her knees. She started to rise and her torso canted forward. For one horrifying moment she feared she was going to fall flat on her belly. Thrusting her taped hands back so her shoulders popped, she stayed on her feet, hopping back several steps until she thudded against the wall. It shivered, sprinkling dust on her, but she didn't mind. She was standing. Ignoring a sharp pain in her groin—a pulled muscle, she diagnosed—she took little bunny hops toward the cabinet, careful not to lose her balance.

Six hops brought her to the metal cabinet and she was able to shoulder open the door that Abbott had left ajar. It wasn't totally dark in the shed—sunlight poked through gaps where the boards were poorly joined—and she could make out the metal latch on the right-side door meant to hook over the rod on the left-side door and hold them closed. Bending, she opened her mouth as wide as possible, pressed her cheek against the door's cold metal, and snagged the handkerchief gag against the latch's hook. She drew her head back and the hook dragged out half the gag before it slipped. She repeated the process, poking at the cloth with her tongue as well, and it finally fell to the floor. Thank God.

Giddy with relief, she ran her tongue around the inside of her parched mouth, trying to generate some saliva. What she wouldn't give for a glass of water! Still, she was making progress. Maybe, if she turned around, she could use the metal latch to rip through the tape binding her hands. Confidence surged through her. She could do this. She could save herself and Lila.

"We Frost women don't give up," she told Lila. Saying it aloud gave her courage. As she maneuvered her hands toward the latch, warm liquid gushed between her thighs. Cold stole through her. Her water had broken.

Twenty-Eight

Laurel had expected Ray's hideout to be a squalid building in a dicey part of town, but it turned out to be an upscale condo with a view of the river. Being a DEA informant came with some perks, she thought, parking her car at the drug store across the street and eyeing the property. It consisted of a single three-story building with what looked like four units on each floor, a large pool, a tennis court, and a small parking lot for visitors. Residents must park in an underground garage. Mature trees provided shade, and a trio of Canadian geese nibbled at the grass near the glass door. Locking her car, she headed toward the building, feeling self-conscious. If Ray was such a high-value CI, chances were he was under surveillance. She glanced casually over her shoulder but didn't see an obvious observer.

The glass door was locked and a speaker grille had six buttons on either side, identified by unit number. She punched 3D and fidgeted from foot to foot waiting for an answer. If Ray was out, what would—

"Yeah?"

It was Ray's voice, tense and dark with suspicion.

"It's Laurel Muir, Evangeline's friend. We need to talk."

There was a pause long enough to make her think he might be disappearing down a rear fire escape, and she was thinking about how she could help Ari make it right with his DEA contact, but then a click sounded and she pushed through the door.

She took the stairs to her left, inexplicably averse to riding up in the small elevator that stood open straight ahead of her. The curving stairwell smelled of fresh paint. The flights were long and she was slightly winded when she reached the third floor. Ray had the unit in the northwest corner and she noted a discreet camera as she knocked. She obligingly tilted her face up so the camera could get a good picture, and a moment later the door opened.

"Come in." Ray's voice came from behind the door.

She obeyed, watching him lock it behind her. His hair was caught back in an inch-long ponytail pulled tight enough to stretch his forehead smooth. His skin seemed a shade or two paler than it was when they first met, as if he'd spent the intervening days inside, away from the sun, and a two-day growth of beard fuzzed his chin and jaw. His feet were bare. His dark eyes, red-rimmed and bloodshot, held a wary look, and there was no hint of the grin he'd sported when he interacted with them as Evangeline's fiancé. Most unnerving of all, he held a long-barreled silver automatic in his right hand as he flipped two deadbolts with his left. Laurel swallowed hard. He didn't raise the gun when he turned to face her, but he didn't put it away, either.

"How did you find me?" he asked, remaining by the door.

"It doesn't matter," she said.

A *snick* told her he'd released the gun's safety. "It matters to me," he said flatly.

She couldn't give up Ari and his DEA contact. "Someone shoved the address under my door at the castle," she lied. "I don't know who. I found out who you were through the high school yearbook and talked to some people at the school. Maybe it was one of them. Or someone from Evangeline's office. We talked to them, too."

Distrust and doubt flickered across his face, but he didn't put a bullet through her or kick her out, so she counted it as a win.

Tucking the gun into his waistband, he brushed past her. Heat and the odor of alcohol radiated off him and she wondered if he had a fever. *He's afraid.* The conviction came to her suddenly. He was nervous about the trip to Mexico. He knew as well as the DEA and Ari what the cartel did to traitors. She suspected he might only have let her in as a distraction, to give himself something to think about other than what tomorrow would bring. Feeling a spark of sympathy, but then reminding herself that he was a drug dealer, Laurel followed him into a galley-style kitchen. Although well-equipped, it was dark, with black appliances and green granite countertops. A tequila bottle, half empty, sat on the counter. Ray uncapped it, pulled a glass from the open dishwasher, and splashed two inches into it. "Drink?" he asked, raising the bottle. It shook slightly.

Wanting to establish a rapport with him, Laurel said, "Sure, thanks," and hoped the dishes in the dishwasher were clean. He pulled out another glass, swiped the rim with his shirt hem, and poured her an equal measure of the pale gold liquid. Leaning against the counter, he took a long swallow from his glass, eyes never leaving her. She lifted her glass reluctantly. Straight liquor had never been her thing, and the one time Evangeline had talked her into trying tequila shots, she'd been sick for two days. She tried a tiny sip. It was smoother than she expected, with a warmth and an almost herbal tang that made her think of saguaro in the Sonora Desert. It made her tongue and throat tingle in a pleasant way. "It's good."

The surprise in her voice brought on a ghost of his grin. "Only the best." The smile faded almost immediately, and he paced to a window in the living room that looked out on a tangle of shrubs and the muddy river. He stared down for a moment, focused on the roiling water, but then turned his back to the window and said, "You wanted to talk. So, talk."

Should she tell him Evangeline was dead? She studied him. He seemed a decade older than he had on Saturday. She'd put it down to fear of his upcoming undercover mission, but now she decided it was grief, at least in part. She didn't need to tell him. She suspected he'd known before they found her body. "You knew Evangeline from high school," she said, not making it a question. As she talked, she moved into the living room and perched on an ottoman, not wanting to risk sinking into one of the squashy leather love seats. She needed to be able to spring up quickly and have some range of motion if things went south.

"Hell, I knew Van from elementary school." He rolled his glass between his palms. "Know-it-all little brat with braids and socks with a lace band around the top. We lived on the same block. It wasn't until high school that we became friends, though." His gaze grew unfocused, as if he were looking into the past, and a reminiscent smile softened his face.

Laurel wondered if he was remembering a slow dance at the prom, a first kiss, or something more …

"We were friends," he said, dashing those visions. "I could talk to Van in a way I never could with my girlfriends. We were tight through high school. Then she went off to Grissom, and I … well, let's just say I opted to stay in town and pursue entrepreneurial opportunities." He gave a humorless laugh. "That paid off better for me than school did

264

for her. Well, it did until recently. We stayed in touch, saw each other summers. When she decided she wanted to buy the castle, she even worked for me for a while. When she had enough, she quit."

He paused to take another swallow of tequila, and Laurel fought the urge to ask what Evangeline had done for his business. She remembered how surprised they'd all been when Evangeline had announced she'd "come into money" and had a contract on the inn, how coy she'd been about where the money came from. As a flight attendant she had opportunities to transport drugs, Laurel was sure. Had Evangeline been a drug mule for Ray? Sold drugs? Laurel squeezed her eyes tightly closed against the thought, but opened them when Ray spoke again.

"Then, of course, she came back to live with her mother after the accident and we hung out sometimes. It was tragic what happened to her. She didn't deserve it." He scowled. "I offered to have some of my crew beat the crap out of all of you when she told me one of you pushed her off that balcony, paralyzed her, but she wouldn't have it. Back then, she was sure she would walk again."

"She never did though, did she?" Laurel asked gently.

He shook his head and downed the last of his tequila with a snap of his wrist. "Nah. When the treatments in Mexico failed ... " He grimaced and strode past her, stumbling over the transition from the carpeted living room to the tile-floored kitchen, to retrieve the tequila bottle. With his glass topped up, he said, "She changed then. She'd used up most of her money on those quacks, and she didn't have anyone to help her. She was in pain all the time. I helped her out with some pharmaceuticals when her insurance ran out, but she still hurt every minute of every day. I tried to get her to see a counselor—can you imagine it? Me, trying to talk her into therapy?" Ray shook his head, amazed. "But she wouldn't. With her mother dead and her money gone, and no job, she was looking at having to go on welfare, maybe even into a state facility of some kind. Her face when she told me that anything was better than that, that she wasn't going to rely on some stranger to help her to the crapper … it was then that she started to get mad at you all." He paused, and his thick tongue licked his lips. His expression, as he looked down at Laurel, was unreadable. "She got me out of some tight spots. I owed her."

Laurel sensed an opening in his last statement. "Pretending to be engaged—that was payback?"

His mouth twisted. "She always said you were the smart one, that if anyone figured it out, it would be you."

His esses were starting to slur, and his eyes seemed more bloodshot. Laurel resisted the urge to ask what else Evangeline had said about her, and how she referred to the others. "She decided to kill herself and frame us."

"I tried to talk her out of it, but she said helping her was the last, best thing I could do for her, that her mind was made up. I did what she asked. I drove her out to the castle and made like we were the happiest couple who ever lived. She said it was important that everyone believe she was happy, that things were working out for her." He made a choking sound and turned away to stare out the window again. The glass reflected his face, eyes screwed up against tears, and Laurel looked away. "I offered to marry her for real," he said tightly, "to take care of her. I've got plenty of money, but she wouldn't have it. Said she couldn't do that to me, keep me from finding a 'real' wife. She meant one I could have sex with, have kids with. I didn't care about the sex. Sex is easy to get. And kids? I admit I thought about them now and then, but I'm getting too old for them anyway. I'm too set in my ways, too selfish for kids. I tried to tell her that, but her mind was made up. You knew Van. Once she made up her mind, nothing was going to change it. Nothing."

He turned and showed Laurel a bleak face. "I promised her I wouldn't tell, but here I am, spilling everything to you. Too much tequila, I guess. Too much time alone, thinking about…"

He swayed and didn't finish the thought. Laurel wondered if it was too much time thinking about Evangeline or about his own screwed-up life and what awaited him in Mexico.

He whipped the gun from his waistband suddenly and pointed it at Laurel. She froze.

"You should know you drove her to it, you and those others. You broke her. You broke her. It's your fault—all your faults. She wanted to see you in prison, but maybe it would be easier if you died. Did you push her? Were you the one?" His voice rose until he was shouting hoarsely.

The gun trembled in his hand, and he swayed again. He braced his free hand against the window and the shape of his fingers bloomed against the glass.

"No," Laurel said, her mouth dry. She couldn't tear her gaze from the hole in the gun's barrel, the dark, unblinking eye. "I didn't push her."

He bowed his head and the gun dipped slightly. "Get out."

Laurel set her glass on the coffee table and rose slowly, trying to think of a way to get him to write down what he'd told her, or record it. He was going to disappear into Mexico within hours, and she had no proof of anything he'd said. While she was trying to form the request, he jerked his head up and raised the gun again. His knuckles blanched white on the grip. "Get out!" he screamed.

Without thanking him or apologizing or telling him she was sorry about Evangeline, Laurel backed toward the door, holding her hands out from her sides in a non-threatening way. She kept her eyes locked on his, dredging up some briefing on back-country safety that said to stare down a threatening cougar or bear, not to look away. He held her gaze until she bumped into the door and had to turn away to fumble with the deadbolts. She cursed her trembling fingers that made the task take too long. She felt his eyes boring into her back, and imagined his finger tightening on the trigger. Her shoulders braced for a bullet, but the door came open and no bullet ripped through her back to shred her lungs. As she pulled the door wider, she glanced over her shoulder. Ray was no longer facing her. The gun hung limply from his hand as he stared down into the river, with its swift-flowing water, muddy and opaque, carrying bits of the North Carolina highlands out to sea.

Twenty-Nine

Safely in her car, Laurel took a rib-expanding breath and tried to process what she'd heard from Ray. She'd been right: Evangeline had committed suicide and attempted to frame one or all of them for her murder. She bowed her head over the steering wheel, arms draped around it, feeling stunned by grief. Evangeline had died in anger, pain, and hopelessness. She'd hated the four of them enough to want to see them in prison, to scheme and plot to make it happen. Suspicion had invaded their friendships, making them question how well they knew each other and wonder which of them was capable of murder. Of course, Laurel had to admit, raising her head and starting the car, that suspicion had been slowly poisoning their relationships for ten years.

She put aside her sadness and thoughts, to sort out later, and pulled onto the road. Right now, she had to tell Boone what she'd learned from Ray Hernan. He'd make her tell him where Ray was. She was torn at the thought of burning Ari and his DEA source, but she'd have to tell Boone everything. Mindy! How could she have forgotten about Mindy? She might have learned the truth about Evangeline's death, but someone had killed Mindy Tanger. She dialed Boone's cell phone and got his voicemail. She left a brief message saying she had to talk to him immediately. A sense of urgency invaded her and the car picked up speed. Tree shadows slashed through the windows as the car swung around curves and sped down the straightaways. She reached the gates of Cygne in record time and stomped on the brakes to slow for the turn between the stone pillars.

A cluster of people, including Dawn, Ellie, and Sheriff Boone, were gathered on the front lawn when she pulled up. She was glad to see Boone; she could tell him everything in person. She stopped her car short of the lot and got out into the gathering dusk. When she checked her watch, she was surprised to see it was already six o'clock. Ellie hurried to meet her. She seemed frazzled.

"Laurel, thank God. One friend missing is more than enough."

"Missing? Who?" Geneva. She was the only one not here. Icy liquid sluiced through her veins. "Have you looked for her? How long has she been gone?"

"We were just starting out. When she didn't meet me for a walk like we planned, I checked her room. Her phone's there, her purse is there, but she's not." Ellie blinked hard. "It's just like Mindy."

Boone and Dawn came alongside them. Laurel shot a look at Boone. "I need to talk to you. I found out—"

"Later," he said. "We need to find Ms. Frost. When women disappear around here, it doesn't turn out well."

Dawn put a hand to her mouth and Boone made a moue of apology. "Sorry," he said. "I've called for more officers to help us look. They should be here within ten minutes. "

"She said she was going to talk to Mr. Abbott about the cradle she wanted," Laurel said. "Has anyone checked to see if the Abbotts have seen her?"

They looked at each other and shook their heads.

"You go," Boone told the women. "I'll wait here and split my reservists into teams when they arrive. Call me if you find her. I'll have an ambulance standing by, just in case."

The gravity in his voice made Laurel shiver. He wasn't sure they'd find Geneva alive.

She started toward the house with Dawn and Ellie. Of one accord, they headed for the kitchen. They crossed the threshold together, and found Mrs. Abbott applying a Band-Aid to her husband's arm. He sat in a ladder-back chair at the kitchen table, sleeve rolled up and hairy arm extended. The tea kettle emitted a thin stream of steam, as if it had recently boiled, and several potatoes awaited slicing on a cutting board by the sink.

"Enough already," Stephen Abbott was saying. He brushed his wife aside. "It's a scratch, not a stab wound." He became aware of the women and scowled. "What do you lot want?"

Mrs. Abbott shot him a placatory look. "Now, Stephen ... Can we help you with something? Tea or coffee?"

"Have you seen Geneva?" Laurel asked, addressing Mr. Abbott. "She said she was going to talk to you about buying a cradle."

"Haven't seen her," he said, rolling down his sleeve. He stood.

Mrs. Abbott's brows twitched together. "Did she not find you, then? I told her to check for you down by the shed where we stored the furniture for the auction house people to pick up."

Something about her precision, the way she met her husband's eyes as if trying to convey a private message, struck Laurel as off.

"I wasn't there. I was mowing by the lake. That's how I got scratched." His eyes didn't meet his wife's and the way he held himself reminded Laurel of a coyote she'd surprised in the backyard once. The dun-colored creature had frozen at sight of her, but the muscles in his thin flanks quivered and she'd sensed the spring-loaded energy that would explode into movement if she so much as flinched.

Mrs. Abbott continued, in a voice that sounded like she was trying to excuse herself. "Since the furniture was collected already, I didn't see any harm. I thought you were cleaning—"

"I said I didn't see her!"

Abbott's vehemence rang warning bells for all of them, Laurel could tell. Ellie took a step toward him, hands balled into fists. Before she could say anything, Mrs. Abbott breathed, "She's pregnant, Stephen. You didn't—"

"Shut your mouth, Nerys." He sprang for the door and collided with Dawn, who had started for it as well, perhaps headed for the shed to see if Geneva was there. "Oof." They both staggered, and then Abbott crunched one forearm across Dawn's throat and groped for the potato knife on the counter with the other. His fingers closed around it and he held it aloft triumphantly. The overhead light flashed on the blade. "Stay where you are." He backed toward the door, towing Dawn.

Her eyes were big with fear and her fingers scratched at his arm where it pressed against her throat. She made a coughing noise and Laurel knew she couldn't breathe right.

"Stephen, stop," Mrs. Abbott commanded. "It's over. Too many people know." She made a weary gesture toward all of them.

Abbott's gaze bounced off his wife, hit each of the other women, and darted toward the door beyond them. He looked at the knife in his hand and pressed it to Dawn's throat. She squeaked. A thin cut opened under her chin and oozed blood. "It's your damn fault, Nerys, for letting them come this weekend. We'd have been okay otherwise."

Laurel wasn't sure what they were supposed to know, but she suspected it had to do with Cygne's antiques and their disposition. The Abbotts must be stealing them. Her mind flashed to the "Drummond" on the side of the van that was removing the furniture. She'd seen that name before in connection with the Abbotts but couldn't immediately dredge up where. Mentally reviewing what she'd learned about the Abbotts, it came to her. Ari's report had mentioned their daughter being "Alice Drummond." She'd bet her next paycheck that Nat was their son-in-law, and that he was helping them transport the antiques. To Texas? To some other destination where they could sell them and pocket the profits? It didn't matter.

"The prison time for theft is a lot less than for kidnapping or murder," she said levelly, catching Abbott's wild gaze. Her pulse drummed in her ears and she rocked forward onto the balls of her feet. If he was already guilty of Mindy's murder, he might think he had nothing to lose. "You don't want to do this. Let Dawn go."

For answer, he shoved Dawn toward her. Dawn's weight knocked Laurel off balance and she staggered, her arms automatically going around her friend. In the confusion, Abbott flung the door open and took off in the direction of the parking lot. A cloud of dark hair momentarily obscuring her vision, Laurel separated from Dawn, steadying her with hands on her shoulders. "Are you okay?"

When Dawn nodded, putting a trembling hand to the small cut on her throat, Ellie sprinted out the door, yelling "Geneva!"

Mrs. Abbott stood where she'd been when Abbott left, fists pressed to her mouth, mumbling, "He wouldn't hurt her, he wouldn't do that. My Stephen isn't like that. He wouldn't hurt a baby. It's not as if they didn't owe it to us. Oh, Stephen."

Ignoring her, Laurel slapped her cell phone into Dawn's hands. "Get Boone," she said. "Tell him to have the ambulance meet us at the shed down the hill." Barely waiting for Dawn's nod, she took off after Ellie.

———

Ellie raced down the hill, hair flying. She stumbled some, now that twilight obscured the ground, and almost couldn't stop herself from plowing into the shed where they'd seen the furniture a couple days back and Mr. A had read them the riot act. A length of chain and a padlock secured the doors. She rattled them. "Geneva, Geneva!"

Was that a voice? She stilled.

"The baby." Geneva's voice was thin and panicky and sounded a long way away. "The baby's coming."

"Oh my God," Ellie breathed. She pressed her lips to the crack between the doors and shouted, "An ambulance is on its way." She hoped it was. "We're going to get you out of there. You and Lila will be fine, just fine, you hear me?"

Voices made her look over her shoulder. She could make out Laurel sprinting from the house, arms pumping, and Sheriff Boone jogging around the front corner, talking into his cell phone. Dawn trailed him. *Thank God.* When they reached her, she said, "She's in there. Geneva's in there. She says the baby's coming. It's locked." She pointed to the padlock. "Can you shoot it off?"

Backing off a step, Boone brought his booted foot up to waist height and slammed it into the wood near where a thin metal plate with a loop for the chain was screwed into the door. It splintered slightly and one of the screws loosened. He did it again, and again, and a fourth time, his face grim and jaw set, and finally the wood disintegrated around the plate, freeing one half of the door. Ellie yanked it back. Blundering into the shed, she was thrown off-stride by the emptiness. A second later, she spotted the crumpled shape slumped against a cabinet on the far wall. "Geneva."

With the others close behind, she hurried to Geneva, using her phone screen to light the way until someone found the light switch and a single bulb lit up. She sank to her haunches and stroked Geneva's face. "Hang in there, honey."

Geneva was arched in on herself, apparently in the throes of a contraction, but she looked up and tried to smile. "Hey."

Memories of the twins' birth, the fear and pain, leached into Ellie's thoughts. It remained the most painful experience of her life, and she'd been in a hygienic military hospital, not a grubby shed crawling with who knew what bacteria. Laurel, Dawn, and Boone crowded around.

"Water broke about two hours ago," Geneva panted. "Contractions coming every eight minutes or so. It's too early. She's not due for almost a month." Panic shivered beneath the words.

"Three or four weeks early is nothing," Ellie reassured her. "Nothing. Lila will be just fine. There's an ambulance on its way." On the words, she heard a siren's whoop. "See?"

As the contraction eased, Ellie and Laurel helped her into a sitting position.

Laurel began struggling with the tape at Geneva's wrists. "Need a knife," she muttered.

Boone snapped open a Swiss Army knife type gadget and sliced through the duct tape. With a sigh of relief, Geneva pulled her arms to the front and wrapped them around her belly.

"It was Stephen Abbott," she said, her eyes on Sheriff Boone crouched in front of her. "The Abbotts were stealing the antiques. He thought I knew what he was up to and locked me in here. I don't think he's playing with a full deck. That's technical psychologist talk."

Ellie chuckled. Geneva couldn't be too bad off if she was making jokes.

"He said he'd come back to deal with me when it was dark." Her voice caught. "It sounded like Mindy figured it out. I think he killed her. Do you think he killed Evangeline, too?"

Ellie brushed damp hair off Geneva's brow. "Don't worry about any of that. Save your energy."

"We'll find out," Boone said, at the same time Laurel said "No." Everyone looked at her, and she said, "I'll explain later."

Ellie was taken aback by the certainty in Laurel's voice, but she was more concerned with Geneva and her baby at that moment than with murder. She urged Geneva to breathe as another contraction seized her, and counted off the seconds on her watch.

The EMTs rushed in then, and Ellie and the others backed away to let them work. One of them murmured when he saw the condition of Geneva's wrists and hands. Within minutes, they had an IV line running and were trundling Geneva to the ambulance on a collapsible gurney while asking questions about the contractions and her due date. Their calm professionalism seemed to reassure her.

"I'm going with her," Ellie announced and climbed into the back of the ambulance without waiting for permission. Geneva's smile was her reward. She reached for Geneva's hand and held it tightly. "I'll be with you the whole way," she promised.

"I'll call Geonwoo," Laurel called as the doors clanged shut, "and Dawn and I will meet you at the hospital."

————————

Boone charged away after the ambulance left, setting his troops in motion to find Stephen Abbott. As she and Dawn left for the Asheville hospital, Laurel saw an officer handcuff Nerys Abbott and load her into the back of his car. The woman looked deflated, her hair flat and head bowed, and Laurel felt a momentary pang of sympathy. Bitterness and resentment had taken the innkeeper far down a path she couldn't have foreseen, and her retirement would be spent in a prison cell rather than walking on the Galveston beach and bonding with her grandchildren. Remembering the way Nerys had talked about her move to Texas and her next chapter, Laurel depressed the accelerator hard and cut the corner too close when turning into the hospital parking lot. Dawn grabbed the dashboard but didn't complain.

They arrived to find that Geneva was still in labor with Ellie serving as her coach. A nurse assured them that everything was going fine and advised them to get something to eat or drink. "It's a first baby," he said, "and she's in no hurry. It's gonna be a while yet." With a toothy grin, he gave them directions to the cafeteria on the second floor.

Dawn said she wasn't hungry, so Laurel left her in the waiting room and headed downstairs alone. Emerging from the elevator, she bumped into Sheriff Boone. She bounced off his solid chest, and he steadied her with his hands on her upper arms. He smelled faintly of butterscotch and clean sweat.

"Whoa."

"Sorry," she gasped, absurdly aware of the strength in his hands.

"Good timing," he said. "I put an APB out on Stephen Abbott and I was coming up to find you. You said you had something to tell me, and it sounded urgent."

He released her and she felt momentarily bereft. "I was headed to the cafeteria," she said quickly, to cover her confusion. "They say the baby won't be here for a while, and I'm starving."

"I could eat." He led the way down a linoleumed hallway and she wondered how many meals he'd eaten in the hospital, waiting to interview a beaten, stabbed, or raped victim.

The cafeteria was a pleasant space with colorful molded plastic chairs, and plants and windows. Even at seven o'clock, a fair number of people in lab coats or scrubs carried trays or conversed at the tables as Boone and Laurel got in line. With a chef salad on her tray, Laurel impulsively gave into the appeal of a cup of chocolate pudding topped by a stiff dollop of whipped cream. It reminded her of childhood desserts, and she knew exactly how it would taste and feel on her tongue. The stress of the past few days had her craving comfort food. They paid and settled at a table near a dusty corn plant.

"So, talk," Boone said, biting into his burger.

"You're going to be pissed off that I didn't tell you in advance," Laurel warned, "so let's stipulate that you've chewed me out and I'm sorry, but I didn't think I had an option at the time."

Boone looked at her from under his heavy brows. "I reserve the right to rip you a new one if I deem it necessary, Your Honor."

Laurel bit her lip and talked, occasionally pausing for a bite of salad. She told him about her conversation with Ray Hernan and how she'd found him. Midway through her recital, Boone paused her with an upraised finger and called the station to issue orders for officers to proceed to Hernan's address and pick him up for questioning.

"Consider me pissed off and yourself chewed out," he said when he hung up.

His unsmiling gaze rested on Laurel's face as she finished telling him what Ray had told her about Evangeline's desire for revenge and her suicide plan. "She wanted one or all of us to stand trial for her 'murder,'" she said sadly, "so she tried to frame us. I didn't think to ask Ray, but I suspect he's the one who bought the rat poison near San Antonio to implicate Dawn."

"If you'd called me when you got his contact info, we would know all the details," Boone bit out.

"The point is that Evangeline killed herself."

"We have no proof of that." He wiped ketchup off his fingers.

"You think I'm lying?" Laurel was hurt by the thought, but hid it. Boone was doing his job, and he was right: there was no proof, nothing beyond Ray's confession as relayed by her. Any competent lawyer would object to it as hearsay, and she'd sustain.

"I didn't say that."

"You have no proof she was killed, either," Laurel said, swinging into lawyer mode.

"In fact, I do."

"Too much proof," she responded quickly. "Pointing to too many people. Reasonable doubt. In fact, there's such a cloud of reasonable doubt hanging over this case that you'll never get a DA to take it to court even without Ray Hernan's testimony."

Boone pushed back from the table. "You may be right." Standing, he loomed over her. From this perspective, the bags under his eyes seemed heavier, the lines carved around his mouth deeper. "The person who should go away for this is the one who pushed the vic ten years ago. She put in motion the chain of events that led us here." His brown eyes pinned her. "I think you've figured out who it was."

Laurel stilled. The whir of a soft-serve ice cream machine and snippets of conversations drifted between them. After a long moment, she dipped her head. "Maybe."

"Are you going to tell me?"

"When I'm sure. I have to be sure."

"I'll hold you to that, Laurel," he said. Unsmiling, he turned and walked out of the cafeteria.

Thirty

Lila Marigold made her appearance shortly after eight thirty, at seven pounds even and twenty inches long. They all crowded in to admire the baby and congratulate Geneva when she and Lila were transferred to a room on the maternity ward. Laurel held the swaddled bundle, surprised by the baby's solidity, awestruck by her tiny little nose and delicate fingers, and dazzled by the silky lashes fanning against her cheek as she slept. Holding the baby gave her a deep sense of peace, and she knew she'd made her decision. Blinking away tears, she reluctantly handed Lila back when a nurse shooed them out saying "Mom needs her rest." Indeed, Geneva looked exhausted. Happy, but pale and shaky after her dual ordeals of imprisonment and giving birth. They left her facetiming with Geonwoo and promising to join them for a memorial to Evangeline the next day before they all scattered to their own states.

Laurel drove Dawn and Ellie back to the castle, taking the opportunity to fill them in on her meeting with Ray Hernan.

"I'll bet he's the one who sold Evangeline and Geneva the coke," Ellie said.

Dawn's phone ringing interrupted their exclamations and speculations. Puzzlement creased her face when she examined the number, and she murmured, "Sorry, I've got to take this." She answered and listened in silence for several seconds, but then exclaimed, "Oh my God! How badly is she hurt?"

Laurel got a sinking feeling. The call was about Kyra, she was sure. She eyed her friend worriedly in the rearview mirror. After another thirty seconds of mostly listening, Dawn hung up.

"Tell us?" Ellie slewed in the front seat to see Dawn.

"It's Kyra," she said, voice trembling with tears. "She was in a car accident Sunday afternoon."

"Oh no. Is she … ?" Ellie didn't finish the question.

"She's in the hospital in Alabama," Dawn said, almost panting. A passing car's headlights blanched her face dead white. "That's where it happened, the accident. She's going to be okay. A couple of broken bones—her leg and her scapula, a lacerated spleen. I didn't catch everything. She was concussed and totally out of it. Her phone was destroyed in the crash. The police traced the license plate to our address, and the nitwit staying at our house found them Kyra's parents' phone number but didn't bother calling me." She ground her teeth. "Her parents assumed I knew, and they were surprised I hadn't been in touch. That was them." She waved the phone. "She—she woke up today and told them she was coming here, to surprise me. She's afraid to fly, always has been, so she was driving. All this time, I thought—I thought she was—" Dawn pounded both fists on her thighs. "She's going to be okay, she's going to be okay," she said, obviously trying to calm herself.

"Of course she's going to be okay," Ellie said, and Laurel smiled at her calm certainty. She made the tight turn between Cygne's pillars and began guiding the car up the winding driveway. *What a day.*

Her smile faded abruptly when they came around the last curve to find a strange car parked in the circular driveway. They got out hesitantly.

"Police?" Ellie asked in a whisper as they neared the castle entrance. Gravel crunched loudly underfoot, undercutting their attempt at stealth.

"I don't think so." Laurel shook her head. Could Stephen Abbott have eluded the police somehow and returned to Cygne? She felt tension vibrating off the women on either side of her.

The porch light snapped on, casting a net of golden light that snared a dozen moths and other bugs. The women jolted to a halt. The door creaked open. Dawn grabbed Laurel's arm. "We should—"

A man's silhouette appeared in the doorway. Laurel took a step back, bumping into Dawn. "Ellie? Is that you?" a man's voice called. "Where the heck is everyone?"

Ellie gasped. "Oh my God, he must have driven after all." She hurtled toward the entrance and flung herself into his arms. "Scott! I'm so sorry. My phone was off because I was at the hospital. Geneva got kidnapped and had her baby, and Mr. A tried to kill her and Dawn, and the police arrested Mrs. A ... "

Laurel and Dawn followed more slowly and greeted Scott Ordahl, who was clearly bemused by his wife's recital. Ellie suddenly burst into tears. "I'm so glad you're here," she said, clinging to her husband. He patted her back and made soothing noises.

"It's been a long day," Laurel said with a tired smile.

"A very long day," Dawn echoed, her voice teetering on the brink of tears. "I'm going to pack and go to bed."

Laurel and Dawn went around the embracing couple and headed back to their rooms. Light glowed from the sunroom, where Laurel presumed Scott had been sitting, but the rest of the rooms were dark. She flipped on every light switch they passed and refused to feel guilty about it. They had earned a little light.

———

Alone in the foyer, Ellie clung to Scott as if she'd never let go. "I'm so glad you're here," she said. He was warm and alive and solid, and tension drained out of her as he held her.

"Let me turn out the light and we can go to bed," Scott said, disengaging himself and walking toward the sunroom.

She followed and paused inside the door while he retrieved the *Aviation Week and Space Technology* he'd left face-down on the coffee table. The table lamp highlighted the strong bones in his hand as he reached for the magazine and left puddles of shadow outside its golden circle. An earthy odor rose from the potted plants, richer, it seemed, in the near dark than during the day. It was the first time they'd been together in this room since Scott came to Cygne with her for spring break their junior year. So long ago.

"I saw you here," she said, the words spilling out without prior thought. "You and Evangeline. On that couch. Well, not that one, since it's new, but the one that used to be there. It had rolled arms, that revolting upholstery with the pink and yellow roses, and thirty years' worth of suspicious stains."

Scott turned slowly. Light winked off the lenses of his glasses, hiding his eyes. He was silent for a long moment, brow furrowed. "You never said anything."

"No," Ellie agreed. "I should have. Instead, I made love with you, and got pregnant, and married you and had the twins, and gave up my scholarship and my education." The words spilled out, as if seeing Scott in this room again had dynamited the dam holding them back. The truth, at last. Out in the open. She took a rib-expanding breath, and there seemed to be more room inside her for air.

"You blame me." He hadn't moved, and the distance between them felt wider than an Olympic pool.

"I did." She nodded. "For a long time. You and Evangeline." An unfamiliar peace flooded through Ellie as she talked. "I blamed you, and especially her, for changing the course of my life, for me ending up near forty with no career, no focus, no purpose." Scott started to interrupt, but she talked faster. "But I was wrong. I might as well give Evangeline credit for the boys, for nearly twenty wonderful years with you and them, for a life full of inconveniences and disruptions—too many moves!—but also lots of adventures and love." She cocked her head. "Something about spending time with my friends this weekend, maybe Evangeline's murder, has helped me take a good hard look at myself. Never a fun task." She made a wry face. "Evangeline didn't make me sleep with you, and you didn't make me give up my education. I made those decisions. Me, myself, and I—no one else. Talking to Evangeline's coworkers, I could see she let herself get bitter—she practically stewed in it. I mean, who works for an orthopedist if they're stuck in a wheelchair? I don't think I'd have done that, but if I only spent half as much energy figuring out who I wanted to be and making that happen as brooding about your one-night stand with Evangeline ... " She shot him a look. "It was just once, right?"

Scott nodded. Small clicks sounded from the windows and it took her a moment to realize it was insects batting themselves against the glass, attracted by the light.

"Well, if I'd done that, or if I'd had it out with you on the spot, or, well, not right on the spot, but if I'd told you the next week that I saw you and asked you what it meant to you—

"Nothing. *Nothing*."

"—then I could have moved on." She put her hands on her hips. "Well, moving on starts right here."

"I'm sorry I cheated on you," Scott said, taking a step toward her. "But, good God. You've been holding this against me for twenty years without ever telling me?" Hurt drew his brows together. "Letting me think we were good, solid, and now you tell me—" He balled his hand into a fist and struck his thigh.

His obvious pain and confusion and anger—totally justified—saddened her. She hadn't been fair to him, to them. "I'm sorry," she said, also taking a step. "It wasn't fair. We *are* good. Better than good. It's not like I thought about it every day, or even every month. Just now and then." She licked her lips. "I'd be willing to see someone when we get back to the Springs—you know, a counselor. This is, well, probably too much to, on our own … A therapist might help us hash it through, teach us to communicate better, I don't know. Elizabeth and Jamal worked with a woman they liked a lot." With two feet between them, she added, "I want to have a career, maybe my own sports nutrition business. I don't know for sure what I want to be when I grow up, but I want to be more than 'Mrs. Commander.'"

"Go for it," he said, his face relaxing. "When you get your business up and running, I'll retire and be Mr. Whatever You Need Me to Be."

She blinked away tears. "You're already exactly who I need you to be—my Scott, my husband." She bit her lip. "What if I'm a failure?"

He put his arms around her. "You've never failed at anything, Ellie. Quitting school to have the boys was not 'failing.' It was a choice, the right choice. You're a better wife than I have any right to, and the best mother in the world. You're a great friend, a good leader and organizer—how many Spouse Club events have you chaired, and how much money did you raise for the Boy Scouts and the swim team?"

"Quite the résumé," she murmured drily.

He pressed a kiss on her lips. "Yes, it is. And if you did fail, well, I'd help you pick yourself up again. We'd evaluate the circumstances, look at the courses of action, and—I'm doing it again, aren't I? Mentoring you. I'll try to stop."

Smiling, she let her head rest on his shoulder and inhaled the familiar scent of him—Dove soap, warm skin, and spearmint gum. "Can we still do that weekend away?"

"I told the colonel I'd be gone for at least a week, and ordered my deputy not to call unless a satellite falls out of the sky," he said, squeezing her tight. "We can leave here tomorrow and head for Charleston or anywhere else you want to go."

"Charleston," she said. Lightness invaded her. "You remember the first time we made love?"

"Like I could forget." His lips curved.

"Well, there's no pool here, but there's a hot tub … "

Thirty-One

Laurel woke later than she expected and blinked in the sunlight glaring through the drapes. It took her a moment to get oriented, but awareness trickled in in spurts. Geneva and her baby. Stephen Abbott holding Dawn at knifepoint. Finding Geneva. Mrs. Abbott's arrest. Kyra's accident. Swinging her legs out of bed, she dressed, brushed her teeth, and splashed water on her face, and then hurried toward the breakfast parlor. She heard voices coming from the dining room and poked her head in. She found Boone sitting on one side of the table with Ellie across from him, looking unselfconscious in a cotton camisole, pajama bottoms, and rumpled hair. Between them was a flimsy box holding assorted donuts, and a carrier with three cups of coffee with the Starbucks logo. Ellie held the fourth Starbucks cup, and Boone had his insulated *Frozen* cup.

"For us?" Laurel asked, entering and pointing toward the coffee.

When Boone nodded, she said, "Oh thank God," and reached for one of the coffees. Unable to resist a chocolate cake donut, she picked one up with a napkin and took a large, sugary bite. She almost moaned with pleasure.

"I figured you wouldn't get much of a breakfast here this morning," Boone said. "Not since I put your innkeepers in jail. It seemed the least I could do."

"Thank you," Laurel mumbled around a mouthful of chocolatey goodness. "Where's Scott?" she asked when she'd swallowed.

"Off to the hospital to pick up Geneva for the memorial," Ellie said with a smile that suggested their reunion had been hot despite the late hour. "She called first thing and says she feels fine—take my word for it, she's lying—and that the doc has signed her out. Baby Lila will stay at the hospital until we're done."

"Do I smell coffee?" Dawn stood in the doorway, dressed and made up, gripping her roller bag by the pull handle. Something in the way she held herself, canted ever so slightly backward as if determined not to enter the room, gave Laurel the impression of a deer about to take flight.

Laurel passed her a coffee cup. "Courtesy of New Aberdeen's finest," she said.

"Thanks," Dawn murmured, cracking the lid and blowing on the steaming liquid.

"I've got a search to organize, so let me fill you in," Boone said, sitting up straighter. He kicked a chair out in mute invitation.

Clearly reluctant, Dawn entered, towing the suitcase as if it were a lifeline connecting her to the highway and freedom. "I have to hit the road. Kyra gets released from the hospital today and I *am* going to be there to take her home, if she's up to it. I don't have time to stay for the memorial." She kept her eyes on the table, not looking at Laurel or Ellie.

"You're having a memorial for Evangeline Paul?" Boone asked.

Ellie nodded. "Who knows when or if there'll be a funeral? We want to remember her together." She looked straight at Dawn, who met her gaze briefly and shook her head.

"Did you catch Stephen Abbott?" Laurel asked.

"We did. At the South Carolina border. He was headed for Mexico with seventy-eight thousand hidden in the door panels of his car. According to Nerys Abbott, they have more in an offshore account. She broke down and told us everything before we brought him in. They were bitter about the castle being sold out from under them, about being forced into retirement. They didn't have much of a nest egg, apparently, and they talked themselves into believing the corporation owed them. Stephen Abbott came up with the idea of siphoning off some of the furniture and other antiques and selling them for their own profit. He has a buddy in the antiques business in New York City, and he was making the connections with the buyers. They 'only' took about a fifth of the castle's contents, Mrs. Abbott told us, all self-righteous, because they figured that's what they had coming to them after twenty-plus years of running the B and B."

"And now what they've got coming is a prison sentence," Laurel murmured.

"It's sad," Dawn said.

"Don't waste your pity on Stephen Abbott." Boone shifted his jaw to the side. "Although he denies it, in all probability he killed Mindy Tanger. He admits that she was blackmailing him. She told him she'd figured out what was going on, and she had photographs of the truck they were using to haul stuff away—"

"From their son-in-law's business," Laurel said.

"Right." Boone's mouth ticked up at one corner, saying she'd surprised him yet again. "We haven't found her phone, so we can't verify that part of his story. He says they were supposed to meet by the lake Sunday night, where he was going to hand over twenty-five thousand in cash to keep her quiet. His story is that she never showed. It's likely their real rendezvous was the fifth floor. It looks like he whacked her with a two-by-four and then dragged her body to the elevator shaft and shoved her over."

"I hope she was unconscious," Ellie said. "Poor Braden."

Boone acknowledged her concern with a nod. "Abbott was probably hoping that a fall similar to the one Ms. Paul suffered ten years ago, plus the murder and the four of you here as likely suspects, would confuse the issue, at the very least."

"Likely?" Ellie asked with affront.

He ignored her, rubbing his bristly jaw. "He'll confess, eventually. His wife admits he was out Sunday night, so he doesn't have an alibi. Regardless, we've got him on the charges related to you"—he nodded at Dawn—"and to kidnapping Ms. Frost."

"And Evangeline?" Dawn asked, her voice pitched low. Her head was slightly bowed and she looked at Boone from under her brows. Her fingers plucked at her cup's rim, peeling away the rolled edge.

"That investigation is still open, but I'm leaning toward the suicide theory," Boone replied. "Unfortunately, Ray Hernan, who was apparently Ms. Paul's accomplice in staging the suicide as a murder, is out of the country for an unknown period." He gave Laurel a slit-eyed stare. "When I get a chance to talk to him and verify what he told Laurel—Ms. Muir—I'll close the case. Until then, it's still open. I know where to find you if I need to." He made eye contact with each of them for a long moment.

"So it's okay if we leave? We're free to go?" Dawn asked, making as if to stand.

"You've always been free to go."

The sound of the front door opening, and then footsteps, presaged Geneva's entrance. "You didn't start without me, did you?" Dark circles under her eyes testified to a sleepless night, but she looked utterly happy, Laurel thought, with a grin wider than the Mississippi splitting her face. Her maternity top billowed over her deflated belly.

"Sit down," Ellie said, sliding a chair out.

"Should you be walking around?" Dawn asked, her brow puckering.

Geneva waved a dismissive hand. "I'm tired and sore, but fine. Better than fine. Before we all got so germ-phobic and precious, women had babies out in the fields and went back to picking cotton, or they popped out a baby in the covered wagon and went back to goading the oxen." Moving a little gingerly, she seated herself. Her gaze landed on the remaining coffee cup and she sniffed. "Coffee. Oh my God, real coffee. Please tell me that cup has my name on it."

"Be my guest." Boone smiled and pushed it toward her.

Geneva cracked the lid, inhaled deeply, and then took a long swallow. "Ah, bliss, thy name is coffee," she said, making them all laugh.

"Does Geonwoo know you left the hospital already?" Laurel asked shrewdly.

Geneva looked sheepish. "Scott's picking him up at the airport. He'll bring him back here and we'll go get Lila. The pediatrician's a little worried about jaundice, so they want to do another blood test or two this morning. I need to be back to feed her in a couple of hours."

"That's my cue," Boone said, pushing to his feet. "I'll leave you ladies to it. We're searching this place today to see if we can turn up Mindy Tanger's phone. A hopeless task, but we've got to try."

"You might start with the housekeeping cart," Laurel said, the idea coming to her suddenly.

"Not a bad thought." He dipped his chin in thanks or farewell and strode out of the room.

A strange pang hit Laurel as she watched him go. Was that good-bye, or would she see him again before she returned to Denver?

When the door closed behind him, Ellie cleared her throat. "Where shall we do the memorial?" she asked. "Geneva suggested the lake, and I think that would be lovely, but I'm not sure she can—"

"I'm not staying." Dawn stood.

"Dawn! You have to—" Geneva started.

Dawn shook her head, tendrils of dark hair bobbing around her face. "No. I wanted to say goodbye to Evangeline, but that was before we found out what she tried to do to us. She tried to have one of us convicted of murder. She plotted and schemed and found ways to implicate all of us." Her hand clenched and flexed on the suitcase handle. "She sent Ray to Texas, for God's sake, to buy rat poison to make it look like I poisoned her. And she put you in her will, Ellie, not because she wanted to help you out but to give you a motive for murder! I can't remember the good times or celebrate her life, not now." She shook her head and her curls tossed wildly. "Maybe not ever. I can't believe you want to say nice things about her, either." Her gaze challenged each of them in turn.

"Maybe not," Ellie agreed slowly, "although I'll never forget how kind she was when she found out I was pregnant. She helped me make up my mind to leave school and have the baby. She bought your paintings, Dawn—"

"That wasn't kindness," Dawn shouted, throwing her arms out so the suitcase spun away and cracked against a table leg. "I was so happy, over the moon, when the gallery owner told me my showing had sold out. I finally knew I could make it as an artist, that people liked my work, my art. And then to get here and find out that she'd bought them all, every one, kept other people from buying them, even…it broke something inside me. By buying out the exhibit, she was saying she knew no one else would want my art. It was pity, the equivalent of a mercy fuck. Well, she fucked me over, all right. I knew then that she was right, that I didn't have what it took, that spark, that vision that sets a true artist apart. I was a hack, suited for teaching or advertising or what I'm doing now. I wasn't a real artist and I was never going to be. You expect me to revere her 'kindness' in showing me that?" She paused, panting.

"You were so hurt and so mad that you pushed her off the balcony, didn't you?" Laurel said softly.

Ellie's eyes widened. "Laurel! You can't say—" She stopped, her gaze resting on Dawn, who had half turned away. "You did," she whispered. "Oh, Dawn."

Laurel leaned forward. "You pointed out that there didn't have to be a link between what happened ten years ago and Evangeline's death this weekend. That's because you pushed her ten years ago, but you had nothing to do with poisoning her, right?"

It felt almost like a courtroom: the three of them, sitting, impaneled as jurors, and Dawn, standing, the prisoner in the dock.

Dawn's lower lip trembled and she bit down on it. "I was drunk, furious, humiliated. Heartbroken—I was heartbroken. I didn't set out to hurt her, you have to believe that." She swung in a semicircle, meeting each of their eyes in turn. "I didn't! I went to her room, planning to have it out with her, that's all. I wanted—needed—to tell her what she'd done, make her understand how she'd, she'd *crushed* me. I knocked, but she didn't answer, and I knew she was avoiding me, knew she didn't think it worth her time to even talk to me."

She flung her hair back, thrusting her pointy chin up. "Well. I went in. I was going to make her listen whether she wanted to or not. I didn't see her at first, but then there was the breeze and I knew she was on the balcony. I called her name, but she couldn't even be bothered

to turn around and talk to me. I … I'm not sure what happened next."
Her gaze shifted to her hands, clasped together so tightly every bone
stood out. "Before I knew it, I was on the balcony, leaning over the
rail—the stone was rough under my hands, so rough." She rubbed her
hands together lightly, as if the palms were sore. "I could see her
sprawled on the ground, broken." She let out a single loud sob and
swallowed the next one with a sound like a hiccup. "I didn't mean to."

A hush fell over the room. No one moved, and Laurel figured they
were all visualizing the scene.

"You're not sure what happened? You didn't 'mean to'?" Ellie's
voice, loaded with scorn, exploded into the silence. "Is that a 'the
ghost made me do it' defense? Total BS. I'll tell you what happened:
you came up behind your best friend, shoved her between the shoulder blades as hard as you could, and watched her fall five stories." She
stopped, shuddering, and turned away from Dawn.

Laurel could see that Dawn's confession had quenched Geneva's
happiness. Her face solemn, Geneva reached out a hand. "Dawn, why
didn't you come forward? Tell us, the sheriff, what had happened?"
Her hand dropped and anger seeped into her voice. "You let him grill
us, put us through the wringer. Do you know how I fought to stay
sober through that time, how scared I was that they'd arrest me because I was the black woman with a record?"

"I didn't mean to hurt anyone, certainly not any of you," Dawn said,
taking a step toward them, leaning forward like a supplicant. "Not like
Evangeline. Look how she's tried to hurt all of us, tried to send us to
prison." Her voice grew impassioned as she tried to convince them.
"She played God with us—she has for years. She outed me by kissing
me in front of my sister and caused no end of trouble with my family.
She seduced your boyfriend and lost you your scholarship," she said,

294

facing Ellie, who turned toward her. "And what she did to Geneva was the worst of all."

Geneva shook her head slowly. "I take full responsibility for what happened that night. It was Vangie's idea, sure, but no one put a gun to my head and forced me to go on a drug buy, and no one siphoned vodka down my throat for a year thereafter. I'm not proud of any of it, but it's all on me, not Vangie."

A thin silence settled and held for fifteen seconds after Geneva spoke. Laurel steeled herself. An abdominal muscle spasmed, reacting against how tightly she was clenching her abs. It would be so simple to leave things as they were. They knew the truth about Evangeline's fall now. That should be enough ... but it wasn't. Only the whole truth would suffice. Those who remained could never heal their friendship without the whole truth. She licked her dry lips. "What about Mindy?"

Dawn stumbled backward as if struck, sloshing coffee on herself. She set the cup down with a trembling hand. "What about Mindy? Abbott killed Mindy, we know that. The sheriff said—"

"Do we know that?" Laurel asked. "Abbott denies it."

"Of course he does." Geneva frowned at her.

"I think Mindy was blackmailing you, Dawn," Laurel said. She stood, too, so that they were level, facing each other. "She found the rat poison box and receipt that Evangeline had planted in your room. In the trash, I'll bet. I think she was in the habit of going through the trash. She brought them to you, didn't she?"

"No! She ... I ... " Dawn's face reflected her confusion. As Laurel watched, the confusion turned to anger. "How can you accuse me of that? I admit that in a moment of drunkenness, near insanity, really, I ... I pushed Evangeline. I've regretted it every day since then, every day. You can't think that I would—"

295

Laurel swallowed hard around the lump of regret and disappointment clogging her throat. Sadness weighed her down, like the time she tried on a cop's Kevlar vest. She'd felt unbalanced, clumsy, and slow, like now. "When we were in my room, you said something about not being able to prove where you were at 5:08 on any particular Friday. That's the exact time that was on the receipt."

"So? I—"

"The receipt was in my robe pocket. You didn't see it in my room, so you couldn't have known the time on it unless you'd seen it before. In fact, you wouldn't even have known the box implicated you unless you'd seen that the receipt was from San Marcos. Mindy showed it to you."

Dawn's face went expressionless. Laurel couldn't begin to imagine the calculations going through her head. She didn't give her a chance to come up with a story. "Mindy was stepping up her blackmail activities, building a nest egg for when she was jobless, I suspect. She blackmailed the Abbotts, and she came to you, too. She showed you the box and receipt and said she'd give them to the police if you didn't pay up. You didn't know how they'd ended up in your trash can—how could you at that point?—but you knew they were incriminating and you didn't need Boone taking a hard look at you, not with last time on your conscience. Did you suggest meeting on the fifth floor, or did she?"

Dawn licked her lips. "Does it matter?"

"Braden," Ellie breathed, looking sick.

"Mindy was an opportunistic bottom-feeder," Dawn said, slitting her eyes. "She'd been draining me for years—forty bucks for a soccer uniform here, seventy dollars for Braden's college fund there—ever since Evangeline's fall. She knew I wasn't in my room that night like I'd told the police. The morning after, she came in to change the bed and mentioned, oh so innocently, that she'd come by to bring me fresh towels the night before, that the dryer had been broken, which was why she was doing it so late, but I hadn't been there. She didn't ask where I'd been, but the question danced between us. I froze, feeling sick, but I felt relieved, too. It was over. But then, a lie popped into my head and I heard myself telling her I'd gone out to meet a woman, a married woman, and she smiled this tiny smile. She didn't blackmail me outright—she just started talking about an upcoming date and how she wished she could afford a new dress. I asked if I could contribute, mumbled something about wanting her to feel special for her special date, and that was that."

"She probably wanted more this time, didn't she?" Laurel said, conscious of the way they'd all stilled as Dawn recounted her story. "Since she'd been let go, she needed more money."

"You always have to be right, Laurel, don't you?" Dawn said, the words saturated with resentment. "No matter who it hurts. I pity anyone unfortunate enough to end up in your courtroom." Without warning, she picked up one of the heavy chairs and slung it toward Laurel.

Laurel tried to sidestep it, but it crunched into her shins and she fell over it, bolts of pain lighting up her legs. Before Geneva or Ellie could come around the table, Dawn ran out of the room. Disentangling herself from the chair, Laurel went after her, hobbling at first but picking up speed as the pain in her legs receded.

Boone's voice said "What the hell?" as Laurel reached the foyer. Looking pissed off, he was backed against the doorframe as if Dawn had bumped past him. He was staring after her as she ran flat-out for the yellow Mustang.

"Stop her," Laurel gasped. "She killed Mindy."

Boone didn't hesitate. He leaped down the stairs and sprinted toward Dawn, running with a power and athleticism that would have been impressive even if he'd been fifteen years younger. Laurel followed him, dimly aware of footsteps behind her. Dawn skidded to a halt in a swirl of hair and desperation beside the car, wrenched the door open, and gunned the engine before she pulled her left leg inside. The Mustang jumped forward with the door still open. Boone lunged for it, but he missed and almost fell as the powerful car accelerated in a blast of gravel. It caromed down the driveway, fishtailing on the first curve.

Boone was on his radio immediately, vectoring patrol cars toward the Mustang and ordering a roadblock. Ellie came to a panting halt beside Laurel. "Where does she think she's going?" she asked.

Laurel shook her head. She couldn't imagine that Dawn had a plan or a destination. She was running on instinct, running to nowhere.

Boone came up to them, tucking in a shirt tail that had pulled loose. "There's nowhere for her to go. We'll—"

Before he could finish the sentence, there came a screeching of brakes that made Laurel's teeth ache and the gut-wrenching *kee-scrunch* of a high speed crash, of compacted steel and shattered glass, and a scream that might have been human or might have been the car's roof shearing off. A plume of smoke rose from the direction of the stone pillars.

Thirty-Two

The next morning, Laurel folded the last T-shirt and laid it in her suitcase. Her eyes felt gritty, as if she hadn't slept for weeks. They'd sat vigil at the hospital, waiting for the surgeon to emerge from the operating room and tell them Dawn would be okay. They'd all been there—Ellie and Scott, fingers linked and talking softly; Geneva and Geonwoo, sitting with shoulders touching, jiggling tiny Lila when she got fussy; a variety of cops and deputies and hospital personnel rotating in and out. Someone had three pizzas delivered, and it would almost have felt cozy if their reason for being there hadn't hung over them like a damp mohair blanket, heavy and itchy.

Near sunset, Laurel had made her way to a vending machine down the hall. While she waited for it to spit out the suspicious liquid it called "coffee," she leaned her head against the machine's cool metal front. A hand landed on her shoulder, and she turned to find Geneva and Ellie standing behind her. Geneva's hand squeezed her shoulder.

"Buy you a coffee?" Laurel asked with a strained smile.

"I need sugar." Ellie fed coins into a candy machine and retrieved the PayDay bar that plonked into the tray.

"I'm coffeed out," Geneva said, shaking her head. "Never thought I'd say that after nine caffeineless months."

Without talking about it, they settled at the single round melamine table pushed into a corner beneath a window. Its surface was ringed with coffee and soda stains, and Ellie pulled a wipe from her purse to clean it off. The vending machines' humming was soothing. The window looked down on a parking lot and Laurel watched as a man parked haphazardly, ran around his car to the passenger seat, and helped his very pregnant wife out of the car. Life and death, she thought. Life and death every day in a hospital. What an emotional roller-coaster. How did doctors and nurses do it?

"Do you think she'll make it?" Ellie asked.

No one answered her for a long minute, and then Geneva said, "If she wants to, maybe."

They pondered that in silence, and Laurel wondered if Dawn had crashed the car on purpose or if she'd merely lost control and slammed into the stone pillars by accident in her rush to escape. They might never know. "She'll spend the rest of her life in prison if she does," she pointed out.

Ellie twisted her PayDay wrapper, making a crinkling sound. Without meeting their eyes, she asked, "If you find out that a friend wasn't really a friend, does that cancel out all the good times you had together when you thought she was a friend?" She sounded close to tears.

Geneva put a hand over Ellie's hand and stilled it. "Dawn was our friend—"

"Don't say she *is* our friend," Ellie said swiftly, withdrawing her hand.

"I wasn't going to. But she was our friend, a true friend, for many years. She lost her way."

Laurel wondered, as she had fifty times that day, if Dawn would have tried to kill her in the bathroom if Geneva hadn't come by. Thinking about it filled her chest cavity with concrete and she found it hard to breathe. "She crippled Evangeline and murdered Mindy," she said drily, trying to dispel the feeling. "That's a lot of lost."

"You could almost say she killed Evangeline, too," Ellie said.

"However you want to phrase it," Geneva persevered, "whatever she did ten years ago and this week, it doesn't 'cancel out' the times we shared in college, or mean she was faking her friendship. I'll never forget the time she missed her plane to pick me up after I sneaked out the kitchen door of L'Escargot to escape a date who turned out to be a total psychopath. She was supposed to be flying to New York for that gallery internship but when I called, she came to get me. That's the last time I ever went anywhere without cab money, I'll tell you."

"I remember that guy," Ellie murmured. "Ronald."

"Roald," Geneva corrected, giving the word a snooty twist.

"Will you visit her in prison?" Laurel asked baldly, looking from Geneva to Ellie.

After a moment, they both shook their heads. "Me neither," she said. "At least, I don't think I will."

"I'll pray for her and for the grace to forgive her," Geneva said. "Mama Gran would want me to do that."

"I won't forgive her." Ellie's face set mulishly. Tears made her eyes shiny. "What she did ten years ago brought us to today. She's responsible, directly or indirectly, for two deaths, not to mention she split us apart for ten years." She reached out to each of them and took their hands in hers. "Can we be friends again? I mean real friends? Call on the phone friends, go to visit friends, bitch about husbands and kids and celebrate losing five pounds or getting a new job friends? I've missed you guys so much."

Laurel had been thinking the same thing, how much she'd missed these women. It would be hard—they didn't live in the same town and they were at different life points, with Ellie saying goodbye to her kids and Geneva embarking on raising her first baby. *And me about to try to have one, and be a single mom and a judge.* But they were smart and determined and they had FaceTime. "Yes, we can," she said definitively.

"Chicago's only a bit more than an hour from Denver by air," Geneva put in. She smiled and then winced, cupping a hand over her breast. "My boobs hurt—it's time to feed Lila."

They returned to the waiting room to be greeted by Lila's fretful mewling and the sight of a scrubs-garbed woman talking to the men. Geonwoo, taller than the others, looked over their heads as the women entered. He shook his head slowly from side to side.

———

Laurel closed her suitcase and zipped it decisively. Swinging it off the bed, she left the room. The hall was quiet as she strode toward the entryway. Almost eerily so. No construction workers today, and the cops had finished their crime scene analysis, leaving strands of yellow and black tape to rope off the elevator shaft. She was the last one. Ellie and Scott had left before dawn to catch a flight out of Charlotte, and Geneva and her family were returning to Chicago in a rental car, not wanting to expose two-day-old Lila to the hazards of airline travel and being cooped up with a couple hundred coughing, sneezing, possibly infectious people. "I'm turning into Ellie," Geneva had laughed as she hugged Laurel goodbye. She held her at arm's length and gave her a little shake. "Go be the thoughtful, fair, and compassionate person you are on that judge's bench. You're going to be a damn fine judge."

"I'm going to try," Laurel had said with a smile. "It feels like what I'm meant to do." She was eager now to take the oath and tackle her new duties. She might not always get it right, but she would try her damnedest. Same with being a mom.

She resisted the urge to go from room to room and say goodbye to Cygne. It was sentimental and, truth be told, she wasn't sure she was entirely sorry to be leaving the castle and its memories behind. She glanced up the curving staircase as she reached the foyer and was captivated by a spiral of dust motes dancing in the sunshine streaming through the arched windows. A clank from the direction of the kitchen broke the moment; the new manager, sent by the corporation to oversee construction, as he'd officiously told them last night, must be fighting with the espresso machine. No need to let him know she was leaving.

Pulling open the heavy door, Laurel stopped on the threshold, startled by the sight of Judah Boone leaning back against his patrol car, arms crossed over his chest. A sheen of sweat made his dark brow shine, and his uniform was as rumpled as always. The gray threaded through his hair gleamed brightly under the sun's glare. Her heart beat a little faster at the sight of him and she couldn't hold back a smile, although she asked, "Come to follow me to the county line to make sure I'm permanently out of your hair?"

Boone straightened and came to her, taking the suitcase without asking. His brown eyes searched her face. Apparently satisfied with what he saw there, he gave a shallow nod. "No." They walked slowly toward her rental car, parked beside what must be the new manager's SUV. "I came to see you off."

"To say goodbye?" She made a visor of her hand to shade her eyes and looked up at him.

"I hope not."

She sucked in a tiny breath and looked a question at him.

"I've got a brother in Aspen," he said nonchalantly. "I visit him on occasion."

"Aspen? La-di-da." She tried to keep the moment light, although her heart thudded against her rib cage.

He grinned. "Yeah, he's the filthy-rich venture capitalist and I'm the cop. Mom swears she loves us both the same, but Micah made a lot of points when he bought her a Mercedes for her seventieth birthday." He paused, tugging at his lower lip. "Anyway, it's been too long since I've been out there. I'm about due for a visit."

His gaze swept her face and she sensed an unusual uncertainty in him. His vulnerability made her swallow hard. "If you come through Denver," she said, "you should call me. I suspect you can find the number," she added with a hint of asperity.

"If I put my mind to it." He shoved her suitcase onto the back seat and then opened the driver's door. "Drive safely."

She touched his upper arm, feeling his solid biceps tense under her fingers. "I'll look forward to seeing you," she said with simple sincerity. She hesitated, somehow feeling awkward and uncertain and happy and hopeful all at the same time, conscious of the warmth and scent of butterscotch emanating from him. Giving in to impulse, she stood on tiptoe and pressed a kiss to the corner of his mouth. His skin was firm and the hint of stubble tickled her lips. She pulled away and scanned his face. "See you soon?"

"Micah smokes a twenty-five-pound turkey every year for Thanksgiving, and his wife Cassie makes the best sweet potato casserole you ever tasted," he said.

With a smile of acknowledgment, Laurel slid into the car. Boone closed the door with a solid thunk. As she started the engine, he slapped the trunk twice and stepped back. She pulled away, driving slowly so the car wouldn't spit gravel at him. On the driveway, she pressed on the accelerator and started into the first curve, her eyes on the rearview mirror. Boone was heading toward his car, Cygne golden and substantial and impervious behind him. A shadow moved behind a fifth-floor window, catching Laurel's eye and making her foot hesitate over the brake pedal. *Has to be a trick of the light.* She blinked twice and looked again. Now the windows were opaqued by the light's angle, with nothing visible behind them. *Of course not.*

She guided the car through the curve, picking up speed. There was a flash of blue lake after the second bend, the silhouette of chimneys behind a scrim of red leaves as she curved to the right, and then she lost sight of the castle.

THE END

Acknowledgments

I owe a huge thank-you to all the folks at Midnight Ink who have helped to make *That Last Weekend* the novel it is, especially Terri Bischoff and Sandy Sullivan for their editing efforts, Bob Gaul for the spiffy interior design, Ellen Lawson for the stunning cover, Katie Mickschl for her outreach activities, and everyone else who works behind the scenes.

I am also supremely grateful for my friends who have taught me so much about myself and friendship through the years. This book, which is as much about friendship as it is about obsession and murder, would not have been possible without Amy, Cindy, Jill, Katie, Linda, Nancy, Patrick, Sam, Steve, Susan, and so many more. You enrich my life greatly. (Family members: you're not listed here, but you're all friends as well as kin. I love you!) As Hubert H. Humphrey puts it, "The greatest gift of life is friendship, and I have received it."

Photo by bluefoxphotography.com

About the Author

Laura DiSilverio is the national bestselling and award-winning author of twenty mystery and suspense novels and a YA dystopian trilogy. Her 2015 standalone, *The Reckoning Stones*, won the Colorado Book Award for Mystery, and *Library Journal* named her most recent title, *Close Call*, one of the Top Five mysteries of 2016. Her books have received starred reviews from *Publishers Weekly*, *Library Journal*, *Booklist*, and *Kirkus*. She is a former Air Force intelligence officer and past President of Sisters in Crime. She can be found online at www .LauraDiSilverio.com.